THE IMAGINARY FRIEND

MICHELLE DUNNE

Boldwood

First published in Great Britain in 2025 by Boldwood Books Ltd.

Copyright © Michelle Dunne, 2025

Cover Design by Lisa Horton

Cover Images: Shutterstock

A CIP catalogue record for this book is available from the British Library.

Paperback ISBN 978-1-80600-724-0

Large Print ISBN 978-1-80600-723-3

Hardback ISBN 978-1-80600-722-6

Trade Paperback ISBN 978-1-80656-084-4

Ebook ISBN 978-1-80600-725-7

Kindle ISBN 978-1-80600-726-4

Audio CD ISBN 978-1-80600-717-2

MP3 CD ISBN 978-1-80600-718-9

Digital audio download ISBN 978-1-80600-721-9

This book is printed on certified sustainable paper. Boldwood Books is dedicated to putting sustainability at the heart of our business. For more information please visit https://www.boldwoodbooks.com/about-us/sustainability/

Boldwood Books Ltd, 23 Bowerdean Street, London, SW6 3TN

www.boldwoodbooks.com

For Emily always, with love

PROLOGUE

Eve Holland stood bloody and trembling in her darkened kitchen. The sound of rain beating against the window made her feel cold to the bone, and this space, which had always been home to her, now looked strange and unwelcoming. There was a pool of blood on the cream tiled floor, with bare, bloody footprints leading away from it. Her breathing came in short, jagged bursts, her thoughts, too. But the pain. My God, the pain.

What had she done?

'Eve?'

Eve's eyes found Pennie, her frail little body still shrouded in the yellow, polka-dot nightie that Eve had bought for her. That was just after their once large family had decreased in size yet again, leaving just Pennie and Eve to fend for themselves. The nightie had blood on it, and Pennie was as pale as a ghost, her blonde hair matted to her head.

'Eve?' she said again in a soft, trembling voice. She wasn't crying, but at ten years of age, her little sister Pennie managed her fear with far more stoicism than Eve ever could.

The long-bladed kitchen knife fell from Eve's hand as she dropped to the floor. Her vision started to fade and the sound of Pennie's voice got further and further away. She blinked in an effort to stay awake, but the last thing she saw were Pennie's bare, blood-soaked feet being lifted off the floor, replaced by heavy, black boots. Someone was standing over her, their steel toecaps less than an inch from Eve's face. Then the darkness that had followed her around for most of her life closed in around her until, at last, it swallowed her whole.

1

SIX WEEKS EARLIER…

'It'll be fine,' Eve assured Pennie, as she paced the kitchen, stopping from time to time to wipe or tidy something that had already been wiped and tidied. 'I know it feels… different, being here without Ellen, Pennie, but… you know, I… well, I love you and you know, you're my sister and I'm sure… I mean, we *will* be absolutely fine here, the two of us and…'

'How will we be fine?' Pennie asked, her voice small and delicate, just like her. Pennie rarely spoke, so the fact that she was asking meant she must really be worried.

Today was their first day alone in that house, without Ellen or anyone else, and her absence seemed enormous suddenly. A physical thing that weighed heavily on both of them. Pennie was sitting at the kitchen table with two cooling cups of cocoa between her and the seat opposite, which Eve had recently vacated for a second time since setting the drinks down. She could not sit still. How could she? Her mind was on fire with all the things she did not know about managing a household and caring for Pennie, without help.

Pennie's penetrating stare burned through her as she moved from surface to surface, cloth in hand. 'We just will be, Pennie.' Eve flung the cloth at the sink. She stood for a moment, staring at the plughole, trying to translate her thoughts into a coherent sentence. Something she always struggled to do, even in the best of circumstances. 'We have to be,' was the best she could come up with. She spoke the words softly, glancing at her precious ten-year-old sister.

Poor Pennie was one of those kids who never seemed fully aware of what was happening around her. She'd spent most of her life lost in her own little world and there were times when Eve envied her that. It wasn't easy being an unwanted child, which was what all the Hollands were at one time or another. Like Eve, Pennie had been dumped by her mother not long after she was born, so really, her own little world was probably the best place to be. Eve had no such place to hide. There was an age gap of thirteen years between them and though they'd both been given the Holland name, they'd also been reminded often enough about where they came from. Eve wondered if that was why Pennie was such a quiet girl. Was it that she simply had too much to think about?

Now she had even more.

'But *why* are you so sure?' Pennie asked.

Eve raised her eyebrows and went to sit down again. 'Do you know how many foster kids came through this house, Pennie?'

Pennie shook her head, her wavy, blonde hair pulled back into a messy ponytail, the way she always wore it. Her bright-blue eyes were pleading with Eve to give the reassurance she desperately needed.

'Seventy-three,' Eve said, forcing resolve that she didn't necessarily feel into her voice. 'That was the number Ellen gave me before she... well, before. Some only stayed a day, others stayed for months, but Ellen remembered all of them. And so do I.' She jabbed a finger into her chest. 'Or at least the ones who came after me. Because who do you think helped to look after them, eh? I did.' She wrapped her hands around her cooling mug and closed her eyes tightly, in search of a few seconds of peace and some darkness. Her head had started to throb yesterday, and it hadn't stopped yet. There was a pattern to Eve's headaches, so she knew that it would only intensify throughout the day, but would then start to ease off by morning. 'That's why I know...'

'Is it your head?' Pennie asked, her voice barely above a whisper now, collapsing under the strain of all these words.

Eve opened her eyes and went on pretending she was fine. She didn't answer because she didn't want Pennie doubting her capabilities any more than she already did. Eve had always suffered from headaches. But over the past few weeks, they'd increased in both intensity and frequency. To the point where Pennie had started to notice them when she never did before. Some people might consider frequent, mind-blowing headaches a good reason to visit a doctor. But the Hollands didn't believe in doctors. Neither Eve nor Pennie had ever been to see one, no matter what ailed them, so it didn't occur to Eve to seek medical advice now. Still, Ellen kept enough medication in the house to cure just about anything – temporarily, at least. But none of it could help with the voice in her head. The one screaming at her now, telling her that when it came to caring for a child, especially a child like Pennie, she'd never be as capable as *they* were.

'You don't have to take care of me while your head is...'

'My head is fine, Pennie.'

Pennie returned a slow, stoic nod. One designed to appease Eve, rather than a sign of agreement, and she wished that the child wasn't so much more intelligent than she was. Eve was stupid. She'd always known this and she'd come to terms with it a very long time ago. But Pennie – Pennie was the smartest person in the world and the time had come for Eve to figure out how the hell she was going to take care of her in a way that she deserved. And how she was going to answer questions like these without letting Pennie know for sure just how stupid her big sister, and now her guardian, actually was.

'My point is, Pennie, I've been helping to take care of children since I was even younger than you are now. Believe me... I know what I'm doing.'

Eve did not know what she was doing.

'I don't remember that many kids being here,' Pennie correctly pointed out.

Eve nodded and bobbed her head from side to side. 'Yeah, well, there weren't nearly as many kids here since you came along. But *before* you, this house was full nearly all the time.' She tried to force some animation into her tone by using hand gestures that didn't necessarily align with the type of conversation they were having. 'The bedroom that you're in now,' she continued, 'there used to be two sets of bunk beds in there and they were nearly always full. That was the boys' room.'

'I know,' Pennie muttered, looking down into her cocoa. She'd heard all this before, but Eve continued anyway because she didn't know what else to do.

'And the room *I'm* in – well, that was the girls' room. At one time, I remember having three boys and two girls, plus me, and it was that way for months.'

'Why didn't they keep any of them?' Pennie asked, looking at Eve again. 'Like they kept me and you?'

'And Amelia,' Eve said, her face falling along with her spirits. She looked away towards the kitchen window and took a breath before continuing. 'I wish you could have known her, Pennie.' She looked at the girl again, not sure if she'd ever really talked about Amelia with her. Pennie was only a baby when Amelia disappeared, so there was no way she could remember her. 'Amelia was kind of outgoing, if you could believe it.' She smiled at the memory of her big sister. 'She could make friends absolutely anywhere. Not real friends, mind you. Not the kind who stuck around when you needed them or anything. But people always liked her when they first met her, you know?' She looked at Pennie to see if she was listening, but it was hard to tell. It always was, but Eve continued anyway, for her own benefit, if not for Pennie's. 'Amelia could make strangers believe that she was someone worth knowing, whereas I was the complete opposite.' Her smile faded then and she looked at her fidgeting hands. Ellen used to say that Eve's brain wasn't quick enough to come up with responses to anything, and Eve supposed she was right about that. But she omitted that detail now. 'But Amelia always seemed to have somewhere to go and someone to go there with, do you know what I mean? Once, she even brought a friend home for dinner.' She looked up again, her eyes a little wider with something like excitement. 'A real friend, from a proper family.' She paused and looked to her hands again. 'That only happened once, though, and she picked a really bad night for it.'

'Why?' Pennie asked, surprising Eve.

'Eh, well, you know, depending on who was staying here, anything could happen at our house back then. Which was why it wasn't a great idea to bring normal people back here. Not if you wanted them to stay friends with you. Raven's Rock was anything but normal and on that particular night, when Amelia's friend, Millie-something, came for dinner, this one kid threw an absolute fit.' She became a little animated again, despite the terrible memory she was describing. 'She punched Ellen in the throat *and* bit her face seemingly for no reason. By the time Millie-whatever recovered from witnessing it, Ellen was already cooking dinner for Millie and Amelia as if nothing had happened.' Pennie was watching her intently and Eve felt her stomach fall again. Why had she started this story? 'There she was,' she continued in a lower voice, 'scrambling eggs with one hand, and patching up the teeth marks on her cheek with the other, like this was just another night at Raven's Rock.' Eve supposed it was. 'Needless to say, Millie never set foot inside our house again. Amelia became far less busy, too, as her social invitations dried up.' She paused then, getting lost in the past. 'She was fourteen years older than me,' she said in mild wonderment. 'She'd long aged out of the foster-care system by then. But for reasons only Amelia knew, she stuck around anyway, and Ellen and Peter let her.'

'So why just us?' Pennie asked again. 'Why didn't they keep any of the other seventy children?'

Eve shrugged. 'Because they were foster parents, I guess. And fostering is only ever meant to be temporary. That's just the way it works.'

Pennie nodded, but Eve could see that even now, after a lifetime in this house, she still didn't really understand it. Perhaps that wasn't altogether a bad thing either.

Eve leaned towards her and made herself smile, even though there was absolutely nothing worth smiling about. 'I guess you and me were just special, eh?' She reached out and took Pennie's hand.

'And Amelia,' Pennie reminded her. Then she looked at Eve's big hand engulfing hers and she slowly pulled out of her loose grasp. Eve sat back, too. She'd always been really bad at holding conversations, which was probably why she had no friends. Even her little sister found it difficult to be in her company for too long, and now here she was, stuck with Eve as her guardian. Eve Holland, a substitute for nothing, let alone a mother.

After all these years and all those people, Raven's Rock had finally been reduced to just two. The name, Raven's Rock, just added to the stigma of the Hollands' house. That, and the troublesome nature of the kids who passed through it. But now all that was gone, too. There was nothing left and Eve honestly had no idea whether this was the beginning of something new, or the end of everything.

Pennie's eyes were on the tabletop, and she was swirling her untouched drink around in her cup.

'Pennie?' Eve pulled herself upright again and spoke in a low, unconvincing tone. 'What I'm trying to say is that I helped take care of a lot of those kids. There were often so many here that Ellen needed all the help she could get. And that help was me.' She jabbed a finger this time at the tabletop. 'Now if I could take care of that crazy bunch of kids, then...' she raised her eyebrows and smiled a crooked smile, 'then me and you are going to be absolutely fine, okay? Trust me. I promise you.' She was almost pleading with Pennie now, so she stopped talking, sure that she didn't sound anywhere near as reassuring as she'd set out to.

Pennie nodded, undoubtedly just to stop Eve from saying any more. But still, she did.

'Peter is gone and now Ellen, too,' she said, feeling the sudden weight of it. She furrowed her brow as she realised that Pennie was right to be worried. Ellen and Peter Holland were the kind of people you'd expect to live forever. But then Peter went to work one day and just never came home. Killed in a hit-and-run on his way back from the shop. He was carrying six breakfast rolls: elevenses for his workmates on the building site, even though he himself never ate things like breakfast rolls. Now Ellen was gone, too. She'd been recovering from a recently fractured ankle when she fell from the top of the stairs. She should have been resting her foot with the heavy boot on it, not walking around carrying loads of laundry. But she'd decided to carry on as normal and that was her all over. Bury the head and carry on. Eve glanced towards the stairs, remembering the thumping sound of her falling down them, and the sight of her twisted body on the hall floor. Now Eve and Pennie were alone in the house they grew up in. A house that had never seen a quiet day in its existence before then.

'So, we're going to stay here then?' Pennie asked tentatively. 'Me and you? With no one else?'

Eve frowned again. Where did Pennie think they might go? Where *could* they go? 'Pennie, I'm twenty-three years old. That makes me an adult and, well...' She reached out again, to take the girl's hand. 'You're my sister. So you have an adult relative who'll take care of you and that means, you know,' she exhaled a shaky breath, 'it's you and me, Pennie. And that's the way it's going to be.'

Pennie withdrew her hand and stood up slowly from the table. She walked through the open-plan ground floor of the house and took the stairs slowly up to her room. For Eve, sitting there watching her go felt like the loneliest moment of her life. But her mind didn't turn to Ellen and Peter. While their absence was huge, the person she desperately missed at that moment was her own big sister, Amelia. My God, how she missed her, now more than ever before.

Eve continued to watch the stairs long after Pennie's bedroom door closed, and when she managed to pull her eyes away, she took out her phone and opened the photo of Pennie that was now her screen saver. They were Hollands in name only, but Pennie was her sister nonetheless. She stared at the beautiful, pale face of a girl who seemed so much older than her years. Her blonde hair neatly combed, resting on her thin shoulders, her blue eyes wide and fearful. Always fearful. And mostly silent. That was Pennie.

Eve felt a heaviness in her heart each time she looked into those eyes, as the weight of responsibility crept down upon her. She had to do everything in her power to make Pennie feel safe now, and that was something she desperately needed to figure out. Because Eve had no idea what safe felt like. She'd never felt safe a day in her life.

2

Pennie's room, or the boys' room, as it was always called, was the largest of the four bedrooms. More beds meant more heads, and more heads meant more monthly payments received into the Hollands' bank account. As far back as Eve could remember, that room had been magnolia in colour. It never got a fresh coat of paint and so it always looked grubby and run-down. But these were different times. Now the room was clean and fresh and painted in pale lilac. Eve took it upon herself to redecorate, now that it was just the two of them. That was how she'd busied herself for the first week after things died down, regardless of the fact that painting and decorating were not among Eve's very limited skill set. True, there were dabs and dashes of lilac on the ceiling edges as well as the four walls, but the place still looked a million times better than it had. She used relatively neutral colours, so that Pennie would see it as a space to make her own, at last. Some of their past lodgers had done that by kicking holes in the plaster. Others hung photographs, posters, anything they liked up in there and Ellen never cared either way. It was up to the next kid to change it if they felt strongly enough about it.

Eve had scraped the ancient Blu-Tack and tape off before repainting the room in anticipation of their fresh start, this daunting new chapter, and as she stood at the door, looking at the freshened space, a pink, unicorn duvet cover adorning the second-hand, but new to them, single bed, she still saw all the faces of the kids who'd occupied that room in the years before.

'Do you like this room since I did it up, Pennie?' she asked from the doorway, wondering if maybe she might feel happy somehow, despite all that had happened.

Pennie frowned and looked around, like she hadn't even noticed the change. The room hadn't been used at all since Peter died six years earlier. That was when Ellen stopped taking foster kids and the boys' room became surplus to requirement. But she left the room pretty much untouched. Thankfully, Pennie and Eve were allowed to stay, but they'd continued to share a room. It never occurred to Eve to change that until now. It wasn't a room that Pennie routinely went into before moving in there, but surely she must have seen the difference. If not, then she must have felt it at least. It was such a different house now, fresh paint notwithstanding. Even the air tasted different.

Eve shook her head at her own ridiculousness. Of course Pennie wasn't happy. The only family she'd ever known was gone. All except for Eve and while Pennie had always been pretty void of emotion, she'd always been particularly indifferent to Eve. So, rather than standing there all day, waiting for the love and affection that would probably never come, Eve went next door to her own room. There, she put on a warm jacket and took her green, canvas, cross-body bag from the wardrobe. That bag had been Ellen's once, and she never went anywhere without it. It was the only item of hers that Eve took as her own.

She stopped at Pennie's door again, on her way back to the stairs. 'Okay, I'm going to work,' she said with a small smile. The girl was still sitting on the bed with her ancient old Barbie doll in her lap. That doll had belonged to so many people before Pennie got her hands on it, but she still seemed to like it. She busied herself pulling wiry hairs from its head, which came away so easily that the doll would soon be bald. 'Don't open the front door while I'm gone, no matter what, okay?'

Pennie nodded. Of course she knew that.

'I'll be home to make you something to eat before bed.'

Pennie nodded again, without looking up.

Eve pulled her bag higher up on her shoulder and took the stairs slowly down, hesitating over whether or not she should be leaving Pennie alone in the house now. But the urge to go was too great and she reasoned that she *had* to work. Now more than ever, they needed the meagre income that her job provided. Besides, Pennie didn't *really* want her there anyway.

'Are you sure you'll be okay while I'm gone?' she called back when she reached the bottom step.

'Fine.'

Pennie didn't raise her voice. Eve only heard her response at all because she strained to listen for it, knowing, too, that it might be the last word she'd hear from Pennie for the rest of that day and most of tomorrow. If Pennie could help it.

Finally, she did let herself out the front door, locking it carefully behind her. She walked down the front steps, but before walking away, she turned to look back at the old house, which looked so out of place in Ireland. It was on stilts, for one thing, with just enough space underneath it for a low-ceilinged base-ment, which had never been built. Five wooden steps led up to the wooden porch that wrapped around the entire house. It was built by Peter's great-grand-father, who apparently designed it based on a homestead from the Australian outback, where, apparently, he'd spent some time. Luckily, their closest neigh-bour was some distance away, so it didn't look like a boil on the butt of an other-wise normal, rural Irish community. To everyone's relief, which was expressed often and in hushed tones, Raven's Rock was tucked away behind some trees, also planted by Peter's great-grandfather. Hidden away all on its own, leaving ordinary, decent people to pretend it wasn't even there.

Kids turned up at that house at all hours and in all conditions over the years. Some looked like they'd been living in a bin and carried nothing but the rags on their backs. Others carried their belongings in a black refuse sack. Eve often tried to remember how Pennie had come to them. She imagined that she had arrived in a dirty pyjamas, a bottle of milk in her bony little fist and nothing else. But the truth was, she didn't really know. It's like Pennie just appeared in the house one day. This tiny, newborn baby, with a gift for somehow keeping herself on the peripheral of everything. So much so that the rest of them, Eve included, sometimes forgot she was there. But like a flower trying to grow from the worst kind of soil, Pennie never quite managed to bloom.

Eve's head throbbed viciously, reminding her why she was outside the house and not inside, where she usually was. She needed to walk. Fresh air and clear thoughts were the only remedy, aside from Ellen's pills, of which she'd already taken three. As of yet, they'd failed to take effect, but the walk would help things along. But aside from her sheer desire to be out of the house, Eve also had a job, for which she *had* to go to town. It was a job that had been handed down from foster child to foster child until, eventually, Eve turned sixteen. The job had been hers ever since.

Every Monday, Wednesday and Friday, Eve went to a post office box that was in Ellen's name. There, she collected a canvas sack filled with paper flyers advertising anything from the Hoi Sin Chinese Restaurant to a circus making its way through the city. She delivered them to as many houses as she could, whether the occupants wanted to receive them or not. She enjoyed doing this, because it gave purpose to the meandering walks she loved to take. She took a modest cash payment, which accompanied each canvas sack. The cash was in an envelope, taped to the bag, with Ellen's name on it. Eve did this job diligently, knowing only too well that it was a rapidly dying form of advertising. She heard this being pointed out to the old postmaster once, to which Mr Frederickson replied, not as subtly as he could have, that it was a form of charity, to which several local businesses were happy to contribute. Eve didn't care what it was. She needed the money, and she needed to be out of the house. So she continued to do the work.

She turned her back on the house and started to walk.

The Irish summer sun was struggling in the sky as the afternoon came to a close. Eve buttoned up her jacket and pulled a grey, knitted hat from the bag. The hat was Ellen's as well, and Eve still wasn't sure how she felt about wearing it. She'd never claim it as her own or anything. Not while it still held Ellen's scent, which was the most uncomfortable thing about it. But she put it on anyway and tucked all her hair up underneath it. It wasn't that she didn't want to be recognised. No one really knew her anyway and those who did were always happy to avoid her. The same could be said for anyone coming or going from Raven's Rock. She buried her hands in her pockets and picked up the pace. She'd put the hat with the rest of Ellen's things once she returned home.

Eve knew her walking route like the back of her hand because it was the same walk she did most days now. This same dark, country road into the nearby town of Carriglen, through its main street, first to the Hollands' post office box to pick up today's flyers, and then into the park where she'd spent so much of her childhood. If Eve wasn't at school or at Raven's Rock, then she was at that park, sitting on the swings, usually with Sparrow. Sometimes, she even went there while she was *supposed* to be at school. Now, it was where she broke up her outward walking journey, with the walk home, through some housing estates and back along the same dark road. A full loop that took as long as she wanted it to take.

When she reached the town, she lowered her head further, avoiding the eyes of the people milling around, while at the same time, imagining where they might all be going. Some were probably making their way home from work. Others, she imagined, were going to meet with friends, making all sorts of exciting plans, like dinners out, and trips to the cinema. She breathed in the cold, evening air and could already feel her headache subsiding and her thoughts becoming less muddled. She smiled as she passed the Centra shop with its bustle of teenage kids gathered in the doorway. They were either arguing and about to break into a brawl, or they were just taking the piss and having fun. It was always such a fine line, as Eve knew all too well. But the boys didn't bother her as she continued past. She startled when a car horn blasted loudly, just feet away. Her immediate thought was that the car was about to hit her, despite the fact that she was on a busy footpath. She leaped out of the way as the group of boys cheered and waved at their boy-racer friend as he sped past in his ridiculously souped-up Ford Fiesta. But it was too late for Eve to slow her panicked reaction, and as she jumped into a nearby doorway, she collided hard with a person who was already there.

'Ouch!' yelled the woman, as Eve landed practically on top of her.

Eve startled again and found herself grabbing the woman by the arm as she tried to steady herself and not knock her over. 'Sorry!' she half-shouted with the stress and the fright of it all.

Before the woman could react further, or perhaps push Eve away from her, Eve stumbled clumsily back, out of the doorway and hurried away with her head down, deeply flustered. When she was far enough away, she straightened her jacket and pulled her hat further down on her head as she glanced over her shoulder. The boys were laughing and shouting good-humouredly among themselves. Most likely, they were totally oblivious to the minor panic caused by their road-hogging friend. But the woman in the doorway had stepped out onto the footpath and was staring after her, her keys in her hand poised to lock up the door to the workplace she'd just left. Her long, bouncy, ginger hair clashed garishly with the red blazer jacket that was expected to be worn by all employees in that place. Not that Eve ever had cause to visit the Homestead Building Society before. But she was familiar with their uniform because she saw people coming and going from there all the time.

Eve turned and continued shakily on her way, walking a little faster now. But she could still feel the woman's eyes on her until she rounded the bend at the end of main street and was finally out of sight.

It was late when Eve arrived home, later than she'd planned anyway, and she blamed the idiot in the Ford Fiesta for that. He'd shaken her. Eve hadn't let herself be shaken by teenage boys in a very long time, but his stupid car getting that close to her without her realising it made her feel jumpy even now, hours later.

She stood just inside the front door for a moment, listening for signs that Pennie might still be up. Not that Eve would have minded if she was, but she didn't need any more surprises. The house was silent and so she moved quietly through it, removing her bag and her coat as she went. She was trying to heed the advice of the Internet about how to deal with a grieving child. *Give her space, but not too much. Give her time, but* again, *not too much. She might want to talk about it. She might not want to talk about it. She might be quiet as a mouse, or she may lash out.* Eve was no stranger to any of it. As someone who had grown up in one of the busiest foster homes in the county, she was pretty sure she'd seen it all. But that was all in the past. Eve had only one job now and it was to love what little family she had left. Even if that family was entirely incapable of returning the sentiment.

3

Eve woke the next morning feeling somewhat groggy. Like she'd been fighting in her sleep and the state of her sheets made her think that she probably had. Eve never slept well. Her mind always conjured something to keep her switched on. And then there was the dog. She had no idea who owned the thing, but she suspected it might be wild. He only showed up from time to time, but when he did, he howled and barked like a feral beast outside the house. Eve didn't know the different dog breeds, but this was a big, black mammoth of a thing. One she wouldn't want to get close to for any reason, but luckily, he never stuck around once the sun came up. No doubt he skulked off back to whoever was feeding him and that wasn't Eve. The Internet had warned her not to. But whether it was the dog, or just her dreams, Eve felt wretched when she got up that morning. She could hear Pennie moving around down in the kitchen as she herself lumbered out of bed. She shuffled like an old woman, to her wardrobe first, then down the stairs.

Pennie glanced over her shoulder but said nothing as she went about preparing a bowl of cereal for herself. When she was done, she brought it with her to the table and Eve took a seat opposite her. Eve still hadn't gotten used to the silence in this kitchen and she doubted she ever would. It was a lot of things, but it was rarely quiet and at times like this Ellen's absence seemed to fill the place, stifling everything in the room.

'Are you okay, Pennie?' Eve asked, not for the first time and for lack of anything else to begin with.

She nodded, keeping her eyes on her Cheerios.

Eve took a breath and leaned forward, her elbows on the table. 'Look, I know you're worried. It's daunting, I get it.' She leaned back in the chair again, feeling awkward, like she always did when she tried to *lead* a meaningful conversation. *Any* conversation, for that matter. She wasn't cut out for it, but like it or not, she had to try now. She had to be the adult in the room. 'We never really talked about, you know...' Eve gestured between the two of them, 'the whole sister thing, did we? And you know... the fact that I'm now your guardian.'

Pennie's hand froze halfway to her mouth. She glanced up momentarily, then the spoon continued on its painfully slow journey.

'You don't need to,' she said after a while, so quietly and with her mouth so full, that Eve hardly heard it.

But she heard enough to nod her head, and her shoulders sagged with relief. Pennie grew up here, too. Of course she knew how the world worked, and she didn't need Eve explaining the birds and the bees to her. Or lack of birds and bees. How they could be sisters, without sharing the same DNA. Eve had been in Pennie's life from the very start. As far as Eve was concerned, that made them sisters. It seemed Pennie understood that, too, which meant she also understood that she wasn't alone in the world now and Eve could stop trying to figure out a way to explain that to her.

There was silence for a few minutes before she could think of anything else to add. There was so much she wanted to say, but words, sensible ones at least, never came easy to her, which is why she'd been watching *Gilmore Girls* obsessively of late. Lorelai Gilmore *always* knew the right thing to say. She and Rory were like best friends, rather than mother and daughter, and that's what Eve imagined being a big sister would be like. It's what she *wanted* their relationship to be.

'It's my job to protect you now,' Eve said at last, channelling her inner Lorelai. But that was where she would leave the conversation about their sisterhood. There was a lot more to it than that, of course there was. But she could share the rest with Pennie in time. The bits she was sure Ellen would have omitted, Eve would eventually tell her. Like how they'd both come about and why they were only forging a relationship with each other now. But for today, the important thing was that the child knew she was safe and that nothing bad would ever happen to her. Once she got her head around that – and of course, the loss of Ellen, which was an adjustment for both of them – then there would be time enough for everything else.

'There's something I want you to have.' Eve half-smiled and reached behind her back, where she'd stuffed the small brown bear, with the denim dungarees and the red hat that she'd taken down from the shelf in her wardrobe that morning. It belonged to Amelia and then it belonged to Eve. According to Amelia, they were the only two people *ever* to own it, which couldn't be said for many of Eve Holland's possessions. She held it towards Pennie.

'His name is Casey.' Eve smiled. 'And he's the best listener.'

Pennie looked at the bear and frowned. Like, how could an inanimate object *listen*? But she didn't say anything like that, because Pennie was never unkind. She just reached out slowly and took the bear, staring at it all the time, like maybe it would come to life in her hand or something. They sat quietly for another minute, while Pennie examined the bear, and when the silence was finally broken, Pennie was the one to do it.

'I need another bed in my room,' she said, pulling the bear close to her chest and holding him there with both hands.

Eve, a little stunned by the sound of Pennie's voice, just sat there like an idiot, staring at her. Then she looked at the bear again and thought, *oh*. 'Well, I think Casey would like to sleep in your bed, with you,' she said, again trying for a smile that might look more reassuring than weird.

Pennie looked down at the bear and loosened her grip on him. 'It's not for Casey,' she said. 'It's for Angel.'

Her voice was so small that Eve wasn't sure what she'd actually said. Plus, she was still a little surprised to have heard her voice at all today. She'd spoken quite a bit yesterday and Eve wondered if maybe this was a turning point for Pennie. If maybe she'd start coming out of herself, now that it was just the two of them.

'What, Pennie?'

But all too soon, the girl seemed to disappear inside herself again.

'It's okay,' Eve said gently. 'Whatever you have to say, please don't be afraid to say it.'

'Angel. I want somewhere for Angel to sleep,' she said softly.

'Who's Angel?'

'My friend.'

Eve took a second before answering and rewound through Ellen's playbook once more. She'd never heard the name Angel before, so she was pretty sure it wasn't a friend. Not that Pennie had many of those either. She had none, in fact. At least none who felt like getting in touch during the school holidays.

'I don't think I've met Angel yet, have I?' she asked, knowing that neither of them had.

Pennie shook her head. 'Angel is just *my* friend,' she said, her eyes on the bear again.

An imaginary friend, Eve thought. They'd had as many of those staying with them over the years as actual, physical humans. 'Oh. Well, friends are very important, aren't they?' her inner Lorelai said wisely.

Pennie's eyes filled with tears and she started to sob quietly. Eve, stunned, got up and hurried around the table. She put an arm around Pennie's shoulders and the girl stiffened. But Eve's heart filled with a kind of warmth she hadn't felt before. *This* was what being a big sister was about. *This*.

Eve encouraged her to stand and when she did, she led her towards the stairs and up to her room. If Pennie wanted to talk about beds, then that was the best place to do it, surely. She sat Pennie down on her bed and Eve sat alongside her.

'What is it, Pennie? Tell me what you need and I'll do it for you.' Eve meant every word of it and her words sounded just as determined as they were supposed to.

'I don't have any friends. Only Angel.'

Pennie's school was twenty-five miles away from Raven's Rock. That was by Ellen's design. None of them had gone to school locally, because Ellen didn't like nosy teachers prying into their business. 'What about your friends from school?' she stupidly asked anyway.

Pennie shook her head, her tears drying up as suddenly as they'd appeared. 'They all think I'm weird, so I don't have friends from school. And even if I did, it's school holidays.'

Eve was back on shaky ground now, which was pretty much where she lived. What was she supposed to do with all of these words pouring from Pennie's mouth? More than she'd spoken all year! She tried to remember what the Internet had told her... It definitely said something like, *let them lead*. 'Why would they think you're weird?' she asked, keeping her voice low and soft, but her self-doubt was overwhelming now. Why would she ask her that when she knew exactly why they thought she was weird? She was from Raven's Rock. That was enough, but added to that, Pennie never spoke. She *was* weird. They all were.

Pennie shrugged. 'I just am. I don't know how to play like they do. I don't know how to talk like them, and I don't know any of the cool stuff from like, TV, or YouTube or any of that. My clothes are always old and never have the proper names printed on them. I'm poor and I'm stupid and I'm weird and now I don't even have a mum or a dad! I'm not like any of them! I'm not like anyone,' she said, far more calmly than Eve could have if she'd tried to articulate all of that.

I know, Eve thought. Her chest tightened and her heart hurt so much for her little sister. Eve knew exactly the loneliness that Pennie described, and the girl was so much more articulate at ten than Eve felt at twenty-three. She nodded while she tried to come up with the right thing to say. 'I know what that feels like,' she said softly, immediately feeling like she'd said the wrong thing. But what was the *right* thing?

Pennie let out a *humph* and turned away. Having something in common with Eve was probably little consolation to her now. Maybe it even made matters worse.

'Some people just don't *want* to understand other people, Pennie,' she found herself saying. 'They only want to know about people who are exactly the same as they are. People who come from the same kinds of families as they do and think the same thoughts.'

Pennie didn't respond. Was she done speaking?

'We don't need people like that,' Eve insisted, reaching out a hand and touching Pennie on the shoulder.

Pennie looked at her with more uncertainty and Eve felt a pang of hurt. But she kept it to herself and tried to keep it out of her voice and her expressions. But there was a heaviness in the room suddenly and Eve could find no words to help lift it. She reminded herself that she needed to be patient. Pennie needed time to get her head around this massive change in their lives. As did Eve.

'Pennie, I...'

'It's okay. I know.' The girl was looking at the floor, at the relatively new, rainbow-coloured rug under her feet. New to them, at least. It, like everything else, had come from the charity shop in town, but it looked clean and lovely in this room.

'What do you know, Pennie?'

'I know that you'll tell me I'm safe.' She glanced at Eve through hooded eyes. 'That nothing bad will happen to me, but I also know that it won't really be true, will it? Because bad things happen all the time.'

Eve frowned and that was when she realised that, although quiet, Pennie was sharp. Much sharper than Eve had ever been. At ten, Pennie seemed to know exactly what kind of world they lived in, while Eve was only just figuring it out. She'd seen and heard enough in her ten short years to know that, in fact, life really was a fairy tale. A true fairy tale, as fairy tales were intended to be. Grim and often scary, cautionary tales with some genuinely catastrophic happenings. And enough other kids came through Raven's Rock to let them know that other homes and other lives were no better than theirs. Pennie had been conditioned to think that things could never improve, and it was up to Eve now to convince her otherwise. To show her that she was loved, no matter what.

'You're right,' she said at last. 'Bad things do sometimes happen. But they won't happen to you, okay?'

Pennie shrugged, and while she didn't seem overly convinced, she didn't look too worried either.

Eve repositioned herself on the bed, straightened her back and took a moment to silently rehearse what she wanted to say, before saying it. When she was satisfied, and before an awkward amount of time passed, she cleared her throat and said, 'Well, Pennie, I *promise* that you are safe. I *promise* that I am your family. And I *promise* that everything will be better soon.' She arched her body in search of some rare eye contact, which Pennie expertly avoided as always. 'Okay?' she asked, placing an arm around Pennie's shoulder and jostling her gently, desperate to bring some lightness back into the room. 'Okay?' she asked again, when no response came.

Finally, Pennie nodded.

'So.' Eve looked around, scrabbling for ways to cheer the child up. 'How about we go about making up a bed for Angel then?'

Pennie smiled at last and stood up. The surprise of her reaction caused a swell of emotion that Eve wasn't quite sure what to do with. She wanted to both laugh *and* cry. Pennie never smiled. Even as a small child, she was always so serious. This smile meant that Eve had gotten something very, very right. More right than Ellen, or anyone else, ever had. Pennie was smiling!

Eve hurried up off the bed and led the way to the linen press on the landing.

She took out a spare blanket and handed it to Pennie. Then she led the way to her own room and to the window box where she kept her spare pillows. Eve's was another larger-than-average bedroom, but it was also the coldest, with a draughty bay window taking up most of one wall. That window should have been replaced decades ago, but because of its ridiculous size and shape, any replacement would have had to be bespoke. Therefore it would always remain financially out of their reach, meaning that Eve would always need a decent stock of spare blankets. But this was important enough to make Pennie smile and, for that, Eve would happily freeze to death.

Pennie stood in the middle of the room, her bare feet surely cold on the thread-bare carpet. She looked around like she'd never seen the room before. Of course she had, but not since she had moved into the boys' room. Theirs wasn't the type of house where everyone mingled in each other's bedrooms at night – doing each other's hair, talking about their day and their latest crush. Theirs had been a house of strict curfews and regimental routines. It was probably time for that to change as well, but one step at a time. Eve needed time, too, to adjust to all this upheaval. She turned her back to give Pennie enough privacy to take in her surroundings in peace. The ancient, blue and white, floral-patterned wallpaper clashing garishly with the floor-to-ceiling, heavy, velvet curtains in olive green. There was the dark wood dressing table against one wall, on top of which was a stand-up mirror with foldable flaps on either side. A beast of a thing, all curves and drawers. That, and the matching free-standing wardrobe, wouldn't have looked out of place on the *Antiques Roadshow*, which Ellen used to watch religiously. She was always so sure that some of their belongings would turn out to be worth a fortune. But Eve knew that all of it would end up in the *yes, well, it does look ancient, but it's actually worth fuck all* category. The room was nowhere near as nice as Pennie's room was, now that Eve had done that up for her. Maybe she would do this one up in time, too.

She removed the long bench cushion from her window seat, which doubled as a storage unit. She opened it up, then she looked at the bench cushion and smiled. She tucked it under her arm and pulled out a pillow with her other hand. 'This lot will do nicely,' she said with genuine enthusiasm. She crossed the landing again to Pennie's room, with Pennie trailing after her. On the floor opposite Pennie's bed, Eve knelt, put down the long cushion and covered it with a pink sheet. She frowned and looked up at Pennie. 'Wait, is Angel a boy or a girl?'

Pennie didn't respond, but she smiled again. She was clearly pleased by Eve's efforts, which in turn made Eve want to dance. Or something of that nature. Do something joyful at the very least. She didn't, of course, but she thoroughly enjoyed the feeling of wanting to.

'Do you think Angel will mind having a pink sheet on their bed?'

Pennie shook her head, her small smile still there.

'Phew.' Eve smiled back. She placed the blanket over the cushion and tucked it in all around. Then she placed the pillow on top and leaned back on her heels, pleased with what she saw. It looked like a little toddler's bed, but she was sure it was perfect for an imaginary friend. 'What do you think? Will this do?'

Pennie looked to her own single bed and back. She shrugged and nodded.

'What do you think, Angel?' Eve asked, looking at the air beside Pennie.

Pennie frowned and looked behind her.

Eve's smile faltered as she caught herself too late. She'd gone too far. She could see it in the girl's face.

'Angel's not here?' Eve asked, feeling stupid suddenly.

Pennie shook her head.

'How long has Angel been your friend?'

'Since Ellen.'

Ellen. She was the only mum that either of them had ever known, but they were never permitted to call her by that title. She was Ellen, always. Still, it made sense that Pennie's imaginary friend would turn up just as she lost her mother figure.

Eve reached out and gave her shoulder a gentle squeeze. 'I'd like to meet Angel sometime.'

'Angel won't let you see him. Only me.' There was an uncharacteristic hint of petulance in her tone. A ten-year-old who'd lost everything, claiming something that was now hers and hers alone. But it seemed Angel was a *him*. At least Eve now knew that much.

'Ah. I see.' Eve nodded and smiled, bringing them back on an even keel. *Thank you Lorelai*, she thought.

'Angel will always be my friend,' she responded sternly, as if Eve had suggested otherwise.

'Okay, well...'

'She'll mind me. She promised she will and I...' Her eyes filled with tears again.

Okay, Angel was a *she* now, but Eve said nothing. Clearly, Pennie's imagination wasn't quite done with creating Angel yet. They were still a work in progress.

'And so will I,' Eve said, gently reaching for the girl again. 'I'll mind you, too.'

Pennie surprised her then by letting Eve hug her. Usually, she wriggled away whenever she tried, but now she stood there, perfectly still as Eve wrapped her arms tightly around her. Again, warmth spread through her entire body and her heart, so suddenly full it felt like it might burst. This was it. This was love.

'We're a family, Pennie. We'll keep each other safe.' She spoke into the girl's hair, holding her close. 'Me, you... and Angel.'

4

Over the next few days, Pennie returned to her usual self, hardly speaking, no matter how much Eve tried to coax her, and when Monday came around, she cried at the thought of going on a day out to the park. Eve couldn't understand how Pennie never loved the place like she did. She never craved the freedom from this old house or the fun that could be had on those swings, old and rusted though they may be. Did Pennie even know what it felt like, soaring high up into the sky like that? And then that moment at the very top, where your body pauses in mid-air, before rushing back to earth? Didn't she know how good that felt? Didn't she *want* to know? They'd never been allowed to go there together when Ellen was here. She didn't like the idea of both of them being gone at the same time, so she always came up with some chores for one of them to do, while the other went out. Or perhaps it was her way of making sure that Eve always came back. A totally irrational fear when Eve quite literally had nowhere else to go, even now. Eve was never really the independent type. Not like Pennie. But seeing her tear-filled eyes and crumpled face, Eve let go of the idea of a day out of the house together. Pennie was a home bird and maybe she always would be. If she had her way, she wouldn't leave the house from the time school broke for summer, until the first day of a new term was forced upon her. But what could Eve do about it?

Eve was different. No matter how much she wanted to spend her time with Pennie, she couldn't spend all day inside that house. But following her near-death experience with that Ford Fiesta, she'd switched her working hours from night-time to day. Luckily, she had the freedom to do that. No one cared *when* their advertised services reached the letter boxes of potential customers. So long as they did. She'd also started bringing her car with her so that she could get home quickly if Pennie ever needed her. Now, if Eve were still at home come lunchtime, the walls would start closing in. Even on rainy days, she'd find herself happily swaying back and forth on the swings in the park, lost in thoughts of Sparrow, her bag of flyers wrapped in plastic on the ground beside her. She thought that when the new school term started, she could drop Pennie to school each day then head to the park after her rounds and spend the whole day there, while she waited for her to finish. Then they could drive home together in silence. Always in silence. She could never imagine that changing by much, even if Pennie had spoken to her more this week than ever before.

Before leaving, Eve went to the kitchen and packed an old, teal-green lunchbox with a ham and cheese sandwich. It was the same lunchbox she'd had throughout her school years and now it was Pennie's. But she only used it during term, which meant that Eve could make use of it now. She placed it carefully in her green canvas bag. She then made a second ham and cheese sandwich, which she covered in tinfoil and placed in the fridge, for Pennie's lunch. Next, she filled two water bottles with orange cordial. She put hers in her bag and brought Pennie's to her bedroom, where Pennie sat fully dressed on her bed.

'Are you sure you don't want to come?' Eve asked, for the second time that morning. 'The park is fun!'

Pennie didn't answer and Eve threw a look of uncertainty at the carpet. 'I mean, we don't *have* to go to the park. We could do something else.' She said it in case it was what Pennie wanted to hear, though she had no idea what that something else might be. There wasn't much by way of children's entertainment nearby that she knew of. At least none that didn't compel you to buy coffee and food on top of an unjust entrance fee. They could get a bus to the city, but everything there cost money, too. Every single thing seemed to come with a price tag and whatever that price was, they couldn't afford it. Except for the park. There were no fancy horsebox coffee bars there. No monetised distractions at all. Just swings, a slide, a wonky roundabout and a wooden balance beam that wobbled when you stood on it. And lots and lots of clean, fresh, free-of-charge air.

Pennie shook her head as she fingered Casey's red hat. Seeing her holding him so tightly made Eve feel happy. She'd always loved Casey, because he was given to her by her own big sister. Passing it down to Pennie felt like a real family-like thing to do.

'Okay, well... you call me if you need me.'

'I don't have a phone,' Pennie reminded her. Not that she'd ever asked for a phone.

'I know that,' Eve said gently. 'My number is on the board beside the kitchen phone.'

She hadn't mentioned it, or made a *thing* of it, but she'd rubbed out Ellen's number, which had always been there. Not that Ellen had ever left the house either. Certainly not for long enough that any of them might desperately need for her to come back. Well, they *had* desperately needed her at times, but Ellen was a funny old sort. She always had been. Eve was different. She'd replaced Ellen's number with her own now, so that Pennie could always reach her, no matter what. And Eve would always come.

'Okay, well, I'll leave you to it then,' she muttered, when Pennie failed to respond to her telephone instructions.

Eve could have made a handy list of suggestions for her. Things that she could do to pass her day, like go out to the garden, or build a fort. That kind of thing. But she didn't want to be one of those try-hard adults. If she was honest, she was finding the whole thing mentally draining. How could two people be in each other's lives forever, under the same roof, and hardly know how to just *be* in each other's company? Had Ellen engineered it that way, she wondered? Had she purposely kept them so busy and regimental in their routines that now they hardly knew each other?

'Your lunch is in the fridge,' she added, sounding embarrassingly desperate to please.

Pennie replied with another slight nod, her eyes still on the bear and the string that she was slowly pulling out. Eve worried briefly for Casey. Was he headed in the same direction as the balding Barbie? Would the hat slowly begin to disintegrate, after all this time?

'Okay,' she echoed, her eyes on the bear now, too. But eventually, she made herself move along. She made herself leave the house and get in her car and start driving without really knowing where she was driving to. She'd circle round to the post office box at some stage, but for now, she just followed the road.

As she drove, her phone started to ring. She slowed the car and glanced at the screen, but there was no name to go with the number. Not that she had many names saved in that thing. But this was the same number that had been calling her non-stop for the past three weeks. Eve let out a frustrated moan and stabbed the red button with her thumb, declining the call. There's a reason why people don't pick up calls from unknown numbers. Eve had made that mistake before and was hit with a barrage of horrible name-calling and shaming from someone who'd been spending too much time online. She would not make that mistake again. Her phone was for her to search for information online, to call Pennie, and to receive calls from Pennie. That was it. To the rest of the world, Eve Holland could not be reached at this time.

Her head started to throb again, and Eve decided that fresh air was the first thing she wanted to try today. Before the pills and before taking herself off someplace dark. She needed to try to get a handle on her headaches in a way that didn't take her away from her responsibilities. So, she made her deliveries on foot first, then she drove to her favourite place in the entire world: the park. Once there, she parked up and took her canvas bag containing her lunch off the back seat and brought it with her, through the park, and over to the swing set. She set the bag on the ground, sat on a swing – always the same swing – and gently pushed herself off.

As she glided back and forth, a small smile grew on her lips. This was where all her happy memories were made. It was where she got to be alone with Sparrow, side by side swinging up to the clouds and back down to earth. She imagined he was here with her now, swinging alongside her. That was his swing and this one was hers. Sparrow and Eve. Eve and Sparrow.

Hours passed while she lost herself in thoughts of him. It was late in the afternoon and lunch was long since eaten, when she thought to return to her car, and the road back to Raven's Rock.

When she got there, Pennie was nowhere to be seen, as usual. Eve tidied the still-tidy kitchen, then headed to Pennie's room. She wasn't in there, but Eve could hear the shower running. She peered around the bedroom door and saw that Pennie's bed was made up as neatly as it had been that morning. Eve had set a ground rule for herself, to respect the privacy of her sister, knowing only too well how it felt to have adults poking their noses into every thought in your head. So she'd planned to take just a quick glance into her room each morning, just to make sure the girl had a clean and comfortable space to call her own. Ellen would call her an idiot for that, and Eve knew exactly why. This house had been home to children who'd gotten up to all sorts while under their roof, including drug-taking, drug-storing, food-hoarding, some had been self-harming, weapons-stashing – one girl was found to have a handgun under her pillow. Lord knows where she had got one of those around here. So with this in mind, Eve opened the door a little further and peered around the entire room. She frowned when she saw the makeshift, toddler-sized bed looking like it had been slept in. She stepped into the room and looked again at the two beds, wondering now if Pennie had been sleeping there, and if that was why the single bed had been perfectly made up each morning. Eve had assumed that it was because Pennie was conscientious when it came to keeping her room tidy and her bed made. But instead, was it because she'd stopped sleeping in it?

Eve frowned as her eyes came to rest on the two plastic bowls sitting on the windowsill. It seemed her ground rule of total privacy had lasted no time at all, but she didn't hesitate in stepping fully into the room now. She walked to the window and looked into each of the bowls. One contained cornflakes, mostly eaten, and one held some of last night's cottage pie, untouched.

'Damn it,' she muttered.

She thought back through each of their mealtimes since Ellen, looking for signs that Pennie's relationship with food held any red flags. Pennie just pushed her food around the plate for the most part, but that was normal given what they were going through, wasn't it? Lord knows, Eve didn't have much of an appetite herself. Still, she pulled her phone out of her pocket and googled, *eating disorders*.

She was bombarded with results, all far more extreme than a bowl of cornflakes and some cottage pie. She was being ridiculous. Her head throbbed again, harder this time, and Eve brought the heels of her hands to her temples. The time for pills and darkness was fast approaching. And anyway, what the hell was the problem here? Aside, of course, from Eve's overexposure to the world of troubled kids, the upshot of which was that she saw problems where there probably weren't any. There was only a grieving child and her inept big sister. She tucked her phone back in her pocket, feeling as stupid as ever, then she took the bowls from the windowsill, shook her head again at her own ineptitude and left the room. But still, she would remove the privacy ground rule. Or at least, relax it. Ellen was right about this one thing: she did need to keep an eye on things.

Eve dropped the bowls in the sink and went in search of her pills. She deposited two in the palm of her hand and washed them down with water. Then she went to her room and closed the door.

Pennie was outdoors when Eve finally emerged from her room an hour or so later. She was sitting on the front steps with a thin smile on her lips. It was almost imperceptible, but it *was* there, and Eve felt her own shoulders sag, unaware of the tension she'd been carrying in them.

'You look like you had an okay day?' she said from the front door. She wanted to go and sit alongside her, but was unsure whether or not she'd be intruding on the girl's moment of mild contentment.

'I don't want to go to the same school next term,' she said, like she'd just been discussing this very thing with someone cleverer than Eve. 'Isn't there another school I could go to?'

Eve's relief dissipated and the tension returned. She dithered for a moment more, before finally going and sitting below her, on the bottom step. 'Really? Why?' was all she could think to say. *Why not?* That was what her brain asked. Her school was miles from her home and she had zero friends there. Why wouldn't she want a fresh start in a new school? But instead of acknowledging any of that, she waited for Pennie to respond while Eve ran the idea through her baffled mind. *Could* she remove Pennie from her school and start her at another? She was Pennie's guardian, so technically yes, she probably could. But what kind of paperwork would that involve? A lot, probably. As far as Eve knew, neither of them came with papers like birth certificates and the like. Her headache intensified at the idea of trying to obtain anything like that now.

'I want to go somewhere where people don't know me. Where they don't know where I come from and that I'm an orphan.'

Eve understood exactly what she meant and why she would want to move schools. There was comfort in anonymity and Eve had to agree that it might be the best thing for both of them. But still, there would be paperwork.

'Okay, well... let me see what I can do,' was the answer she settled upon. And she would see what she could do.

'Angel said everything will be better when they're not all watching. He said there are too many chiefs and not enough Indians when it comes to people like me.'

Eve frowned. 'Oh. Angel is here?' And he was a *he* again.

'Angel is always here now.'

'Course he is.' Eve smiled. 'But there are some good reasons to stick with your old school, Pennie,' she tried. The more she thought about the red tape involved, the more she scared herself off the idea. 'Your *real* friends will be there for you, too, in time.'

'Angel *is* my real friend.'

'Oh, I know that.' Eve glanced up at her, her little face serious as she turned to look towards the treeline that ran around three sides of the house. 'I just mean... well, Angel found you. That's great!' she said, scrabbling for the right words, but they remained just out of reach.

'Angel said you wouldn't know what to do.'

Eve frowned, confused. 'I wouldn't know what to do about what?'

'Moving me to another school. Angel said that you just need to call up another school and ask them. Tell them I want a fresh start and that having people staring at me and whispering about me all day isn't helping me.'

Eve repositioned herself in a bid to ease her discomfort, physical and otherwise. She threw small glances over her shoulder at Pennie, wondering how an imaginary person, one who'd only recently come to stay with them, was so articulate when it came to Eve's ineptitude. Pennie, for her part, looked like she was losing hope. She was still looking towards the trees, with her chin resting on her closed fist.

'Angel said that?'

Nothing. Not even a nod.

Eve looked straight ahead towards the narrow road that ran past their hodgepodge old house, her brain scrabbling for a response. The only one she could come up with was, 'You know, it's not nice to assume that someone wouldn't know what to do.' *Or for a ten-year-old girl to think her big sister is stupid.* Wasn't it a rule somewhere that younger siblings were supposed to idolise their older sibling? Weren't they supposed to think that they were cleverer than anyone else and that they were right about everything, whether they were or not?

Pennie turned to look at her and Eve could feel her eyes on the side of her face, but she said nothing. Neither of them did. Pennie just stared for a minute, before turning back to the more interesting landscape beside their house. It was pretty to look at. A thick copse of evergreen trees behind a low, quaint stone wall which had been built by Peter's grandfather and repaired in places by Peter himself. But Eve couldn't see the beauty in it now. All she could see was Pennie's disappointment. She thought Eve was stupid and she was right. Not that that made it hurt any less, but the fact that Angel was the one who had brought it up meant that he was textbook as far as imaginary friends went. That was according to the Internet, *and* all she'd learned from her years at this house. Pennie was unable to voice her own concerns, so she used *Angel* to voice them for her. Textbook. Exactly the kind of thing that imaginary friends were invented for. But Eve couldn't dwell on her own pain now. Not when her job was to manage Pennie's.

So how could she possibly tell her that a new school wouldn't help? The stories that circulated about their home were legendary and not in a good way. Stories of witchcraft and devil worship had been rife for a time. So were stories of organised crime and a dozen other ridiculous stereotypes were attached to their home and its occupants over the years. So a school where no one knew either of them simply did not exist. Not around here, at least.

'Angel says I need a fresh start,' Pennie whispered, to the trees rather than to Eve.

Eve exhaled, slowing her thoughts. 'Okay,' she said, putting the bad news off for another day. At least until she, too could use someone else's words to relay the message.

'Okay?' Pennie looked at her, a hopeful lilt to her voice.

'I mean, obviously I'll need to check with some of the other schools in the area. We can't just turn up there and assume they'll have a place.' Truth was, Eve had no idea how school admissions worked. 'It's not rocket science, though,' she mumbled.

Pennie glanced in her direction.

'I just mean... we'll figure it out.' She reached behind her and gave Pennie's knee a gentle squeeze. 'Don't worry,' she said instead of breaking the news that they would never be accepted anywhere. 'I'm in full agreement with Angel. I think a fresh start would be amazing. I'll start making calls first thing tomorrow, okay? It might not happen overnight, but I'll do my best.' Yes. That's exactly what Lorelai would have said. Exactly.

They sat quietly for a while then, Pennie staring into the trees and Eve looking up at the old house. A wildflower garden grew all around it, and it had a patch at the back where Ellen had planted cabbages, carrots, onions, lettuce and more herbs than Eve knew how to use. It was low maintenance and Eve vowed to start using it more, to nourish her little sister. She needed to start taking better care of herself, too. She was Pennie's guardian now. Eve was all she had, and she could not let her down, no matter how much Pennie expected her to. The wrap-around deck had a timber railing that was handmade by Peter. He had been handy that way. A jack of all trades, he'd called himself, many times. The deck and the railing were his attempt at making it look even more like that Australian homestead that his great-grandfather had had in mind. The idea had seemed to sit well with Peter. He'd always had a thing for Aussie culture. It even had a rusting swing chair beside the front door and a large chunk of black slate nailed to the railing beside the steps, with the name *Raven's Rock* etched on it in white paint, beside a depiction of an actual raven. Peter might have been a jack of all trades, but an artist he was not. Still, everyone knew what it was supposed to be. To Eve, it was home and it always would be. Raven's Rock was as much a part of her as her arms or her legs were. At this point, she wasn't sure she'd survive without it. She wondered briefly if Pennie felt the same way. Or did she picture a life away from this place and, if so, what did that life look like?

'What if they say no?' Pennie said, breaking the peaceful silence.

'Well, then...'

'Angel says you'll give up too easily.'

Eve was starting to dislike Angel. 'I won't give up,' she replied sternly. 'And you can pass that on to Angel because, clearly, he doesn't know me very well.'

Pennie looked at her like she was deluded, which of course was understandable. Then without another word, she got to her feet and went inside.

Eve watched her walk away with more confidence than she seemed to have had earlier in the day. Or earlier in her life. Was that because her *friend* had found her, Eve wondered?

In that moment, she envied her little sister. Real or not, Eve wished she had a friend who could do that for her. Where was *her* Angel?

5

'I understand this is a very upsetting situation for the poor child.'

This was the third school administrator she'd spoken to that day and this one sounded tired. Or perhaps annoyed, it could be hard to tell sometimes. But it was school holidays. Perhaps she didn't appreciate being contacted about work during this time, despite the last one saying that *there was no rest in the department of education.* Yeah right, Eve thought. This woman sounded like she dealt with queries like this every day during the holidays and was losing the last of her patience.

'But surely routine and continuity are crucial at this important juncture.' She sighed loudly down the phone. 'You're that woman from Raven's Rock, aren't you? Mrs Holland?' Her dark fascination made good its escape at last and Eve didn't correct her on her assumption. The woman didn't wait for confirmation either, before ploughing on. 'I really think pulling her out of her school, just because she asked you to, would be a mistake.' She sighed again, like this was the most trying part of her day. 'At this age, introducing a new student from such a... well, one who needs special attention...' She was fumbling in her own condescension now. 'Well, it would just be too disruptive to the other students, I'm afraid. We just don't have the resources here at St Ethans to give her the help she would need.'

'She's not thick, you know, Mrs Hayes,' Eve cut her off finally. She'd been biting her tongue, trying not to be *difficult.* But she didn't particularly want to be told yes in the first place. Not if it meant having to figure out all the baffling and torturous red tape. She just needed to be able to tell Pennie that she'd tried. That was it. But she refused to let this woman talk about her sister like she wasn't one of the cleverest people she knew. Hell, Pennie was probably cleverer than Mrs Bitchy Hayes. 'She wouldn't *need* any special treatment,' Eve insisted, against her better judgement. But she was tired of people treating them like pariahs. 'She needs a fresh start because she's being treated like a freak at her current school. Do you think that's okay?'

'Please don't ever use that word around me again,' the woman said, like the word *freak* was so much worse than her own distaste at the words *Raven's Rock*. In schoolyards everywhere around here, the two used to mean the same thing. One equalled the other.

Eve's face contorted from the effort of keeping her frustration and annoyance at bay. She brought the palm of her hand to her forehead and clutched the phone tightly in her other hand. 'Freak isn't *my* word, Mrs Hayes,' she lied. 'Pennie told me that that's how she feels every day when she has to go there. I just think that letting her start at a school where nobody knows her might help her to...'

'Well, that may be. But I'm afraid I can't make a place magically appear in one of my classrooms, Mrs Holland. And I'd imagine you'll get the same response from each of the other schools in the area.' She heaved another exasperated sigh into Eve's ear, sending what was left of her nerves teetering towards the edge. 'May I ask, how come you never got in touch before? Haven't you always sent those kids to St Mary's?'

'What does that mean?'

'Well, no disrespect, Mrs Holland, but I'm sure this isn't the only child who's suffered the same treatment from their peer group. How come you never looked to change schools for any of the others?'

None of the Raven's Rock kids had ever attended St Ethans, and yet Eve didn't need to ask how she knew that they had all been mistreated in the schoolyard of St Mary's. When it came to them, everyone seemed to know everything. Or at least, they imagined they did.

'Well,' Eve said, her voice low and questioning now, 'if you're aware of how other children are being mistreated, then how come *you* never questioned the ways in which you might be able to help, Mrs Hayes?' She shouldn't be asking this and she knew it. Still, she couldn't stop herself. 'Isn't that what teachers are supposed to do? Look out for the well-being of their students?'

There was an icy pause before the insufferable woman spoke again. 'Well, they were never *my* students, were they? Anyway, I'm very sorry, Mrs Holland, but I'm unable to help in this instance. I will certainly place Pennie's name on the waiting list for St Ethans. But I warn you that it is quite long. Now you have a lovely summer, won't you. And best of luck finding a new school for Pennie.'

There was a long pause, while Eve choked down the words she wanted to throw back at the woman. Instead, she made a note on the page in front of her. The other three schools had said pretty much the same thing about their waiting lists. But each of them had mentioned Raven's Rock in a way that said, *don't hold your breath waiting for a place to come available*. All of them had assumed, too, that she was Ellen, and Eve hadn't corrected any of them. Their house was so much quieter now than it used to be and it seemed news of their grief wasn't so quick to travel. She wondered if any of them had ever actually met Ellen in the flesh. She so rarely left the house, preferring instead to have the kids do her errands for her. And she'd never attended parents' night at the school. Never. Eve could see why now.

She folded away her notes and got slowly to her feet. She smoothed down her clothes and mentally prepared herself to deliver this news to Pennie. In the words of multiple school administrators, rather than her own.

When she was ready, she went upstairs and knocked gently on Pennie's door. She waited this time to be invited inside, which she was, in a tiny voice that sounded very far away. Eve pushed open the door and Pennie was sitting on the makeshift bed, legs crossed and the brown bear, Casey, being fidgeted with in her hands.

'Hey, mind if I come in?'

Pennie nodded and Eve went and sat on Pennie's actual bed, glad to be off her feet again. Surely, she was too young to feel this old.

'Have you been sleeping in that bed?' she asked.

Pennie nodded again.

'Well, don't you think this bed might be more comfy?' She smoothed her hand along the colourful bedspread. She would have loved a bed like this at Pennie's age, and she desperately wanted to lie down on it herself now.

'That's Angel's bed,' Pennie replied as a matter of fact.

'Oh. But I thought we made *that* bed for Angel?'

Pennie shook her head. 'She's too big for this bed.'

'She is? So... how big is Angel then?'

'Bigger than you.'

Eve made herself smile. 'Well, I'm only five foot five, so it's not hard to be bigger than me.'

'Angel is bigger than everyone. Angel is a watcher, that's why.'

The Internet told Eve several times that imaginary friends were a good thing. They helped make a child feel safe and they lent their voice when the child lacked the confidence to speak for themselves. Angel, the watcher, sounded like a father figure, Eve thought. Or a mother figure, depending on the day. Maybe even a fairy-tale knight the way Pennie described them, her voice sounding younger than her ten years whenever she spoke about Angel.

'A watcher?' Eve said with interest. 'What's that then?'

Pennie didn't look like she'd heard her and Eve didn't really expect her to respond. But she did. 'Angel watches people. Minds them, like.'

Eve nodded. 'Oh. Hence the name, right?'

Pennie started pulling again at that thread on the bear's hat as they sat quietly for a beat. Eve watched her fingers move and worried again that Pennie might ruin the bear, after it had survived so much before her. There were times when that bear felt like Eve's only friend in the world, and she worried for him now. But she said nothing.

'Well, I'm glad that Angel makes you feel minded,' Eve said, her voice soft. 'I hope someday, you'll trust me to mind you as well. I *am* your big sister, after all.' And that made her feel better. Those words always brought her comfort, which was why she was throwing them around so much now – *big sister*.

But Pennie didn't look up.

'So.' Eve frowned. 'Is Angel a boy or a girl?'

Pennie shrugged, nonchalant, her eyes still on the bear.

'That's okay. Gender isn't what it used to be,' Eve said, her voice filled with uncertainty. Again, this information came from the Internet. She'd never met anyone who'd changed genders or identified as anything other than what they were born as. But when she thought about it, it made her wonder just how big and strange the world outside this house might actually be. A world where people could literally be anything they want to be.

'Sometimes, when Angel speaks, she's a woman. Sometimes, when she speaks, she's a man,' Pennie explained.

Eve nodded, her brain picking slowly through the meaning of that. What it came up with was that Angel was a substitute mother *and* father figure. Angel was the full package, making Eve feel ridiculously insecure. More so than usual, that is.

'I spoke to some schools today,' she said, changing the subject with a hopeful lilt. 'They're all going to rejig their waiting lists and get you into the next place that comes available.' It wasn't a total lie, because they had all mentioned putting Pennie on their waiting list. It was just that none of them had sounded in any way convincing.

Pennie looked up then, surprised.

'Yeah.' Eve smiled. 'A fresh start.'

Eve wasn't sure she believed in those. *She* certainly wasn't likely to get one. Not while she couldn't bring herself to leave this house, but she had often thought about changing her appearance. It wasn't like anyone knew *her*, exactly. Perhaps they knew the outline of her with her brown coat and her canvas bag, working her way through town, delivering flyers. But they wouldn't have paid attention to the detail of her. Most people were too self-conscious to stare. But they knew Raven's Rock and, vaguely, all the troublesome people who came and went from it. Perhaps it was their aura which identified them. Or some stench that they carried unknowingly with them wherever they went.

'But in the meantime, you and I could do some stuff together over the summer, I'm sure? A day out at the beach or something.' What beach, she couldn't imagine.

Pennie shook her head, no.

'Won't you be lonely here by yourself all summer while I have to work?'

'I'll have Angel,' she responded with a slight, almost happy smile.

Eve looked around the room again, trying to think of another suggestion. As much as Eve knew she'd never leave Raven's Rock for good, nor could she hang around inside it all day. And Pennie didn't want to leave it. So from a guardian's perspective, *should* she be leaving Pennie home alone at the age of ten? Was that safe? Ellen had never left anyone home alone, but Eve was sure that that was more to do with Ellen than her fear of any harm coming to them in her absence. But what choice did Eve have? For at least three days out of every seven, she *had* to work. And sometimes, when she didn't get all her flyers delivered, she had to roll over into the next day. But they'd be in far more trouble without that money.

Eve would have given anything for friends and play dates when she was younger. Even now, she'd kill to have a friend. A *real* friend. But Pennie seemed very accepting of her life. Had she always been like that, Eve wondered? She didn't know and, again, she questioned how they'd lived before. Separate lives in such close proximity to each other. For such an unassuming-looking woman, Ellen had been a mastermind when it had come to engineering their circumstances in such a way that no secret had ever escaped the house, and no bond had ever been formed inside it.

Well, in that one at least, she'd failed. Eve thought again about Sparrow and Amelia and her heart became heavy with loss and longing.

'Angel will be my friend,' Pennie said, as if reading Eve's thoughts and bringing her back into the room.

Eve nodded silently. 'Okay,' she said, sounding as tired as she felt suddenly. She stood and walked to the door. 'Come on then. It's dinner time.'

6

The television in the corner of the kitchen was on with the volume low while Eve cooked, and she purposely didn't turn it off when they sat down to eat. It was one other thing she would do differently to Ellen. She'd always insisted on no distractions at the table. But Eve always found silence so awkward, and she felt immense pressure to fill it. She had yet to experience a so-called *comfortable* silence and doubted very much that they even existed. Not that there was ever a lot of silence in their house, but when a new kid came and they didn't feel like talking, that silence was as loud as a ticking clock as far as Eve was concerned. So now ads played on low in the corner of the room, while Eve scooped lasagne out of a dish in the centre of the table. She wouldn't mention Angel again, or ask if he'd be joining them for dinner, or anything stupid like that. She'd been wrong every time she had, so instead, there was enough lasagne for the invisible man, or indeed, the invisible woman, should they deign to show up. And when they didn't eat it, it would be their dinner for tomorrow as well.

'She's that woman,' Pennie said, nodding towards the TV. She said it like someone who initiated conversations often. Like speaking without first being asked a question was perfectly normal for her.

Eve raised her eyebrows in surprise and turned to look at the TV, which was behind her. The news was on, and a picture of a glamourous, red-haired woman, whose bouncy curls looked like they belonged on a shampoo commercial, smiled back at them.

Eve's heart stopped momentarily, she was sure of it. The sudden pain in her chest was too great for there to be another explanation. She stared at the smiling face looking back at her as Pennie reached for the remote and turned up the volume. It was her. The woman she'd bumped into on her walk, after that car horn sent her stumbling. The picture disappeared and a highly polished man sitting behind a news desk took its place.

'Twenty-six-year-old Leslie Granger was last seen leaving work at around 6.30 p.m. yesterday. She was found dead at her home early this morning when a passing neighbour became concerned at seeing the front door to the woman's house wide open, while walking her child to school. When she returned twenty minutes later, the door was still open, with no sign of Miss Granger.'

'What, did you know her?' Eve peeled her eyes away from the screen and looked worriedly at Pennie. Her mind raced towards the impact this news might have if she did.

Pennie shook her head and took a mouthful of food, looking nervous suddenly. Eve's heart thumped heavily against her chest as she studied Pennie's face. When she turned back to the TV, the newsreader was handing over to a more windswept woman, standing on a well-lit, suburban road. Behind her, a row of semi-detached homes that looked vaguely familiar to Eve. Familiar in the sense that they resembled all the houses she visited on her delivery rounds. They were the standard blueprint used in house-building in Ireland over the past few decades. Houses like those made their home look even more ridiculous. Or marvellous, depending on your architectural taste.

'Yes, Fred, that's right,' the woman said, squinting into the camera as it started to rain on her, just as gentle drops began tapping on their kitchen window, too. 'Miss Granger was last seen leaving her place of work on Carriglen's Main Street at around six thirty yesterday evening. She was wearing the Homestead Building Society uniform at the time. The alarm was raised when a neighbour noticed that Miss Granger's front door was wide open when they passed this morning. They went to investigate and found Miss Granger inside her home, still wearing her work clothes, deceased on her living-room floor. Although there was no sign of forced entry, Gardaí are treating Miss Granger's death as suspicious. They have not yet confirmed whether they have any suspects in mind, but it is believed that the woman lived alone and had only recently moved to the area, having lived overseas in New Zealand for the past number of years.' The reporter gestured to the house behind her again, keeping her eyes trained on her captive audience. 'The cause of death is unclear at this time, but the State Pathologist, Dr Carrie Howard, is due to carry out a post-mortem early tomorrow morning. Forensics are currently at the scene and Gardaí are appealing for anyone who may have been in the Carriglen area between the hours of six thirty yesterday evening and seven o'clock this morning, or indeed if they saw anything suspicious, to please get in touch at the number below, or to make contact with any Garda station. We'll bring you more details as they emerge.'

The reporter handed back to the studio and Eve turned the volume down again. Her efforts to control her breathing made each of her movements feel robotic. But if Pennie noticed, then she didn't say.

'That's not too far from here,' Eve said, trying to sound more normal than she ever actually was. Meanwhile, her headache poured into her eye sockets. Murders don't often happen in Cork, so she imagined they'd be hearing about this for days. 'Where did you hear about her?' she asked Pennie, gently stabbing a forkful of food that she no longer felt like eating, her eyes on Pennie and her barely touched meal.

Pennie shrugged. 'Someone did something to her.'

Eve frowned and nodded. That was an understatement, and she immediately questioned the wisdom of letting Pennie listen to the full news report, lacking though it was in detail.

'It was a secret,' Pennie said, her eyes averted. 'That's why she's dead.'

Eve's fork froze halfway to her mouth. 'What?' She closed her eyes and shook her head, confusion stealing her coherent thoughts. 'What do you mean, that's why she's dead? How do you know this?'

Pennie shrugged again. She pushed her food around on her plate, looking more upset suddenly. Eve continued to stare at her, wondering if perhaps she *did* know the murdered woman. But how could she? And why would she say she didn't?

'You're looking at me,' Pennie mumbled.

'What?' Eve hadn't heard her. She was thinking about the fact that she'd physically touched that dead woman just days before.

'You're *looking* at me.' Pennie lowered her fork, keeping her eyes on her plate.

Eve snapped out of her thoughts.

'Like the kids at school look at me,' Pennie continued, her voice shrivelling again. 'Like you think I'm a freak or something.' Her eyes burned with unchar-acteristic anger while she spoke.

Uncharacteristic. That word was beginning to sum up a lot of Pennie's behaviours over the past few days and Eve couldn't help wondering what was bringing about this change in her. Was it down to Ellen's sudden and unex-pected absence? Or was it Angel's sudden and even more unexpected presence? Either way, she was right. Eve *had* been staring, but in wonder. Or maybe, discomfort?

'I'm not... You're not a freak, Pennie, and I'm not staring at you. I'm just wondering how you knew so much about that woman. That's all.'

'Angel says we all need to be careful about knowing stuff. If someone thinks you know their secrets, then they can kill you.'

Eve's warm skin cooled rapidly and pricked with the appearance of goose-bumps. 'Angel said that?'

Pennie nodded and took a small bite of her food, her stomach growling loudly as she did. 'Secrets make people die, like, all the time.'

'And how do you and Angel know that she had secrets? The newsreader didn't say anything about that.'

'There's different newses, you know, aside from the one on the telly,' she said, sounding younger than her age and far more chatty. Again. 'Plus, Angel knows a lot. He knows more than you.'

Eve nodded slowly, gathering her thoughts. Her stomach had cut itself off entirely now from the idea of food and what she *had* eaten began churning slowly in there. 'So, how did Angel find you then?'

Pennie frowned, like it was a stupid question. 'Angel is my friend,' she said, as if that explained everything. 'Can I go to bed? I'm tired.'

Eve felt sure she needed to probe more on this weird conversational path that they'd found themselves on, but she had no idea what else to say to the girl. Truth be told, she was freaked out. She never wanted to admit that, knowing how damaging things like that were to a child. Especially one that already thought of herself as a freak. But she was.

'Sure,' she said after a beat too long. 'But you didn't eat much.'

'I'm not hungry.'

'Okay, but you need to eat,' she insisted.

Pennie looked at the plate for a moment, then back up at Eve. 'I don't like lasagne.'

That was a lie. She'd always eaten it before, but Eve didn't push that fact.

'I'm not a very good cook, am I?' she tried instead, with half a smile which travelled no distance at all past her lips. 'I'll leave it in the fridge. If you get hungry,' she looked at the plate of barely touched food, 'or desperate later, just come and get some.'

Pennie nodded and mouthed something that looked like, *thanks*. Then she walked upstairs and, seconds later, her bedroom door closed.

Eve sat there until the light outside died completely and the chill in the air became harder to ignore. She couldn't get the woman's face out of her mind. Leslie. Her eyes looked right into Eve's as they bumped into each other that night. She'd frowned, as if wondering who Eve was and what her intentions were. Eve remembered the smell of her perfume. Something floral and sweet. She roughly rubbed her eyes with the heels of her hands and got up from the table at last, her legs tingling in protest after too long sitting in one position. She went to get her pills from the kitchen cupboard, took two and then retrieved her phone and brought it with her upstairs. She was done with this day and needed sleep, but as she walked through the house, she did a Google search for Leslie Granger and a string of bold headlines filled her screen.

Woman Dies in Suspicious Circumstances at her Rented Carriglen Home.

Death on her Doorstep.

Woman Found Dead in Carriglen. Murder, or Accident?

Death in New Home. What Happened to Recently Relocated Leslie Granger?

Eve clicked on the first headline and started reading. Leslie Granger worked for the Homestead Building Society, specialising in mortgages and loans. She'd only been working there for six weeks and, according to her co-workers, she was quiet and kept to herself. She'd been living in New Zealand for the past five years, prior to moving back to her home city of Cork. Eve frowned again. This story was only published a few hours ago and Pennie didn't own a phone. How could she know anything at all about this woman? And just what secrets did Pennie and her imaginary friend think might have gotten her killed?

7

Eve woke with a start. It was still dark outside and when she tapped the screen of her watch, it came to life, confirming that it was indeed too early to be awake. Still, it wasn't far off the time she woke at most mornings. She rolled on her back and roughly rubbed her face. She didn't remember if she'd been dreaming, but her heartbeat was elevated, and she felt unsettled. As if her subconscious mind had conjured something awful, just to rouse her from an otherwise peaceful sleep. But then the silence of the night was broken by a loud creak, followed by a dull thump coming from somewhere else in the house. Eve bolted upright and swung her legs out of bed. She sat there, clutching the sheet on either side of her, listening for a minute. This old house made lots of noises, but none of them sounded like that. Was that what had woken her? The sound of someone moving around inside her home? She looked at her watch again. Twelve minutes past three in the morning. She usually made it till just after four and she resented the stolen hour. Until she heard a scrape, like furniture being moved across one of the old and uneven floors that ran throughout this old house.

Eve jumped off the bed and hurried to her closed bedroom door. She stopped before going outside and looked around the room, lit only by the moonlight that shone through her flimsy net curtains. She moved quickly to her bedside locker and picked up the ceramic lamp that had been there since forever. She pulled its plug from the socket on the wall and wound the cord around her hand. She tested the weight of the lamp, which wasn't overly impressive, but it was all she had to hand. If she needed to defend herself, then it probably wouldn't do much good. She thought about Pennie in the room down the hall and she wondered if it was just her, moving around. But she never got up in the middle of the night. She'd been conditioned not to by a lifetime of not being allowed to leave her bedroom after lights out. That was a house rule and while Eve had no intentions of keeping that rule in place now, she still found it hard to believe that Pennie would stray from a lifelong habit. But either way, Pennie was Eve's responsibility now, so if someone was in their home, then it was Eve's job to protect her sister. The thought was enough to almost paralyse her with anxiety.

So, before she could think too much about it, Eve took a deep breath and flung open her bedroom door. The rest of upstairs was illuminated by the landing light, which was left on for Pennie's benefit, lighting the way from her bedroom to the bathroom. Or indeed the stairs, if she did feel like eating shit lasagne in the middle of the night. Either way, a light being left on was another small step towards breaking away from old habits. They just hadn't discussed it yet.

Tightening her grip on the lamp and with her back to the wall, Eve moved quietly towards Pennie's room, her eyes trained on the stairs, her senses on high alert. She listened intently for signs that someone was in their house, but all she could hear was blood pulsing in her ears. She paused momentarily and looked towards the locked door opposite Pennie's room. That room had been locked for as long as Eve could remember and she had no plans to change that now. Not unless she absolutely had to. Still, she moved as deftly as she could across the landing towards it, and placed her ear against the door, holding her breath as she did so. She strained to listen, but as expected, there was no sound coming from in there. When she crossed again to Pennie's room, she tapped gently on the door and shoved it open with her foot.

She startled when she saw Pennie sitting up, cross-legged on the makeshift bed, pulling more strings from the bear's hat, which did nothing to ease Eve's mounting anxiety. Pennie had been smiling, but her smile melted away when Eve stepped inside the room. Now she just looked disappointed.

'Pennie? Why are you awake?' Eve asked, her eyes darting around the room, lit by the low-light lamp in the corner. Another light to be left on all night, if required. Which it seemed it was.

Pennie shrugged and shifted her concentration to the task of pulling threads.

Eve tilted her head to see the girl's face and wondered if she'd imagined the smile that had been there. When Pennie refused to look at her, Eve glanced again around the room, feeling more unsettled, rather than less. Her stomach was bunched tight and her chest with it. Pennie's bed hadn't been slept in, but the covers were creased in the middle, near to the edge of the bed. Like maybe she'd sat there for a while before deciding to sleep on the floor again.

'Were you moving some furniture around?'

Pennie shook her head, no.

'Did you hear anything – scraping or thumping or... something?' What actually *had* she heard?

Pennie shook her head again, eyes still cast downwards.

Eve took in every detail of the room, from the made bed with the crinkled cover to the wardrobe against the wall, the chest of drawers and the closed, but unlocked window. 'Why aren't you sleeping in your bed?' she asked, yet again.

Pennie's response was the same as before. 'That's Angel's bed.'

Eve felt a flair of annoyance now. Being dragged from her sleep at three in the morning, when she hardly slept to begin with, was one thing. But having to explain why she didn't want the child sleeping on the floor was another. Eve wanted to tell her that she was too old to really believe that an imaginary friend needed her bed more than she did. But she held her tongue, knowing that it would be a mistake to do so. Also, what the hell did she know? Maybe all this was perfectly normal, because what the fuck was normal anyway?

'Okay, well... go to sleep, Pennie,' was all she could muster. She placed the lamp gently on the floor and went to tuck her in. Eve guided her to lie down, then she went and pulled the warm duvet off the single bed and draped it over her. Angel would just have to deal with the chill tonight. 'Sleep,' she said softly.

Pennie turned on her side, facing away from Eve, and Eve watched her for a minute before clambering to her feet. The pain in her head, which had plagued her for days now, was subsiding finally, and perhaps that was due to the pills. Or maybe she'd actually had a restful sleep prior to being woken. But there was a tension in her now and it bore down upon her shoulders. She also had the unsettling feeling of being watched, neither of which she liked. She left Pennie's door ajar, letting some more light seep through the crack, then reluctantly, she went to look around the rest of the house. The fact that Pennie was so wide awake made her think that she *had* made those noises, entertaining herself and her imaginary friend on a sleepless night. Eve was being silly thinking that someone else might be roaming around inside the house. Of course she was. But she would check the other rooms anyway, because life had taught her to always trust her gut. Plus, she needed to *try* to sleep in peace when she finally got back to bed, so she checked the bathroom, pulling aside the shower curtain and feeling ridiculous for doing so. She glanced again towards the locked door before moving reluctantly towards it and pressing her ear against it again. After a few seconds, she moved away and crept downstairs, checking the front door at the bottom, which was locked. She moved carefully through the living room, checking each window, and into the kitchen. It was in darkness, with again just the low glow of moonlight leaking through. She checked the back door, which was closed but not locked. She must have forgotten to turn the key, but she did that now. Everything was as she'd left it the night before and she was being an idiot.

She exhaled loudly and was about to turn and go back to bed when she looked towards the kitchen table. Her heartbeat quickened again and the hair on her arms slowly stood. The oven dish, which contained leftover lasagne, sat in the middle of the table. Green washing-up liquid had been poured all over it, ruining the food. On either side of the table, a bowl – one scraped clean, the other holding the remains of some cornflakes and milk. Both chairs were pushed back from the table, as if the diners had only just upped and left. Eve walked over and stood for a long minute, studying the table and this apparent destruction of dinner for two. Finally, she pushed the nearest chair back into the table. She knew the sound it would make, because she'd been hearing it all her life. Still, her body stiffened as the wooden legs scraped their way over the floor, just like they had when they'd woken her. Then, aside from the sound of her unsteady breathing, the house fell silent once more.

8

Eve sat at the table the next morning, still wearing the T-shirt she'd slept in, with a pair of jeans that had been discarded on the floor. Her knees vibrated against the underneath of the table as she sipped her coffee and waited for Pennie to come down. She'd lain awake for the rest of the night, staring at the ceiling and thinking far too much. It was somewhere close to 6 a.m. when she'd calmed herself with the reminder that Pennie was a classic. They'd had numerous kids come through their house, with various types of eating disorders, so Eve already knew that they could present themselves in different ways. Ellen had taken no notice of disorders and the like, because she'd said it wasn't her place to fix anyone. Plus, they wouldn't be with her long enough to make a difference anyway, so why bother? But that wasn't the case with Pennie, and thankfully, the Internet explained it better than Ellen had. It told Eve what to look for now, with Pennie.

According to one website, Pennie was feeling like she'd lost control of her life when she lost Ellen. But food was something she *could* control. She could decide when to eat and how much. She could even control whether or not to keep that food inside her body. Eve had examined the bathroom more closely than she usually would before coming downstairs that morning, and she'd determined that Pennie hadn't purged during the night. Or if she had, then she left no trace of it behind. The other thing she realised when she thought about last night, was that imaginary friends were there for comfort. To always be on the side of the child and, at times, to take the blame for things that the child does not want to admit to. Like destroying a double portion of lasagne in the early hours of the morning. So, now that she knew what it was, Eve could handle this. Still, she consulted the Internet incessantly while she waited for Pennie to come down, skipping over the paragraphs about seeking counselling. Counsellors were technically doctors, and doctors took people away from their families. Eve and Pennie did not require their services.

'Hi.' Pennie's soft voice pulled her from her scattered thoughts and the blue screen held far too close to her tired eyes.

'Hey! Morning.' Eve smiled, turning in her chair to face her. 'Cornflakes or Cheerios?' she asked, a little too brightly. *Chill out, try-hard,* she warned herself.

Pennie just shook her head and held the brown bear close to her chest.

'Well, you should eat something,' she said, getting to her feet. 'What about some toast?'

'I'm not hungry,' Pennie said.

Eve was about to ask if she was still full after her late-night cornflakes binge, but she didn't. She'd made the decision not to make a big deal out of the fact that she was out of bed in the middle of the night. That rule was no longer in place, she reminded herself. Perhaps she should insist they have a *talk*. But the very idea made Eve squirm. Surely all kids hated *talks* as much as Eve did. Besides, it was Eve who told her to help herself if she got hungry, so she wasn't about to food-shame her about the fact that she'd eaten almost two bowls of cereal. But she couldn't let the destroyed lasagne slide. That was intended to be dinner for another night, and they didn't have money to throw away on food waste.

'Pennie, why did you pour dish soap on the lasagne last night?'

Pennie paused momentarily, then busied herself with her bear. 'I didn't,' she replied after a silent moment.

'Well, someone did, because I just put it in the bin.' *After removing the top layer and spending five minutes googling whether or not it could still be eaten.* She kept that bit to herself but having to admonish someone was unfamiliar territory for Eve. She sounded so unsure of herself that she wondered if Pennie, or anyone else, could ever take her seriously as a disciplinarian.

Pennie's back was to Eve as she pretended to examine the different cereal boxes on the countertop. But Eve saw the rigidness in her body, the tension as she moved aimlessly. Like any child being scolded, she was scrabbling for a story that might get her out of the trouble she was in.

'Angel did it,' she said at last.

It was exactly what Eve expected her to say. 'And why would he do that?'

'Angel said I shouldn't eat the lasagne.'

Eve brought a fidgety hand to her throat and fiddled with the tiny silver cross she'd been wearing since her first holy communion. It was Amelia's communion cross before it became Eve's and it brought her comfort at times when she didn't know what to do. She was running out of words for this situation and felt even more out of her depth than usual. 'Angel isn't in charge around here, Pennie,' she said, not sounding as authoritative as she would have liked. 'When it comes to feeding and caring for us, *I'm* the one in charge. Okay?'

Pennie took a banana from the fruit bowl and turned to face Eve at last. 'Won't you be late?'

'Late for what?'

Pennie shrugged. 'Your walk.'

They looked at each other in silence, Eve with no idea what else to say or do. She did desperately want to leave the house and get some much-needed fresh air. But she felt that to do so now would be giving in somehow. Handing the balance of what little power they had between them over to the child. Eve didn't know much, but she suspected the Internet would frown upon that. Eventually, she turned away and she too went to get some fruit from the wooden fruit bowl beside the fridge, just so she didn't have endure the girl's scrutiny any more. If that's even what it was. Was she being paranoid? Because that wouldn't have been unusual for Eve. Loads of people had told her that she was paranoid over the years and they couldn't all be wrong. But her gut was telling her that something was happening here, and right or wrong, she was having a hard time ignoring it. But then she turned again to face Pennie, who looked so small in her polka-dot nightie, with a brown-spotted banana in her little hand. She was so pale and fragile, and Eve suddenly thought that, yes, maybe whatever what going on inside her head was just that. All in her head.

'Are you feeling okay?' she asked at last. Pennie did not look well. How was she just noticing this?

'I'm fine,' Pennie said, but Eve knew she was lying.

But why would a child lie about feeling unwell? Didn't they all want care and attention at that age, especially when sick? Or maybe that was only when a loving mother was there to give it and not a woefully under-equipped sister.

Eve looked at the apple she was holding and offered it to Pennie. 'In case Angel gets hungry as well.' She forced herself to smile at the child, not wanting to leave the house on an awkward note.

Pennie nodded and she made herself smile back, which Eve appreciated. Even though forced smiles were not what she imagined Lorelai and Rory Gilmore gave each other over breakfast. This morning, however, it would have to do.

'Are you sure you don't want me to stay home?' Eve asked, after a short but awkward silence. 'Because I can. I really don't mind. It's not like I have anywhere important to be, and my deliveries can just as easily be done later, or even tomorrow.' Which was true. But for Eve, the act of leaving the house and staying out for as long as she liked *was* the important bit. To be *able* to do that.

Pennie shook her head and walked to the stairs. 'I'm fine. You can go.' She made her way slowly up and didn't look back. Eve was dismissed.

Why was it that people on TV always knew the perfect thing to say at times like this? They never seemed to have the kind of strained relationships that Eve and Pennie had, just trying to coexist and figure out how to love one another. Not that Eve needed to figure out her love for Pennie. She just loved her. The problem was figuring out what to do with that. How to convey it, when neither of them had had much experience with love in any of its forms. Eve desperately wanted to say something clever now, but she just felt awkward and clueless, trapped in some kind of limbo between parent, stranger, and fun big sister. None of which she was.

She turned and took her jacket off the peg on the wall and quietly let herself out the door. A part of her was disappointed that Pennie hadn't chosen to confide in Eve about last night, choosing instead to blame her imaginary friend. She desperately wanted to be that cool big sister. The one who instantly improved the life of her grieving sibling. A silly and childish notion, she knew. They weren't the Gilmore Girls, as much as Eve wanted them to be, and Eve was an idiot, she knew that. But still, she was a disappointed idiot.

Eve turned on the radio in the car to drown out her own thoughts as she drove slowly away from the house. The hourly news bulletin was on and the newsreader was already halfway through her dramatic telling of the Carriglen murder. That was what it was called now, apparently.

'Miss Granger was last seen leaving the Homestead Building Society, where she'd worked for less than two months, at around 6.30 p.m. on the night she was killed. Gardaí aren't releasing exact details of the crime scene at this time, but they've confirmed that they have launched a murder investigation. A post-mortem is currently being carried out at Cork University Hospital and Gardaí are awaiting those results before commenting further on the cause of Miss Granger's death. In the meantime, they're asking for the public's assistance – if anyone was in the Carriglen area, particularly the area around Meadowview Road and Meadowview Woods, between 6 p.m. on Tuesday and 7 a.m. yesterday, or indeed, if they noticed anything suspicious over the past number of days, please contact Gardaí immediately.'

Eve wondered briefly if she should contact them and tell them about the souped-up Ford Fiesta that was driving erratically outside the Homestead Building Society that night. It was just as Leslie Granger was leaving work, wasn't it? Or the group of boys standing nearby, maybe. Were they just hanging around, as teenagers do, or were they up to something? She soon dismissed the idea, though, when she thought about what going to the police would entail for her. The Gardaí would want to take her details. They'd want to know who she was, where she lived, who she lived *with* and what she was doing in the area herself. Why she took such long walks alone, day and night. Why she had nothing else to do with her time but deliver useless flyers that no one wanted. Why, why, why? No. She'd let the police do their jobs and find the person responsible. Those kids probably had nothing to do with it anyway and Eve felt a momentary pang of guilt for thinking like one of *those* adults. The ones who always threw blame at the kids, just because they dressed in tracksuits and hoodies and were loud and a bit thick.

Naturally, the news bulletin brought her back once again to Pennie. How did she know so much about Leslie Granger? The way she spoke about her, it was as if she'd just been having a coincidental conversation about the woman with someone else, only for her to then appear on television.

Someone did something to her. It was a secret.

Eve tried again to picture the woman's face as it had looked on the night she bumped into Eve. Her eyes seemed to travel over every inch of Eve's face in the seconds when they'd stood so close, perhaps searching for signs that they might know each other. Had she looked like a woman who carried dark secrets around with her? Eve glanced at her own face then in the rear-view mirror. Did *she*?

Instead of the radio drowning out her thoughts, like it was supposed to, things were happening the other way around, so she slapped it off. She needed to have a proper conversation with Pennie. One where she could convince the girl to trust her. To trust her with her fears and her grief. To trust her to cook for her and to care for her when she felt unwell, which was all well and good as a thought inside Eve's head. It worked perfectly well in there. But Eve's experience with heartfelt conversations was limited to what she'd learned from Lorelai and Rory. Ellen Holland wasn't the heartfelt type. Her approach had always been more bull in a china shop. Peter had tried at times, but his approach had never really worked either.

Before Eve could give any real thought to where she was going, she found herself back on Carriglen's main street. She was about to drive past the Homestead Building Society, which was open for business as usual, despite the recent loss of their colleague. Eve pulled into the kerb and sat there for a while, staring at the doorway where she'd bumped into Leslie Granger. Was that the last thing that had ever happened to her before she'd died: some random woman slamming into her because of a poxy Ford Fiesta?

Eve picked up her phone from where she'd discarded it on the passenger seat. She opened her Internet browser and entered the name *Leslie Granger*. She didn't have to wait long for a string of results, all pretty much telling the same story, using slightly different wording. The update was that the cause of her death was thought to be pharmaceutical. That was the one word they all had in common. Pharmaceutical. Why didn't they say, *drug overdose*? Maybe because Leslie Granger didn't appear to have a drug problem. Each article mentioned the fact that no drugs were found at her home. Nothing stronger than an aspirin at least, so maybe that was why they used such vague terminology. Either way, an official murder investigation had been launched and now it seemed it was the only story that mattered.

Before she could stop herself, she opened her phone app and dialled the house phone at Raven's Rock. It rang out and she tried again. For a second time, it rang out, but when she hit redial for a third time, Pennie answered on the first ring.

'What did you know about that woman?' she blurted, without thinking to say hello first, or come up with any kind of preamble.

'What?'

Eve squeezed her eyes shut, remembering their need for a proper conversation. Already, this was not one of those. 'Sorry, Pennie. Hi.' She made herself smile in the hope that it would travel in her voice, through the phone, and reach Pennie intact.

'Eh, hi.'

'It's just that, well, I'm in town and I'm near that building society where she worked. That woman who was killed?'

'Why are you there?' Pennie asked softly.

Eve shrugged, even though Pennie couldn't see that. 'I don't know. It's just kind of where I ended up.'

Pennie said nothing. Instead, she just waited in the kind of silence that Eve needed to fill immediately.

'Well, you said that she died from her secrets, or something like that. But what did you mean by that?'

'Angel says that's why she died,' Pennie said. 'Angel says that's what happens when people have secrets that belong to other people. Those secrets can kill them.' She paused and Eve could hear her breathing. 'That's all I know.'

Eve's stomach tightened and her blood pulsed in her ears again. But she kept her eyes on the windscreen, ignoring her whitened knuckles as they gripped the phone too tightly. She couldn't think of a response and she was beginning to wish she'd never heard the name Leslie Granger. Now, it was all anyone talked about. The news. The Internet. Pennie. Fucking Angel.

'Well... do *you* think she died because of a secret?' was all Eve could come up with to ask. Eve wondered at what age kids realised that death was a permanent thing.

Pennie shrugged. 'She's not the only one.'

There was a pause in Eve's breathing, and she felt a slight tremble work its way through her body. 'What do you mean? Who else?'

'Like that fella who did loads of drugs,' she said as a matter of fact. 'He used to sell drugs to other people, too, just so he could buy more for himself. Everyone gets hurt when there's that many drugs and that's why some people think people like him deserve to die. But really, it's because of their secrets. And that's why they do the drugs in the first place. Then after a while, they die from the secrets, but the drugs get blamed. No one ever wonders about the secrets.'

Eve's hand ached as she gripped the phone tighter. *All* of these words pouring from her otherwise silent sister were jarring. Eve was drowning in their conversation now and had no idea what the right thing to say was. Where was this coming from? What she'd said sounded far too specific to be rhetoric.

'Did you know that, Eve?' Pennie continued, sounding cautious as she did. 'Some people take too many drugs to help them with their secrets. Then they die.'

'Wh… they take drugs to help them with their secrets?' Eve closed her eyes and shook her head. This was too surreal. Pennie was ten. Ten!

'To manage them, like.'

'Are you talking about your birth mother?' Eve stupidly asked. She was pretty sure Peter would have told Pennie the story about her mother being a heroin addict. He'd told Eve the same thing. But her unknown mother wasn't the one who came to mind now. Sparrow was.

'No.'

Eve tapped the heel of her hand roughly against her forehead as tears pooled in her eyes. 'Well, the Gardaí arrest people like that,' she tried, knowing full well that that wasn't even true.

'Because of secrets?' Pennie sounded incredulous, rather than confused.

'Secrets? No. For selling drugs. Or for hurting people because of drugs.' Eve's words were tumbling out now, desperately tripping over each other. How was Pennie, who hardly ever practised speaking, still better at speaking than Eve was?

'How do *you* know that?'

She inhaled deeply, trying to slow things down so that she could bring an end to this torturous conversation. 'Because that's what happened to the person who was driving the car that crashed into Peter. Remember?' Of course she wouldn't remember. Pennie was only four then. All she knew was that Peter was there one day and gone the next. So, Eve explained as best she could, which wasn't very good at all. 'He'd taken drugs before driving his car, he hurt Peter, and he was sent to jail.' Eve tried never to think about that and she certainly didn't talk about it, as a rule. Not that she had anyone left to talk about it with. Her headache was coming back and it seemed angrier than usual. But who could blame it.

'Yeah, well,' Pennie breathed shakily through the phone, sounding like she was about to cry, 'that doesn't change anything. By then, it's too late, isn't it.'

Eve frowned and brought her knuckles to the side of her head, digging them roughly into her temples. 'Does Angel talk to you about people dying, Pennie?' she asked, trying to bring the conversation back around by asking an intelligent question, surprised to be able to think of one.

Pennie didn't answer, but Eve thought she was definitely crying now. She could hear her.

'But he did talk to you about that woman – Leslie Granger?' Eve pressed. 'And drug users?'

'Angel is a watcher. I told you that.' Her words were filled with frustration, as if Eve was being stupid. Or that perhaps she hadn't been listening to Pennie when she told her this the first time.

'What does that mean, though?' Eve asked beseechingly.

'It *means* that she watches people. She knows where the bad ones are and what they're doing and that's how she minds me. She keeps them away from me, until...' Her voice trailed off.

'Until, what?'

'Until she doesn't need to any more.'

Only for the fact that Angel seemed to switch from *he* to *she* from one conversation to the next, Eve might start to worry that Angel wasn't all that imaginary. But she did wonder where all this was coming from, given that the girl had hardly spoken at all for the first nine and a half years of her life. Now suddenly, in Ellen's absence, she'd become some kind of oracle, determining when and why people died.

'Are you on the Internet, Pennie?' she suddenly thought to ask. Was there some kind of predator injecting themselves into Pennie's life, online?

'I don't have a phone. Or anything else,' Pennie replied, deadpan.

She was right. Of course she was right. Eve had a phone and their TV wasn't hooked up to the Internet. *Stupid, stupid, stupid, Eve.*

'You know when I was a kid, I used to be scared of the dark,' Pennie said, so quietly that Eve had to think what the words meant.

'Oh,' was all she could think to say in response.

Pennie huffed out a humourless laugh, like she couldn't believe she'd ever been that silly. 'But Angel says that people who mean the most harm come out by day. Angel says, they're not lurking under your bed or in your wardrobe.' Pennie sounded like she was telling a scary story around a campfire, and Eve was listening just as intently. 'Instead,' she continued, 'they just walk around the place, like normal people. Normal people that no one would suspect.'

'Oh,' Eve said again, like a robotic idiot this time.

'Some people know who they are, but they have to keep it a secret. If they tell, then bad things will happen to them.'

Eve sat there silently waiting, feeling a chill right through to her bones. But it seemed Pennie was done. She had nothing more to add to this ghastly story.

'Bye,' Pennie said at last, and the line went dead.

Eve sat there gripping her phone dangerously tight for God knows how long. Long enough for the same man to walk into the building society, complete his business there and leave again sometime later. Did he ask where that lovely red-headed lady was? The one who served him last time. Or did he even notice that she was no longer there? Did anyone inside that building miss her?

Eve loosened her grip on the phone and opened her browser. Again, she looked up Leslie Granger. She clicked into images and for the next ten minutes she acquainted herself with the woman's smiling face, which Eve worried might haunt her now for the rest of her life. When she couldn't look any more, she exited the search. She then brought the cursor back to the search bar and let her thumb hover over the keys for a while, unsure of which ones to strike. Finally, they typed in *drug-related death* and hit search. Eve had no idea what she expected to find and, at first, she found exactly nothing of interest aside from the Leslie Granger story. Certainly, nothing else that raised any questions. Only a string of barely-there stories about drug deaths and overdoses. Stories like those didn't tend to get a lot of coverage and most were just a few lines long at most. In fact, Eve would wager that fifty drug addicts could be murdered in one night and no one would bother to report on it with any great interest. But on the second page of results, right at the bottom, she found it. A bold headline above a story that made her blood run cold.

9

The remains of twenty-five-year-old Jack Logan were discovered in Carriglen Park in the early hours of last Saturday. Mr Logan, of no fixed abode, was known to Gardaí at the time of his death, which is thought to be linked to his heroin addiction. Multiple complaints had been made to Gardaí in recent years about antisocial behaviour in the park and the fact that drug use is all too common in what was intended to be a children's amenity. Discarded needles are commonplace, according to one local resident, who says that she can no longer bring her children to the park, as it's just not safe. The grim discovery was made by nineteen-year-old Graham Crowley, with an address on the north side of the city. Mr Crowley describes himself as Mr Logan's 'best friend' and insists that Jack was 'clean' at the time of his death, which was why it was such a shock to discover him in the park as he made his way home after a night out. He says he's been left traumatised by the discovery.

The story was four weeks old. Eve's next search was for Jack Logan.

What Really Happened to Jack Logan? the bold headline asked. Beneath the recap of the story was an interview with Graham Crowley, the man who discovered Jack Logan's body. This interview was dated two weeks ago.

'I'm in recovery now,' said Mr Crowley when he met with me in a Costa coffee shop near where he lives with his parents, Noel and Maureen Crowley.

'Jack was my friend, and finding him like that, it scared me, you know. That could've been me. It still could be if I don't get straight.'

'What was he doing in the park that night? You say he was your friend – had you arranged to meet him there?'

'We didn't really make arrangements like that. The park wasn't exactly somewhere we went for fun, you know. When you're an addict, the only thing you try to arrange is your next fix: where it might be coming from and how you're going to get it, know what I mean? And the only friends you have are as unreliable as you are, so it's not like we saw each other every day and went for coffee and stuff like that. But it wouldn't have been a shock to see him there either. It's where most of us went to score. But like I said, Jack was clean. Had been for a few weeks at that stage, so I was surprised to see him there.'

'At what point did you realise that something was wrong?'

'Well, from where I entered the park, I just saw this dude on the flat of his back, with his legs hooked around the seat of the swing. You know, like he'd been sitting there and fell backwards onto the ground. I just thought the guy was high, you know. But then I saw that it was Jack and I thought, wait a minute, Jack is off the gear. Then I realised he wasn't breathing and, you know, that he was like, dead.'

'It's thought he'd been there for a few hours by the time you discovered him. How did no one else see him?'

'Well, like I said, he just looked like he got high while sitting on the swing and fell off. A bit of a rookie move, but not unheard of, like. Plenty of people saw him and thought the same thing, you know. Only for the fact that I knew Jack and I thought he was clean, I might have just carried on past myself. I mean, it's sad and all, but that's just the way it is.'

'So you think Mr Logan relapsed? You agree that he died from a heroin overdose?'

'Well, yeah, kind of. I mean, that's what they're saying and that's what it looked like. But I mean, it was strange.'

'What was strange?'

'Well, there was no needle, no strap... you know, no signs that he'd just injected himself.'

'So what does that mean?'

Mr Crowley shrugged then and said, 'Well, I have yet to meet an addict who manages to shoot up and then take the strap off their arm and tidy away their needle and their spoon and all their gear, then just slide off the swing and onto the ground. You shoot up, you go to the moon. No time for house-keeping, if you know what I mean.'

'But the Gardaí didn't seem to find this unusual?'

'The Gardaí didn't give enough of a shit to think about that, did they? As far as they're concerned, it's just one less addict to think about. But I'm telling you, man. Something about all this just isn't right.'

A post-mortem showed that, while Mr Logan did have traces of heroin in his system, his cause of death was ruled as inconclusive. When this reporter spoke to Gardaí, they confirmed their belief that Mr Logan's death was a heroin overdose, contrary to post-mortem findings. What do you believe?

That was the end of the semi-investigative article and when Eve looked back on some of the earlier search results, she discovered that four of those stories were also about Jack Logan. The focus of each short piece was the fact that he was found in a children's park. All of the comments on the article were aimed at the Council and not the Gardaí. There were a few words about his overdose and a touch of outrage about the city's drug problem. But the rest of the comments were to do with a lack of policing and the upkeep of public parks and ameni-ties. No one seemed to cast doubt on the nature of Jack Logan's death, and no one seemed to give a damn either. The fact that no drug paraphernalia had been found near him was only mentioned by that one reporter and a nineteen-year-old former addict, while the post-mortem results seemed to count for nothing. Traces of heroin in a long-term user's system was all the proof they needed.

Eve kept scrolling through the Jack Logan search results. She found some social media links to several other Jack Logans around the world, and one court report. Eve clicked into that. Jack Logan was indeed known to the Gardaí. He'd been charged with drug possession and distribution. So had the man who'd discovered him, Graham Crowley. According to at least one reporter, Jack's death looked suspicious but there were no other red flags or stories of suspi-cious deaths in Cork. So was Jack Logan the drug user that Pennie was referring to? Raven's Rock hadn't had a drug addict in years, so really, Pennie shouldn't know much at all about them. Let alone dead ones.

Eve physically shivered as a chill ran through her again. She closed her browser, done with these stories. They were affecting her mood and muddling her thoughts further, which was the last thing she needed. She opened up a new browser to distract herself from all she'd read and typed *camping holidays in Cork* into the search bar. Perhaps she could take Pennie somewhere for a few days. Get her away from all the dark thoughts being conjured up by her imagination. A little holiday might even give them a chance to get to know each other, in a way they hadn't really been able to before now.

Eve remembered going on holiday once, when she was about thirteen years old. It was to a mobile home in Kerry with Ellen, just the two of them. From what she could remember, they went purely to decompress after a particularly annoying kid, a girl, who'd been staying with them, left. Eve used to call her 'the screamer'. All night, every night, she screamed. She wasn't so bad when she first arrived, but by the time Eve and Ellen left for Kerry, she'd become so insufferable that Ellen just woke Eve up extra early one morning and told her they were leaving. She was already in the car with a packed bag by the time Eve made it downstairs. Eve didn't remember much else about that holiday, except being woken up to go, and stepping into a bright-green mobile home with a yellow stripe all the way around it. The rest just seemed to fade into an unreachable part of her mind. But by the time they returned to Raven's Rock, the screamer was gone.

Now Eve wanted to take Pennie on holiday, too. Maybe not as far away as Kerry, but somewhere where they could relax, just the two of them. She just needed to come up with the money to do it. She had her unemployment benefit, of course, which Ellen made her apply for as soon as she was old enough, and the cash-in-hand she collected for her deliveries. She also had Ellen's bank cards which she could tap and use online up to a certain amount without a PIN number. She had no idea how long that money would last because she had no idea how much Ellen and Peter had left behind. Deep down, she knew that a holiday would be frivolous right now, but she vowed that she would plan one as soon as she possibly could.

Though maybe not today. She dropped her phone on the passenger seat and started the engine. She pulled out onto the quiet road and drove straight home, much earlier than she usually would and without much walking or fresh air to sustain her. She just really wanted to be with Pennie suddenly. To physically be there, keeping an eye on things, and it didn't take her long to get home.

When she let herself inside, she dropped her keys in the bowl on the hall table and stood looking around the seemingly empty house. She walked slowly towards the stairs and up to the landing. Once there, she stood outside Pennie's closed bedroom door. 'Pennie?' she called quietly.

There was no answer and only silence all around. She must have gone outside, which made Eve wish she'd stayed out, too. She hated being in this house all day.

'Pennie?' she called again, louder this time. But again, no one responded.

She knocked on her bedroom door and pressed her ear against it. She didn't hear anything and debated with herself for a moment about whether or not to go in. Pennie was a scared kid who happened to have seen some news stories before Eve had. That's how she knew about Leslie Granger and Jack Logan. Or maybe she didn't know about Jack Logan at all. Maybe she was talking about drug users in general. Ellen had warned them about drugs often enough. She'd made it perfectly clear that if she found any sign of drug use in Eve and Pennie's room, she'd bury them in the back garden. She probably didn't mean that she'd *literally* bury them in the garden, but it was enough to scare them into making good decisions when it came to drugs. So *maybe* Eve had put two and two together and gotten a rectangle when she took Pennie's story and ran to the Internet with it. The child had just lost the only mother she'd ever known. It was normal, surely, that her mind would go to a morbid place. Eve's mind had darkened, too, for a time, so why now was she looking for problems that probably weren't there at all?

Eve was already in Pennie's room while she entertained that thought. Her legs moved of their own accord and her hands helped themselves to Pennie's closed wardrobe doors. Her eyes roamed over the clothes hanging neatly inside, before she found herself crouching to look through the shoes, lined up in pairs beneath them.

'What are you doing?' she muttered, standing up and closing the wardrobe again.

But still, she didn't leave the room. Instead, she stood there, looking around. She cast her eyes on the makeshift bed on the wooden floor. The one intended for an imaginary friend, but being occupied by Pennie. Then she looked at the actual bed. She went and ran a hand over it, checking for any reason why Pennie might not want to sleep in it. It didn't hold any painful memories of being tucked in and read to by Ellen, because Ellen was already gone when Eve bought it from the charity shop. Plus, Ellen was never the tucking-in or storytelling kind. Maybe Pennie was put off by the fact that other bodies had lain in it before her. But the same could have been said for her previous bed. That had been at Raven's Rock for longer than Eve had.

She reached to the top of the bed and pulled back the duvet. The pink sheet was smooth and tucked in at all four corners. She replaced the cover again, tucking it in, and then she stood with her hands on her hips, looking around the room. She puffed out her cheeks and exhaled slowly, shaking her head. Finally, she left the room, pulling the door closed behind her. Pennie had always been the constant in this house. Quiet, obedient, relatively contented and always there in the background. Now every single thing about her was so far out of character, from speaking regularly, to the way she acted. Eve's head was spinning from all the recent changes, and she wished that, despite Ellen, she'd made herself get to know Pennie over the past ten years. Then maybe things wouldn't be so damn hard now.

She stood on the landing with her back to Pennie's door, taking deep, calming breaths, and staring straight ahead at the locked door opposite her. She pictured the room beyond that door as it had looked the last time she saw it, which was several years ago. Grey carpet matted with age, its stains covered over with an equally matted, brown rug. A white, timber-framed bed against one wall, with an off-white comforter, dotted with panda bears. Grubby walls painted in a shade of yellow that clashed with everything else in the room. She pictured the rust-coloured splatters at the bottom of one wall, near the skirting board, and she pushed herself off Pennie's door and walked quickly to the top of the stairs. Yes. A few days away would definitely do them good. She'd start saving this week.

10

'Where have you been?' Eve asked when Pennie came through the back door a few minutes later.

Clearly, Pennie wasn't expecting Eve home so soon and she startled at the sudden sound of her voice. But she gathered herself in the long seconds it took for her to respond.

'I was outside, in the woods.'

Eve glanced out the kitchen window, at a view that might look to some like a framed painting. A row of evergreen trees behind that little stone wall. The space between the house and the wall was so overgrown that Eve could see exactly the route Pennie had taken, because she'd left a meandering trail of flattened grass in her wake. It led from the back door of the house to the section of wall that Peter had replaced a few years before he died. It was weathering now, but it still looked newer and slightly out of place compared to the rest of the wall, which had been there for a hundred years or more.

Eve looked to Pennie again. 'What were you doing out there?'

Pennie shrugged. 'Nothing.'

She went and took a glass from the countertop and filled it with water. *Her* glass. The Minnie Mouse one she'd had since she was four. They all had their own cup, their own glass, their own plate, bowl and cutlery. Even now, with Ellen gone and at twenty-three years of age, Eve still used the Mickey Mouse stuff and Pennie still used Minnie. That was another rule that Eve needed to change and perhaps she would in time. But she figured there'd been enough upheaval for now.

Pennie took slow, tentative sips of water and Eve didn't think she looked very well.

'Are you feeling okay, Pennie?'

Pennie nodded, with the glass still pressed to her dry lips. Eve wondered if that was why she'd been outside. Perhaps she was hoping the fresh air would make her feel better, in the absence of a mother with a magic touch. Guilt took its rightful place among Eve's emotions. Looking after Pennie and showing her all the love she'd missed out on was the one thing she'd promised she'd do with Ellen gone. That was what gave her purpose. It was why she got out of bed every morning and continued to do the chores she'd always done. Cooking, cleaning and maintaining domestic order in the house. All the things she hated but continued to do anyway, for Pennie. Now the child was sick and what was Eve doing? She was leaving her home alone, with only the trees for company. *Stupid, stupid, stupid.*

'Let me make you something to eat,' Eve said, gently placing a hand on Pennie's shoulder. It felt so small and bony. Pennie had hardly eaten since the last time Ellen cooked for her, and again, Eve felt all of her failings at once.

'I don't want anything to eat.'

As she said it, her stomach rumbled so loudly that they both looked down at it.

Eve frowned. 'Pennie, you have to eat.'

'Angel says I can't eat.'

Eve clenched her jaw in annoyance. 'Why not?'

'Angel said that if I eat, I'll die.'

All the fresh air that Pennie had brought inside with her was sucked violently out of the room and Eve stood there, mute for however long it took for Pennie to haltingly drink the full glass of water. It was the most unnatural silence, and it dragged endlessly on. Pennie added nothing more. She just stepped around Eve and made once again for the stairs.

'Pennie?' Eve stammered, her voice shaky and unfamiliar. 'Wait... why would Angel say something like that? How will you die if you eat? People die from *not* eating.'

As soon as she said that, Eve doubted herself more. Were you supposed to say things like that to children? That they might die from something? Pennie stood on the bottom step, watching her and listening obediently to her fumbling warnings. But as soon as Eve finished speaking, she started silently up the stairs.

'Pennie!' Eve called, more urgently now. What was she supposed to do here? Was it normal for imaginary friends to threaten children with death? *Was it?*

Pennie stopped her ascent, again obeying as she'd always done. But she didn't turn to look at Eve this time, so Eve strode over to the stairs and gripped the spindles as she spoke, her eyes just about level with Pennie's knees. 'Why does Angel talk about death so much?'

Pennie crouched down and peered through the spindles at Eve, their faces just inches apart. 'Sometimes, Angel knows if someone is going to die *before* they die,' she whispered, like she didn't want her words to be overheard.

Eve felt like she was suffocating. 'And Angel thinks *you're* going to die?' she whispered shakily back, the violent thumping in her chest almost painful now.

Pennie nodded, her expression grave. 'Only if I eat. But Angel will keep me safe.'

'No!' Eve shouted, making Pennie jump. '*I'm* the one who'll keep you safe. Me! Not Angel.' She reached through the spindles and caught Pennie by the ankle in sheer desperation. 'Do you hear me, Pennie?'

Pennie tried to pull away from Eve's grasp and only when she saw the fear on the girl's face did Eve release her. But she couldn't stop the flow of her probing and panicked questions. 'Why did Angel tell you about Leslie Granger?' she blurted. 'And drug addicts? Why are you talking about them, Pennie?' Her eyes were filled with tears and she sounded slightly unhinged herself. Why was Pennie doing this? Why was she making it so hard? She'd never been a delusional child, as far as Eve was aware. Never particularly imaginative either, so what had changed, aside from Ellen? Was she having some kind of a breakdown?

'Because...' Pennie said, as calmly as if this was just a normal conversation, 'people think they died from something normal. But they didn't.'

Eve was unable to formulate a response. She couldn't even sort Pennie's words into an order that made sense.

'They never saw the other pinprick,' Pennie said quietly. 'The one on his thigh.' Then she lowered her voice further and said, 'And they won't even look for the secret drug. The one they died of.'

'Wh...' Eve was going to be sick. Her almost-empty stomach roiled, and words could not battle their way out.

Pennie glanced cautiously over her shoulder again. 'So you see, Angel knows everything about people who die,' she whispered.

Eve turned and dashed for the kitchen sink, fear causing her entire body to revolt against her. She heaved towards the plughole and, though nothing came up, she retched until she thought her ribs might break.

By the time she stopped, Pennie was back in her room with the door firmly closed. Eve dismissed the idea of going up there, and instead, she fell into a kitchen chair, unable to hear another word about Angel and death. The Angel *of* Death.

In that moment, Eve desperately wanted someone to talk to. Someone who would know what to do. Someone who could take it all off of Eve's shoulders and fix it. Amelia came to her mind, as she always did, and Eve never missed her more. Eve was not equipped to deal with whatever was happening to Pennie. But she hadn't seen Amelia since she disappeared nearly a decade ago. In truth, Amelia hadn't been the same since that time her friend came over and had to witness Ellen getting bitten in the face. That Millie girl was probably the only friend Amelia had, and this house ruined that for her. That, and everything else. But if Amelia were here now, she'd know exactly what to do. She was the best big sister who ever lived. Right up until she vanished, leaving Eve behind.

Eve opened her phone again and a search engine. She was about to look for updates on the Leslie Granger story. To see if they'd found the *pharmaceutical* reason for her death: the *secret drug* which, according to Pennie, they wouldn't even look for. She also wanted to look up that reporter who wrote about Jack Logan's death. *Had* someone seen a second puncture wound in his thigh? Surely, the reporter, who was so suspicious, would know the answer to that, if anyone did. It *must* be written somewhere. Otherwise, how could Pennie possibly know about it? How could Angel?

As Eve's heart slowed to something like a normal rhythm, she realised that *this* was the most important question right now. And she wouldn't get the answer from the Internet.

She put her phone face down on the table, shoved her chair abruptly back and hurried to the stairs. She took them two at a time and, without knocking, she shoved open the door to Pennie's room, ready to get the answers she needed from her. But Pennie wasn't there. Her window, however, was wide open.

Eve hurried across the room and slammed her body into the windowsill. 'Pennie?' she called out into the shadow of the hulking evergreens. She reached out and clutched the ladder that leaned against the wall of the house, between Pennie's window and the garden below. A ladder far too long and cumbersome for a ten-year-old to wrestle across the garden and into place like this. 'Pennie!' she screamed.

But Pennie was gone.

11

Panic gripped Eve as she searched every inch of their garden and the surrounding woods, beyond the tracks in the grass. But she found no trace of Pennie. Even the wildlife seemed to have left this place and the woods were completely still. All the time, Eve's mind raced to the darkest of places and her stomach felt like it was on springs. When she'd exhausted her search of the area, ducking under the house and through the treeline several times, she got in her car and drove for almost two hours, circling nearby Carriglen and the entire surrounding area. Before long, everything blurred so she pulled over and started to search on foot. She didn't even bother to shut the car door as she hurried away from it, towards the park first. When that yielded nothing, she ran to Pennie's school building. She searched all around it and through the sports grounds, stopping only briefly when the janitor paused his summertime grass cutting to challenge her. He was the same janitor who'd once told Eve that she was *so mature* for her age when he'd caught her skipping class during her time at St Mary's. She was about fifteen years old and was hiding out at the back of the sports grounds. She'd responded by driving her knee into his crotch and getting herself suspended for two weeks. She'd never done anything like that before. It was purely impulsive, and she hadn't felt a rush of strength and power like it since. She never explained to the multitude of angry adults *why* she did it either, but now he looked at her with the same wary disdain he always did after that.

Pennie wasn't at the school and Eve didn't feel like explaining herself to the janitor, so she left. Then for reasons she couldn't explain, she returned to her car, got in, and drove to the cemetery. She parked up, but rather than going inside, she walked around the wall of the cemetery until she came to a little detached cottage that sat all alone beside it. Eve didn't know which one was put there first, the house or the graveyard. But she couldn't imagine why anyone would want to live there. It was on a narrow country road about a mile outside of town with nothing but graves and sky between them and everyone else. No one *had* lived in that cottage for a very long time, which was why it had always been a favourite with Raven's Rock runaways. They'd all hidden out there over the years, Eve included. She didn't think Pennie knew about this place, but Eve wasn't certain of anything. Not any more.

Eve let herself in through the buckled front door, with a different and much older feeling of foreboding. There were clear signs of squatting in there, with scattered bean cans, filthy sleeping bags and other rubbish, but the place was abandoned right now. Pennie wasn't there. She wasn't anywhere.

'Where the hell are you, Pennie?' Eve muttered, getting back in her car and driving a slow lap of the short, quiet road, which ended at the entrance to a field. There were no trees or places to hide there. Just wide-open space, ready and waiting for more graves to be dug. Eve turned her car around and drove past the house again. She paused when she came to the junction onto the main road, while she decided whether to turn left or right. She chose right, towards town again, thinking it was where she might have gone at that age, if not to the cottage. Her hands shook while she drove and Eve muttered to herself, as she'd always done when she was scared.

Her headache was back, too. Usually, she had a few weeks between episodes, but they were becoming far more frequent, and she wondered if the weight of her new responsibilities were to blame. Perhaps the stress of her new living situation and the worries that came with it. Ellen told her once that worrying about other people's children could suck the soul right out of your body. It was starting to feel like she might have been right. Being a big sister without parental support was heady stuff and it was taking its toll.

'This is what you wanted,' Eve reminded herself out loud to make sure she was listening. 'This is what you *always* wanted. To be the kind of big sister who always stuck around. Who *always* cared.'

Eve always craved the kind of bond that, apparently, sisters share. Real sisters. Not temporary ones, of which she'd only had a few, Amelia being the most significant. But Ellen stopped taking girls when Eve was about thirteen, after the screamer left. The screamer accused Peter of molesting her, but the girl had apparently done the same thing at another home she'd been at before coming to Raven's Rock. Once she was sent away, Ellen refused to take any more girls. They were trouble, she'd said. They were all too fond of crying wolf whenever things didn't go their way. That was partly why Eve never told on the janitor. What he'd said, *or* how he'd looked at her. She didn't want to be one of *those* girls. Instead, she'd dealt with him herself, took the consequences both at school and at home, and she'd carried on. Amelia disappeared around the same time as the screamer left and so then it was just Eve and Pennie. Eve wondered now if all those wasted years spent keeping Pennie at arm's length had done irreparable damage. Could Pennie ever trust Eve to take care of her, when she must have seemed so indifferent for most of her young life? They'd both been indifferent to each other. She frowned, wondering if that was normal. Did that happen in normal families?

Pain burst through her brain in a particularly violent wave, putting a stop to her rambling train of thought. She reached in the glove box and pulled out the pills that she kept there in case of an emergency. They were Ellen's pills, of which she'd had many. But these particular ones always seemed to take the pained look from her face. Now they helped Eve to feel a little less, too. She popped two in her mouth and swallowed them dry, grimacing as they clung to her parched throat. But she kept her eyes on her surroundings, not wanting to become distracted from her search.

It was on her second lap of the town when she spotted Pennie at last. She was sitting at a bus shelter, her feet together and her hands, fidgeting as always, in her lap.

'Pennie!' Eve exhaled heavily, pulling the car into the nearest parking space, which was opposite the bus shelter, outside a greasy-spoon restaurant called Carver's Kitchen. Eve knew the place well enough that the smell of fried food in the air outside made her already fragile stomach do an unnatural turn. It was well after lunchtime and all she'd had so far today was coffee, having shunned breakfast that morning while waiting for Pennie to come downstairs. But any hunger she might have felt was chased away by the stench of that place.

'Pennie!' she called, as she walked quickly across the quiet road, not allowing herself to break into a desperate run. When she reached the bus shelter, she sat down beside Pennie, her head swirling and diving like she'd just stepped off a rollercoaster. But relief flooded through her. Relief at having found the girl safe and well, and relief at not having to call the police or anyone else. She should have been angry with Pennie for worrying her like that, but she wasn't. Eve had run away from home at least twice by the time she was Pennie's age. Usually when Ellen and Peter took in a child that she didn't get along with. Back when she was too young to understand the importance of what they actually did. Of how those kids put food on their table and allowed the Hollands to keep Eve and Amelia from a life on the street. Pennie, too. She wasn't used to being on the other side of that childish behaviour and just how exhausting it could be.

'How did you find me?' Pennie asked.

'Never mind that. Where were you planning to go?' She indicated the bus timetable and route plan.

'Nowhere.'

'You're not waiting for a bus?'

Pennie shook her head.

Eve nodded. 'Okay. You just needed some space, eh? I get that.' It sounded like a very Lorelai thing to say. In fact, she *had* said it. Many times. *I get that.*

Pennie looked at her, seeming a little surprised by Eve knowing exactly the right thing to say, and Eve felt her spirits lifting ever so slightly.

'Did you think you were in trouble?'

'Aren't I?'

'Not with me. I get it, Pennie. Everyone needs some time to themselves. But I want you to know that you can tell me when things get too much. All I care about is that you're safe. And you're safer at home than you are sitting alone at a bus shelter at ten years old. I know what can happen to someone like you, okay?'

Pennie frowned.

Shit. She'd gone too far again. 'I just mean... it's not safe.'

'Okay,' Pennie said, but she didn't sound convinced.

Pennie was looking straight ahead and Eve followed her stare, which landed at the door to Carver's Kitchen.

'Do you know that place?'

Pennie shook her head.

'You don't ever want to eat in there. Trust me.' Eve smiled a little unnaturally. Goosebumps tickled her skin again and the nausea that she'd been feeling since their earlier conversation came on slightly stronger now, too.

Pennie crinkled her nose, shook her head and stood up. She walked into the road and across to Eve's car, all without so much as a cursory glance in search of oncoming traffic. She opened the passenger door, sat in and waited for Eve to join her.

Eve looked again towards Carver's Kitchen. It looked awful even from the outside. If there was any joy in that place, then it was well hidden behind years of grease and grime. It was as if the building itself was depressed. She pulled her eyes away before that depression spread to her, and got in the car beside Pennie. Before starting the engine, she sat and watched the girl for a moment. Her eyes were downcast, and she was fidgeting with something green between her fingers.

'What's that you've got?' Eve asked. Whatever she was holding was partially stuffed inside the bulging sleeve of her jumper.

'Nothing really,' she said, pulling it further into her sleeve.

Eve didn't push it. Whatever it was, it looked like it was made of long grass, or maybe reeds. From what she could see of it, it reminded Eve of the St Bridget's crosses that they used to make at school when she was there.

'Right. Come on then,' she said, pulling on her seat belt and starting the engine. 'Let's go home.'

Pennie sat in silence for the whole drive and Eve gave up probing after about five minutes. She glanced at the girl from time to time, as she looked out her window with her chin resting on her loosely closed fist. She looked far too deep in thought for someone her age, but then Eve was, too. Now that the panic of losing Pennie had passed, she couldn't *not* think back on their earlier conversation about secrets, drugs and death. Extra pinpricks and postmortem drug tests? Imaginary friends didn't tend to know much more than the imagination they were born from, so how did Pennie know about things like that? And what voice in her head was threatening her with death if she ate?

A sudden and uncomfortable feeling came over Eve while she drove the last hundred yards to Raven's Rock. It felt like her entire blood supply was draining from her head, slowly down towards her feet, leaving her body heavy and lifeless, and cold to the bone. Her limbs weighed a ton and every one of her senses dulled. Terror gripped her, but she couldn't respond to it in any way.

'Eve?' Pennie asked warily.

Eve mounted the curb outside the house and the car stalled. She'd felt blankets of fear before, of course she had. But never like this. She wondered briefly if she was having a stroke or something. Her eyes moved to the bound, grassy item poking out of Pennie's sleeve. Pennie noticed and concealed it further, as far inside her jumper as it would go without tearing the cuff.

'Are you okay?' she asked.

There was worry in Pennie's barely-there voice, and perhaps it was that worry which breathed a little life back into Eve. Whatever feeling had moved down along her body just then, sucking her strength, seemed to move in reverse now. Not as obviously. But that feeling of being sand on the shore, getting sucked out by the tide, was gone. The tide wasn't rushing back in or anything, but she felt some of the life returning to her body and her arms unlocked from the ten-to-two position on the wheel. She inhaled sharply, like she'd been starved of oxygen.

'Eve?'

'Yes.' Her voice was high-pitched and filled with stress, but it was a response at least. Her eyes were still on Pennie's sleeve, but she was too thrown by whatever medical emergency she'd just had. Or not had. She couldn't think of anything else. Certainly not a way to ask Pennie about a lump of grass.

Pennie saw her looking and a very small part of Eve expected her to volunteer the information and just show her. But she didn't. Instead, she opened the door and went to get out of the car, but paused before stepping out. 'Maybe you shouldn't take so many pills,' she said, without so much as glancing back.

Eve blanched. She didn't take too many pills. She was always careful only to take enough to cure her pain. 'No, I didn't... I mean, I don't...'

Pennie got out of the car and closed the door on Eve's explanations. Eve took another minute to compose herself and when she felt it was safe to do so, she started up the car again and pulled it down off the curb. Inch by inch, she drove it, with far more revs of the engine than usual, into the short driveway.

It was after dinner time by then, so Eve took some different pills, when Pennie wasn't watching. Ones that might undo the ultra-calming effect of the ones she'd taken earlier, in perhaps too high a dose. Eve didn't want Pennie to see her taking any more because she didn't understand. Pennie was just a child.

She didn't know enough about pain and medication to know how much was too much. But Eve knew, and she only took what her body needed. Then she made herself cook chicken fajitas with roasted garlic potatoes for their dinner. It was a recipe she found online, but of course, her end result didn't look nearly as nice as it did in that video. She had no garlic for one thing, and very few potatoes. She also lacked the red and yellow peppers that went into the fajita wrap along with the chicken. But she substituted with the foods they did have, and it wasn't all that bad. But again, Pennie just looked at the food and picked. Her stomach had been growling earlier, yet apparently she wasn't hungry now. So, what was she eating when she wasn't eating what Eve made for her? Or was this so-called Angel trying to starve her to death? Eve needed to pull herself together. She *had* to do something about this.

'Not hungry?' she asked, as if they hadn't had their earlier conversation at all. Discomfort squirmed through her. She'd been putting a lot of effort into Pennie's food. Far more than she ever put into her own, but still, she shunned it.

'Not really,' Pennie responded, with her eyes on her plate, like she was examining each piece she pushed around with her fork, before finally picking up the smallest potato she could find and placing it in her mouth.

'Do you want to tell me why you left like that today?'

Pennie shrugged, keeping her eyes on her plate.

'Did Angel tell you to go?'

She shrugged again. Pennie speared another potato and shoved it a bit more forcefully in her mouth.

'You know, you...'

'Angel says I'm stronger than you think.'

Eve paused. 'Did he?' she said, sounding too uncertain. 'Well... Angel is right about that one. You are. We both are.'

'Angel says that everything comes out in the end.'

Eve slowly put her fork down and wiped her mouth with the tip of her thumb. 'And what does Angel mean by that?'

Pennie shrugged again.

Eve watched Pennie while Pennie watched her plate, the pair of them wound tight like springs, fearful and untrusting of each other. The more Pennie spoke Angel's words of wisdom, the more unsettled Eve felt. Eve thought she seemed too mature for a ten-year-old girl. But then Pennie wasn't just any ten-year-old. She'd always been the most silent member of the Raven's Rock family.

Almost like an interloper, in that the rest of them could, and often did, forget she was even there. She stayed out of everyone's way and rarely got in any trouble, which was miraculous in their house. So maybe she was the kind of child who sat all day with her nose in a book, learning the kind of words that *Angel* spoke to her now, while Eve and the rest of them were busy trying to muddle through. Plus, her maturity had been accelerated in recent times following the loss of Ellen. Maybe...

'Can I bring this to my room with me? I might feel like having it later,' Pennie asked, standing up and picking up her almost-full plate.

Eve was momentarily torn between responses. She could give in and allow her to bring her dinner to her room. She probably needed some space. Truth be told, Eve did, too. But who was to say she wouldn't climb out her window again? What if she actually got on a bus next time and what if Eve never saw her again?

'Actually, Pennie, I'd rather you didn't,' she said, too quickly.

Pennie's expression darkened. In fact, her expression had been darker than usual all afternoon. Ever since Eve found her sitting at that bus stop. She seemed angry today and that anger overshadowed the sadness she'd worn like an oversized coat up until now.

'I'll cover it up and put it in the fridge. If you feel hungry later, then come and get it. Or, whatever else you feel like eating. Plus,' she looked at her watch, 'it's still early. You don't need to go to bed...'

'I'm tired,' she said, putting her plate back on the table and walking away.

Eve watched her go, unable to think of a way to stop her. But as soon as Pennie was halfway up the stairs, Eve went to the back door, unlocked it and went outside. The ladder was still leaning against the wall, from the ground, all the way up to Pennie's window. Eve grabbed the sides of the ladder and pulled it away from the wall. She struggled as it swayed this way and that, threatening to drag her down to the ground with it. But then she remembered how she saw Peter doing this once, and she steadied herself. She stepped slowly and carefully backwards, away from the house, with her arms over her head and a tight grip on the ladder. Once she'd lowered it to the ground, she dragged it away from the house, back as far as the stone wall. There, she inched it across the top, shoving it as far as she could, until its own momentum took over from her. She ignored the loud clang as it crashed to the grass on the other side.

She stood for a moment wiping her hands on her pants, the absolute darkness of their garden broken only by the dim light from the kitchen window and the upstairs light from Pennie's room. Eve glanced up to see Pennie watching her, her hands limp by her sides. They made eye contact for the briefest moment and Eve raised her hand in salute.

But Pennie didn't return the gesture. She looked behind her, back into the room, then turned and moved slowly out of sight.

12

Eve knocked once and then opened the bedroom door.

'Pennie?' she said softly, peering around to see Pennie, sitting cross-legged on the makeshift bed again. It was just after 9 p.m. now and Pennie hadn't come back downstairs looking for food, or anything else. Eve couldn't take it any more. 'I thought you might be hungry, so I made you this.' She held a plate towards her. She'd made a toasted bagel with lots of melted cheese on top. Everyone loved grilled cheese, surely.

Pennie stared at the plate for a long minute, then finally she got to her feet and took it from Eve. 'Thank you,' she said, turning and going back to her spot.

As she walked away, Eve spotted the grassy creation that had been stuffed up her sleeve earlier in the day. It was resting beside the pillow on the floor. She tilted her head to see it properly, while Pennie's back was turned. It had a triangular base, semicircular wings and a round head. Far more impressive than she'd realised. Was it an angel?

'Did you make that?' Eve asked, nodding towards the little sculpture. Her scalp tingled uncomfortably and, again, she had that intense feeling of being watched. So much so that she instinctively looked behind her.

Pennie glance at the little doll and shook her head. She sat back down on that miniature-sized bed, blocking Eve's view of the green angel.

'So, where did you get it from? It doesn't look like the kind of thing you could buy in a shop.'

Pennie shrugged and took a tiny bite of her bagel.

Eve could think of nothing else to say and Pennie clearly did not want to speak to her. But the more Angel invaded their lives, the more irritated and unsettled Eve became. She stood there for another minute, watching.

Pennie looked questioningly back at her.

'I want to see you eat some of that bagel, Pennie,' Eve said, sounding impressively authoritative.

Pennie's expression soured further, but she picked up the bagel. Then keeping her eyes on Eve, she made a show of stuffing far too much of it in her mouth. But Eve didn't stop her or pander to her childish behaviour. Instead, she watched while she chewed it up and eventually swallowed with some difficulty brought on by her own actions.

'Well, goodnight then,' Eve just about managed to say at last.

Pennie didn't respond. She just sat there with a face like thunder and eyes like hot lightning on Eve's back as she turned to go.

Eve went downstairs and turned on the television. She played a recording of *Gilmore Girls* with the sound turned down low, but before long, she found herself googling Leslie Granger again. She jumped from one article to another for about a half-hour, but there was still no update on her cause of death. She followed up with a search for Jack Logan. There were no new results on that search, which wasn't surprising. Jack Logan was an addict. His death was old news five minutes after it happened.

There appeared to be no connection between their deaths. At least none that any news story pointed to. There was no way in hell Leslie Granger would have been seen dead in any of the places where Jack Logan hung out. They appeared to be from completely different worlds. The only thing that connected them was that Pennie had spoken about them both. She was the link between the two.

According to what she'd read, Gardaí had contacted some of Leslie's former work colleagues in New Zealand and, according to them, Leslie kept to herself. Her new colleagues here in Cork said the same thing. She didn't socialise much and never dabbled in drugs. Further toxicology tests had been ordered, according to every article she'd read, which debunked Pennie's theory that they weren't looking for the so-called secret drug that killed her. She thought about running up the stairs, waving her phone in Pennie's face, going, *Look! Angel is wrong!* But of course, she didn't. She focused instead on Leslie Granger. This woman who seemed to have invaded Eve's life.

To Eve, she looked like a high-end kinda girl, what with her bouncy curls and shining eyes. Someone found a photo of her at the top of a mountain wearing shorts and a white vest, looking sun-kissed and beautiful. According to that particular article, the photo was taken during her time living in New Zealand. But she was originally from Cork and had returned home only a few weeks before she died. Another brave and adventurous woman, Eve thought almost enviously. Until she wasn't. Very different from the drug user. The furthest he seemed to have travelled was to his nearest street corner, which was where he hung out for the most part, either dealing to feed his habit, or shooting up. But they'd both died drug-related deaths, that much seemed true. And like Jack Logan, no family had yet come forward claiming their grief over Leslie's death either. No boyfriend or husband. No one. The main difference that Eve could see between how their deaths were handled seemed to be down to the fact that Leslie was a beautiful, adventurous woman with a job and a life. A combination which guaranteed her a spot on many front pages and loud demands for action. Jack Logan, on the other hand, was quite an ugly-looking drug addict. The only person who seemed to give a damn about him was a reporter by the name of Nicole Hammond. She was the one writing about his death and asking questions like, *what really happened to Jack Logan?* Nicole Hammond was the one calling for his death to be investigated as suspicious. She'd even asked for his remains to be exhumed just after he'd been buried in a pauper's grave. A request which, unsurprisingly, went unacknowledged by the authorities.

Ellen often said that coppers loved nothing more than playing dumb. They didn't want to waste their precious time and resources looking into society's deep cracks and crevices for the likes of Jack Logan. Not when they had more decent, upstanding citizens to be thinking about. Like Leslie Granger. Perhaps that was why Ellen seemed to get along so well with the cops in their area. They always believed her when she had to come up with explanations and apologies on behalf of their more troublesome kids. All the ones from the wrong side of the tracks, the likes of whom gave Gardaí so much trouble when they were loose on the street. They couldn't help but empathise with Ellen, the woman who tried so hard to keep them on the straight and narrow. Perhaps that was why they always came down on Ellen's side of a dispute.

Eve's stomach muscles bunched up tight when she read Nicole Hammond's article for the third time. She certainly seemed to be screaming murder, but who was listening? Aside from Pennie's imaginary friend, that is.

Eve opened a new page and searched for Nicole Hammond. She was nowhere on social media, but she did have a LinkedIn profile. She clicked in and read through some of her posts. Nicole came across as a *save the addicts* type, but her focus was mostly on Jack Logan. Nicole definitely seemed to think that his death was not accidental, despite the involvement of heroin and the fact that he was addicted to it. Eve clicked into her profile picture. She was a striking woman, in an untamed kind of way. She looked like the type of journalist who was happiest running through a war zone with her hair on fire, even though her LinkedIn profile didn't point to much of that type of action. Eve couldn't tell if her hair was blonde or grey, but it was definitely bleached, tightly shaved at the sides with a bit of a bouffant on top. She had a face that could only be described as weathered, with sharp, steel-blue eyes that looked like they'd seen it all. She had a bit of a haunted look about her and Eve wondered if that was down to her work, or her life in general.

The last article that Eve read on Nicole Hammond's profile did make her sound like a bit of a conspiracy theorist, though. It was a rambling piece about a 'puppeteer' pulling strings and controlling vulnerable kids. It sounded so far-fetched that Eve was left in little wonder as to why no one was listening to her on her murdered-junkie theory. If she hadn't seen her photo before reading that one, then Eve might have imagined a dishevelled, middle-aged man, living in a caravan in the woods. Proud owner of a wide collection of tinfoil hats. But she had seen her picture. And it was one that she knew she'd have trouble getting out of her head.

Eve wondered about reaching out to Nicole, to see what she had to say for herself. She opened the direct-message page and stared at the screen for a minute, trying to come up with any explanation, other than the truth, as to why she might send a message to a reporter. She got a prompt from LinkedIn asking her to log in. She surprised herself by doing so. Eve had a degree in social science, which she'd gotten at some online college during the pandemic. She wasn't sure it would hold up to much in the real world, and she had little interest in finding out. But it was the one good thing that their so-called child welfare officer, Ashley Evans, had done for her. She'd signed Eve up and got the cost of the course covered by the state. Eve knew that

Ashley was just preparing her to enter into the Holland family business, but she took her up on her charitable offer anyway. Ashley wanted Eve to become another understanding foster parent. One who would keep the wheels turning on Ashley's journey towards an easy life. Something she always seemed desperate for. The trouble was that fostering was getting harder and harder to get into. The Hollands began fostering kids back when the state didn't really care where the children went, so long as it was out of their sight. Nowadays, you had to jump through a lot of hoops just to be considered. Probably because of the fact that the state had to pay people to take those kids into their homes, and they were starting to pay out even more in the lawsuits that followed. All those girls who cried wolf and the boys who just cried. The authorities had to be seen to do something to appease the do-gooders. That's what Ellen called the people who never took a feral person into their home, but liked to tell everyone else how it should be done. Those were her words, and she repeated them often.

Anyway, Eve had never actually used that degree in social science and could remember none of what she'd learned on the course. She certainly wasn't active when it came to professional networking, but that's where Nicole Hammond was. According to her profile, she was a freelance journalist with credits in some well-known national press. Her most recent post was the article she'd written about Jack Logan.

A thump overhead pulled her attention away from the screen. She looked to the ceiling and frowned. What was that? She hesitated for a second, before getting up and walking quickly towards the stairs.

'Pennie?' she called up.

There was another thump, though not as heavy as the last one.

She moved a little quicker until she reached Pennie's room, sure that she was climbing out the window again. She knocked brusquely but didn't wait for an answer before opening the door. Pennie was standing by the open window, her torso leaning out and her hair blowing in the cold night breeze.

'Pennie, what are you doing? Do not go out that window!'

Pennie turned to look at Eve. She'd been smiling, but that smile was fading quickly. Again. She seemed disappointed to see Eve in her room. Again. It seemed Eve had interrupted something far more fun than *she* was.

'I asked you a question, Pennie,' she said, sounding sterner than she would have liked, as she walked towards the girl and pulled her gently back from the open window. Eve looked outside, slowly scanning the treeline. It was pitch-black out there, but she saw no movement. No ladder either.

'I was hot,' Pennie replied softly.

Eve could see her breath hanging in the air before she pulled her head back inside, but not before also seeing the remains of the bagel on the grass below. She paused, looking at it, then pulled the window closed.

'You threw your bagel out the window.' Her voice was low, her words measured.

Pennie shook her head. 'It fell.'

Her tiny voice, and the way she lowered her eyes when she spoke to Eve, made Eve want to channel her inner Lorelai again, and smother the child with love and understanding. But at the same time, she felt so sure now that Pennie was hiding something. The question was, would that something help either of them, or would it just bring more heartache to their door?

13

Eve walked slowly through the woods again the following day, not knowing exactly what she was looking for, but sure all the same that something was there. Beyond the trees lay acres and acres of land. It used to be a farm but had since been sold to developers and so the city inched ever closer. But it wasn't upon them yet. Peter told her once that his great-grandmother came from the heart of Cork city, and the fact that she'd married a farmer did not mean she wanted to become one herself. So he created this oasis for her, behind these trees. The *oasis* being Raven's Rock and Eve had trouble thinking of the place in those terms. But Eve knew every inch of this little wood because most of her childhood had been spent out here. As she moved slowly through it now, her eyes were trained on the pine-covered floor, looking for any sign that someone had been there more recently than she had. But there was nothing that she could see.

Her phone buzzed in her pocket. A LinkedIn notification, which she'd switched back on after she managed to connect with, and DM, Nicole Hammond. She'd acted like someone who'd read her article and had her interest piqued by it. Which was more or less true. She opened the app and checked the response that presumably had just come from Nicole.

Nicole Hammond, Freelance journalist – *Sunday Times, Irish Times, Irish Examiner*

Hi Eve,

Thank you for reaching out. Yes, I am very interested in JL's death, and I do believe that it's linked to others. If you have any information, I'd love to meet you to discuss.

She thought for a minute before tapping out her response.

Eve Holland, BSc Social Science
Hi Nicole.

Thank you for coming back to me. I'm not sure I have information, but I would be very interested in meeting up with you to hear what you think.

Nicole Hammond, Freelance journalist – *Sunday Times, Irish Times, Irish Examiner*
I'm in Cork city for the morning. Where are you?

Eve looked at her watch and walked back inside the house. She checked the pot of soup that was simmering gently on the stove. Soup was the one thing that Eve made relatively well and this one was packed full of vegetables and all the goodness Pennie needed today. Eve had woken to the sound of her vomiting in the early hours and had insisted the girl move into the proper bed. She did and was still there now. Eve hoped she'd stay there for the day and get some of her strength back. She would have liked to be there with her, sitting on her bed, stroking her hair and making her feel better. But Pennie didn't want that. She made that very clear without saying anything at all on the matter.

She half-filled a bowl, placed it on a tray with some water and took it upstairs. Balancing the tray precariously on her hip, she knocked gently on Pennie's bedroom door, and went in.

'How are you feeling?' Eve glanced at the old washing-up basin on the floor. Pennie had been sick in it again and now she was pale and looking miserable.

'A little better,' she said, sounding like that wasn't really the case.

Eve went and sat on the edge of her bed, despite herself. She placed the tray on the bedside locker and touched her hand to Pennie's forehead. She tried to ignore the flinch, focusing instead on the fact that she did feel a little cooler so perhaps she was on the mend again.

'Will you try some soup? It'll help bring your strength back up.'

Pennie shook her head.

Eve found herself stroking the girl's hair gently. She couldn't help it. She wanted so badly to bring the child some comfort, even though this was probably doing the opposite. Pennie didn't appear to like being touched. Ever. She never said as much, but her body language spoke volumes.

'Okay,' she said softly, pulling her hand back. 'I'll leave it here if you change your mind. Maybe get some rest and I'll bring you something to make you feel better later, yeah?'

Eve sat with her for a while, until Pennie's breathing became heavier and more rhythmic, then she stood up and quietly left the room. She glanced back at Pennie and smiled, before closing the door. She took her phone from her pocket as she walked downstairs and opened her LinkedIn app. She tapped out a quick response to Nicole Hammond.

Eve Holland, BSc Social Science
I'm in Cork. I can come now if you're free? Let me know where.

Her response took a little longer this time, and Eve used those ten minutes to go back upstairs and change into something that didn't scream of another sleepless night. Fitted, black jeans with a teal-coloured wrap-around shirt. It was an outfit she'd picked up at the charity shop on the same day she found Pennie's new bed. It was what she imagined herself wearing to a meeting, or perhaps a job interview. Not that she'd ever come close to one of those. Eve didn't do well with people and she certainly couldn't imagine being stuck in an office with them day after day. What would they talk about for eight whole hours? Still, she knew what they looked like, so she brushed out her long, mousy-brown hair and pulled it back into a neat, low ponytail. She brushed her teeth and applied minimal make-up, which was the most she ever wore. It wasn't that she was trying to impress Nicole Hammond or anything. If she was, then she would have chosen a lower-cut top because she found herself strangely attracted to Nicole's profile picture. A feeling that was entirely new to her.

Nicole Hammond, Freelance journalist – *Sunday Times, Irish Times, Irish Examiner*
I'm near the Opera House. I'll be in Costa for the next hour.

Costa again. That was where she'd interviewed Graham Crowley, too. It seemed Nicole Hammond was as much a creature of habit as she was. Eve checked her watch, took one last look at her reflection and walked quickly downstairs, typing her response as she went.

Eve Holland, BSc Social Science
   I'll be there in twenty minutes.

* * *

Eve spotted her instantly when she stepped inside the café, which was quiet for a Wednesday morning. Nicole Hammond cut an impressive silhouette, at her table beside the window. She wore a sleeveless T-shirt over wide, blue jeans with chunky, black boots. But it was her bare arms that commanded the attention. Nicole looked as if she could easily bench-press Eve's Opel Corsa, and she had a full tattoo sleeve on each arm. She looked impressive, to Eve's eyes at least, and a small part of her wished she had gone for the lower-cut top. She straightened her clothes, quietly cleared her throat and was about to head over to join her when her thoughts were interrupted by the young woman behind the counter.

'What can I get you, hun?' She smiled.

Eve blinked and looked to the woman. 'An Americano, please. Hun,' she said, just about managing not to roll her eyes. *Hun.* She glanced towards Nicole again. 'Large.' She walked to the top of the counter, tapped her card and waited impatiently for her coffee, glancing over her shoulder at the woman, who seemingly hadn't noticed her yet. Or maybe she had and just hadn't acknowledged her. She had her laptop open on the table and was glancing from her screen to the street outside her window. She seemed completely lost in her own thoughts.

'Here you go. Enjoy,' the barista said, with a less friendly smile now, as she handed Eve a steaming cup. It was roughly the size of a baby's bath.

Eve returned the unfriendly smile, picked up her coffee with both hands, and walked over to Nicole's table.

'Nicole?' she asked, with a proper smile that said, *You'll want to talk to me.*

Nicole visibly pulled herself from her deep thoughts and finally smiled back at Eve. 'Eve?' She got to her feet and held out her hand.

Eve put her cup on the table and took her hand gratefully. The strength in the woman's handshake caught Eve off guard and she found herself staring at her like an idiot. Nicole Hammond was mesmerising. But the troubled look on her face said that she had more important things on her mind than Eve Holland and when she released her hand, Eve had to force herself to look away.

Nicole gestured towards the seat opposite and they both sat down. She closed her utilitarian-type laptop, which looked like it could survive a fall from a helicopter, and she shoved it into an equally utilitarian-looking backpack on the floor beside her.

'Thanks for meeting me.' Eve smiled nervously. She picked up her cup and held it, just to give her hands something to do. She wasn't an outgoing person by any stretch of the imagination, and her discomfort wasn't helped by how attractive Nicole was. She couldn't get her thoughts in order. What was her plan here? In what way would she explain her interest in this story?

'So, you wanted to speak to me about Jack Logan?' Nicole asked, topping her mug up with hot tea from a pot on the table.

'Eh, well, yes...' Eve stammered like a fool. 'I suppose I did.'

Nicole tilted her head and looked mildly amused, and Eve felt a touch of irritation. But she wouldn't show her that. 'I mean...' She smiled again and shook her head almost imperceptibly. 'I read your article and I just, well, I found it really interesting.'

'Did you?' She took a large sip of her tea. 'Why's that?'

It was Eve's turn to look questioningly at Nicole now. 'You think it's strange that people find your articles interesting?'

She shrugged. 'Oh, I'll take all the interest I can get. But not many find my writing interesting enough that they ask to meet with me.'

'Oh. That, well...'

'You're here for a reason,' she said, still with a friendly half-smile. 'And I think that reason might be that you know something about Jack, or maybe the person who killed him.' She leaned across the table, closer to Eve, her eyes alight with curiosity. She didn't sound accusatory in the least. Just interested.

Eve looked nervously around to see if anyone might have overheard what she'd just said. They didn't. She cleared her throat again before answering quietly. 'I'm afraid I don't. I just wondered what made you think his death was suspicious.'

'And?'

'And what?' she said, a tremble in her voice suddenly. Why hadn't she been expecting an interrogation? The woman was a journalist, after all. Why the hell would Eve ask to meet with, of all things, a *journalist*? What was she thinking?

'And,' Nicole continued, 'why are you here?'

Despite the way she spoke, Nicole Hammond had a kind face and a genuine smile while she spoke to Eve. Her gaze, those eyes... they felt almost familiar somehow. Or perhaps it was her many facial expressions, but it felt suddenly as if they'd known each other for a lot longer than these past five minutes. But she would have remembered meeting Nicole before. She seemed like a woman who lived an exciting and unpredictable life and, suddenly, Eve wanted some small part of that. She didn't want her polite smile. Eve wanted Nicole to be interested in what *she* had to say.

The Internet told her that the best way to lie was to stick as close to the truth as possible. 'Okay,' Eve said, placing her heavy cup on its saucer again. 'I met someone recently. I can't and won't tell you anything about them, so please don't ask. But they spoke about some recent deaths in the city that don't seem to be related in any way, but...'

'But...?'

'It was the way they spoke about them. The reasons *why* they died...' She shook her head and frowned. Was she making any sense? Probably not. None of this *made* sense. But she found herself really wanting to hook Nicole Hammond in. As ridiculous as the idea was, she wanted to fascinate her.

'Who is this *someone*?' she asked.

'I can't tell you that. I can only tell you that they couldn't possibly be involved in any of the deaths that they spoke about.'

'What makes you so sure?'

'I'm sure, okay? Can you take that as a given for now?'

Nicole held her palms up and gave a slight bow of her head. Her white-blonde hair, though tightly cropped on the back and sides, looked impossibly soft and bouncy, and perfectly styled on top. Nicole Hammond might have been the coolest woman Eve had ever seen, let alone spoken to. 'Go on,' she said.

Eve wrapped her hands around the warm cup, but didn't pick it up. Things already felt too heavy. The weight of expectation, perhaps. Or the weight of her stupidity. The weight of it all. 'I don't know how to explain this,' she said, her stomach fizzing and jumping now as Nicole's cool gaze intensified.

'Let's start with the deaths. Which ones are we talking about? I presume Jack Logan is one of them, seeing as you reached out to me.'

Eve nodded. 'Okay. So first, it was Leslie Granger. Remember that woman who was found...'

'Dead from an apparent drugs overdose inside her home. Or should I say,' she made air quotes, '"pharmaceutical-related death". Yes, I know the one.' All traces of her easy smile gone now. Eve had her full attention. Suddenly, she was the most interesting woman in the world. A feeling that was entirely new to Eve.

Eve smiled and gave a curt nod. 'Well, they spoke about Leslie Granger's death in pretty much the same sentence as the one you wrote about. I just thought that was strange, as they have absolutely nothing in common.'

Nicole frowned. 'They spoke about them, how?'

Pennie said that Leslie Granger died because someone had done something to her, and it was a secret. Her secrets killed her, basically, but saying that out loud would prompt far too many questions from someone like Nicole. Eve did not want a journalist prying into Pennie. She couldn't run the risk of some do-gooder coming and taking Pennie away from her, now that Ellen was gone. She just wanted Nicole to tell her what *she* knew. *And* to continue looking at her like that, which she both enjoyed and loathed in equal measures. Nicole looked at Eve as if she was unlike anyone she'd ever met before.

Eve shrugged as nonchalantly as she could manage. 'I can't remember exactly what they said, but they basically compared Leslie Granger's death to your one.'

'My one?' She smiled, bemused.

'You know what I mean.'

'Well, I think anyone would find it hard to connect Leslie Granger with Jack Logan. Their lives didn't look like they'd have anything in common, did they? Aside from their causes of death maybe, but even then... Jack was a heroin addict who died from an *apparent* heroin overdose. Leslie Granger was not a drug user, who died from something that wasn't detected in the usual toxicology tests carried out at post-mortems. My sources tell me they found a huge amount of insulin in her blood. Much higher than what's normal, I mean, but that hasn't been confirmed.'

'Insulin?' Eve asked. 'So she was diabetic?'

Nicole arched one eyebrow and shook her head. 'Apparently not. But again, that's not been made fact yet either.'

Eve nodded thoughtfully. 'That's what I thought.'

Nicole made a curious face. 'What, that she wasn't diabetic?'

Eve fumbled her cup, sloshing coffee onto the saucer. Fantastic. She sounded stupid and now she looked stupid, too. 'That they have nothing in common, I mean.' Her voice was shrinking, along with her confidence. But Nicole continued to watch her, waiting for her to explain further, so she tried. 'Well, that's why I wanted to meet you.' She picked up a napkin and mopped up the coffee, just so she wouldn't have to look at her. 'I was hoping you could tell me a bit more about Jack Logan.' She said his name like she was hazarding a guess, rather than sounding like she'd been googling him obsessively, along with Leslie Granger. 'Are the Gardaí investigating his death? Do you have any idea who might have killed him, or why?'

Nicole twisted her mouth in thought and Eve couldn't help it when her eyes rose to watch the movement of her lips.

'How did it come up?' she asked after a while.

'The conversation, you mean? Eh, I think it was when the news report came on TV on the day Leslie Granger's body was found.'

'Okay. What others?'

She was avoiding answering Eve's questions, but Eve couldn't bring herself to point that out. Or to insist she do so. 'Oh, eh... just *drug users*. That was pretty much all they said, so I started looking up suspicious drug deaths and that's how I came upon your story about eh...' She squeezed her eyes shut, trying to remember the name. Nicole Hammond was affecting her and she'd genuinely lost her train of thought this time.

'Jack Logan,' she offered.

'Yes. Sorry. Jack. They said that they take drugs and sell drugs and everyone gets hurt. That kind of thing.' She held back the bit about them using drugs to manage their secrets, which seemed to be the theme of Pennie's thoughts when it came to both Leslie and Jack. But Eve hadn't come here to *give* a journalist information. She had come to try and *get* some. 'So when I looked up drug deaths, the only suspicious one I could find was that one. And actually, you're the only one who seemed to find his death suspicious.'

Nicole frowned again and shook her head. 'They said they take drugs and hurt people? But as far as I know, the only person who was intentionally hurt by Jack, was Jack.'

'Intentionally?'

Nicole placed her palms flat on the table and looked as if she were about to let Eve in on a secret. 'Jack had a sealed juvenile record,' she said quietly, gluing Eve to her chair with intense eye contact.

Eve felt something like butterflies taking off in her stomach. She was very much aware that this was a totally inappropriate response to what she'd just said. But she *was* letting Eve in on something that wasn't mentioned online. 'For what?' she asked, keeping her tone level. 'Do you know what he did?'

'Well, that's what sealed means, isn't it.' Nicole topped up her tea again.

Eve nodded. 'So maybe he did hurt someone?'

'Most addicts do at some stage. Usually out of sheer desperation and the urge to feed their own habits. Course, they're easy enough to coerce, too, so who knows.'

'So... do you think maybe if he did hurt someone, that maybe someone got revenge by killing him?' This didn't really tally with what Pennie said about secrets, but she wanted to keep Nicole talking.

Nicole crinkled her nose and looked girlish suddenly. 'Even if they did, what would that have to do with Leslie Granger? She's been in New Zealand for the past five years, and as far as anyone knew, she wasn't on the drug scene either here, *or* over there.'

Nicole was right.

They sat quietly for a few minutes, Nicole watching Eve and Eve watching the tabletop.

'I shouldn't have come,' she said after a while.

'I'm glad you did come.' Nicole smiled, and that was exactly what Eve wanted to hear. 'I don't know if there's much to what you're saying, though. I mean, it sounds like this *person* might know something that no one else does, which in itself is quite worrying, or...'

'Or?'

'Or,' she shrugged, 'they're full of shit.'

Eve nodded and started to stand. 'Maybe you're right. There's probably nothing to it. To any of it.'

'All the same, if this is someone that you met eh... socially, I'd consider how close you want to get to a person who thinks that way,' Nicole said softly. 'I mean, it's absolutely none of my business. I know that. But...'

Eve smiled, feeling those strange butterflies again. The kind she'd read about in library books and heard about on TV. 'It's not. I'm not seeing anyone.' She said it too quickly, too desperately, and she felt her cheeks flushing red.

Nicole smiled.

'It's just a young person that I met through work,' she added, again too quickly. 'Like I said, they couldn't possibly be involved in any of it. But I worried that someone they knew might be... well,' she picked up her bag and slung it on her shoulder, 'telling them scary stories.'

Nicole stood with her and reached into her back pocket. She pulled out a card and handed it to Eve. 'Here. Use this anytime, okay? I like conversations like this one and I can tell that you didn't make the decision to come here easily. If that person waves any more red flags in your face, please do call me.'

Eve looked at the card. It was plain white, with *Nicole Hammond* in bold lettering, and *Investigative Journalist* in italics beneath it. Her phone number and email were closer to the bottom. 'Thanks.'

Eve slid the card in her back pocket and said the briefest goodbye, her feet fumbling over themselves as she tried to extract herself from the table. By the time she left, she was fully convinced that Nicole was watching her go, feeling eyes on her back all the way to the door. What she *didn't* know, was whether she watched Eve because she interested her, or was it because she thought that Eve was someone to be pitied?

14

In the days following her coffee with Nicole, Eve spent more time than she should have thinking about her. She'd looked her up on all social media platforms and was annoyingly disappointed when she still couldn't find her anywhere, except on LinkedIn. She was even more disappointed when she realised that she couldn't continuously look at her LinkedIn profile without Nicole being alerted to the fact that Eve was stalking her online. Still, their conversation played on a loop in her mind. Sometimes, Eve cringed at how badly she'd explained her reasons for contacting her. Other times, she managed to convince herself that Nicole had hung on her every word. Sometimes, she found herself thinking about what it might be like to touch her. To be touched *by* her. It had taken a while for Eve to figure out what exactly she hated about so-called *intimacy*. But then she realised that she'd just been doing that with the wrong types of people. In that they'd all been boys. Now she thought she might really like to be in a relationship with someone who looked like Nicole Hammond. *If* she could ever bring herself to seek out another intimate relationship, that is. But that wasn't what she wanted from Nicole now. Not really. She wanted her help to decipher the things her strange little sister had said. Still, it *would* be nice if Nicole were to like her. Not many did because of where she came from, but maybe, just *maybe*, Nicole might feel like getting to know Eve Holland, the person.

Eve wasn't someone who craved attention. Quite the opposite, in fact. She was far more comfortable in her own company than in that of other people. She'd learned to be that way from a very young age, when Ellen was busy with their foster kids, who came and went so frequently that Eve never really made friends with any of them, except for Amelia. And they weren't really friends. They were just sisters. Kids at school never wanted to be friends with her either, and Eve knew that it was because their parents had warned them against playing with kids from Raven's Rock. Somewhere along the line, Eve came to know, and she was told often enough, how bad she was around other people, *and* at acting like a normal girl, from a normal family. Now, as an adult, she never went out socially. She didn't drink alcohol, hated group settings and had nothing in common with anyone. But Nicole Hammond seemed to have struck a chord with her, and now she found herself wondering what her life might be like if she had someone to share it with. Someone to be her partner and to help her with Pennie. Someone to make them a family again. A *normal* family. But situations like that required intimacy. That word again. But it was such a big word and one that Eve struggled with most of all. All the people she'd ever been *intimate* with were men and boys and Eve had no interest in either. But Nicole Hammond was in her head now and she showed no signs of leaving.

'Eve?' Pennie's small voice pulled her from her thoughts as she sat on the couch with her stockinged feet on the coffee table, staring at Nicole's business card and trying to come up with excuses to call her. *Gilmore Girls* was muted on TV. It was a rerun and Eve had seen it so many times, she could practically recite the script.

'Hmm?' She turned to look at Pennie, who was standing at the bottom of the stairs. She'd been spending nearly all of her time in her room and had been unwell on and off for weeks now. Some days, she begged to be allowed to go out to the garden, and Eve let her if she agreed to eat something before going. She firmly believed the fresh air would make her feel better. But it seemed, at times, like maybe Pennie was making herself sick. Purging the food Eve gave her. But Eve would care for her through this phase and would let her sister know that she was loved. Whatever else, she wanted her to know that.

'Can you please make a stew for dinner tonight?' Pennie asked softly.

Eve pulled her feet off the table and turned her whole body to face Pennie. She smiled, feeling a small sense of relief. Pennie *never* asked for food. Some nights, when she was well, she'd come downstairs late at night, when she was sure that Eve was asleep. Then she and Angel would eat anything *other* than the food Eve prepared for them that evening. Usually cornflakes, which was why there were two boxes sitting on the countertop for Pennie to help herself to. So, to hear Pennie requesting a specific food, *any* food finally, made her smile.

'A stew?'

Pennie nodded, still holding on to the banister, ready to retreat back to her bedroom at the earliest opportunity.

'I can do that,' Eve said, standing up and heading to the kitchen.

Pennie started back up the stairs without saying anything else.

'Would you like to help me?' Eve called after her. 'Do you like cooking?'

'No, thanks.'

Her reply was barely above a whisper, and she kind of hovered on the third step, as if waiting for permission to continue on up. She was much thinner than she had been when Ellen was here. A sure sign that Eve was failing at the task of caring for her.

'Okay,' she said, sounding as disappointed as she felt. But she turned her attention to finding the ingredients she needed for a stew. 'You go and rest then. I'll call you when it's done.'

If Pennie responded in any way, Eve didn't hear it, as she padded softly upstairs.

Eve closed her eyes briefly, then turned towards the stairs again. She smiled as kindly as she could. 'Pennie?'

Pennie stopped moving again, but didn't respond. She just stood there, waiting.

'I'm your big sister,' she said, with that desperately hopeful lilt to her voice. 'I'll take care of you, and I love you. You know that, right?'

Pennie, with her eyes cast down, started moving again. One step at a time, like the effort was almost too much. A few seconds later, her bedroom door closed quietly and Eve exhaled a shaky breath, fighting the overwhelming feeling of inadequacy that plagued her, always. She forced herself to get going on the stew, keen to get it made and to see Pennie actually eating it. Nicole Hammond was temporarily moved to the back of her mind. But no doubt, she wouldn't stay there for long.

A couple of hours later, Pennie joined Eve at the kitchen table. Beside her, as always, was her grass angel figure. It had quickly become one of the most important things in Pennie's life and was ever-present now, replacing Eve's old brown bear. Eve ladled the stew from a serving bowl into two cereal bowls, filling them both almost to the top. There was still plenty left for tomorrow. She seasoned Pennie's for her, then slid it across the table.

'How was your day?' A stupid question, considering that Pennie's day was spent in her room. But she kept a small smile in place as she pushed the food in front of Pennie. 'Did you feel all right?'

Pennie shrugged, picked up her fork and started fishing through the watery stew. She soon found a carrot, but rather than putting it in her mouth, she pushed it back down to the bottom of the bowl. Eve watched her closely while she ate her own. Pennie would nibble a piece, clearly just to appease Eve, and then she'd continue stirring the rest slowly around.

'You're not hungry?' Eve asked at last, her disappointment very clear.

'Not really.'

'When you asked me to make a stew, I thought it was because you were hungry.' She tried to keep the irritation out of her voice.

Pennie shrugged again. 'I had a big lunch.'

Her packed lunch, which Eve always left in the fridge for her, was no bigger than usual. A ham and cheese sandwich, with some fruit. Eve took pride in making up Pennie's lunch each day before leaving the house, remembering how disappointing it was to find that you didn't have one. Ellen sometimes did that if Eve had done something stupid. She'd have Eve make lunch for everyone else, and then tell her that there was nothing for her when she was done. Lunches had never been Ellen's strong point. But Pennie's lunch was always gone from the fridge when Eve got home and there were times when she wondered if she just dumped out all the food, rather than eating it. She'd asked her a few times, and Pennie always responded with, 'I'm eating it.' Eve was beginning to feel more like a nagging mother than a big sister and she was trying not to resent the fact. This wasn't what she imagined their relationship becoming.

'So why did you ask me to make this?' she asked anyway.

'I thought I wanted it.'

Eve looked down and started pushing food around in her own bowl now. She wasn't hungry either. It was too early for dinner, but she'd jumped to it because it was Pennie who'd asked. She took a breath and decided not to push it. She didn't want to put Pennie off asking for food, no matter how frustrating the outcome was.

'Is it okay if I go to my room?'

Eve dropped her fork and it sent soup splashing onto the table. Pennie jumped and Eve was immediately sorry. *Don't be annoyed with her.*

'Are you cross with me?'

Eve closed her eyes and exhaled. 'I'm not cross with you, Pennie. I'm just worried about you. You don't eat much and I...'

'I do. I eat when I get hungry...'

'In the middle of the night,' Eve said as gently as she could. 'You know, most people don't eat dinner in the middle of the night.'

'Yeah, well, I don't have to be like most people.'

Eve felt a heaviness in her chest suddenly and her shoulder slumped. 'You're right about that.' She smiled sadly. They were *never* like most people. Not in any way. Eve considered her words carefully. 'I suppose what I mean is that, it's not healthy for you to be having dinner in the middle of the night, when you should be asleep. Even I know that, and I don't seem to know very much at all.'

Pennie looked at her hands, which were fidgeting with her angel figure. 'I know, but I can't help it. When I go to sleep, I see all those dead people. Then I wake up and I get hungry.'

Eve inhaled sharply. 'Pennie, if you're having nightmares, then you should wake me up.'

Pennie shook her head. 'I don't want to.'

'Why not?'

'Adults get tired more than kids do.'

As strange as it seemed, Eve wasn't used to be referred to as an adult. Even though that's what she was.

'I'm not tired,' she said reassuringly. It wasn't true, of course. Her headache seemed to have become a permanent thing, alternating between a dull, throbbing annoyance and blinding torture. She did sleep, but never restfully enough that she didn't wake feeling exhausted, and Pennie's night-time escapades weren't helping. But she kept her mouth shut.

'Can I go to my room now?'

'Pennie?' Eve said softly. It was time to have *the talk* with her. The one she'd been rehearsing for a while. She needed Pennie to see that they were the same.

Kind of. And that she could trust Eve. 'I know you were never really told much about where you came from, but...'

Pennie seemed to sag back into her chair.

'When I was a small baby, maybe around two years old, my mum decided she didn't want me any more and I was taken in by Ellen and Peter.' She gestured to the house around her. 'I was about thirteen when you came along, but there were so many kids coming and going that I didn't really think about where you'd come from. Ellen and Peter never explained it either, but then they never did explain where the kids came from. Like I said, kids just came and went. But I was permanent and so was Amelia, so I didn't think too much about the fact that you became permanent as well.' She looked down at her fidgeting hands. 'I just assumed that your real mother never wanted you back either. Just like mine and just like Amelia's. Ellen never said anything, but...' She inhaled and blew out hard. This wasn't how she'd rehearsed it. 'But of course, it made so much sense. You must have been sent here because you already had a sibling living here. Me. They do that, you know. They try to keep siblings together whenever they can.' She gestured towards Pennie and gave her a soft smile, her eyes quickly filling with tears. The girl was riveted to the spot. 'I should have asked Ellen. I wish I had, even though she probably wouldn't have told me. You know what she was like. You were such a tiny baby.' A tear ran down her cheek. 'She might have thought you wouldn't want to know about any of it, and she was probably right. But then all this happened and now it's just the two of us, so I suppose... well, we need to know these things now, don't we?'

Eve's words poured like a running tap and Pennie said nothing in return. But she was breathing heavily, her shoulders noticeably rising and falling.

'*Did* you want to know? Are you glad to have a sister?'

Pennie shrugged and looked at her bowl again.

Eve nodded and looked around the room. 'Well, if you think of all the kids who came and went from this house, we must have been pretty special to have been kept, right?' she said, trying to bring things back onto a more positive track. 'Did you know that Peter always wanted a daughter of his own? I think it was him who talked Ellen into keeping us long-term.' There was a pause then before Eve added, 'There was another girl who was here even longer than I was. You remember I mentioned Amelia? But she's been gone since you were a baby, so you wouldn't remember her.' Eve licked her lips, which felt dry suddenly, and she lowered her eyes to her still-fidgeting hands. She clutched them tightly in order to still them. 'I thought of *her* as my sister, but...' Eve shook her head and brought one shaking hand to her forehead. This was getting too hard. 'Anyway, Amelia left.' She always felt vaguely unwell whenever she thought about Amelia. Her sudden disappearance hurt Eve more than any other event in her life. She always thought she'd hear from her eventually. That she'd send for Eve to come and join her in some fabulous new life she'd forged for herself. But she never did. 'Sisters shouldn't leave each other, should they?' The words sounded hoarse with emotion.

'Did you love them?' Pennie asked, her voice barely more than a whisper and her face becoming pale and clammy again. 'Ellen and Peter – like a real mum and dad, I mean?'

Eve's smile faded. Pennie knew them. She'd lived with them all her life, but Eve sometimes wondered if she understood them as well as Eve did. Pennie was always so quiet and withdrawn, and always on the outside of just about everything. But despite her chosen *profession*, Ellen Holland appeared very much like she hated children. She had no patience for them or the drama that so often accompanied them. She lost her temper at the drop of a hat and gave little or no sympathy, regardless of what any child had been through before finding themselves on her doorstep. But did Pennie notice any of that? Ellen did feed them and put a roof over their heads, there was no denying that much. Peter, on the other hand, was rarely home because he had a job. He worked on various building sites doing whatever needed doing. But he never had friends that she knew of. Eve had gone with him once when he'd had to make a stop at one site to check his rostered hours for the following week. While she waited in the car, with the window rolled all the way down, she heard one man say to another, 'Look at that odd fucker.' But Peter wasn't odd. He was just quiet, and Eve was his girl.

But she didn't tell Pennie any of that. Instead, she said, 'They were nice, weren't they?' with an enthusiastic nod of her head. 'But my point is, I think we have the same *blood* in our veins, which means, we're a proper family. You're my *actual* sister, Pennie, and I love you.' She reached her hand across the table, hoping that Pennie would take it. She didn't. She just looked at it and Eve could see tears pooling in the girl's eyes. Had she said too much again? Eve slowly pulled her hand back. 'The truth is, Pennie, I've never done this before.' She gestured between the two of them. 'I'm not sure I know how to *really* take care of another person. Not on my own, at least. But we can figure it out together, can't we?' She smiled hopefully.

Pennie shrugged and gave a small nod. But there was so much uncertainty in her expression that Eve found it impossible to ignore. Still, she tried. She cleared her throat before she could continue.

'So in order for us to do that, you need to trust me, okay?'

Another shrug and another nod, then they sat in silence for a minute, Eve hoping that Pennie would give some indication that things were about to change for the better. That she was about to let Eve in and give her a chance. But she didn't.

Eve pulled her hand all the way back and let it fall off the edge of the table and into her lap, where it immediately found its counterpart and started fidgeting again. 'Okay, well, you don't look so good. Why don't you go back to bed and I'll be up to check on you shortly.'

Pennie immediately got to her feet and left looking painfully relieved.

It was the end of yet another one-sided conversation that left Eve wondering if bloodline meant anything, to anyone but her. No matter how hard she tried, Pennie did not want her. Surely, Pennie had to *want* her for this to work.

Eve stood up and returned her portion of stew to the serving dish. She placed Pennie's in the fridge and then went to rinse stew off her fingers. She leaned heavily against the kitchen sink and caught her own reflection staring judgementally back at her. 'She's ten years old,' the woman in the window told her. 'She's lost the closest thing she had to a mother. Go easy.'

Eve lowered her eyes and poured some dish soap on her hands. Didn't it matter that the same could be said for Eve? Yes, she was technically an adult but, really, what did she know about adulthood? Should she automatically be able to manage the transition with a bit more grace? Did being an adult mean that you *always* knew the right thing to do? Eve rinsed her hands and shook them dry. No. She was doing the best she knew how. Pennie, too, was coping as well as she could at her age, and Eve needed to have more patience with the girl. And with herself. If Pennie wanted to stay in her room with an imaginary friend all the time, then Eve should let her. If she didn't want to eat, fine. But Eve would keep on providing food for her. Plus, she would give her love and comfort when she was sick *and* when she wasn't. Perhaps that's what would eventually turn the tables. The rest... would take care of itself. Her irritation turned towards herself now for becoming so emotional and desperate during their conversation. That was Eve in a nutshell. Often emotional, *always* desperate.

She could hear Pennie moving around overhead and Eve looked towards the ceiling. Compared to some of the kids who'd come through this house, really, Pennie was no problem. Pennie had *never* been a problem. So why now, in the absence of Ellen, did she set Eve's instincts on such high alert? Why did her very presence suddenly feel big enough to fill any void?

15

Eve sat in her car facing the park at around lunchtime the following day. Pennie was sick again early in the night and Eve had sat with her for hours after, while she slept. But she said she was feeling better by the time Eve started thinking about leaving the house. That was around mid-morning, which was the time the walls usually started to close in on her. Pennie ate some cereal just to appease Eve and then she encouraged her to go, knowing full well how desperate she was to do so. She wondered if Pennie knew *why* Eve was like this. Why she couldn't settle and just *be* at home. She hadn't always been like this. When Ellen was here, Eve was kept so busy that she never had time to go anywhere except on her delivery round, which was timed each day. It was only when things died down and it was just Pennie and Eve alone in the house for the first time, that Eve started to feel claustrophobic. Perhaps it was knowing that she no longer *had* to stay there that suddenly had her feeling like she *couldn't* stay. Plus, there was her job. She *had* to go. But she no longer had to race through it, and after a day out, even if most of it was spent traipsing around the estates and watching people going about their normal lives, she was content in returning to Raven's Rock and settling back in.

She glanced up from Nicole Hammond's LinkedIn page as a boisterous group of young girls bustled past her car window, on their way towards the gate to the park. She lowered the phone when she saw a girl she recognised. Her name was Lauren something. She was in Pennie's class at school. She went bouncing through the park, smiling and talking enthusiastically to the two girls who walked alongside her, basking in her popularity. A small part of Eve would have loved to see Pennie there with them. Smiling and chatting like a child who had friends. But as she watched them bobbing along, all smiles and cheers, her thoughts turned less friendly towards those girls. They were like clones of each other and Eve imagined them as a scene from a teen movie, their movement through the park a slow-motion scene. Three hair-flicking, smug, smiling, *perfect* girls, leaving the rest in their wake. Not even in Eve's imagination did Pennie fit anywhere among them.

Eve looked away from the girls and down at her phone again. She was reading one of Nicole's older articles about a cyclist who was killed when his bike left the road during a training cycle. The article said that the man was preparing to take part in the L'Étape du Tour de France, whatever that was, but he failed to return home from his last training cycle. The Cork man was found days later in a field just outside Dungarvan in County Waterford. Any physical injuries he had occurred *after* he died, according to Nicole. She wrote that investigators believed he suffered a medical emergency and died very suddenly. *Sudden adult death syndrome* was the phrase that was used. The delay in finding him was due to the fact that he'd left the road and entered into a field below. That, and the fact that he wasn't reported missing for three days. Not until his work colleagues noticed that he hadn't been at his desk in that long. Only that one of them knew his training route, he might not have been found at all. His death appeared to be an accident, and while tragic, it seemed like a deviation from the kinds of stories that Nicole liked to report upon. Eve couldn't help wondering what made her cover it. Perhaps she was asked to, by *The Independent*, which was where the article was published. Clearly, that's how freelancing worked, in a writer's world. It was a sad story for sure, but it didn't look like it had gotten much attention.

Eve glanced up at the park again. The girls were hogging the swings and Eve had to remind herself that they weren't *her* swings. She went back to the article. Nicole Hammond disagreed with the findings of the investigating team. Now there was a surprise. Nicole seemed to disagree with people for sport. Here, she claimed that the cyclist Brian Merriman's death was not properly investigated, and her frustration was clear in her writing. This was another article that made Nicole look like a conspiracy theorist. Why did she think that every death she wrote about was suspicious? Didn't she believe in accidents?

She went on to write that no one was listening. That they'd made a mistake. The article was two months old, and while Eve wasn't one to buy into conspiracy theories, she resolved to look up more details on Brian Merriman when she got home.

Eve put her phone down and let her eyes drift to the group of tweens, playing on the roundabout this time, like a bunch of five-year-olds. They were laughing and screaming like idiots. Trying to be cool, while also letting their inner child out. Again, they made her think about Pennie, and she picked up her phone again and dialled the house number.

It rang out. She dialled again, knowing that it might take a little while for Pennie to get out of bed and downstairs to reach it. They'd never had a second extension, and Eve still hadn't thought to add one now that they had full use of the phone. It rang out a second time. The third time, however, the phone was answered on the first ring. She heard Pennie saying, 'She won't stop if I don't,' before saying, 'Hello, Eve.'

Eve's temperature cooled again as she was plunged back into Pennie's world. Who was she speaking to? 'Pennie, who's there?' she asked, fear causing her pitch to rise unnaturally high.

'What do you mean?' Pennie asked.

'I just heard you saying, "she won't stop if I don't". Who were you speaking to?'

There was silence but she could hear Pennie's breathing. 'I was talking to Casey,' she said at last.

The brown bear. Eve paused, her senses on high alert. 'Casey?' she asked sceptically. 'Not Angel?'

There was another pause from Pennie, longer this time.

'Pennie?'

'I'm fine. I'm feeling better. Is that why you called?'

Eve put the key in the ignition and started the car. She didn't like this. Pennie was lying to her and Eve could sense the other person in the house as if she were standing there in the kitchen, looking at them.

'Pennie, I want you to tell me who's there,' she demanded, pulling recklessly out onto the road without looking. A horn blasted nearby, and she jumped, pulling the wheel the wrong way and narrowly missing a parked minivan. The same horn blasted a second time as she regained control of the car and sped off.

The line went dead.

'No!' Eve cried at the windscreen and brought the car up to an uncomfortable speed. Her mind raced along the road with it until she reached Raven's Rock ten minutes later. She screeched into the driveway and as she jumped from the car, she left the door wide open as she ran up the steps, two at a time.

'Pennie!' she called as she all but fell through the front door. There was no answer. 'Pennie!' Her voice cracked this time as she ran through the ground floor. The phone in the kitchen was off the hook, but everything else looked just as it had earlier. She rushed upstairs, tripping and falling on the top step. Her shin cried out in pain as it slammed against the hard edge of the top step, but she didn't stop. She hurried to Pennie's room and burst through the door without knocking.

'Pennie!' she panted. Both beds were neatly made, but there was no sign of Pennie. 'Pennie!' she screamed, embarrassingly loud and screechy.

Again, there was no answer. There was no sound at all in the house, because Pennie was not there.

Eve ran through each of the other rooms, knowing that she wouldn't be there, yet she stopped in her tracks when, lastly, she entered her own bedroom. There, sitting on her pillow, was her old friend and confidant, Casey. She walked slowly to the bed and picked him up, studying him closely. His hat was barely hanging on by a thread and he was practically bulging with secrets, none of which he would relinquish. It was why Eve had loved him all her life. And it was why she resented him now. She opened her wardrobe and placed him back on the shelf. It was less than he deserved, but it was all she had in her to do for him now. She left the room, closing the door behind her and then she stood there on the landing, looking around. Pennie wasn't here. She walked in circles, clutching her hair in both hands. Pennie was not here.

Finally, feeling utterly spent, she leaned against the wall outside the locked room and slid to the floor. She brought her arms over her head and buried her face in them. Was there another voice on the phone that time? Did someone respond to Pennie when she said that Eve wouldn't stop calling if she didn't pick up? *Who* was she speaking to?

Her breathing stopped when she thought she heard a sound. She whipped her head to the side, as if that would improve her hearing somehow, and she rested her cheek against the locked door. She held her breath, listening intently. House noises. Raven's Rock was filled with them and that room in particular. Perhaps it was because the air was never allowed to circulate in there. It didn't get any heat either, so perhaps it was damper than the rest of the house and thus it creaked more in protest. Either way, the place was so old. She struggled to her feet and went back downstairs. She couldn't worry about the creaks and groans of this old house now. Not when Pennie was out there somewhere, with God knows who. The only thing Eve needed to worry about now was finding her.

'Where are you, Pennie?' Eve called as she hurried around the garden and through the trees. But she wasn't there. No one was.

She hurried back to her car and drove off again in the direction of town, but much more slowly this time, her eyes scanning the streets. She was passing the park again before she knew it and Pennie's classmates were coming out now. Eve pulled in close to the footpath and got out of the car.

'Lauren?' Eve called.

All three girls stopped and turned to look at her. They didn't know her. Eve only knew Lauren's name because Pennie pointed her out one time when Eve dropped her to school. Eve made herself smile in a semi-friendly way so as not to intimidate the girls, even though really, she was the one intimidated by them. Even now, as an adult, girls like them still bothered her, which was ridiculous. But they were so like the girls who'd ousted Eve every chance they got during her own school days. Girls like them were the reason why Eve was such a social misfit. One of the reasons at least. Yet here they were, looking at her like she was a character in a 'stranger danger' ad.

'Hi.' She walked towards them, her worry for Pennie overshadowing all the other feelings and her natural instinct not to interact with them. 'I'm Eve. Pennie Holland is my sister.'

The three girls glanced at one another.

'Oh, hi,' Lauren said, with a bright, friendly smile that Eve knew was manufactured to make adults think she was a nice girl. But she kept her own smile in place, regardless.

'Have you seen Pennie today?'

All three shook their heads, but it was Lauren who answered. 'We haven't seen Pennie since school.'

Eve nodded, her stomach bunching into a tighter knot. 'Do you know where she might be?'

One of the other girls huffed out a sarcastic laugh. 'Isn't that *your* job?'

Eve wanted to slap her, but she ignored her instead. 'Are you her friend?' She directed the question to Lauren.

Lauren shrugged. 'We don't have that much in common really.' Her voice was so full of confidence and her own self-importance. She did not sound like the kind of girl who was a good friend to anyone.

'Have you seen her with anyone else recently? During the school term, I mean. Anyone unusual?'

'She's been acting weird,' the sarcastic one said, and to Lauren's credit, she rolled her eyes and sighed at her friend.

'That's just Pennie.' She huffed, silencing the other girl. Clearly, Lauren was the alpha in this little pack. But then Eve had already guessed that much.

'Weird, how?' she asked.

'Weird like, her whole life went down the toilet on the day she was born.' The third girl finally added her voice to the conversation.

Lauren rolled her eyes again. 'She doesn't play with anyone, so no, we're not friends. At break time, Pennie just walks off and sits by herself over by pitch. Sometimes, she goes all the way to the far side, as far away from anyone as she can get, like she doesn't want anyone to even try talking to her.'

'Joel Henry said he saw her talking to some weirdo over the fence there once.' The other girl again.

Lauren rolled her eyes. 'You can't believe anything Joel says, Kate. He's a twat.'

'What kind of weirdo?' Eve asked, unintentionally holding her palm up to silence Lauren, who looked massively offended by the gesture.

Kate shrugged, looking like she wished she'd kept her mouth shut. 'I don't know. Like Lauren said, no one listens to Joel. Plus, it was all the way at the end of the sports pitch, by the fence. You can barely make anyone out from that distance, so it might not have even been Pennie.'

'Eh, the only person Pennie Holland talks to is herself,' Lauren said, in the bitchiest tone she could muster. 'I mean like, constantly.' Clearly, no one silenced Lauren.

Eve ignored her and instead tried to think what else to ask them. Her breathing was heavier now, and her panic had risen up several notches.

Lauren started to turn away. She was about to lose them.

'Did you see her today?' she asked quickly, the pitch of her voice slightly higher now.

'You asked us that already,' one of them said, looking Eve over from head to toe, making her want to shrivel up and disappear.

'Is there anywhere you can think of where she might go?' Her desperation forced her to continue.

Lauren frowned. 'We're ten,' she said, like Eve might not be aware of that. 'We're allowed to walk to school and walk home now that we're in fifth class, and to this park at weekends and holidays, and then home again. School is the only place I've seen Pennie, full stop. So no, we didn't see her today.'

Eve could think of nothing else to ask them and she could feel her face reddening as the interaction dragged on.

'Anyway, I have to go. If I'm not home before three, Mum will start coming to pick me up again. She's only just started letting me leave our estate by myself. Good luck finding her.'

Eve nodded, but as the girls walked away, she felt whatever hope she'd had disappearing with them.

16

It was getting dark by the time Eve pulled into her driveway. She'd driven around the town several times and walked the entire park and surrounding area. She'd driven for so long that she had no recollection of parts of her day. That happened from time to time. Her memory was struggling with her sudden freedom during the day, and so some days, this one included, were a blur. But she knew she had gone to the park and also to that abandoned cottage again, just before coming home. She hadn't really expected Pennie to be there, but given the house's history with Raven's Rock runaways, she couldn't not check. It must have been such a pretty house at one time. A relatively small, detached cottage sitting on a garden that could easily accommodate an extension. It had once been painted white with lemon trim around the windows and it had a red front door, all in ruins now. Eve went inside the house, checked the wildly over-grown garden and even climbed a ditch this time, to get into the small field beside the house. In the far corner stood the remains of an outbuilding. Sparrow told her that there'd been horses in there once, and a stable made sense of the size and shape of what was left.

Sparrow. She hadn't really thought of him in so long and now he seemed ever-present. This was where he came each time he ran away. He told her once that he was going to stake a claim to it someday and fix it up for the two of them to live in. Just as soon as they aged out and passed whatever duration was required to claim squatter's rights to a building. Sparrow knew things like that, and while Eve never really expected it to happen, she'd listened to him anyway without dampening his enthusiasm with her doubts.

Her feet felt soggy from tramping through the overgrown grass as she'd let herself into the stable, through the gap where a door used to be. It had been a very long time since there were any horses in there and Pennie wasn't there either. She probably didn't even know the place existed.

Eve felt sick to her stomach as she climbed out of the car and went inside her own house. She desperately tried to think of an alternative to calling the Gardaí, but what if something had happened to her? *Had* she even run away, or was she taken by someone?

'Pennie?' she called out from the hall and stood listening for a second. Her heart beat loudly enough that she could actually hear it in the silence of the house. She jogged upstairs, her wet shoes leaving a trail of footprints behind her. *She won't stop if I don't*: the words replayed themselves again and again in Eve's mind. 'Pennie?' she called again from the landing, her voice cracking this time. Silence was her only response.

Eve's first attempt at being a big sister and she'd lost the child, not once, but twice. What if something terrible had happened to her? What if she'd been taken? What if this morning was the last time anyone would ever see Pennie Holland again and it was all Eve's fault for thinking she could actually be someone's guardian?

'Pennie?' she cried this time, sounding utterly desperate. She hurried into all three bedrooms and the bathroom, but all sat undisturbed. Then she pressed her ear and the palms of her hands to the locked door. She held her breath and listened, before shoving herself away. She wasn't in there. No one was in there.

Eve leaned against the wall and slid to the floor in exactly the same spot as she had earlier. Tears brimmed her eyes as she brought her phone up and began a search for her local Garda station. This was it. This was where she had to lose Pennie, in order to keep her safe. And out of the wrong hands.

Just as she was about to hit call, there was a knock on the front door. Eve jumped to her feet and ran downstairs, her heart pounding in her chest. She was practically panting by the time she got there and opened the door.

'Pennie!' She dropped her phone and it landed with a loud thud, as she dragged the girl into a tight hug. Eve felt like she might vomit with relief. But that relief soon turned to anger. Ten seconds later and the Gardaí would have been on their way. Then what? She pulled back and held Pennie by the shoulders at arm's length. 'Where the hell have you been?'

That was when she noticed that Pennie looked even worse than she had this morning, her skin almost translucent, and her eyes red-rimmed. The child looked quite unwell, but more than that. She looked to be in shock. Eve's emotions swung wildly away from anger and back to panic. 'What happened?' she panted.

Pennie didn't answer. She just stood there with her hands limp by her sides, her face completely blank.

'Pennie?' Eve shook her gently to snap her out of it, fear again rising up. Something had happened to her. Someone had hurt this already broken child and it was Eve's fault. She *should* have made sure she was safely tucked up in her bed, where she should have been, *with* Eve, all day. 'Pennie, please tell me what happened?' She straightened up and led Pennie inside the house. Before closing the door, she looked outside and scanned the road in both directions. She didn't see anyone, but that didn't mean they weren't there. Theirs was an unlit street, and the moonlight was lost behind clouds now, so all she saw were shadows. And they were everywhere. She closed and locked the door and led Pennie to the couch. She lowered her onto it and knelt on the floor in front of her.

'Pennie?' Eve forced calm into her voice and placed her hand gently on Pennie's forehead. How sick *was* she?

Pennie looked at her at last.

'Are you all right?' Eve rewound to the question she should have asked first, before launching into her panicky barrage.

Pennie nodded.

Thank God, Eve thought. *She's coherent.* 'Where have you been?'

'At the park,' she all but whispered.

Eve held back the sharp response that she wanted to give. She wasn't at the park because Eve had been there, multiple times. She wanted to raise her voice and press home the details of the day she'd just had, running all over town, through fields and into stables, trying to find Pennie. She wanted to scream about how close she'd come to calling the police! That would have been a life-changing call for both of them and Pennie seemed to have no concept of any of it! But Eve kept it all to herself and, instead, she said, 'But you weren't there,

Pennie. I checked the park. Then I checked it again, and again. If you were there, I would have seen you.'

Pennie looked to the floor again and Eve could see that she was scrabbling for excuses in a head that was already too full. It was all written in fear on her babyish face.

'Who was here with you today, when I called? And please don't say no one because I heard you speaking to them.'

'No one was here,' Pennie barely said. 'I wasn't talking to anyone.'

Eve tilted her head to look at her with an expression that said, *I know you're lying*. 'I'm not mad.' She lied now, too, in a way that she hoped was more convincing than Pennie's. 'I just want you to tell me who was here and where you went today?'

Pennie's eyes filled with tears and her gaze at the floor intensified. Her lower lip jutted out and trembled.

Eve sat up beside her on the couch and pulled her into a hug. Pennie didn't reciprocate as usual, but the feel of her small trembling body made Eve's anger evaporate. Hugging wasn't something that Eve had experience with either, but she desperately wanted to change that. Pennie stiffened in the embrace, but that was okay. She wasn't used to it either. But while her tears soaked into Eve's jumper, dampening her skin beneath, it was the closest Eve had ever felt to anyone. That was when her anger actually dissipated for real. Her sister had been through so much lately and things weren't easy for her. No more than they were for Eve. Lord knows, Eve had tried to vanish from this house many times when she was Pennie's age, always without success. She'd always been too scared of getting caught and feared having nowhere else to go. But Pennie seemed to be playing to a different set of rules now. Imaginary or not, she had someone whispering in her ear, and Eve couldn't begin to imagine how it all might end.

'Tell me, Pennie. I promise I won't be cross.'

'I didn't go anywhere,' she said in a voice that seemed to be shrinking by the day. Just like her body. Eve could feel her shoulder blades protruding through her thin jumper.

'Were you alone?'

Pennie shrugged.

'I was scared today,' Eve said softly. 'I was so worried that something might have happened to you. Like maybe you'd gotten lost or hurt. You're only ten years old, Pennie.' She used her thumb to gently wipe tears from the child's cheeks. 'It isn't safe for you to spend the day alone out there, without anyone knowing where you are.'

'Angel was with me,' she said softly.

Eve stiffened. She had asked Pennie once if Angel was real and the girl became hysterical. She'd cried that Angel *was* real and was *always* minding her. But then she'd said that Angel was right there with them, and Eve felt herself relax slightly. He *was* imaginary. But still, she was tiring of him. 'Did Angel tell you not to let me know where you were going?' she said after a moment.

Pennie shrugged.

'Was Angel with you all day?'

'Not *all* day.'

'When was he not with you?'

'Angel had to go mind someone else for a little while.'

Eve frowned. It was when Pennie said things like that that Eve's skin tingled and crawled in a way she couldn't explain.

'I see. Who else did Angel have to mind?'

Pennie shrugged.

Eve paused again. She had so many questions. She wanted to know *exactly* where Pennie had spent her day and what she'd been doing. She wanted to know if Angel was an actual voice in her head, or if he was just a child's manifestation of their need to feel safe. She wanted to know so much, but she had to choose her questions carefully because she wouldn't get to ask too many more before Pennie shut down. She always did, sooner or later.

'Angel said that I can be a watcher, too,' she said, before Eve had a chance to put her concerns into any more words.

'Did he? And how do you become a watcher?'

'Angel will teach me.' A small smile appeared on her lips and her glassy eyes looked suddenly hopeful. 'All I have to do is be brave.'

'That's great,' Eve said, with zero conviction. 'When you're a little bit older, it will be nice to be able to take care of someone who needs it.' She turned it into something far more banal than it sounded coming from Pennie. 'But you know, you need to focus on being a child for now, Pennie. And *I'm* the one who can help you with that.'

'I'm not...' she started, defiantly now.

'Sorry, I know you're not a child.' Eve closed her eyes, wishing she'd chosen less inflammatory words. 'And I'm not saying you can't be a... a watcher. I mean...' Eve was stammering again, all traces of confidence gone.

Pennie looked to the floor, her expression neutral again. Her hopefulness and her defiance lost, along with Eve's will to continue this conversation.

'You need to rest and let me help you to feel better,' she said, standing up and pulling Pennie to her feet. 'But you always need to let me know where you are.' She tilted Pennie's chin so that they were looking at each other again. '*I'm your watcher, too. I need to know you're safe. Okay?'*

Pennie nodded finally. 'Can I go to bed now?'

Eve nodded, not sure what else she could say, except, 'I'll make you some soup and bring it up when it's ready.'

She desperately wanted Pennie to like her. To *love* her even, and to know that she, too, was loved. But it seemed nothing was further from Pennie's mind. She didn't trust Eve enough to tell her where she'd been and why she looked like she'd seen a ghost. She didn't trust her enough to tell her why her hands were trembling so violently either. Eve had seen the same haunted look on the faces of a dozen kids before. That look that told the world that something terrible had happened to them. Ellen had a *don't mention it* policy, so Eve had no idea how to ask in such a way that might make Pennie respond. But as she watched her walk away and climb the stairs like a sad, elderly woman, Eve was sure that today wasn't just a ditch day. Every instinct she had screamed that today, something terrible had happened. And for now, only Pennie knew what that was.

17

Gardaí have cordoned off a café in Carriglen Village this morning, following the discovery of a man's body late last night. The identity of the man has not yet been released, but the discovery was made at around 11 p.m. yesterday at a well-known establishment called Carver's Kitchen in the heart of Carriglen. It's believed that the proprietors of a neighbouring business raised concerns about the welfare of the man after he failed to open up for the past three days, which they say is out of character. Gardaí have said that they'll await the results of a post-mortem before determining the course of their investigation. They have not yet said whether foul play is suspected, but we'll bring you more on this story as it emerges.

Pennie retched into her cereal bowl, Cheerios pouring from her mouth.

Eve dropped her spoon and hurried around to the other side of the table. 'You're okay!' she consoled, not really having any idea if that was true. In fact, she was pretty sure that Pennie was anything but okay. Meanwhile, her own thoughts were whirling having listened to the morning news report. The TV was off, but the radio was on, and Pennie started throwing up not long after the newsreader started speaking. Eve tried to remember if she'd passed Carver's Kitchen yesterday and surmised that she must have. She didn't *remember* it, but she'd been through the town so thoroughly that it would have been strange if she'd missed it.

'Pennie, were you there?' Eve asked, the words clawing their way out.

Pennie heaved and silently retched again. She looked deathly sick.

'At Carver's Kitchen. Were you there that day when I found you at the bus stop?' Eve pleaded with her.

'H... he had secrets, too,' she cried, milk running off her lip and down along her chin, chased by tears.

There was a long pause as Eve's own breakfast starting to look for a way out. 'What?' she said after a while. The word sounded so precise. Like hours of thought had gone into its pronunciation.

'It was the secret.' Pennie drove the palms of her hands into her eye sockets.

'What secret?' She took a hold of Pennie's shoulders. 'What are you talking about, Pennie?' She shook her, not as gently as she should have. Should she have been shaking her at all? Of course not. But she couldn't stop herself. She wanted to drag the answers from her. 'You're the only one keeping secrets, Pennie!' she half-shouted, her words filled with fear and frustration. 'You have to tell me!'

Pennie shook her head and cried a silent, heaving cry.

'Tell me, Pennie!' Eve demanded, nauseous to the point of throwing up now, too. But Pennie didn't answer. With her mouth open, her sobbing was completely silent, and her head just kept slowly shaking from side to side. She got up and stumbled for the stairs.

As soon as she was gone, Eve ran to the sink and brought up what little breakfast she'd had time to eat. When she finished, she swung her arm out, swiping the radio off the top of the microwave and onto the floor. It crackled for a bit, but it didn't break. Nor did it switch off. She bent to pick it up and stabbed roughly at the off button, before placing it back where it was. Where it had always been.

The morning dragged slowly on, while Eve did her best to nurse Pennie. She desperately tried to recall her drive around from yesterday. She would have at least glanced in the direction of Carver's Kitchen and certainly at the bus shelter opposite, where she'd found Pennie the last time. But she couldn't recall either, which made no sense. Distracted, she tucked Pennie into bed and placed a damp cloth on her head. Then, with more focus, she gave her some medicine from Ellen's ample supply. She sat on her bed, soothing the girl into a fitful sleep and, by lunchtime, Eve was back at the kitchen table, the remains of their breakfasts exactly where they'd both left them, including Pennie's upchucked Cheerios.

Eve knew with certainty that any outsider would scream that Pennie needed a doctor. But they were the kind of people who never had to worry about their family being torn apart. She wouldn't be calling a doctor. But Eve knew exactly what Pennie needed in order to get well. Love. That was all. And Eve had love in abundance for her sister. But if Pennie wasn't going to tell her what she knew, then Eve would need to learn what she could from the Internet. She'd been putting it off, not sure she really wanted to know, but she had to. What was Pennie keeping from her? What did she know?

She opened Facebook and didn't have to look any harder than that. The image of Garda tape surrounding the grubby greasy-spoon café was the first to greet her when she opened up the app.

Dead man named locally as thirty-five-year-old Henry Carver. Mr Carver opened his café in Carriglen nine years ago and is a well-known businessman in this part of Cork. When he failed to open up over a three-day period, neighbouring businesses became concerned. Sheila Hogan, owner of Perfect Pastries in Carriglen, said that Mr Carver frequented her shop daily and had ordered a specific pastry for the day before yesterday. He did this often and never failed to show up. His café was closed, which, according to Ms Hogan, was highly unusual and he wasn't answering calls. Ms Hogan became concerned for his welfare and called the Gardaí to carry out a welfare check. They arrived several hours later, at close to 11 p.m., and that was when the discovery was made. Ms Hogan said that Mr Carver is well known in the area, although he was a very quiet man and kept to himself for the most part. But he had a sweet tooth, Ms Hogan smiled as she recalled this. According to Ms Hogan, Mr Carver lived alone above his café. He didn't have family and didn't entertain or invite any friends around. 'He was a loner, but we all liked him well enough,' she said. Gardaí are refusing to speculate on the cause of the man's death and have yet to say whether foul play is suspected. But the post-mortem is due to be carried out later today.

Beside the article was a candid picture of an unsmiling man. It looked like he was caught unawares by the photographer. Like perhaps they called out his name, and when he turned, they snapped that awful picture. It certainly wasn't a flattering image, and it made Eve wonder if that was the best they could do for a dead man. But if he was a loner, like the woman said, then maybe there weren't any other photos that they could have used. Henry Carver also looked like he ate nothing but deep-fried food. And pastries, clearly. A heart attack seemed like the most obvious cause of death. Or at least, it would have if Eve hadn't seen Pennie sitting there, staring at his café the week before. And if she hadn't said what she'd said about him. *He had secrets, too.*

A chill ran right through Eve. What was she going to do about this? Pennie wasn't telling her anything and it seemed Angel was calling all the shots. Angel. Eve was sure that everyone had voices in their head. She certainly did at times, but she needed to find out how the voice in her sister's head had become so dark. And so specific in the things they shared with her. Was it that Pennie was more damaged than Eve could ever have imagined? Either way, all these people were being put right in their path now. Dead people. But why? What did their deaths have to do with the Holland girls?

18

Eve spent that entire day sitting cross-legged on the floor outside Pennie's room. For hours, she stared at her closed bedroom door, hoping for answers, which of course never came. Questioning Pennie over and over again wasn't getting her anywhere either and by the time evening came around, Eve had come to the only conclusion she could think of. She needed to back off. If she wanted answers, she'd have to get them for herself and that meant standing back and watching Pennie like a hawk. Or at least, standing as far back as she could, while they lived together under the same roof, and while Pennie was so unwell. She was so weak now, refusing to eat for the most part, and unable to keep down anything when she did eat. Something was happening under Eve's roof, and it scared her. She needed to know what it was and that meant she'd have to curtail her days away from the house, too. That wouldn't help Eve much, but she'd have to deal with it. Pennie was more important now. But she couldn't let Pennie know that she'd be staying close. That was it! That's what she was going to do about all this. She'd let Pennie go on believing that she was alone in the house. That way, Eve would see exactly what she was getting up to.

Darkness fell so gradually that Eve found herself still sitting there in the pitch-black. Her stiff legs complained when she pulled herself into standing and turned on the landing light, before quietly opening Pennie's door to check on her. She hadn't made a sound all afternoon. Now she was either asleep or pretending to be, curled up on the makeshift bed with her back to the door.

Only when she was feeling very unwell could Eve get her to sleep in her actual bed and tonight was not one of those nights. But she was perfectly still, aside from the gentle rise and fall of her shoulders. Eve gently closed the door and went downstairs, pins and needles still prickling her lower limbs. She took her jacket from the hook on the wall, put it on and went outside, closing and locking the door behind her. She stood on the porch for a moment, letting her eyes adjust to the darkness.

Eve knew about night vision. She knew that the longer you stayed in the dark, the more you could see through it. Eve's night vision was better than most, and the moon was high tonight, so she didn't have to wait long to adjust to it. She turned and walked slowly around the deck, which wrapped around the entire house. There were no hiding places there and when she returned to the front of the house, she walked slowly down the steps. On the grass, she got down on all fours, turned on her phone's torch and shone it under the deck. Then she crawled all the way around the house again. There were no signs that anyone had been under there. No prints in the dirt. No disturbances of any kind. She turned off the torch and stood up again. When she slowly circled the house for a third time, her eyes were trained on the trees which surrounded it on three sides. When nothing obvious caught her eye, she walked into the treeline.

Ellen had shown her this methodical search method when she was very young. Lots of their foster kids tried to run away. Several more tried to sneak people into the house. People who brought them whatever contraband they wanted during a time when they didn't have the freedom to leave the house and get it for themselves. Sometimes, they left those deliveries out here for the kid to find when they could. Groundings were common in their house during Ellen and Peter's reign, among other punishing reprimands.

Eve scanned the earthy floor looking for any sign that someone had been there. She'd stopped going into those trees years ago and she didn't like being back among them now, for a second time in as many days. This was where she used to come when she was in the midst of one crisis or another and just being here now brought such a feeling of foreboding.

It wasn't until she came to the edge of the trees on the opposite side of the house that she saw it. An angel figure made of reeds, identical to the one Pennie carried everywhere with her. Was this her one, or another one just like it? Eve's breathing quickened and she looked frantically around. The angel had been placed on the grass, beside the treeline. Not *inside* it, and Eve felt sure she would have seen it if it had been there that day. It was directly opposite where she parked her car. She would have been facing it when she stepped out of her driver's side door so, yes, she would definitely have seen it. Fear gripped her. That same fear she'd so often felt when hiding among those trees. Fear that someone was coming to get her. That they were already here, watching her. Toying with her. Waiting for their moment to pounce.

She turned and ran, back towards the house. She took the porch steps two at a time and had her key in her hand by the time she reached the front door. But her hand was shaking too much for the key to find its way into the lock. 'Come on!' she said, her voice quivering. She looked around again, then gripped her wrist with her other hand, steadying it enough that she could finally get the key in the door and unlock it. She stumbled inside, slammed the door shut behind her and locked it. She stood with her back to the door, panting, her mind racing through too many possibilities, none of which made any sense.

She frowned and hurried towards the stairs. Her legs felt weak as she made her way up as quickly as she could and opened Pennie's door, not worried about waking her this time. If indeed she *was* awake, then she pretended to the contrary. Eve walked over to the makeshift bed, got on her knees and leaned over her. In Pennie's hand, clutched tightly to her chest, was her angel.

So, it wasn't Pennie who'd left her creepy doll in the garden. But where the hell had it come from?

Eve spent the rest of that night sitting in that same spot, on the floor outside Pennie's room, with her back resting against the wall. Adrenaline pulsed through her, not letting her eyelids droop for a minute. All her senses were on high alert. Several times, she heard Pennie getting up and moving around the room. She could sense her standing just inside the door, which was slightly ajar so the light from the landing could make its way in. But it seemed she could sense that Eve was there, too, because she didn't come out of her room and Eve said nothing. When she wasn't holding her breath and listening to Pennie's movements, she was looking at the locked door straight ahead of her. Her breathing came no easier thinking about that room, which held some very mixed memories for Eve. Some of the worst times of her life were spent in, or near, that room. But it was also where she fell in love, for the first and only time. She had no idea whether or not it was the kind of love that people craved on television. Or whether or not that love went both ways. But she told herself every day that it did.

It wasn't that Ellen and Peter were cruel people. Peter was as soft as they came, especially with Eve. He just had a few quirks that other people wouldn't understand. But he was the one who'd always wanted a daughter, and he'd talked Ellen into keeping Eve and Amelia and probably Pennie, too. Ellen was a much more complicated woman, who never would have made Eve a permanent member of the family of her own volition. She'd been raised in the system herself and spoke often about how hard she'd had it compared to kids nowadays. There were no families like theirs who were willing to take a child in when *she* was young, and she made sure the kids who stayed with them knew that. She told them again, whenever they went to her with the kind of stories they thought she might be interested in hearing. Stories about that room.

But Ellen Holland had an incredible gift. She only ever had to hear things that she liked to hear. Like when Peter told her how much more money the Internet could bring them, she heard that. And when he explained that there was one less room for Ellen to have to clean, so long as the door stayed locked. She heard that, too. More money, less cleaning. She liked hearing things like that so much that she'd respond with an approving nod. Just one, mind you. She was stoic, even when happy. If she *didn't* want to hear something, then she'd just keep talking. Sometimes, she'd even smile and nod, like the person wasn't screaming at her, begging to be heard.

Eve spent plenty of time in that locked room, too, but she was more privileged than any of them. *She* was Peter's favourite. Most of those kids could only ever dream about the stability that she enjoyed, knowing that she wouldn't be sleeping under a bridge on the whim of an angry foster carer, because Peter would never allow it. And so, Eve knew how lucky she was. She also knew that she had more to lose than any of the others, so she took the time to understand Ellen better than any of them did. And to set Peter apart from his bad habits. Unlike any of their other kids, Eve always knew how to just get on with things.

But she had a lot more quiet time these days. Now when she looked at that door, she tried to picture Sparrow's face and not the stained carpet and those little splashes on the wall that other people might not notice at first glance. She conjured up the memory of him taking the blame for something Eve had done, knowing full well what the consequences would be. Then after, him, sitting on the floor in that room, with his back against the wall and his ankle cuffed to the radiator. Sparrow wasn't particularly handsome or anything. He had a scar on his bottom lip from where a grown man had hit him with a leather belt, and his freckles were outlandishly orange. Clusters of them had joined together in places, though he didn't seem to care much about how they looked. They made his brown eyes stand out like dark, bottomless pools, filled with useless fury. But when those eyes were looking at her, she saw nothing but kindness in them. He always tried to protect her. He had a nice smile, too, which really, he only ever showed to Eve. She'd had to wait three days before she was alone in the house that time, and able to go in there by herself. Three days before she could bring him some food and something to drink. The smell had erased itself from her memory, but it probably still lingered in that room, which creaked and groaned now of its own accord. All the house noises converged like ghosts on that one, haunted space. But as she continued to stare at the door, all she saw was his open face and those brown eyes that seemed to adore her. She'd lost her virginity to him while he was tied to that radiator. She remembered straddling him, like she'd seen women doing on TV. She didn't particularly like that ugly little thing that boys kept between their legs, and she had no idea what to do with it on that occasion. But Sparrow did. Sparrow always knew what to do.

That was the first of many times he took the blame for Eve, and living right alongside the guilt she felt for that was the knowledge that at least someone, at some time, had loved her.

19

The following morning, Eve made a breakfast of cereal and toast for Pennie. She put it on a tray, along with some orange juice, and brought it with her to Pennie's room. She was awake, but she lay there like a discarded rag doll, hardly able to sit up. She was becoming weaker by the day and Eve knew that, really, she should be considering a doctor by now. But her fear of losing Pennie was too great. Doctors tore families apart. Hadn't Ellen warned her of that often enough? Doctors were the reason why so many kids were shoved into the system, and why they ended up at places like Raven's Rock to begin with. Course, Eve never questioned how it was that Ellen always had just the medicine she needed, when she needed it. Why would she, when Ellen knew a way to get just about anything? All she knew for sure was that doctors assumed kids were being hurt by the people in charge of them. It didn't matter what evidence there might be to the contrary. That's what Ellen always said, whenever one of them was hurt. Eve just knew that they'd take one look at Pennie and decide that Eve wasn't fit to take care of her. When, in fact, taking care of Pennie was the *only* thing Eve really wanted to do now. She wanted to nurse her until she felt better. She wanted to give her the tender, loving care that both of them had missed out on during their lives. She wanted Pennie to feel the kind of love that Rory Gilmore felt from Lorelai every single day. But Pennie wasn't letting her do that. She wouldn't eat the food Eve made for her and she didn't want her hugs and reassurance. It seemed the only *person* who could comfort Pennie now was a figment of her imagination. Eve was beginning to feel like she was running out of time. What if today was the day when the decision about a doctor was taken out of her hands? What if Pennie got so sick that she couldn't breathe? The thought made Eve feel nauseous. She couldn't lose Pennie. Not to a doctor and not to an imaginary friend. Not when she hadn't yet had the chance to show her how much she loved her.

Eve sat with Pennie for as long as she could without feeling totally unwelcome. At which point, she told her that lunch was in the fridge and that Eve would be back at around dinner time, like she always did. She wondered if the words sounded as natural as when they were true. She avoided Pennie's eyes, just in case, and she left the house, fighting the urge to run. She locked the door, got in her car and drove for about half a mile in the direction of town, before pulling into a lay-by, locking it up and walking quickly back towards home. She approached the house from behind, through the trees, and that was where she stayed. She realised that she'd found the perfect vantage point for anyone who might want to *watch* their house or any of its residents. From where she was, Eve could see the approach to the house and Pennie's bedroom window, which was at the back of the house. She was fairly sure that, unless someone was really looking, they wouldn't see her standing there beneath the evergreen canopy. They wouldn't see *anyone* standing there. The thought gave her a shiver down her spine.

She stood for a while, scanning the entire area, searching for anyone else who might have been there. When she was sure she was alone, she sat on a tree stump and rested her chin in her hand. She took her phone from her pocket with the other hand and started to scroll, her eyes glancing from her screen to the house and back again. It didn't take long for the Henry Carver story to grab her attention. It was all over her newsfeed as if it were purposely trying to push Leslie Granger to the back of people's minds. One particularly brash headline screamed:

Overdose Killed Carver.

Thirty-five-year-old Henry Carver is thought to have died of a drugs overdose. It is unknown at this time if he intentionally ingested the drug, but residents of Carriglen Village who either worked near Mr Carver or frequented his café have described him as a quiet man who liked to keep to himself. One woman describe him as 'a depressive sort' who angered easily. The same woman said they'd had to leave the premises once after her husband returned a dish to the kitchen because it was, in his opinion, reheated, and not freshly cooked. She described Mr Carver's reaction as 'overly sensitive'. Others who claimed to know him have said that his occasional bad moods were directed mostly at himself and that he was generally a 'nice man'.

We know that some prescription medications were found on the property; however, it is unknown which particular drug was found to be in his system at the time of his death.

Was Henry Carver a depressed man seeking the ultimate escape, or the victim of an accidental overdose? Follow us to find out more.

The same awful photo of Henry Carver was pasted halfway down the article. At the bottom was a smaller image of a woman with the worst hair Eve had ever seen. It looked exactly like a bird's nest had been taken from a tree, and placed without care on top of her head. Eve would easily believe that the woman had been given less than fresh food at Carver's Kitchen. But she couldn't see how using her complaint here was responsible journalism. Or telling the world about the man's depression. This article represented more victim shaming to Eve, but she didn't feel strongly enough to comment on it. In fact, she was slightly relieved. They appeared to think his death was accidental. That perhaps he'd sent himself on a one-way trip to the moon. Still, she found herself scanning through the comments. There were a few who called out the shameful way the so-called journalist had covered Carver's death, while others piled on the character assassination. They all pretended to be respectful of the fact that he was dead, when they called him things like *strange* and *sad* and *lonely*, but the undertone of their disgust was quite clear.

She was just about to click into the next Henry Carver story when her phone rang and Nicole Hammond's picture, the one from her LinkedIn profile, filled her screen. Eve sprang to her feet, holding the phone away from her. She looked around, as if Nicole could see her, sitting there in the trees, spying on her own house. Logic finally returned on the sixth ring, and she answered the call.

'Hello?'

'Hi, Eve?'

'How did you get my number?'

'Oh, I think you might have called me a few nights ago, but you got cut off.'

Eve closed her eyes and brought her hand to her face. She'd been staring obsessively at Nicole's business card, trying to come up with reasons to call her. She'd put her number in her contacts and attached a screenshot of her profile picture. Then she did press call, but she hung up as soon as it started to ring.

'Oh, yeah. Actually, I was putting your number in my contacts because your card got ripped.' Why was she lying? 'I must have hit call by accident.' She closed her eyes and covered her face with her hand.

'I'm glad you did. To be honest, I was only guessing it might have been you. I could just as easily be phoning a call centre in India right now. I get a lot of calls from them, too. They're very concerned about various issues with my computer.'

She could hear the smile in Nicole's voice but had no idea what she was talking about. 'Well, it's me all right.'

'Well, good then.'

'Why did you call?' She squeezed her eyes shut again. Eve sounded like she didn't want Nicole to call, when actually she'd been thinking about her constantly. Even when she was searching for Pennie, she thought about what it would be like to have someone like Nicole there to help her. To share some of the responsibility... and maybe even the love.

'Have you seen the latest headline. The Henry Carver story?'

Eve blinked, bringing herself back to the conversation of now. 'I was just reading it,' she said, sitting down on the stump again.

'Jeez, Cork is really making headlines these days, aren't we?'

Why was she making small talk? What did she really want?

'Seems like his Special K was a bit too special,' Eve said and immediately wondered why she'd said it. She knew the street name for just about every drug on the market. Or at least, she had. It had been a few years since they'd had a drug user at Raven's Rock, so there were probably new ones by now. Either way, it was yet another stupid thing to say.

'You know your Special K?' Nicole asked, sounding impressed.

Eve shook her head. 'Not really. But my parents used to foster kids. Some of them used drugs and they liked to talk about them. A lot.'

'Wow, okay. Sounds like you grew up in an interesting house.' Nicole was smiling again. Eve could tell. Then there was an awkward silence that stretched on for seconds, which felt like minutes.

'Do you want to get some coffee?' Nicole said at last.

Eve stood up again, her stomach contracting. 'What, now?'

'Sure. If you're not busy.'

She looked around the messy but deserted garden. All was quiet. She looked behind her and beyond the woods. She could see right to the other side of the wide, open space, and the backs of some houses way off in the distance. She was alone. No one was here.

'If you *are* busy, then—'

'I'm not,' Eve cut her off. She wanted to know Pennie's every move. She also wanted to be perched on the edge of her bed, with a cool, damp cloth and a bowl of chicken soup, which she lacked the skill to make. But her own weaknesses were far more powerful than the best of her intentions.

Was Nicole Hammond another of her weaknesses now? Sparrow was the only other person who'd looked at her like she might have something interesting to say. But Sparrow wasn't really... well, he wasn't Nicole Hammond, and she'd looked at Eve with interest, too. She'd *called* her! She *wanted* to see her again.

'I'm not busy,' Eve said again. 'Where are you?'

'Right where you left me.'

Eve found herself smiling. Nicole was being familiar, and she liked it. 'Costa?' she asked, walking to where she could see the front of the house. The door was closed. Pennie wasn't going anywhere for now. 'I'm on my way.'

20

Nicole was sitting at the same table as before, with her laptop open in front of her. Eve ordered the same coffee, from the same woman, with a keen sense of déjà vu. The difference this time was that Nicole wasn't staring blankly out the window, and Eve wasn't skulking onto the premises unnoticed. Nicole was watching out for her, and she smiled at Eve as she came through the door. She was already packing away her stuff, making space on the table for Eve and her giant coffee cup.

'I'm glad you came,' she said, as Eve wrestled with the mug and saucer and sat down opposite her. 'I wasn't sure if you would.'

'Well... here I am,' Eve replied, with no idea how else to respond. She had butterflies in her stomach, and it took a lot for her to look the woman in the eye. She couldn't let Nicole know how much she liked her. Not until Eve knew exactly what she wanted from her.

As much as Eve would like to think that she was interesting and beautiful, and attractive to other people, she just wasn't, and she knew that. Convention-ally good-looking, yes. But it was like the baggage of her past had attached itself to her, and its presence glowered at people through hers. Anyone who got close, even for a short time, was afflicted with a sudden discomfort that they couldn't quiet explain. That was the effect that Eve had. She imagined, too, that she smelled of disadvantage, which in itself was enough to make most people want to move quickly on. Which was why she couldn't *but* suspect that Nicole had an ulterior motive for wanting to see her. How could she not?

'Here you are,' Nicole agreed, nodding with a small smile and her mug at her lips.

'So, why did you call?' Eve asked, taking a sip of her steaming coffee.

'I don't know. To talk about dead people?' Nicole laughed and when Eve didn't respond, she said, 'Sorry. That was in poor taste.' But she was still smiling.

The closer Eve looked, the more she realised that there appeared to be very little joy in Nicole's smile, and it made her wonder when she'd lost it. Was there one event in her life that had taken it from her? Or, like Eve, was it a combination of many?

'I used that Carver guy as an excuse to pick up the phone, if I'm honest,' Nicole continued. 'I've been trying to think of a reason to call you all week.'

Eve lowered her cup so that it wouldn't shake in her hands, but there was nothing she could do about her reddening face, except to lower that, too. 'Really?' she asked, her eyes on the table now.

'Yes, really.' Nicole angled her head, making a show of seeking out more eye contact.

Eve glanced up, despite her discomfort. Nicole Hammond was even more stunning than she remembered. That said something, because her imagination had come up with all sorts of scenarios involving this woman. She wasn't conventionally beautiful in the sense that her skin was quite leathery and some of her teeth were crooked. Plus, she was a decade or more older than Eve was. But she had a presence that filled the room and made Eve want to bask in it all day. Eve had imagined Nicole sharing her home and her life, and the care of her beloved little sister, who would grow to love them both. But despite her smile, Nicole looked tired today. Exhausted, even, and Eve wondered what was keeping her awake at night, sure that something was. She had that look about her. Like maybe she was haunted, too.

'So... have you seen your friend again?' Nicole asked, interrupting Eve's rambling train of thought.

'Hmm?'

'Your friend... the one who keeps talking about, you know...' she gestured with her hands, 'dead people.'

'Oh... they're not my friend. They were just someone I met through work and, no, I haven't seen them again.'

'Where do you work?'

Eve's face warmed again and she was sure a red flush was making its way rapidly up her neck. 'I *did* work in social services,' she lied. 'I still pop into the office from time to time to see some old colleagues, but now I just look after my little sister.' Those words buoyed her up like they always did. She loved how that sounded. *My little sister.*

Nicole smiled. 'And, it's just the two of you?'

She shrugged and nodded, but she didn't want to talk about this. 'What about you?' she asked, before Nicole had a chance to continue.

Nicole inhaled deeply and raised her eyebrows. 'Wow, my turn already.' She smiled. 'Okay, well...' she held her hands out, palms up, 'it's just me. Only child. My parents emigrated a few years ago, and I suppose my work kind of took me all over the place. It didn't really leave me with much time to settle down, so...' She laughed quietly then and added, 'Actually, that's bullshit. I just like being single.'

Eve didn't know what to say, but her honesty was like fresh air, dancing across her boiling-hot skin.

'Now I'm living here in Cork and just,' she shrugged, 'doing what I do.'

Eve nodded and picked up her cup. She'd been looking Nicole up incessantly online and she hadn't seen *that* much in the line of globe-trotting work adventures. Certainly, nothing that warranted a lonely life. But that seemed to be what Nicole wanted, so what did she know? Eve sipped slowly to kill some time while she tried and failed to come up with a good response. So she just continued to nod and smile like the idiot she was.

But if Nicole noticed her discomfort, she didn't say. Instead, she talked about herself in such an unselfconscious way that Eve couldn't help but envy her. What she wouldn't give for just a fraction of that self-belief. Would her life have been all that different, she wondered? She stared in awe at the woman while she spoke about the type of stories she liked to cover – the gritty kind, showing the darker elements of life, was how she described them. She talked about how her family had moved around a lot when she was a kid and how she'd never really put down roots.

Eve sensed the conversation was making its way back around to her and she felt uncomfortably hot again. This was why she was so terrible with people. Inevitably, it always came around to Eve's family life, which she never spoke about. Not to anyone. So how could she possibly know how to respond to conversations like this when she'd avoided them all her life? When she did have to endure them, they always came to a painfully awkward end, whereby the other person would make their excuses and leave. Even now, while Nicole was still speaking, Eve's mind was scrabbling for something to say when she finished.

When she did finish, the only thing Eve could think of was, 'So do you think that Henry Carver fella just accidentally overdosed?'

It was entirely the wrong response to *I never got along with my father*, and the way Nicole looked at her said that she agreed wholeheartedly. It wasn't that Eve hadn't been listening. But she honestly couldn't come up with anything better. Plus, she didn't think it was any of her business to ask why she felt the way she did towards her parents. That was family business, and Eve knew all too well how complicated a thing that could be. But now there was another awkward silence and Eve wished she could disappear. She always ended up feeling like this when she was alone with one other person for too long. Even when it was with someone that she liked.

Nicole cleared her throat and put her cup down. 'Well... unbelievably, they say he had elevated levels of insulin in his blood, so I suppose.' She shrugged, as if she was thrown by the change of topic and didn't quite know what else she could say.

'Sorry. I don't know why I changed the subject like that,' Eve said with a shake of her head, feeling like she needed to give some sort of explanation. Otherwise, Nicole might suddenly realise how weird she was and bolt, never to be seen again.

But she smiled kindly. 'That's all right. Not everyone likes talking about their family. I get that.'

Eve shrugged. There'd been a knot of tension in her gut since she'd seen Nicole's number lighting up her screen, and it had been growing in size and weight ever since. Her kind understanding should have helped, but it didn't. Eve still felt that Nicole's interest in her couldn't be real, no matter how much she wanted it to be.

'Have you ever eaten in that place?' Nicole asked, crinkling her nose and looking a bit goofy suddenly.

Eve frowned. 'What place?'

'Carver's Kitchen?'

'Oh, no.' She shook her head, her stomach clenching again. 'The smell in the air outside it was enough for me.'

Nicole laughed and nodded, taking a drink of her tea. 'Jack used to love that place.'

There was a pause for a moment before Eve thought to respond. 'Jack?' she asked, at last.

Nicole nodded with a sad smile.

'You mean, Jack Logan?'

'Yeah. He had a stomach of cast iron, that boy. He went there all the time. I think the owner pitied him or something, but whenever Jack turned up there, he got fed.'

'Why would he do that?' Eve frowned. 'I mean, from what I've read about the man, he didn't seem the charitable type.'

Nicole's bottom lip jutted out and she shrugged. 'I think maybe he wasn't as gruff as people made him out to be. Or at least, not to Jack, he wasn't.'

'You knew him?'

'Carver?' She shook her head. 'Not very well. Only from listening to Jack talking about him from time to time.'

'But you knew Jack?' Eve's hand tightened around her cooling cup, the tension becoming more visible in her shoulders.

Nicole put her cup down, still smiling a nostalgic smile now. 'Sorry. Didn't I mention that? It's why I'm trying to keep his case in the public eye.'

'Oh. So, how did you two know each other?'

She shrugged. 'We met a few years ago. He was clean then. He'd been in recovery for a while and was just such a nice guy. Really funny.'

'Oh.' Eve lowered her eyes to the table again, unsure what else to say.

'I just find it so hard to believe that he'd...' She raised her eyebrows and blew out hard.

'That he'd relapse?' Eve offered.

Nicole shook her head. 'I know that seems naïve. He was an addict. Addicts relapse more often than they don't. And he'd been clean and relapsed countless times from what he told me. It's just that, he was doing really well and...'

'There was no needle found with him. None of the, eh...' Eve waved her hand around stupidly, 'drug stuff that you'd expect to find near someone who OD'd,' she offered, surprising herself with the ability to offer *anything*.

Nicole's eyes widened and she nodded more vehemently. 'Right?'

Eve nodded in agreement, desperately wanting to keep up this new momentum. To seem interesting again, rather than just plain weird. And then the perfect thing occurred to her. 'Wait, did you say that a high level of insulin was found in Henry Carver's system?'

Nicole grinned, her gaze intensifying. 'You picked up on that, eh? Well, according to my source at the coroner's office, yes.'

'I didn't read that anywhere.'

Nicole put down her cup and leaned enthusiastically across the table. 'That's because they're not releasing that detail to the public.'

Eve narrowed her eyes, thinking.

'Can you think of a reason why that might be?' Nicole half-whispered, sounding like a teacher presenting Eve with a surprise pop quiz.

But the answer had already come to her. It came to her when Nicole first mentioned it, but her mind was far too distracted to process it. 'Didn't they also tell you that they found insulin in Leslie Granger's system?'

Nicole put her cup noisily back in its saucer. 'Bingo,' she said. 'Which is why they're not making the cause of death public.'

'You mean they...'

'It'll probably be announced later today that Henry Carver's death is being upgraded to a murder enquiry.' She leaned back in her chair, her smile less jovial now. 'And Gardaí think they're looking for one killer. Not two.'

Eve had stopped listening moments ago, as all her thoughts returned to Pennie. How did she know about these deaths?

'And have you spoken to the guards, or are you just writing about it?' Eve asked at last, her voice sounding more urgent suddenly.

'You mean about Jack? Yeah, I went to the guards about him.' Nicole was becoming upset. 'I know now that whoever killed Henry Carver and Leslie Granger killed Jack as well.' She slapped her palm on the table, but gently enough not to attract attention. 'I know it. Jack did not die from a heroin overdose, because he was clean. And like you said, there was nothing drug-related *anywhere* and the post-mortem only showed *traces* of heroin in his system.' She stabbed the table this time, with her finger. 'It takes more than a trace of heroin to kill a user. But he's dead and buried now and they never tested him for insulin.'

'Why not?' Eve asked. 'Don't they test for drugs when they do a post-mortem? What's it called? A tox screen?' That was a phrase she'd heard many times on TV.

'They do. But it doesn't include insulin. Everyone has insulin in their blood, I guess just at different levels depending on whether or not someone is diabetic. So it's not something they routinely go looking for. They only checked for it at all, because Leslie's death was otherwise unexplained. She had no health problems, no other medication in her system... but my source says they found a puncture mark on her thigh. That's what made them look deeper.'

'And she was all over the news,' Eve added, knowing that public interest had a lot to do with how much attention someone received, whether they were dead or alive.

'Exactly,' Nicole agreed. 'And you know what, I'd bet if they dug up Brian Merriman, they'd find the same deal with him. Clever really if you think about it.'

Eve frowned. 'What's he got to do with the others?'

Nicole threw her hands out wide. 'What have any of them got to do with each other?'

There was a long pause while Eve tried to come up with something else to say. Nicole was so passionate about this, but all Eve could think about was Pennie. She'd never mentioned Brian Merriman. Or a cyclist or anything that suggested she knew about him. So maybe Nicole was wrong. Or maybe...

'They're just not interested.' Nicole's voice broke through her thoughts once more. 'That's why *I* write about it.'

Eve nodded again. 'Did he have many friends?' she asked. 'Jack, I mean.'

Nicole bobbed her head from side to side. 'Not in the true sense of the word, I don't think. Other addicts mostly, but he did have a way about him when he was sober. Like I said, he was funny, and he had a certain charm.' She smiled again and Eve wondered if Nicole might have loved him in some way. 'So I suppose he could draw people in, for a time at least,' Nicole continued. 'But eventually, he'd slip up and those people would vanish. And who could blame them, I suppose. It's not easy to be friends with an addict, trust me.'

And Eve did. Looking at her now with her strong, tattooed arms bared to the world in another sleeveless tee, her cropped hair and her thick skin, Eve wondered if some part of her own life might have been spent on the other side of the tracks. Eve's side. But where Eve wore her past like a bad smell, Nicole wore hers like a badge of honour.

'But you were,' Eve said. 'His friend, I mean.'

She bobbed her head again and puckered her mouth. 'We weren't friends as such. Like I said, I just knew him. And I liked him. He was dealt a shitty hand in life, and if someone did something to him, then I believe he deserves some justice. Don't you?'

A few might agree with that. Many more would think that the world was better off with one less addict in it. Eve's own thoughts ventured towards the idea that Jack Logan left the world doing what he loved. Drugs. But she wouldn't say any of that. *She* wanted to be the one asking the questions, not answering them.

'And did you pick up on another common thread between all four of them?' Nicole asked in a low, urgent whisper.

Eve frowned and shook her head.

'They were all referred to as loners, weren't they? No one missed Brian Merriman or Henry Carver. Not for days! They were only reported missing because their work wasn't getting done. Likewise, none of Leslie Granger's colleagues seemed to know her socially either. They all just said things like, *she kept to herself.* No family, no close friends. And as for Jack, well... we just spoke about Jack. Now tell me that isn't an alarm bell right there.'

Eve nodded slowly, as Nicole's alarm bell clanged loudly in her head. She hadn't picked up on that, but Nicole was right. Now Eve was certain she wouldn't be able to think about anything else, ever again. The very same thing could be said about Eve and Pennie. They were the very definition of loners. She frowned again and couldn't help wondering who, if anyone, would ever miss them?

She got haltingly to her feet. 'I'll be right back.'

Eve didn't need the bathroom, but she did need a moment to shake this new, unsettling feeling. She was suddenly desperate to check in with Pennie, too. She should be there with her and not here, drinking coffee with Nicole Hammond. But if she hadn't come, then she never would have discovered the links between those people, at least three of whom were brought up in conversation by Pennie. But all four were definitely connected. That much was becoming very clear.

Eve found a cubicle and locked herself inside. She lowered the toilet seat and sat down, resting her chin on her closed fist. She brought her phone to life and opened up her recent call list. This time, the phone back at Raven's Rock was answered on the fifth ring.

'Hi, Eve.' Pennie sounded almost robotic. Like she'd been drained of life.

'Pennie, you're up. How are you feeling? Are you all right?' She forced something resembling cheer into her voice and wished again that she could have been contented to just stay there with her. To just *be* with her, in their home, like she so desperately wanted to be.

'I'm feeling better,' Pennie said. But that's what she always said.

'Is anyone there with you, Pennie?' She asked the question, even though she dreaded what she might say.

'No,' Pennie replied, like she was tired of being asked.

All Pennie's talk about secrets and Nicole's talk about loners filled Eve's mind, distracting her from her phone conversation. Eve had secrets. Plenty of them. Pennie, too, probably. She squeezed her eyes shut, desperately trying to calm her thoughts.

'Are you still there, Eve?'

She shook her head and stood up. 'Yes! I'll be home soon, okay. I left your lunch in the fridge. Try to eat something, yeah?'

'Okay.'

Pennie ended the call before Eve could say any more. She flushed the toilet, even though she hadn't used it, washed her hands and went back to their table. The barista had just replaced Eve's coffee with a fresh one and swapped out Nicole's teapot for a new, steaming-hot one.

'I got you another Americano. I hope that's all right?' She smiled as Eve sat down, with a questioning look on her face.

It wasn't all right. Not really. Eve needed to get back to Pennie. But what if Nicole had more to offer? 'Eh, sure. I suppose five more minutes won't hurt.' The tense knot moved around in her stomach at the idea of prolonging this conversation, to which she would surely be expected to add something more.

'So, what's your sister like?'

Eve picked up the cup and thought about that while she took a drink. If Nicole hadn't spoken about that common thread, then Eve would be sitting here now thinking about the fact that Nicole thought she was *so* interesting that she wanted her to stay. She tried to think about that instead, as she answered as honestly as she could. 'Beautiful,' she said softly.

Nicole smiled.

'And clever. Far more clever than I am.' She put down her cup. 'She's witty and outgoing and...' She stopped then, realising that she was describing the version of Pennie that she wanted her to be. The Rory Gilmore version. She shook her head and shrugged. 'You know... she's a little sister.'

Nicole nodded. 'And how long has it been just the two of you?'

Eve made a non-committal sound, like a mumble, directed into her coffee, followed by, 'A while.'

'Sorry,' she said. 'You really don't like talking about your family, do you?'

Eve inhaled deeply and let it out as inconspicuously as she could. She'd have to give the woman something sooner or later, so better to get it out of the way. Plus, perhaps it was time for someone to know them. Well, maybe not *know* them, but someone who could at least potentially miss them should anything happen! 'It's not that I don't like talking about them,' she started slowly. 'It's just upsetting. My parents passed away and I... well... it's just been me and Pennie ever since. She took it really hard, and I suppose I did, too.' She shrugged, her face burning from the pressure. 'It's just not easy to talk about.'

'I get it,' Nicole said softly. 'What happened to them? If you don't mind me asking.'

She did mind. But she answered anyway, beginning with another shrug and some further mumbling into her cup. 'My dad was killed in a hit-and-run six years ago. He was crossing the road from a deli to the building site where he was working. My mum, well, she was more recent. She was hobbling around on a fractured ankle. She was wearing one of those boot things that they put on at the hospital. You know the ones?' Even though she didn't *go* to the hospital. But she *did* get a boot, and Eve made the shape around her own leg, to describe it as best she could. Nicole nodded. 'She couldn't walk properly in it, and she tripped at the top of the stairs and fell. She broke her neck and died before the ambulance arrived.'

'Jesus.' Nicole sounded genuinely horrified. 'I'm so sorry. No wonder you don't like talking about it.'

Eve nodded and picked up her cup again. She didn't really want the coffee any more. It was pooling sickeningly in her stomach, but the cup was giving her something to do with her hands. And her mouth. As she took another halting sip, she told herself that that was it. It was done. Out of the way. Now they could move on.

'Did they ever catch the driver responsible for your father?'

The question threw her, and she found herself swallowing coffee down into her lungs, triggering a coughing fit that lasted an eternity. It left her red-faced and tear-streaked.

'Christ, are you okay?' Nicole was on her feet, patting her on the back, which only made the situation a million times more uncomfortable. Eve never wanted to disappear more than she did now. But she nodded anyway, gasping to catch her breath and recover as well as she could.

The barista arrived with a glass of tap water, for which Eve was more grateful than she came across. She took a series of small sips, while Nicole sat there watching her, unwittingly making Eve wish she were dead.

'Okay?' she asked, at last, when it all seemed to have passed.

Eve nodded, bringing her hands to her face to hide her mortification. But nothing could. 'Sorry,' she said, when she was able.

'For what? That happens to me all the time.' Nicole smiled kindly and, again, those eyes looked as if they'd known her all her life. Which of course, she hadn't. 'So, did they?' she asked after another quiet minute.

'Sorry?'

'The person responsible for your father's death. Did they ever find them?'

The coffee she'd drunk churned its way towards her throat and she worried she might start choking again. Nicole Hammond was a reporter. She could find out the answer to that any time she liked through public records. Knowing this, Eve nodded.

'Well...' Nicole reached out and squeezed Eve's hand gently, but only for a second. 'That's something, I suppose.'

Eve nodded and felt her shoulders sagging with relief that Nicole didn't respond with yet another question. But Eve was done. She couldn't do this any more.

But before she could make her excuses to leave, Nicole *did* come up with another question.

'So how is Pennie now? How old did you say she is, ten?'

Eve frowned. She didn't remember telling her how old Pennie was.

'She must need a lot of care, given what she's been through at such a young age?' Nicole continued, sounding genuinely concerned. But Eve couldn't come up with a response. Not until she could first answer the question of whether or not she'd told her Pennie's age. And if not, then how did she know?

'So, Jack Logan was a friend of Henry Carver?' Eve asked, frowning, her own thoughts scrambling.

'Okaay... another rapid change of subject.' Nicole raised both eyebrows and smiled a strange smile. Not the same one she'd been using up until now.

'You said he used to go there all the time. That Henry Carver took pity on him. So, it's a bit strange that they both ended up dead like that, isn't it?'

Nicole's smile faded now as she began to sense the hostility that was sliding into Eve's voice. 'Eh... well, both deaths were *unofficially* caused by an insulin overdose, when neither one was diabetic. I'm saying that even though they never tested Jack. But in my opinion, that was what connected their deaths.' Nicole frowned and looked quizzically at her. 'We just went over this. There's quite a few links if you look.' She made a face like she was about to humour someone. 'I suppose the rest *could* be coincidence. Cork is a small place after all, but...'

'An investigative journalist who believes in coincidence?' Eve said with uncharacteristic sarcasm.

Nicole was frowning deeply now and looking at Eve like she was some strange and exotic creature. Like maybe she was questioning her own wisdom in buying Eve a second coffee and prolonging their time together. 'I didn't say that.' Her own tone lost some of its lightness. 'I *said* that there are a few links that could be made, but I think I made it clear where I stand on the matter. Why are you...?'

'I never told you how old my sister is.' The conversation jumped track again.

Nicole opened her mouth but seemed lost for words suddenly. Eve didn't offer any to bail her out with. 'I'm sure that you did,' she said at last.

'When?'

'The last time we met.'

Eve's mind jumped back to their previous conversation, but she couldn't get their spoken words to stand still. *Had* she told her? She might have.

'Eve, are you all right? Did I say something to offend you?'

Eve looked at her, but didn't respond. She didn't know what to say, because she didn't know which one of them was right.

'I'm really sorry,' Nicole said again, more softly this time. 'Honestly, you did tell me that your sister was ten, but I apologise if I freaked you out in any way by mentioning it. I just...' She sat back in her chair and let her hands fall into her lap. 'I happen to have a really good memory for details, but especially when...' she puffed out her cheeks and closed her eyes, 'especially when I'm speaking to someone that I like.'

Eve felt like she'd been harpooned. Nicole Hammond was telling Eve that she *liked* her, and Eve was acting like a lunatic. But she still couldn't trust this entire situation. People like *her* did not like people like *Eve*. Was she telling her the truth about their past conversation or was she really investigating Eve for some reason? Or, worse, Pennie? Reporters had been digging around Raven's Rock for years. So was she the stranger that had been talking to Pennie at the school that day, when that horrible girl saw her by the fence? Was hers the unknown number that had been calling Eve for weeks before finally giving up?

'Are you investigating my parents?' she asked, her voice low and sounding nothing like her. It sounded like it belonged to someone angry. Someone broken.

'I'm... what?' Nicole leaned towards her, perplexed. 'Why would I...?'

Eve shoved her chair back and got to her feet. She hurried from the café and soon after she started to run. Eve wasn't a runner, but that day, she ran, and she didn't stop for nearly forty minutes. Not until she was back inside the door of Raven's Rock, where she slid to the floor, battling for breath and sheer survival. Something bad was happening here and, once again, it was triggered by this house. So why the hell did she ever think it was safe for her to leave it?

21

An hour later, Eve was still sitting on the floor in the hall with her back to the front door. It took that long for her to gather herself back up, but she couldn't shake the intense feeling that something terrible was coming for them. She felt suddenly like everyone was watching *her*. Like she was at the centre of some weird game that fate had signed her up for. Pennie was playing it, too, only she seemed to know the rules. She wondered if Pennie was always like this: floating around the house like a strange little ghost girl? In truth, Eve didn't know. She'd been kept too distracted to know, or to care, at the time. It hurt to realise that, but she knew it to be true. Eve went out of her way *not* to care about the other kids in this house. She'd cared for Sparrow, and she adored Amelia, but look where that got her. They'd both left and that hurt too damn much to let herself become invested in anyone who came after them. Like Pennie.

But that was all in the past. Eve was older now and things were very different. She didn't just *care* for Pennie. She loved her, and yet she had the unsettling feeling that she and Pennie weren't the twosome they were supposed to be. If anything, it was Eve who felt like the third, unwelcome wheel at times thanks to Pennie's *Angel*. He'd insert himself into their lives in a way that left Eve feeling like she'd never have control over anything in life. Of course, the whole idea screamed of paranoia and Nicole Hammond's string of questions did nothing to abate those feelings.

When her thoughts began to settle and her breathing calmed, Eve used some of her time on the floor to google cheap home security. She went on to spend a total of €120 on the lowest budget nanny cams she could find through Amazon. An enormous amount of money, but she didn't care. She'd gladly starve if it meant she could have some peace. She also downloaded the Ring doorbell app and figured out how to connect it to the one Peter had installed some years back. Both he and Ellen used to monitor it on their phones, so they could keep track of the comings and goings around Raven's Rock. It still worked, but Eve had never made use of its features. She would from now on. She had to.

> Hey. You ok?

Nicole Hammond's WhatsApp message flashed across the Ring app's home screen. Her insides churned again. What did she want? Women like her were not interested in people like Eve. Not unless there was something in it for them.

> Sorry for all the questions earlier. A hazard of my job, but I get that it can be annoying for most people! I really didn't mean to make you uncomfortable and I apologise if you think I was prying. Honestly, I wasn't. I just wanted to get to know you a bit better, that's all.

She inserted a face-palm emoji. She'd be able to see that Eve had read her messages, but rather than responding, she just sat there staring at them. What did she want? What *could* she want? A small part of Eve desperately wanted to take her messages at face value and believe that Nicole actually did like her. *Her*, and not the story of Raven's Rock. But that just didn't seem possible. Not any more.

> Can I come over? Just for 5 minutes. Give me a chance to explain myself?

Eve frowned at the screen. What. Did. She. Want? She looked around the open-plan downstairs of the old house. The battered, green couch to her right, separated from the TV by an equally old, but still shiny, wooden coffee table. The dining table and kitchen straight ahead were clean and tidy as they always were. She knew what *she* saw when she looked around this place. But what would Nicole Hammond see? A run-down old kip? A room filled with unhappy ghosts? Or would she see a homely space shared by two loving sisters? A part of her wanted to know. She typed out a quick response before she could talk herself out of it.

EVE

Fine. 5 minutes.

NICOLE

Thank you! Where do you live?

A flash of relief came with that message. It reassured her to know that Nicole didn't already have her address. Of course, she could just be pretending not to know, but... maybe?

My Eircode is X24NE25. The house is called Raven's Rock and has a wrap-around deck. You'll know it when you see it.

Her stomach fizzed with nervous energy as she sent Nicole her address. Was she making a big mistake, inviting another person here? Was Nicole coming to investigate the rumours and half-baked stories about this house, or was she coming because of... Eve?

She looked at the phone. A minute passed since her message before finally three little dots told her that Nicole was responding.

Ok. I just looked it up and I can be there in ten minutes. Raven's Rock? Wow. Sounds ominous. See you soon.

Eve pulled herself up off the floor and went upstairs to her room, where she stood in front of the full-length mirror. The reflective surface was worn off in places, but she could see enough of herself to want to change it all. But she couldn't. She wouldn't even change her clothes. She didn't want to seem desperate, even though that was exactly what she was. But she grabbed a brush and pulled it through her hair, which was a mass of tangles following her impromptu run from the city to Raven's Rock. Then she took a seat at the old dresser and started fixing her face as best she could, wiping the smudged mascara away from underneath her eyes and brushing some powder over her skin to dull the shine and conceal some of the redness. A touch of lip balm, a lot of deodorant, and then she found herself standing in front of the mirror again, seeing absolutely no difference. Chances are, Eve Holland would always want to change the woman reflected back at her.

The doorbell rang and Eve's phone tingled, letting her know that the door-bell app was working. She opened the app and Nicole's face filled the screen. She was here already. She was standing at the top of the steps with her back to the front door. She was looking all around the garden and towards the treeline. Eve continued to watch until Nicole turned and walked to the door again. She rang the bell for a second time and looked into the camera with a smile this time. She even waved and Eve quickly closed the app, as if worried that Nicole could see her, too, sitting there like a weirdo, watching her. She got up and walked quickly downstairs, knowing first-hand that if she ran, then Nicole would hear her rushed footsteps on the loud wooden staircase and would sense her desperation even from outside on the deck.

Her breath caught in her chest when she opened the door and saw Nicole standing there with a colourful arrangement of flowers held in the crook of one arm. Eve had missed those when she'd watched her through the camera. They were wrapped in the kind of fancy cellophane that made Eve think she'd bought them from an actual florist rather than a service station. Nicole held them towards her.

'By way of apology for being an asshole.' She smiled. 'I'm sorry.'

Eve took the flowers and stared at them. She was twenty-three years old and no one had ever given her flowers before. 'Eh, thanks,' she said, sounding more confused than thankful. 'Come in.' She opened the door wider and stepped hesitantly aside. She'd argued with herself about whether or not to invite Nicole inside her house. Nothing good ever came from bringing outsiders in. But this wasn't *that* Raven's Rock any more. And Nicole was the person who could potentially miss them if they were suddenly gone.

Nicole looked up at the old house, smiled and shook her head. 'That's okay.'

She didn't want to come in. It was the stench. It had to be. The disadvantage that clung to Eve must also permeate the air throughout the house, leaking out through the open front door and assaulting Nicole's senses. No matter how much Eve cleaned the place, she doubted there was any getting rid of it. Or perhaps it was the trained gut instinct of a seasoned investigative journalist that stopped her from stepping over that threshold.

'Why don't we sit out here.' Nicole gestured towards the rusty swing seat.

Eve looked at it. No one had sat on that thing for more than a decade. 'I'm not sure I'd trust it,' she said, frowning. She looked at Nicole again and glanced towards the front door, which was still open. Nicole didn't move and, clearly, she did not want to go inside. Eve's nervous energy dissipated, and her shoulders sagged as she pulled the door shut and went and sat on the steps leading down from the deck. Nicole came and joined her.

'Is your sister home?' she asked.

Was that why she didn't want to come inside?

Eve shook her head. 'She's out.' Nicole didn't need to know that Pennie had been sick for weeks. That she'd barely left her bed, let alone the house except for when she disappeared. Twice. She wondered what Nicole would think if she knew that.

But Nicole accepted her response by nodding as she sat down on the top step, resting her elbows on her knees. She was wearing ripped jeans with one of her tanned knees poking through. Eve could see the edge of another tattoo just above it, but she couldn't make out what it was. She couldn't make out what most of her tattoos were, but Eve admired the confidence with which she displayed them so consistently.

'Can I ask you something?' Nicole said. She was looking straight ahead, rather than at Eve.

Eve placed the flowers gently on the floor beside her. She didn't respond, knowing that Nicole would ask whatever she wanted to ask anyway.

'Why would you think a reporter might want to write about your family?' She turned to look at Eve then. When she didn't look back, Nicole craned her neck encouragingly.

Eve squeezed her eyes shut and exhaled, annoyed at herself for having opened her mouth. 'Is this why you came? To find out if there actually *is* a story?'

Nicole shook her head. 'No.'

Eve looked at her at last. 'My parents devoted their lives to fostering the kinds of kids that no one else wanted.' She rehashed the words Ellen had used many times. 'Then they both died in freak accidents. You don't find that interesting?'

Nicole jutted out her bottom lip and nodded slowly. 'Well, when you put it like that. But, Eve, if I wanted to write that story, I would have just asked you. And I don't mean to sound dismissive of anyone's family tragedy, but...'

'But what?'

'Well, it sounds like your parents were amazing people, taking in all those kids. And their deaths are tragic, like I said.' She ran her hand through her hair, then ended the motion by brusquely rubbing the shaved back of her head. She looked a little uncomfortable suddenly, like this was an awkward conversation. 'But I mean...' she continued hesitantly, 'they arrested someone for your dad, didn't they?' She didn't wait for a response. 'Don't get me wrong, it does sound like an interesting story, but... I don't really write about stuff like that.'

Eve watched her closely while she spoke, her eyes narrowed. To her, theirs *did* sound like the kind of story Nicole Hammond would write about. Their *real* story, that is. But Nicole's eyes, and her apparent discomfort, told Eve that she was telling the truth and, strangely, Eve's gut told her that, too. She felt herself relaxing a little, which perhaps was brought on by her naivety. Or maybe her desperation to be liked. *Wanted,* even.

Because of the way Nicole was sitting, with her colourful forearms resting on her thighs, the bare skin on her upper arm was touching Eve's. The warmth from this light touch spread through her and she found herself imagining what it would be like to be touched by Nicole in a way that was intentional. What would her hands feel like if they were to roam through her hair and down over her face, her neck... her body?

'Do you believe me?' Nicole asked softly. 'Because the last thing I want is for you to think of me as some kind of low-life vulture, because honestly, that isn't me.'

Her voice pulled Eve back to the front steps and forced her to stop looking at her lips while she spoke.

When their eyes met, Eve nodded. 'Sorry for running out like that earlier.'

Nicole smiled. 'That's okay. I can't say I blame you.' She swivelled slightly to look at the house again and this time her entire arm pressed against Eve's. 'So, this is where you grew up? This is Raven's Rock.'

Eve glanced back, too, and nodded.

Nicole turned away again. 'Nice.' The word was barely a whisper, and her eyes found Eve's as she said it. Then they just sat there, looking at each other for what felt like an eternity. Every instinct Eve had screamed that she should kiss Nicole, or that Nicole should kiss her. Her insides churned and burned as she waited with a panicky yearning for her to do so.

But she didn't. Was it written all over her face? That desperation which turned to despair as soon as Nicole turned her face away? Could she see it? Smell it, maybe?

Nicole got to her feet and walked slowly down the steps and across the poorly maintained front garden. She ran her hands through her hair again, doing the same rough rubbing at the end. Then she turned back around to face Eve.

'You're leaving?' Eve asked.

Nicole nodded. 'Yeah, I think it's best that I do.'

Eve lowered her head, her disappointment dripping onto the steps beneath her.

Nicole shoved her hands in the pockets of her jeans and walked back to the bottom step, putting herself right in front of Eve. 'I'm a stranger to you, Eve. And well, you...' She gestured to Eve with a half-smile. 'Christ, I don't think I've ever had to apologise so many times to someone I just met.'

Eve exhaled a shaky breath. *You were about to kiss me*. Those were the words Nicole stopped herself from saying. Eve was mortified. She wanted to tell her that she was wrong, but the lie wouldn't form in her mouth. She couldn't speak at all, without every emotion she had coming rushing out. So she just nodded again.

'So I'll go now, but...' Nicole started to walk slowly, backwards, away from Eve. 'I'll definitely be seeing you again.' She smiled, turning away. But before stepping off Holland property, she turned again and said, 'I hope.'

Eve returned another mute nod, desperately trying to control the emotional turmoil inside. She turned to look at the closed front door, then looked again at Nicole as she walked casually away. Suddenly, the thought of going back inside alone terrified her. She wanted to call out, to beg the woman to come back. To step in there with her. To hold her and tell her that everything would be all right.

But behind her, the house seemed to whisper, *You know it never will be.*

22

It was a while before Eve could bring herself to go back inside the house and for far too long she stood watching the space where Nicole once walked. Finally, she took a walk around the back of the house and looked up at Pennie's bedroom window. In a way, she was annoyed that she'd broken away so soon from her plan to watch Pennie like a hawk. At least until she discovered how Pennie was coming across details of these deaths. Was Angel just a vessel for Pennie's dark thoughts? Perhaps, but that wouldn't explain where the details were coming from. Hidden drugs and undiscovered pinpricks? And now that Nicole had mentioned insulin, Eve needed to figure out a way to get to the truth. Because Nicole finding out those details was one thing. But how could a child, who never left her room, possibly have known first?

But as annoyed with herself as she was, Eve also knew that if she had the chance to do this day over again, she wouldn't change a thing. Not even the bit where she ran out on Nicole at the café, because even though it was embarrassing and unplanned, it was what brought her to Eve's front steps today. It was what led to Nicole's arm brushing against hers, and the electricity that sparked something in Eve, making her see possibilities where there'd never been any. In that split second before Nicole had jumped to her feet, Eve felt alive. More alive than ever before. Eve Holland was no virgin. But nor had she ever been on a date. She'd never been with a woman either, despite often fantasising about sharing her life with one. She'd never had someone invite her for coffee, for no reason other than to be in her company, which she now believed had been the case. What's more, Eve had never really wanted *anyone* to kiss her. Not before today.

Pennie's bedroom window was closed and there were no ladders leading up to it. Eve was sure that Pennie wouldn't be able to lug their one over the stone wall and back to the house by herself, but she checked anyway, and it was still exactly where she'd left it. Eventually, she went back inside the house and upstairs, where she knocked once before letting herself into Pennie's room. She was there, sitting on her own bed looking like the ghost of a girl who was haunting the room. Eve might have veered from her plan to stay close to Pennie that day, but her intention to find out what was going on hadn't changed. She'd just need to take a more direct approach, because it seemed she wasn't cut out for the long game after all. She stood and silently watched the girl, who had yet to acknowledge her presence. That was when Eve decided, and thus convinced herself, that today, Pennie was going to tell her all that was going on inside her head, and under Eve's roof. Because it *was* Eve's roof now. With Peter gone and now Ellen, too, the job of protecting Raven's Rock and those within it fell to her and her alone.

Eve went and sat on the edge of Pennie's bed. She reached out and gently tucked her limp, greasy hair behind her ear. 'How are you feeling?' she asked softly.

Pennie shrugged and it looked like it took far more effort than it should. Still, she seemed to sense the barrage of questions being held back by the tight line of Eve's smile.

'Pennie, we need to talk,' Eve said, after a quiet moment.

Pennie glanced at her, her face giving little away as usual, then she slid down into a lying position and pulled the covers up around her chin. Whatever energy she might have had that day was disappearing fast.

'Do you want something to drink, or a snack?' Eve asked.

Pennie shook her head.

Eve took a breath and tried to gather her words into some kind of order. Blood was pulsing in her head now and she brought both hands to her temples. It was the beginnings of yet another headache, which was coming on quickly and without the usual preamble. She closed her eyes. Eve was noticing less and less time between episodes these days, but luckily, she still had a good supply of Ellen's pills that she could take. She couldn't help worrying, though, that she wouldn't have them for very long at the rate she needed them now. There were times when she wondered what she'd do when they ran out? She had no idea where Ellen had gotten all those pills, seeing as she didn't believe in visiting doctors. Ever.

'You have another headache,' Pennie said in the same soft voice that never really changed.

Eve snapped out of her own head. She never wanted Pennie to pick up on her headaches. It wasn't like she went around complaining about them or anything, and even if she did, they hardly spent enough time together for it to become obvious. Her observations reinforced Eve's feeling of being watched a little too closely. 'How do you know I get headaches?' she asked, because it was as good a place as any to start this conversation.

Pennie shrugged.

'I'm sorry, Pennie but...' Eve mimicked her shrug, 'this, isn't good enough any more. I want answers.'

'What kind of answers?'

'The kind that let me know that you're all right. That *we're* all right.'

'But we're not all right,' she replied with a frown, like this should have been very obvious.

Eve's skin prickled and the pulsing in her head became more intense suddenly, like one loud whoosh after another. 'Why aren't we all right?' She was the one who sounded like a scared child now.

Pennie looked around, lowering her voice to a whisper. 'Because they're chasing us.'

A cold shroud covered Eve's body, making the hairs on her neck stand up. 'Who's chasing us?' Her voice rose slightly, and she splayed her hands on the bed between them in a bid to make the room stop spinning. For the second time that day, desperation emanated from her, and she didn't like it. Why was she always the one with the least amount of control? Even now, as the big sister of a ten-year-old child and head of the household, she felt like she was along for a ride that she wasn't overly welcome on.

Pennie's face crumpled. Her eyes filled with tears, and she shook her head vehemently. 'The secrets!' She pulled the covers up to her nose, as if the monster under her bed was coming to get her. 'If *I* know them, then I'll die, too.' She brought her hands up to cover her ears and she squeezed her eyes shut, tears rolling off her chin and onto her pillow. 'I don't want the secrets!' She inhaled deeply and screamed, 'I don't want them!'

Pennie jumped out of bed and hurried from the room, leaving Eve open-mouthed and speechless, staring after her. Her head pounded now, and her mind began to race. Something was coming. She could feel it as surely as she could feel the nose on her face. But who was driving it? There was always a marionette pulling the strings at Raven's Rock, watching everybody dance within it. But for the first time in her life, Eve had no idea who that someone could be.

23

Three days passed in a blur and Eve was almost catatonic from lack of sleep. She'd sat on the floor outside Pennie's room each night, staring straight ahead at the locked door, with the sharpest of her kitchen knives resting in her lap. She heard that dog from time to time, howling and growling outside the house, and Eve chose to think of him as an extra layer of security, rather than a beast waiting to devour them. But Pennie hadn't spoken a word since she'd run, screaming, from her bed. She hadn't been eating, or vomiting, but she had wet the bed. Twice. Eve went into her room each morning, brought her food, changed her bedding, tried to convince her to talk, but all she got back was silence and a thousand-yard stare. She had a death-like pallor to her face and her hair had lost what little vitality it might once have held. But Eve still couldn't risk taking her to a doctor. She'd be taken away and shoved in some godforsaken foster home. No. Eve had to do what was best for Pennie, and right now, that was to be right here, in this house with someone who loved her. Someone who would keep her safe, no matter what.

But Pennie had disappeared inside herself, and Eve wanted desperately to do the same. Her headache was violent now and no number of pills could dull the pain. Hours dragged by and then vanished suddenly as soon as the sun came up. During daylight hours, she walked the property. As desperate as she was to escape it for a few hours, she stayed, and she searched for any signs that someone was there. From time to time, she had to lock herself in her room with her shades drawn. That was when the headache got to be too much. Finally, it *all* got to be too much, and Eve knew that there was only one thing left to do.

Pennie had to go. It wasn't working. Eve was not cut out to be anyone's big sister and, try as she might, she was unable to take care of her the way she planned to. Not when the girl refused to eat a single morsel of food. Not when she refused all that Eve had to offer her and instead chose to waste away, miserable and in pain. Because she *was* in pain now. Pain from hunger. Pain from fear. Pain from carrying the weight of the secrets she feared so much. Neither of them could go on like this. This wasn't how it was supposed to be. Eve was no one's guardian and it seemed her life was not meant to be shared with anyone, no matter how much she would have liked it to be. Not a child. And not someone like Nicole Hammond, whom she hadn't heard from since she walked away from the front steps of the house.

Eve got out of bed, took the pill bottle from her dresser and left her room, squinting in what little daylight had managed to find its way up the stairs, getting trapped between all the closed and locked doors on the landing. She stopped briefly outside Pennie's room and stood with her ear pressed to the door. There was no sound and Eve had no desire to investigate further. Her exhaustion had sucked that out of her. She continued down to the kitchen and over to the sink, all the while feeling like she was moving underwater, everything muted and distorted around her. She opened the pill bottle and tipped three pills into her hand. She shoved them in her mouth and drank straight from the tap to wash them down. She stood for a minute, supporting herself against the kitchen counter. She squeezed her eyes shut and took a series of breaths, pulling her shoulders up with each one, and letting them fall slowly. The pain eased slightly, hinting that it was nearing a corner and was thinking about turning it. She stared longingly at her car keys on the table, counting down as many minutes as she could before she picked them up. The keys led to her putting on her jacket, and the jacket led to her leaving the house. The fog went with her, refusing to lift even for a minute.

While she drove, she thought about Nicole Hammond, refusing to count her out entirely, despite knowing better. Maybe when all this was done, Eve could invite her over to dinner. Maybe she'd like it, and she'd want to stay. Maybe.

She arrived at the park with no real memory of the road she'd taken to get there. But it was a road she knew well and that happened sometimes when the headaches wouldn't go away. A side effect of the extra pill, maybe. She reasoned away the guilt of leaving. Pennie was probably better off having a break from Eve and Eve needed a break from Raven's Rock. This was what happened when she had to spend all day there. There would be no end to the headaches and nothing would look clear to her, ever, if she didn't leave that house, just for a while.

She parked her car and walked on autopilot to the swing set. She sat on the one she considered to be *her* swing, wrapped her arms around the chains and let herself sway her with its gentle momentum.

This was where Eve escaped to throughout her whole childhood. On the rare occasions when she was permitted to escape, that is. Usually, it was when she was meant to be at school. Sparrow, too. This was where they'd come to. She sat on her swing. He sat on his. Here was where they made their monumental plans for what they would do when they aged out of the system. Things like travel to Australia, where Sparrow would get a job in the mines and earn his fortune, while Eve would work in a shelter for abandoned cats. She did like cats. Or at least, she liked the idea of them. As far as she knew, Sparrow never did go to Australia, but at least he left Raven's Rock. He left it well before he aged out, but the so-called child welfare people were never able to find him, so they never got to drag him back, or shove him anywhere else. She wondered now what he'd make of Eve if he knew she still lived there, even now, years after she was old enough to leave. Would he be disappointed in her, she wondered? She smiled fondly as the fog gradually started to lift. No. Sparrow wouldn't be disappointed in her. Sparrow never wanted anything from Eve, only for her to be happy. Her smile faded. In that regard, she might well have let him down after all.

'Yes! I said I'm on my way!'

A gravelly voice pulled her from her reverie, and it was a voice she'd know anywhere. She straightened herself up and looked around to see where it was coming from, her stomach tightening, as it was prone to doing. Her heart sank when she saw Ashley Evans, about to get into a car outside the entrance to the park, stopping instead to answer a call in her usual brash manner.

The department of child and family services was ironically housed in a former mother and baby home in Cork city, not too far from Carriglen. It was nearing knocking-off time, which meant that Ashley was on a home visit or something in the area. Or perhaps meeting someone, as her words suggested. Eve jumped up from the swing and hurried as quietly as she could, in the opposite direction, to where a line of bushes separated the park from the supermarket next door. She stood out of sight, watching and waiting for Ashley to get in her car and move off.

Eve had once referred to her as Aunty Ashley, because she turned up at their house so frequently that Eve felt sure she must be related. But Ashley was no one's aunt. She came with a string of children, each one more desperate than the last. She brought the ones that other foster homes refused to take and now her unmistakeable shape was ambling around to the other side of her car. Her arms were laden down with files and a canvas bag hung from her shoulder, weighed down by its overload of contents. In addition, there was a tote bag hanging off her arm. All the baggage she always carried. She was still driving her fifteen-year-old Volkswagen Polo: a miraculous car to have survived for so long. Its appearance gave the impression that it would be too weak to cope with Ashley's six-foot frame and her problem with obesity. But that Polo was motorised proof that looks could be deceiving. Just like Ashley herself, with her smiling face and her shiny trophy for *Social Superstar 1999* which she kept on a shelf in her office. Ashley was the most deceptive of them all.

Right now, she was red in the face and panting by the time she'd shoved her bags and folders into the passenger seat and come back around the circumference of the car. Talking on the phone at the same time was visibly adding to her stress. She paused for a moment and Eve could have sworn she looked right at her, so she moved back a pace, as slowly and as inconspicuously as she could. She stayed there, out of sight, until Ashley's car groaned in protest, indicating that she'd shoved herself into the driver's seat. Eve glanced out again as she heaved her door shut, ending the conversation she'd been having. Her engine coughed to life and revved wildly as she pulled away from the kerb, and Eve started breathing again.

Seeing Ashley, and coming so close to being seen by her, was the wake-up call Eve needed. What was she thinking? How could she even have entertained the idea of handing Pennie over to the likes of Ashley? What if she'd seen her? What if she took a notion to call around, because that was something she'd do! Ashley always acted like she had power over Raven's Rock somehow. Or at least the children there, Eve included. They'd stopped fostering when Peter died, but that wouldn't stop Ashley. Not if she got an idea in her head.

As soon as the Polo was out of sight, Eve hurried to her own car and got in. She drove straight home, her vision as clear as day, finally. But when she pulled into the driveway and stepped out of her car, Eve saw a shape hurrying past the stained glass of the front door. The size and shape could only have been Pennie, who hadn't left her room for days, other than to go to and from the toilet. Eve walked quickly up the steps and opened the door, just as Pennie disappeared around the top of the stairs and her bedroom door closed gently again. Eve stood just inside the door, looking around for signs of what Pennie had been doing before the sound of Eve's car had sent her running. Eve had been assuming that the girl was too ill to get out of bed. But now it seemed she just didn't want to be around Eve.

The TV was on, showing a rerun of *Home and Away*. On the counter in the kitchen, right inside the back door, was one plate with two half-eaten sandwiches on it. She walked over and looked at the food. A plain cheese sandwich, alongside a peanut butter one. An odd combination, even for a ten-year-old. Eve got that sensation again. A kind of self-conscious anxiety that made her palms clammy and her skull feel too small for whatever was inside it. She pictured herself as a lab rat, with all eyes watching to see what she would do. Pennie and her *friend*. Ashley. Even Nicole Hammond. People like her didn't seek out women like Eve, so what was her angle? What was *her* part in all this?

Her thoughts were swinging like a pendulum, back and forth between hopeful and hope*less*, but the fog hadn't fully returned just yet. It would, and probably soon. But for now at least, it was allowing her to function. Just about.

The harsh, blue light from her phone screen hurt her eyes when she brought it out of her pocket and opened her Amazon account. Then she glanced at the sandwiches again. Where were the cameras she'd ordered? She fumbled with her password, entering the wrong one several times as hot tears of frustration came to her eyes. She tried to calm herself. To remind herself that she had a tendency towards paranoia, which was true. She'd always assumed that people were out to get her, when in reality, she was hardly on their radar at all. And it was *she* who'd sought out Nicole Hammond. Not the other way around. But why did everything have to go wrong all the time? Why couldn't Pennie have wanted a sister as much as Eve did? Why did she need the baggage of this extra pseudo-person? Why couldn't everything just be *fine* for once?

Finally, her Amazon account opened, and she clicked into *your orders*. She frowned.

Your items were delivered.

She checked the date. Two days ago. She turned and went back outside and searched around the deck. Sometimes, the delivery drivers placed packages under the swing. One time, they even put one in the wheelie bin at the side of the house. She hurried around the property, checking all the usual places where a delivery guy might leave a package. But there was nothing. Annoyance clawed at her. She needed those cameras. She walked back up the steps and was about to go inside and type out an angry message to the Amazon support robots when she looked at her Ring doorbell. She'd activated it, but hadn't been checking it. She fumbled with the phone before finally managing to open the app. Notifications were turned off, so she switched them back on, then opened the footage. It took a few minutes to work out how to go back in time and see whether or not Amazon did what they'd said they'd done and delivered her nanny cams. She double-checked the date and time from the delivery notification and found the same date and time on her doorbell footage. And there he was. A short, Asian man with a backwards cap and a large pair of headphones, trotting up her steps, placing the package against her front door and leaving in pretty much the same happy, trotting way.

Eve closed her eyes to think. Where was she two days ago at 11.17 a.m.?

'I was here,' she muttered, her frown deepening as she went to sit on the couch, glancing again towards the two leftover sandwiches. She'd been awake all night, keeping watch outside Pennie's bedroom door. She was dizzy with tiredness, even now. But she had lost a few hours each day to her headache and a dark room, so perhaps that was when the package arrived. But it wasn't there when she left the house today. So where did it go?

That's when her eyes were drawn back to the phone. The footage was still playing and movement on the screen caught her attention. She blinked and brought the phone back up. Someone was on her deck. She jumped to her feet and hurried over to the door, yanking it open. But there was no one there. Of course there wasn't. This footage was from two days ago. She walked outside, her eyes still glued to the phone. It was a man for sure, tall and with the kind of posture that looked like he was ready for something. He wore all black. Black, utilitarian-type pants, chunky, black boots and a black hoody with the hood pulled up. He also had a cap on underneath and positioned himself in such a way that the camera did not pick up his face, even for a second. He stood for a minute looking down, then he bent to pick up the package. He stood looking at it and then Eve's stomach collapsed through the floor, as the front door opened, and the man stepped inside.

24

Eve brought her hand to her mouth to muffle the sounds that were coming from her. Someone had been inside their house. And Pennie had let them in. Fear and panic engulfed her, and she ran for the sink. She heaved into it, yielding nothing at first. But then everything inside her came out, including the extra pills she'd taken in the car on the way home. She'd taken too many and her senses were dulled. *That's* how she'd let this happen. She heaved and cried and when she was finally spent, she stood panting over the sink. Again, movement on her phone screen caught her attention. A cat, walking along the railing of the deck. Eve straightened up and checked the timestamp on the footage. A few minutes after the man went inside the house.

She grabbed a tea towel and used it to wipe her mouth and her eyes, then she filled a large glass of water and chugged it back, desperately hoping to clear whatever drug remained in her system and wake herself up. She refilled the glass and brought it with her to the kitchen table. She stood there for a minute, looking towards the stairs. Her fear intensified. Someone had been in her house. While she was here. She looked at the sandwiches again. One cheese. One peanut butter. Her breathing quickened and she took the phone in both hands again. She sped up the footage, moving through the minutes and hours in fast forward. The sun went down and the garden became dark. Flies and other bugs glowed as they swept past the camera until the sun came up unnaturally quickly and a new day started. Yesterday. He'd been in the house overnight. While Eve was sitting on the floor outside Pennie's room, a man was in their house. But where was he? Was he in that room with Pennie? What was he doing? Was he watching Eve? Her breathing was distractingly loud now, and her chest felt so tight, she thought she might be having a heart attack. Or an anxiety attack at the very least. She brought one hand up and pressed it against her sternum, applying as much pressure as she could with her knuckles. Her thumping heart felt like it was trying to break out of her chest, but Eve kept going with the footage. She fast-forwarded through the morning, through the rain showers in the afternoon until darkness fell once more without anyone coming or going from Raven's Rock. Finally, today's sun came up. Eve watched the day crawl by before she saw herself leaving the house. She watched her car pulling away and she watched the next few uneventful hours as the sun started to sink lower again in the sky. Then she watched herself searching the garden for her package. Her face looked like someone else's when she stood with her phone held in both hands, watching what she was watching now. The horror there made her look grotesque somehow. Like an insignificant character in a scary movie. One of the first to be written out of the script and forgotten about.

Two days. Someone was in her house, right now, and he'd been here for two days. Eve pushed her chair quietly back from the table. Her bladder weakened and she fought the urge to let it go. But her legs felt weak, too, as she slowly stood up. Darkness was falling fast and Eve's hands trembled as she reached for the knife block on the kitchen counter.

'Pennie?' she called, her strangled voice catching in her throat. 'Pennie!' The word came louder now, but no stronger. Her voice was that of a child. She was the scared little girl from Raven's Rock, all over again. Would she ever be anything more?

Pennie came to the top of the stairs. She looked different, too. Her hair, which had been pulled into a messy ponytail earlier, hung loose now and clung to both of her cheeks, making her pale, expressionless face appear longer somehow. Plus, she was completely calm, despite Eve's obvious panic. She just stood there, her hands limp by her sides and her eyes following every jerky movement Eve made.

'Come down,' Eve said, with quiet urgency. She was holding the knife against her leg, hidden from Pennie's view. She didn't want to scare her, even though she herself was terrified.

'Why?' Pennie asked, coming down one step and then stopping.

'Someone's in the house,' she whispered.

Pennie's eyes widened but only slightly and she turned to look back towards her room.

'Come down!' Eve said, her fear sounding like anger now.

Pennie came slowly downstairs. She stood near the front door, with her hands clasped in front of her. She was wearing the yellow, polka-dot nightie that Eve had bought for her when she'd first moved into her newly decorated room. She wore that nightie every night, apart from laundry day, when it was left to dry until morning.

'Who did you let in?' Eve asked, lowering her voice to a whisper, her eyes darting from Pennie to the top of the stairs and back.

Pennie spotted the knife in Eve's hand. She stared at it, her face turning even more pale. 'I don't know anything,' she whimpered, shaking her head, tears spilling down her cheeks.

Eve squeezed her eyes shut and shook her head. 'It doesn't matter what you know, Pennie.' She took a few steps towards her, holding her hand out in what she hoped was a reassuring manner. 'Just tell me who's in the house. Please! I need you to tell me who you let in.'

Pennie's tears stopped suddenly, and her body stiffened. She turned her head slowly and looked up the stairs again. Even the sound of Pennie's breathing had stopped and, looking at her strange behaviour now, so did Eve's.

'You're to come with me,' Pennie said then, sounding as surprised as she did scared.

'Wh...' Eve looked to the top of the stairs and the dimly lit landing beyond it. 'Pennie, what?'

'Angel said, you're to come with me.' Pennie turned and walked upstairs.

Eve's breathing quickened again and her eyes darted all around. A kind of humming sound broke through the silence, which she soon realised was coming from her.

'Come on,' Pennie said, like she was asking for a bedtime story.

The air fell silent then as Eve watched her walking calmly up, one step at a time. Was she imagining it, or had Pennie gotten some of her strength back?

'Pennie?' Eve called after her in a strangled whisper.

Pennie glanced over her shoulder and nodded. 'My room,' she said, rounding the corner at the top of the stairs and continuing out of Eve's line of sight.

Eve's eyes darted all around, upstairs and downstairs. Then, with shaking hands, she shoved the knife into the belt around her waist and reached for another, smaller but equally sharp knife on the kitchen counter. This one she slid up the sleeve of her jumper. She felt almost paralysed with fear now, but there was no sign of Pennie.

The light from her open bedroom door just about made it to where Eve could see it, as she braced herself to take the first step on the stairs.

'Pennie?' she whispered. She closed her eyes, gripped the handle of the knife in her sleeve, then with slow, shaky steps, she made her way up.

25

By the time she got to Pennie's room, Pennie was sitting cross-legged on her bed. The real bed, with her grassy angel clutched in both hands.

'You're to sit down there,' she said, indicating the makeshift bed on the floor opposite her.

'Pennie?' Eve's voice shook as she cast her eyes around the room. It was the same as always, with nothing out of place. 'Is someone else here, Pennie?'

Pennie nodded, keeping her eyes on her angel. She was perfectly calm. As if she had full control, which Eve knew couldn't possibly be the case.

'Who is it?' Her words came out on a whimper and, suddenly, *she* was the child in the room, while Pennie seemed to know exactly what was going on.

'It's Angel. And Angel said you need to sit down. If you don't, then you'll never see Amelia again.'

Eve's breathing stopped, and she felt a physical weight slamming into her chest. Amelia. *Amelia*? She turned her horrified glare on Pennie. How did she...? 'How do you know...?' Pennie had only been a baby when Amelia vanished, so there was no way she could remember her, other than perhaps hearing Eve asking about her all throughout their childhoods. *Where did Amelia go? When is Amelia coming back?*

'Angel said to sit down now. It's time for a story.'

Eve started to cry like a child and Pennie wouldn't look at her any more. Instead, she just stared straight ahead towards that other little bed. Her face was almost completely hidden behind her greasy hair and her fingers worked furiously at her angel doll.

Eve moved with uncertainty towards the small bed. The one she wished she'd never made up. She didn't know what else to do, and her legs were threatening to go. Despite being afraid for most of her life, Eve never felt fear like this. Fear, of a ten-year-old girl. And a man, who'd been in her house, watching them both, for two whole days.

'Who's telling the story?' Eve asked, when she could muster the vocabulary.

'Angel is.'

Eve looked towards the door, her fingers touching the handle of the knife as she waited for him to show himself. But he didn't. Instead, Pennie started to speak.

'Chapter one. Brian.'

Eve froze, turning her eyes back to Pennie. She looked like a child. She sounded like a child. But everything about her screamed, *Pandora's box*. Goosebumps pricked Eve's skin and a sudden chill seeped into her bones. She was unable to speak, barely able to breath and was glued to the very spot where she sat.

'Brian's life was never good,' Pennie continued, sounding like she was reading from a book, the way a child might. Slow and automated, like she just about understood the words on the page, sounding each one out. 'But it got even worse when he turned twelve.'

'I don't want to hear this story, Pennie,' Eve said, her lost voice finding its way back.

'Angel says if you interrupt me, you'll never see Amelia again.'

Eve fell back into silence, but her mind raced. Amelia. She was dead. Only the smallest part of Eve believed that she might actually have run away that time, while Eve was on the mobile-home holiday in Kerry. And that was the part she always chose to listen to. But that wasn't the logical side of Eve's mind. The logical side told her that Amelia was dead. That *she* was the one under that unnatural lump in the soil beneath the section of wall that Peter 'repaired', while she and Ellen fought the unnatural summer heat in their rented mobile home. Eve recalled being violently sick on that holiday. She remembered screaming in pain as spasms ripped through her. Maybe that was why they only stayed for three days, but she was over the worst of it by the time they went home.

'Brian liked to annoy people,' Pennie continued in that same robotic voice, pausing from time to time as if recalling the details, or reading a paragraph ahead in her mind. 'Nobody liked him, especially not the other children living in his foster home.' She paused again. 'But then he was sent to The Room, and that all changed.'

Eve's eyes filled with tears and her body shook, but no sound came out.

'Angel said that you're to read the next few paragraphs.'

Eve looked to her lap, her breathing unsteady and coming too quick. 'I don't have the book,' she said in a voice so strained that Pennie couldn't have made out what she said.

'Angel says you know it by heart. You have to speak now. For Amelia.'

A few louder sobs escaped Eve. Undignified and ugly crying was the only kind she knew.

'Angel said you're to tell the story of The Room. Only The Room, he said.'

Eve nodded slowly, thinking of her big sister. If there was even the slightest chance... She inhaled slowly and closed her eyes. 'The Room was where the bold children went,' she started, her voice still unable to reach a normal pitch.

'What did it mean?' Pennie asked. This time, she was an interviewer, reading questions from a piece of invisible paper in her lap. Though her eyes were still on that doll. Eve looked at it now, too, and wondered if it was some kind of evil. Voodoo or something, but then she remembered the footage.

'The Room meant different things for different people.' She made herself go on, speaking now to the room around her and not to the girl on the bed. They were all here now. She could feel them. Each and every one of the Raven's Rock kids were here, hanging on her every word. 'Does that story of yours have a chapter about the house rules?' she asked, feeling bolder suddenly, though she knew it couldn't last. But it was as if someone had whispered in her ear that she had nothing left to lose. Amelia was gone. Pennie was... She glanced at the shadow of a child, hunched and hiding in her hair. She was gone, too.

Pennie glanced up momentarily. 'You can tell that chapter,' she said.

Eve nodded, then closed her eyes. In a split second, she was back there, in Ellen Holland's kitchen. She looked around at the little padlocks that adorned each kitchen cupboard. The fridge had two.

She cleared her throat and started to speak. 'There were a lot of house rules, but the only one that anyone knew for sure was that no one ate anything, unless Ellen handed it to you. The rest of the rules changed day by day.' Her hands started to move now, like they were about to take over the explaining. 'The Room was the consequence of a broken rule. If you ate something that you weren't given, then you went to The Room. The lock was put on and you stayed there without food for one week. So next time, you'd think harder before stealing a cheese slice.'

Pennie wasn't reacting to anything Eve said. It was as if she wasn't even listening. She just rocked gently back and forth, fidgeting with that infernal doll. Eve watched her quietly for a minute and when she was sure that she was paying no attention whatsoever to Eve, Eve began to move very slowly in a bid to get to her feet. But before she could straighten one leg, Pennie looked up.

'What else did The Room mean?' she asked.

Eve froze again and stared at Pennie. Pennie, as usual, gave her nothing in return. She just lowered her head and started gently rocking again.

'You have to talk now and you're not to stop again until it's my turn,' Pennie said, without looking up this time.

Eve exhaled, bringing more tears dripping into her lap. Her own fingers started fidgeting with each other then, just to stop her hands from shaking. 'Like I said,' she continued, crying through the barely coherent words, 'different things for different people. The ones who ate went hungry in there. The ones who were violent saw violence in there.' She brought her hand to her mouth then, stifling her sobs. 'The ones who ran away were...' She looked pleadingly at Pennie, who was still acting as if she were alone in her room, thinking happy thoughts. Eve squeezed her eyes shut and slowly shook her head. 'The ones who ran were shackled to the radiator in there.'

The memory came flooding back. Sparrow. Her love.

Pennie stopped rocking and seemed to freeze for a few seconds. Then she said, 'It's my turn now.'

26

'Chapter two. Peter,' Pennie began again.

Again, Eve stopped crying, stopped breathing and just stared at her, waiting.

Pennie looked up and, for the first time since Eve entered that room, they made eye contact and Eve took it as her chance to speak *to Pennie*. 'Pennie, where are these stories coming from?' she pleaded.

Pennie lowered her head again. 'Angel said no more questions. It's my turn now and you must listen. Then it'll be your turn and you must speak. But no questions.'

There was a silent moment then, filled only with the sound of Eve's erratic breathing.

'You must say you understand,' Pennie added.

Eve brought both hands to her face and nodded. Roughly, she dragged the skin on her cheeks towards her chin. 'I understand.' She cried quietly.

'There were two Peter Hollands,' Pennie began again, in her story-reading tone. 'First, there was the one that his builder friends knew. He was just a bit weird. He didn't know how to be one of the lads, and so none of them wanted to spend any time at all with him.' Her tone rose and fell now, in the way a practised narrator would. 'He just worked and hardly spoke to anyone.' She took another long pause before continuing. 'They used to send him to get their breakfast rolls at elevenses. That was weird Peter. The one with no friends and no power. Peter number one.'

Eve was leaning back against the wall now, her body having slackened as a numbness crept through her. Peter was the story that hurt the most. Well... it hurt a lot.

'Then there was Peter number two,' Pennie added, pulling a reed loose from her angel doll. Eve found herself watching and hoping the ghastly thing would fall apart in her hands. As if that might break the spell that had come over her sister.

'Peter number two was the one who lived here. He was the man who called his wife a pig and forced her to eat twenty-four doughnuts in one sitting, because her kitchen cupboard inventory was one doughnut short the day before.' She paused for a beat, then added, 'But that was how he got her to tell him everything. It was why she controlled the house so strongly while he was away. So that he could save up all his imag... imaginative... im...' Pennie exhaled in mild frustration, 'all his punishments for the children, and not her.'

Eve frowned. *Imaginative*. A particular word that Pennie was supposed to say, but couldn't pronounce. Eve tilted her head to try to see into Pennie's lap, sure now that she must be reading this. But there was nothing there. Nothing but the now less than perfect, grass doll.

'Peter was in charge of The Room,' she continued after a few seconds. 'Peter was the one who liked to watch while children cried.' Another pause, but slightly longer this time. 'Peter was a nobody out there in the world. But he was the master of The Room.'

Again, Eve closed her eyes and travelled back in time. She found herself standing in that room, her back to the closed and locked door. Then she heard his voice coming from behind her and felt his breath in her ear. Her eyes shot open and her hand flew to the back of her neck, as if that breath still lingered there. She covered both ears then, to drown out the memory.

'But the master had a favourite,' Pennie said, her pitch rising slightly at the end as if it were a question. 'One little girl who saw no punishments. One who could eat whatever she wanted, whenever she wanted it. So long as Ellen watched to make sure that it was her, and only her, eating it.' Pennie looked up again. 'That she wasn't giving that food to anyone else.' She paused again, then, 'Now *you're* to say who the favourite was.'

Eve lowered her eyes to the floor. 'Me,' she mumbled.

'Yes,' Pennie agreed. 'But until when?' She didn't wait for an answer. 'It's your turn to speak. You must say when you stopped being the favourite.'

'I was always the favourite,' Eve said without having to think about it.

Another silent beat before Pennie spoke again. 'Yes. But when did that stop being fun?'

Silent tears poured and poured from her and, suddenly, Eve wouldn't have cared if Pennie incarnated as the Devil himself and devoured her whole this very minute. Anything would be better than making public this private hell where she'd spent her whole life. Did she honestly think she could atone for any of it now? Was she so stupid as to think she could escape?

'You're to start speaking,' Pennie urged her, then she started slowly rocking again.

'It was never fun. But everything was worse when the screamer came,' Eve said.

Pennie stopped rocking. 'Robin,' she said and started moving again.

Eve nodded. 'Yes. Robin. Robin Higgins.'

They sat in silence for a few minutes, both still, and both seeming to have given up. After a while, Pennie said softly, 'Robin is your chapter. You must speak.'

Eve nodded, resigned to whatever this was. It was possible that she physically could have gotten up and ran from that room and from the house. Would Pennie have tried to stop her? Would she have been *able* to? Or was there someone on the other side of the bedroom door, waiting for exactly that? Either way, it didn't matter. Eve couldn't move. She was weighed down by the mention of her beloved sister's name at the beginning of this horrendous conversation. Amelia. Plus, the idea of escape was gone from her head. She'd even stopped fingering the knife handle in her sleeve and she no longer felt the length of the longer knife pressing against her stomach, the bare tip sharp against her thigh as it travelled down inside her trousers. She'd forgotten all of it. Except for Robin.

'Robin said that Peter was... abusing her.' The words hurt her throat and left her mouth feeling uncomfortably dry.

Pennie kept rocking with her head down and Eve knew somehow that she was expected to continue.

'But she'd said that before, too. About her uncle, while she lived at home with her mum. That time, her mum and her aunts all said she was lying and so no one believed her. Ellen said she was lying, too, when she said it about Peter.'

Pennie stopped rocking and glanced up briefly. 'Angel said you must tell the truth.'

Eve heaved in a breath and, after a while, it stuttered back out. She gave a small nod of acceptance, which Pennie couldn't have seen because she was looking in her lap again. '*I* said she was lying, too.' It came out as a whisper, riddled with guilt. It was as much as she could manage.

Pennie didn't say anything and she didn't look up. She just continued to move almost rhythmically back and forth, her face perfectly hidden behind her hair.

'But she wasn't lying,' Eve went on. 'She told me about her uncle even before Peter did... before she told on Peter. I *knew* she wasn't lying.' She roughly wiped tears from her eyes, but they were quickly replaced with more. 'Then the screaming started.' Eve cried gently. 'She screamed all the time. She told me that if she did that, then he'd leave her alone. She'd tried not washing, thinking the smell would stop him. She even tried wetting herself one time. None of that worked, but no one could stand to be close to someone who screamed, she said.' Eve tried again to scrub away the tears, but they kept on coming. 'She thought it would get her removed from here and sent to another home. But I couldn't sleep with the screaming.' She sobbed. 'We were together in this room. I couldn't sleep, I couldn't think. I couldn't do anything!'

Eve brought her hands to her face and her whole body shook with crying. She remembered what came next. That feeling of being outside herself, watching on as *she* started screaming, too. One evening at close to dinner time, Eve reached her limit. Robin was screaming upstairs, and Eve started screaming downstairs. She remembered the look of unbridled horror on Millie Grace's face as she sat waiting for her dinner, alongside Amelia. That one friend who came to their house for dinner. That one and only time. From outside herself, Eve could see their eyes following her as she charged towards Ellen. Amelia silently begging her not to do it, and Millie looking like she was watching a car crash happening in slow motion. None of it stopped Eve from launching herself at Ellen, scratching and biting her face in a fit of pure rage and exhaustion. She could taste the blood in her mouth even now, mixed with her tears and mucus.

'I melted down.' Her words were muffled by her hands, and she pulled them slowly away. 'There was no more screaming after that. I was locked in one room and Amelia was locked in another. And Robin... she was put in The Room.' Eve glanced towards the door, picturing The Room again. She took a moment to work through the constricting pain in her chest before she could continue. Her voice and her storytelling were semi-automatic now as she relived those awful days. 'Ellen woke me up early the next morning,' she continued quietly. 'She pulled me downstairs and out to the car without stopping for breakfast, or even to get dressed. There was a packed bag resting on the back seat. I was still in my pyjamas and for a minute, I panicked. I thought they were sending me away. But they didn't.' She stared unblinking at the carpet as she recalled Ellen's clear hatred for her that day. 'Ellen told me that Peter wouldn't allow her to get rid of me, even though she really wanted to.' She breathed out heavily, expelling as much pain as she could. 'We spent the next three days in Kerry instead, and by the time we got back, Robin was gone. And so was Amelia.'

Eve thought again about the repaired section of wall, which Peter was still working on when they arrived home. She remembered the lumpy earth all around it and her breathing became even shallower, too shallow, and the room started to dance and weave before her wide eyes, until they rolled towards the ceiling and, for a split second, she felt herself falling. But Eve had no recollection of landing on her back, on the makeshift bed.

27

'She's awake.'

Pennie's voice was the first thing Eve heard when she opened her eyes, and for a few seconds, she forgot what was happening. In that brief moment of respite, her mind let her imagine that she was waking up beside her sister following a restful sleep. But then the room came into focus, and she saw Pennie sitting there on her bed. Her legs crossed, her limp hair covering her face and that godforsaken angel in her lap, and she remembered. The story.

'Angel says it's my turn,' Pennie said, in her soft, unchanging voice, not giving Eve a chance to come around fully.

'How long was I out for?' Eve asked, struggling to sit up again. As she moved, she realised that something had changed. Not Pennie. She looked like she hadn't moved a muscle since Eve fainted. She hadn't done that in years, but she still knew what it felt like. However, as she went to sit up, she noticed that the discomfort of the knife in the waistband of her jeans was gone. She brought her hand to where she'd kept it, but it wasn't there. She looked at Pennie, but the girl gave no indication that she'd taken it from her. Pennie gave no indication that anything at all was wrong, and Eve didn't know which scared her more: all the unknowns of this night, or Pennie.

'Pennie, did you...?'

'Angel said it's my chapter and you must listen.'

Eve's bottom lip trembled as she looked around the room again. Her fear was replaced with hopelessness now. 'Pennie?' she cried.

'If you want to see Amelia again, it's my turn to speak and you must listen,' she said, cutting Eve off. 'Angel said no questions.'

Eve slumped against the wall behind her, pulling her sleeves further down over her hands. Pennie, or whoever was really here, hadn't found the smaller knife inside her sleeve and Eve fingered it gently, hoping she could stoke some courage to keep going. To keep trying to fix this. 'Okay,' she whispered at last.

Pennie sat quietly for a few seconds before she started. 'This chapter is called, Leslie.'

Eve closed her eyes. Leslie-Anne Williams. She could see her face in her mind as clear as day. Not the face of the woman she tried to become. Not Leslie Granger. Eve saw the eleven-year-old girl who was small for her age, with crooked teeth and a button nose. The girl who hardly spoke a word, because scared was her perpetual state.

'Leslie-Anne was afraid of her own shadow,' Pennie went on. 'She never spoke up for herself, no matter what anyone said or did to her.' Again, Pennie sounded like she was relaying someone else's words, or reading them from an invisible script. But she was making statements of fact now, rather than the rhythmic telling of a story.

Eve kept her eyes closed and kept Leslie's unsmiling face in her mind's eye.

'Other kids used to steal her stuff,' Pennie stated. 'She *had* stuff, because she'd been living with an old aunt who used to buy her things.' She paused again, with her head down. 'Everyone stole from her, but she never told.' Another pause, but Eve kept her eyes closed, dreading the words, *it's your turn*. 'She was too afraid to tell.'

Eve's nostrils flared as her memories moved relentlessly forward. Pennie was right. Leslie-Anne was too afraid to open her mouth. No one knew what she was afraid of, but in no time at all, everyone knew that they could do whatever they wanted to her, without consequence. The boys shoved her and called her names when they ran out of things to steal from her. Taunting Leslie-Anne became a sport. An entertaining pastime and Eve wasn't innocent in that, either. She used to eat food off Leslie's plate sometimes, but only when she was really hungry. Generally, Eve did *try* to be nice to the girl. Or at least that's what she used to tell herself back then. But she knew now that she didn't try very hard, and that weighed heavily on Eve. Another tear rolled off her chin.

'It's your turn.' Pennie said those dreaded words. 'The chapter is called, Leslie-Anne and The Room, and you must speak now.' She paused for a moment, then this time, her body stayed still. Only her head started moving gently from side to side like a metronome.

Eve nodded slowly. Her mind was already there, deep inside her chapter of Leslie-Anne's story. With her eyes still closed, Eve found herself standing outside The Room, with her ear pressed to the locked door. Even now, she could hear the soft crying coming from inside. Leslie's pain travelled through that draughty old door and into Eve's soul, which was why she could hear it so clearly now. It had been living here with her ever since.

'I could hear what he was doing to her in there.' She started speaking before being warned again to do so. 'I could hear him. I saw it on her, too when she finally came back to the room she shared with me. I saw that the person who used to live behind her eyes was gone and only a ghost was left behind.' More tears dripped onto her clothes and started to pool there. She opened her eyes finally and looked towards Pennie. Her head was still down and she was gently moving back and forth, like she was in another world entirely. Not here, listening to the darkest human memories. 'He knew she wouldn't tell.' Eve cried softly, her words bouncing off the top of Pennie's head. 'He took her to The Room every single day, knowing that Leslie would never say a word.'

There was silence for a while then, aside from Eve's keening sobs. She wiped tears and mucus from her face using the sleeve of her jumper.

'By the time someone came to take Leslie-Anne away, back to whatever home had let her go in the first place, there was nothing left of her. Leslie-Anne Williams no longer existed.' There was a tuck in Eve's chest and the sound of it escaped her lips. 'She *never* told,' she cried.

Pennie stopped moving then and sat still for a few seconds. Then, barely lifting her head, she glanced at Eve and said, 'The secret that killed her.'

28

Eve pulled her knees to her chest and buried her face in them. Without realising it, she was rocking now as well, but there was more desperation coming off Eve than there was off Pennie. In fact, something about Pennie seemed reminiscent of Leslie-Anne now. Somewhat soulless. Resigned. Her pain now a protective shield around her emotions. She thought only very briefly that Pennie, or whoever was arranging these chapters, was doing so in no particular order, because Leslie-Anne had been here before Robin. Robin was the last girl the Hollands ever took into their home. At Ellen's insistence, there were to be no more. *At least until Pennie.*

'Ashley Evans agreed,' Eve mumbled, making Pennie stop rocking and hold perfectly still for a moment.

'Speak,' she said after a little while.

'Leslie-Anne. She came before Robin because Robin was the last girl that came into his house.' These were just thoughts being spoken aloud. 'Ellen said she didn't want any more girls, but Peter wasn't listening. Then, one night, a few days after we got back from Kerry, I was awake when I shouldn't have been, and I heard Ashley speaking with them downstairs in the kitchen. They'd reported her missing. Robin, I mean.' Her hands started gesturing again, taking over the explanation. 'They had to, you see, and that's why Ashley came over in the first place. They blamed Amelia, of course. She was aged out by then and they said she took Leslie-Anne with her when she left. But I knew she didn't. If Amelia was going to take someone with her, it would have been me.' She lowered her head and examined her trembling hands for a moment before continuing. 'I heard Ashley saying that she'd been told about the screaming.' Eve frowned then and looked towards the window. 'I wonder who told her that?' The question was no more than another thought and she didn't expect an answer. 'Ashley said, "Between this and the Eve situation, it might be best if we only send boys here for a while."' Eve's frown deepened and she looked at Pennie, who was still sitting with her head down, fidgeting with her doll. 'That must mean that Ashley *knew*, right? She knew. But by not saying it out loud, it meant she could go on pretending that she didn't know. She could keep dumping kids here, and the files on her desk wouldn't get too high.' Eve blew out a long breath. 'She *chose* not to do anything about it. She just didn't send any more girls.' Her words were slow and clear now. Thoughtful. She looked around the room and then back to Pennie. 'But *you* came. And she left you here. She left both of us here.'

Pennie was still again. Then with a small nod of her head, she said, 'It's time to talk about Sparrow.'

'No!'

The force with which she said it surprised them both and they sat there for a long minute, Pennie with her eyes on her grass doll, Eve glaring at her. Throughout that time, it seemed like Pennie didn't know what to do. But then her shoulders sagged again and she said, 'Angel says this is all your chapter. You have to speak now.'

Eve shook her head, bile rising up.

'Think of Amelia,' Pennie said, her head down again, 'and speak.'

Eve's shoulders shook and she cried quietly, but fiercely. The way she always did when she thought too hard about Sparrow.

'I loved him.' Her crying painfully elongated each word, and she shook her head from side to side. She wanted to beg whoever was in charge here, not to make her speak about him. *Thinking* was excruciating enough, but to put Sparrow into words felt nothing less than impossible.

'Speak,' Pennie said. Then she commenced rocking again.

'*He* loved *me*,' she said, a little more forcefully then. There was silence for a while and the words just hung there, dead and useless. But Pennie didn't break the silence or react in any way. There were no orders for her to speak. Perhaps she could tell that Eve needed this time to get her thoughts of Sparrow in order.

She rewound back to the first days she met him and a small smile came to her lips.

'I knew he was trouble the minute he stepped inside the front door. He had these enormous freckles and hair that stuck up in all directions.' Her sadness lifted momentarily, and she remembered that mischievous glint in his eye when he smiled at her while Ashley explained to Ellen that she'd need to *keep an eye on this one*. He was proud of that, Eve could tell, and she remembered rolling her eyes and thinking, *another tough guy*.

'His name was Jack,' Eve said, when she finally found her footing and was able to speak. '*Pirates of the Caribbean* was on TV the night before he arrived and I'd been watching it from the top step of the stairs when I was meant to be asleep. It was me who gave him the nickname, Sparrow. Jack Sparrow, the swashbuckling, troublesome adventurer.' Eve smiled a small smile again, her eyes shut tightly, transporting her back to that first day with him. 'It wasn't love at first sight or anything.' She lowered her head. 'He wasn't a good-looking boy. Not then at least. But after...' She brought her hands to her face and pulled at her skin again. 'After, he was the most beautiful boy in the world.'

'Why?' Pennie asked.

Eve didn't raise her head, but she wiped her damp hands on her jumper. 'Because he always looked right in my eyes. The whole time, he looked nowhere else, but in my eyes.'

Pennie stopped moving again and sat there, still as a statue for a long minute. Then she got haltingly to her feet. Eve felt her entire body stiffen, as Pennie moved fluently at last, like the child she was. She crouched down and reached in under her bed. Eve held her breath and watched as she pulled a cardboard packing box out from under there and lifted it up onto the bed. Whatever was in it didn't weigh much. She could tell by the ease with which Pennie was able to pick it up. She sat down on the bed again, with one hand resting on the lid, and she waited. Finally, she lifted the lid and placed it gently on the pillow. Eve had no idea what was in that box, but she'd subconsciously pressed her body against the wall and was bracing herself with both hands against the cushions beneath her. Her eyes watched Pennie's every move, each one so carefully thought out. She paused between each action she took, as if waiting for instruction on how she should proceed. Remove the box from under the bed, wait. Remove the lid, wait. Reach inside the box, wait. But where were those instructions coming from. And from whom?

Eventually, Pennie pulled a long scrap of red, silky material from the box. She held it up between both hands and gave it a gentle shake, so that it unfolded fully. Then she held it there for Eve to see. It had fancy, white lettering all over it. *Homestead Building Society.* Eve watched in stunned silence as Pennie got up again and laid the silk neck scarf carefully on the floor between them. When she returned to the bed, she reached back in the box. Without saying a word, she took out a cheap digital watch. The kind that cost no more than twenty euro. Eve could feel herself starting to struggle for breath as she watched Pennie place the watch on the floor beside the scarf. She knew that watch. She knew that if she turned it over, *Sparrow* would be scratched into the back of it. Not engraved. Just scratched. She'd used a razor blade to do it herself before she gave it to him. The blade of the knife dug further into her skin as her body tensed.

Next, Pennie pulled out a large, black lump of material. She fumbled with that for a bit, before managing to unroll it and place it on the floor beside the watch. When she stood up, she paused for a second, looked down at it and then crouched again. She turned it carefully over and she smoothed it out so that the embroidered words, *Carver's Kitchen* looked up from what was now clearly a large apron. There were other items taken out of the box and placed neatly on the floor, including a fitness watch with a broken strap, and a silver cross on a chain, which, if Eve were still absorbing information, she might have recognised as the one that never left the neck of Ellen Holland. But she wasn't taking in the rest of the morbid line-up now. Her eyes were still on that cheap digital watch and her thoughts on the man who always wore it. Jack Logan. Her Sparrow.

29

There was silence in the room for at least five minutes after the last item was placed on the floor. A family photo of sorts. But it wasn't Eve's family. There was a smiling woman with both hands resting on the shoulders of a young girl, who was sat on a low seat in front of her. Neither of them looked particularly happy, but like they were trying their best for the camera. The girl was Amelia. She must have been about five when that picture was taken, which would have been right before her mother was arrested. One side said it was self-defence, but the side with more money said it was manslaughter. Either way, it left Amelia in the hands of the state. The silence told Eve that she was being given time to absorb the items being paraded in front of her. But she didn't want the time for that. She didn't want to see them and remember the people to whom they used to belong. She felt sick and started to retch, but nothing came up. She couldn't remember the last time she'd eaten anything, and she felt truly hollowed out in every way. When she stopped, she looked to Pennie for some sign that she recognised the significance of what she was doing and the effect that it was having. She was crying, too, and at last, there was a trace of fear in her expression. A hint of emotion where there had been none all evening.

'Pennie?'

Pennie was sobbing quietly and nodding. Like she was being consoled by a voice inside her head. She wiped her eyes then and got to her feet again. Eve felt herself stiffen as Pennie walked towards the door.

'You have to come with me,' she said, glancing back over her shoulder.

Eve was frozen to the spot. Where was she taking her? Was someone out there on the landing, waiting for Eve? Was this it?

'You have to come with me, now.' Pennie opened the door and stood aside, waiting.

Eve tried to get up, but her arms buckled as she tried to push herself off the makeshift bed. She rolled off the cushions, onto her hands and knees. Pins and needles assailed her, and her legs couldn't seem to find the strength to get her up off the floor.

'You need to come with me,' Pennie repeated.

'I'm trying!' Eve shouted before she could stop herself. 'Where are you taking me?'

Pennie didn't answer.

'Pennie, please?' Eve cried in desperation. Eve had always known helplessness, so this feeling was not new to her. But she'd been so sure that she was done with it. That neither she, nor any of her Raven's Rock family, would ever have to feel this way again. But here she was. Helpless. Useless. Everything she always was. How stupid could she be to think that anything could be different?

Eve needed to use the radiator, and then the freshly painted windowsill to pull herself up off the floor. It only took a few short steps to reach Pennie at the open bedroom door, but they felt like the last mile of a gruelling marathon. Her body trembled and ached, her legs threatening to drop her like a rock. When she was almost upon her, Pennie walked out of the room. Eve stopped at the door and looked up and down the artificially lit landing. There was no one there. She pulled her hand inside her sleeve for the reassuring feel of the knife, hoping again that she could take some strength from it. She gripped it so tightly that the blade dug into the skin on her forearm, but she didn't care. She watched Pennie walk away, towards Ellen and Peter's room. But then she stopped outside the linen press and opened the door. She paused for a moment, her head down and her face mostly hidden again, behind her hair. Eve watched her intently and was sure she saw her nod once before looking to Eve again.

'You have to go up there.'

Eve walked towards her in silence, but the noise inside her head was deafening. The hatch to the attic was inside the linen press. A ridiculous place to put it, but there it was. No more out of place than the house itself. When she reached the door, Eve looked cautiously inside the press and up towards the hatch, which wasn't sitting properly in place. She looked to Pennie again, who was standing there like a remote-control toy, waiting for someone to press a button and spur her back to life. Her head was down and was bobbing slightly. Sleep mode.

'Who's up there, Pennie?' Eve whispered, but she was unable to make eye contact with her.

Pennie didn't respond. She just bobbed along to whatever tune was playing in her head. But then she stopped. 'If you want to see Amelia again, you need to go up now.'

Eve's tears seemed to have dried up and she just stood there now, staring at the top of Pennie's head. She glanced again towards the hatch, her mind searching for answers that seemed just out of reach.

'Go,' said Pennie.

Eve glanced at her one more time, then she thought of her sister, Amelia, and she started to climb.

30

The cool air hit her as soon as her head poked up into the dark and dusty space. It had been years since she was up there, but she remembered the hole in the gable end of the wall, where she'd pulled a vent out once, just so she could see outside. It had never been repaired and was probably a contributing factor to the unnaturally cold temperature in the house, which seemed to linger all year round. Before pulling herself fully up through the hatch, she cast her eyes around, looking for someone she was sure must be lurking among the many shadows. As she moved further into the space, a cobweb blew across her face and did its best to settle there. Eve closed her eyes and wiped it away, then continued to climb until she was on her hands and knees on the splintery attic floor.

'Hello?' she asked, certain that someone else was there. She could sense them. She looked back down through the hatch to see Pennie walking away. Her hands were by her ears and, as Eve watched her go, she saw her pulling her hair back off her face at last. But she was gone from sight before Eve could get a proper look at her.

'You needn't worry about her, Eve.' A voice came from the darkest corner and Eve's entire body stiffened. The voice sounded robotic. Not human. 'She's going to be fine, even though... well, you know.'

Eve's heart hammered against her chest and she was almost afraid to move.

'You're Angel?' she asked, her voice cracking and making her sound as weak and as scared as she felt.

'I am.'

'Where's my sister?' She tried in vain to sound angry and forceful, but instead, she continued to sound desperate and pathetic.

'You mean Amelia?'

'Amelia is dead,' Eve said, more as a question than a statement of fact.

Angel laughed, a strange, echoing laugh that sent a fresh ripple of fear through her. 'Is she? What makes you say that?'

Eve didn't answer, but the sound of her breathing filled the silence.

'Is it because she disappeared at the same time as Robin? Or is it because you *know* that at least one of them is buried under that wall out there? Or... maybe both of them are. Is that what you're thinking?'

'Why are you doing this?' she cried.

'Why are *you*?' Angel responded.

Eve squeezed her eyes shut, then opened them wide and looked again into the darkness. She could see a shape now: someone sitting on the floor against the far wall, but she couldn't make them out.

'I want you to take a seat, Eve.'

'Why?'

'Because I said so.' The tone was reasonable all the time, non-threatening, yet everything about this night felt threatening.

Eve, already on her knees, turned herself into a sitting position.

'With your back to me,' Angel said.

She looked towards the shape again, wishing her night vision had better distance.

'If I wanted to hurt you, Eve, I wouldn't need you to sit with your back to me. I'd just hurt you.'

She closed her eyes again, then swivelled so that her back was turned and she was facing the other end of the house. She kept her eyes closed until she heard a click and a light shone past her. When she opened her eyes, a home movie was being projected onto the wall in front of her. In the movie was a close-up of a brown wooden door and Eve started to cry.

'I don't want to watch this.'

'Be quiet.'

She closed her eyes and shook her head as the movie played on, and a hand reached out from behind the camera and unlocked the door to The Room.

'If you close your eyes then you'll never see Amelia again.'

'Amelia's dead!' she half-shouted, shaking her head more vehemently now.

'She's not. At least, not in the true sense of the word.' Angel's voice held such conviction that Eve could almost understand how Pennie had listened to and obeyed it for as long as she had. Eve did open her eyes but she had to know. *Could* Amelia really be alive?

'If she's alive then why wouldn't she have let me know?' Her tears flowed again. 'She was my sister! Why would she leave me?'

'Watch. Then you'll know.'

Eve lowered her head and cried quietly. Her stomach was a tight ball of hurt and pain. She knew what this movie was. She knew what all of them were and she did not want to see them. Not any of them, but it played on regardless. When she looked up, she could see her much younger self. Or at least she could see the back of young Eve Holland's head, as she walked ahead of the camera, into The Room. There was the squeak of the door as it was pushed closed and Eve's hands shot to her ears when she heard it. That squeak was the haunting soundtrack to her nightmares, even now, along with the sound of the key turning in the lock, which followed. She forced herself to open her eyes again, sure that Angel would know if she didn't. The camera wobbled, taking in the dirty, threadbare carpet and a pair of feet in the corner of the room. But then the camera panned back up from the floor, passed Eve's head and came to land on a young Sparrow just beyond her. He was sitting on the floor with his back to the wall, and his ankle cuffed to the old, tubular radiator.

Eve's sobs grew louder and her body shook with each one. 'Please,' she begged, shaking her head from side to side. 'I don't want...'

'Shh.'

She brought her hands to her mouth, stifling the incoherent sounds coming from her.

'Eve,' came a man's voice from on-screen. 'Take off your top.'

'Hello, Peter,' came the voice from behind her and Eve's breath caught.

Angel knew Peter, and knew what this was.

'Who are you?' she asked, her head turned, but she didn't dare look all the way around.

'I said, shh.'

'That's it,' came Peter's voice again, and Eve glanced back at the projection on the wall. She'd found these recordings not long after Peter died and she'd watched them many times since.

'Now your skirt,' Peter said, his voice soft and gentle, like he was explaining the rules of a family board game.

Eve watched as her younger self did as she was told. She was standing in her underwear with her head down, her limp hair covering her face, not unlike the way Pennie had been all evening.

'Now your underwear,' Peter said, and as young Eve did as she was told, she could hear Peter's breathing quickening slightly, close to the camera's built-in microphone. 'There you go. Now, go over and kneel across him. One knee on either side.'

The first time Eve watched this, she only focused on herself. Her awkward movements as she bent and tried to position herself the way she was supposed to. Seeing herself like that filled her with such shame and self-loathing that now her focus was purely on Sparrow. Eve couldn't look at herself at all. She tried to tune out the sound of Peter's breathing, too, and the memory of what he was doing to himself while filming them. Instead, now, just like all the other times she'd watched, she kept her eyes on Sparrow. The defiance on his face from the moment he came on-screen. The way he turned his face away, refusing to look at Eve as she removed her clothing, one item at a time. The way he glared at the camera, as Eve inexpertly fumbled over him. But the bit she clung to, even now, was the way he closed his eyes for a few seconds, his mouth puckered with rage. But when he opened those eyes, they looked straight up into Eve's and nowhere else for the rest of the time she was there.

She clearly remembered that moment, when he'd closed his eyes. It was the same time that she felt him coming to life beneath her. He'd told her afterwards that he tried to stop it, but he couldn't. And when Peter instructed her to sit on him and told her how to move, there was nothing he could do, except refuse to look at her body. Refuse to make any sounds of enjoyment and even when the moment came when he lost all control, his effort not to let it show on his face was so clear. And his eyes never left hers. Not for a second. Eve told herself that those eyes were filled with love. Love for her.

'That was me, losing my virginity,' she whispered.

'There are a lot just like this,' Angel said and Eve thought she heard a hint of sorrow in the artificial voice. But how could there be?

She nodded and lowered her head. 'Yes. But this is the first.'

'The first of *you*.'

Eve looked up, but didn't turn around.

'There are many more featuring Amelia and Robin and Leslie, aren't there?'

Eve's shoulders started to shake again, and her head bobbed, yes. She'd seen them all.

'Please...' she begged quietly, 'don't make me watch Amelia. Not again,' she keened, pulling her knees closer to her chest and wrapping her arms around them.

'Tell me about them,' Angel said.

'No.' She buried her face in her knees.

'Tell me, or we watch them.'

Eve pulled her arms over her head, desperate to disappear. 'Please.'

'Fine. Up next is... drum roll, please... Amelia!'

'He was different with her,' Eve blurted out.

'Go on.'

'She was, she...'

'She was fat,' Angel said, as a statement of fact.

Again, Eve glanced over her shoulder, though not far enough to see. Something in the tone of the voice seemed familiar somehow.

'Tell me how he was different,' Angel demanded, sounding angry suddenly.

'He was cruel,' Eve said, her mouth turning down at the memory of what she knew to be true, even at the time. 'He directed Amelia's movies differently to mine.'

'How so?'

Eve hugged her knees tighter, wishing she could disappear, just like her sister had. 'He'd tell the boy to be rough with her,' she said into her knees. 'To slap her, bite her...' She took a sharp breath in.

'And?'

'He used to make squealing sounds, like a pig.' Her voice was a high-pitched whine. She'd sat and listened to Peter's excitement growing and growing the rougher they got with Amelia. The weight of it, of all that had happened in this house, was the reason why Eve could never leave it. She simply couldn't carry it all, and there was no leaving any of it behind.

'Mm. And you think that was worse than what he did to you?'

Eve counted her breathing for a minute, unsure if she could go on. But if there was even a chance that she could get to Amelia... even for a minute, then... 'At least he let me fall in love.' That was the only way she could make sense of any of it.

Angel laughed loudly, seeming genuinely amused. Of all the things Eve was expecting, laughter was not one of them. 'Is that what you think?'

Eve's face darkened. Who was this bloody *Angel*? And why question Eve's love for Sparrow or Sparrow's love for her? *How* could anyone question that, unless they'd been there? Unless they knew something that Eve didn't?

'You don't fall in love while being forced to fuck for the camera, Eve.'

Eve's stomach groaned violently and before she had time to react, or prepare in any way, she vomited on the floor beside her, splashing her jeans and her hands, too.

'Finally,' Angel bellowed triumphantly, 'a *normal* response.'

'Who are you?' She gagged, wiping her mouth on her sleeve.

'All in good time, Eve. We have so much more to see.'

31

'What do you want?' she cried, her face wet with tears and saliva. 'Why are you doing this?'

'Tell me how much you loved Sparrow.' There was curiosity in Angel's voice, but also a hint of a challenge. A challenge to make it somehow believable.

But Eve could talk about her love for Sparrow all day. It was painful, because of what that love cost both of them, but it was love all the same. 'You talk like you've seen more of these movies,' Eve said, her voice low and her breathing coming a little steadier now that her body had purged itself. And she was on somewhat steadier ground with Sparrow.

'I'm acquainted with them, yes.'

She closed her eyes while Angel spoke. She *knew* that tone of voice. 'That one, the movie we just watched, that was my first,' Eve continued, wanting now to get this over with. 'But like you said, it wasn't the first time Peter had done that.'

'Go on.'

'No one ever talked about it, because they were too scared. Peter threatened everything, but his favourite one was that he'd make sure the kid's real family never wanted them back.' She paused for a moment then, remembering. 'He threatened to inject Amelia with heroin once.' She lowered her head again. 'He promised her a life of addiction and prostitution on the streets. Something she had a real fear of, because Ellen loved to use that one, too. But then Robin came along.'

'Let's talk about Robin too then, shall we?' Angel said, ignoring the rest.

Eve was sure the end of this torture would spell death for her. What else could the endgame be? And what did she have to lose? She might as well purge her memories, as well as her body. Say it all out loud for the first time in her life. She started talking, before she couldn't.

'The way Robin described it was awful.' She spoke into her knees, but her words were clear enough to render the so-called Angel in the corner, quiet. 'She was made to do that with all different boys. Not just one. And some of those boys were horrible.' She closed her eyes again and tried to picture Sparrow's face. She begged for his help in getting through this. 'But Peter did it to Robin loads of times as well. He was never on camera, but sometimes, she had to do it with him first, as well as making a movie with one of the boys in the same day.'

'What did you do when Robin told you about it?'

Eve shook her head. 'Nothing,' she whispered.

'Why not?' The question wasn't accusatory. Perhaps Angel just wanted to hear her say it.

'Because if I told, and Robin was taken away, then I'd be the only one left.' The delicate and puffy skin around her eyes cried out in protest as she rubbed them dry again. 'Ellen kept saying that if one more girl cried wolf, that she'd be the last one. So that only left me.'

'But it wasn't just you, was it? There was Amelia... and Pennie.'

She shook her head. 'Amelia was old enough to leave and Pennie... well, I don't think she was here then.' She frowned, trying to remember, and she shook her head again. 'Or if she was, then she was just a baby. Peter liked us older. So that only left me, and I had nowhere else to go.'

'So, you weren't surprised when Robin told you what he was doing?'

She shook her head again. 'For so long, I didn't know exactly *what* was happening to the girls inside that room,' she said truthfully. 'I was too young to know for sure. No one had ever given us the birds and the bees talk, if you know what I mean.' She inhaled a long breath, held it and exhaled slowly and shakily. 'But I knew *something* was happening. Something bad. I knew girls before they went in there and...' she paused again, trying to form the words, 'and then I saw how different they were after. Like, a girl would walk into that room and a ghost would come out.' She wiped her painful eyes again. 'I didn't want that to be me, so I kept my mouth shut.'

There was silence in the attic then, aside from Eve's gentle sobs.

'But it was you, wasn't it?' Angel said after a few moments, but Eve didn't respond. 'Go on,' Angel said after another brief silence. 'Back to Robin.'

Eve blew out another long breath and nodded. 'After Robin left—'

'Was killed, you mean,' Angel corrected, sucking the air out of the already stifling room. 'After Robin was *killed*.'

Eve could feel herself starting to hyperventilate.

'Do you feel like that was your fault?' Angel asked, when Eve was unable to continue.

Eve nodded without hesitation, desperately trying to fill her lungs with some of the stagnant air around her.

'Why?'

'Her screaming,' she said, not giving herself time to think. Or to clam up. 'I made such a big thing of it.' Her chest tightened and she brought her hand to her sternum, panic rising up with it. 'I attacked Ellen because of it.' She heaved. 'I did it in front of a normal kid from another house. That was the worst thing I could have done as a Raven's Rock kid. I drew attention. The one thing we were always warned *never* to do.'

'Millie Grace,' Angel said knowingly.

Eve froze. 'You were here, weren't you?' she asked at last.

'What happened after that?'

Eve shrugged. 'Millie was sent home, and I was locked in my room.'

'Who else was here?'

'My sister, Amelia. She was sent to her room, too. Then very early the next morning, I was woken up and taken to Kerry with Ellen.'

'Yes, but should I tell you what happened in the meantime? Would you like to know?'

Eve's body stiffened. She held her breath and stayed perfectly still, waiting with her lungs on fire. How could anyone know what happened next, when even *she* didn't know that?

'While you were in your room, Ellen went to Robin. She was still screaming, as I'm sure you remember.' Angel didn't wait for an answer. 'But then Ellen had the genius idea to place a pillow over Robin's face to shut her up.'

Eve remembered now. She lay on her bed with her hands jammed against her ears, trying to block out the girl's shrieks. Her own anger had boiled over like never before and all she wanted was for Robin to shut up. Then suddenly, she did. Eve didn't even question it. Not that night at least. Instead, she lolled into the deepest sleep she'd had in months.

'Did you ever wonder why only *you* were taken to Kerry, and not Amelia?'

She had. Of course she had. But when she'd asked, she was told that Amelia had work to do. That her older sister couldn't come.

Again, Angel didn't wait. 'While you were taken away on a holiday, Amelia was pulled from her bed and forced to dig a hole in the garden. She was made to dig a grave for a girl who was suffering the same abuse that she had for years.'

Eve's crying became childlike then, loud and unbridled.

'Did you hear that, Eve? *Years.*'

When she could think again, she realised that the only thing that made sense here was that Angel really did know Amelia and had heard all of this from her. It was the only thing that made sense.

'Is she alive?' she asked at last.

'Amelia?'

Eve nodded.

She heard a loud exhale then. 'Amelia watched Peter carrying that girl out of the house and dropping her into the hole he'd made *her* dig with him.' The voice sounded sad now, too, and Eve realised that Angel must actually have loved Amelia. Must *love* Amelia. Why else would anyone be this invested in what happened here? 'You could say that Amelia died that night. Or she certainly became someone else entirely.'

'Is she—' Eve tried.

'So back to Sparrow,' Angel cut her off, the voice growing stronger again.

Eve blinked at the sudden change and her thoughts scrambled to keep up.

'You say that you were allowed to fall in love. Tell me about that? Tell me what that love meant.'

Eve brought her hands to her face and could feel the solid length of the knife handle inside her sleeve. She thought briefly about what she could do with that knife. She could lunge for that dark corner and hope for the best. But she had no strength in her body and the will to do so was gone. Plus, if there was a chance, no matter how small, that this could lead her to Amelia, then she had to take that chance.

'When Peter made me... when I...' She couldn't formulate the words.

'I think we all know what he made you do,' Angel said, allowing her to skip over the sordid details.

'Did you watch the Amelia movies?' she asked.

She heard a sharp intake of breath behind her, which she took as a yes.

'So you know how he... *directed* her ones,' she said, before Angel had a chance to respond. Not that she had any illusions of control here, but she did want to get the story out in a way that required the least amount of explanation. 'Mine were different,' she continued. 'And Sparrow, well...' She pressed her knuckles into her sternum to ease the ongoing pain in her chest. 'He'd just look straight into my eyes the whole time.' She closed her eyes to see him again. 'When I cried,' she shook her head, 'his face became more...' How could she describe this? 'More intense. He'd look at me with defiance when I cried. Like he was trying to pass some of his strength into me. When I wasn't crying, those eyes made me feel like it was just me and him in that room. Like we were there because we wanted to be.' She wiped her eyes again. 'Sparrow could make the whole world disappear. He made me feel...' She lowered her head onto her knees again.

'Loved,' the shadow in the corner finished for her.

Eve nodded, whether it could be seen in the darkness or not.

'He did love you,' Angel continued.

Eve held her breath again, and when no elaboration came, she asked, 'You knew him?'

There was a sound from behind her then. Angel was moving, getting up from the floor. Eve tensed and gripped the knife again, her mind racing ahead, trying to anticipate what was about to happen. She closed her eyes as heavy footsteps started towards her. She was still sitting on the floor, facing away. But the footsteps kept coming and, in no time at all, she could feel someone standing over her. She could hear them breathing.

When Eve opened her eyes, they came level with a pair of knees, clad in black, utilitarian pants. Angel. The imaginary friend was not only very real, but was standing less than two feet from her. But she dared not look up. Only when Angel bent and came eye to eye with Eve would she have sworn that her heart actually stopped beating.

'You,' she said, in total disbelief.

'Me,' Nicole Hammond responded.

32

Nicole hunched down beside her, pulling some sort of box away from her mouth. Whatever it was had been distorting the sound of her voice, making it sound deep and gravelly, like a heavy smoker, or a robot. It must have been the lilt to her words that Eve had found familiar, and not the voice itself. Nicole was holding up a tiny remote control and pointing it to the projector behind Eve. 'I'd like another chapter. Wouldn't you?'

Eve looked at the woman she'd stupidly let herself fantasise about. The woman she imagined sharing her home and her life with. Deep down, she always knew it was a trick and yet she still let herself imagine. Stupid, stupid Eve.

'Before we see any more, let's talk about Sparrow some more, yeah?'

'Why are you doing this?' Eve's voice sounded different now. Almost child-like, the way it always did when she found herself on the receiving end of someone with more power than she had. Power over *her*. 'Why didn't you just ask me when we met before? Why *this*?'

'Ask you what?' Nicole asked.

'Whatever this is about.' Finally, Eve felt a flare of anger and wondered where it had been. She'd been made to think she was losing her mind. 'Why didn't you just ask me?! Why all that stuff with Pennie? And why are you making me watch these tapes?' Her voice rose again as she gestured towards the paused recording on the wall behind Nicole. Thankfully, she'd paused it as the camera panned across the featureless wall, and not on Eve's fumbling nudity. 'Don't you think I see enough every time I close my damn eyes?' she cried, roughly tapping the side of her head.

'It's not the kind of thing you can *really* get into over a pot of tea in Costa, is it?'

'But I...'

'You watch television, don't you, Eve? In just about every American TV programme, someone is off to see their shrink. Did you ever notice that?' She didn't wait for Eve to answer. 'I looked into that, you know. Shrinks, I mean. They cost a bloody fortune, and the outcome is always the same. They spend months beating around the bush, but it's not until the person on the couch confronts every horrible thing in their lives that they can heal.' She paused then and stood up. 'Well, I don't believe in beating around the bush, and even if I did, we don't have time for that.' She stepped around Eve and moved back to her spot by the wall. 'You need to see your life for what it actually was. Only then can anyone begin to heal.'

Eve buried her face in her hands and shook her head.

'I think this is my chapter,' Nicole said.

And that's when Eve thought about Pennie. Nicole Hammond's words were those being spoken by Pennie. 'Why did you have to get Pennie involved? Where is she?'

'You left me with no choice, but don't worry about Pennie. She was listening to some Ariana Grande while you spoke to me.' She smiled then, holding up the kind of charging case that came with Bluetooth earbuds. 'Good idea with the nanny cams, by the way. They kind of took the thinking out of this for me.'

Eve's head was starting to hurt. The pain that had been absent for hours was on its way back, sending her thoughts scrambling once more. Who was Nicole Hammond, really? All the times Eve had stared at that face and imagined it when she wasn't there. She was sure she would have remembered her had she been at Raven's Rock. Yet there *was* something familiar about her.

'I can see your confusion,' Nicole said, lowering herself onto her backside and moving around again so she was sitting beside Eve, facing the projected image on the wall. 'I promise, it'll all become clear before the night is through. But like I said, it's time for another chapter. And it's my turn to speak.'

Eve covered her face with both hands and exhaled noisily into them. She nodded and waited for it to start.

'I didn't tell you the whole truth about who I was. But I never lied to you either. Sparrow was my friend. I hadn't seen him for years, but then one day, there he was. Back in my life and he was clean the last time I saw him. That's when he told me what you did. And I believed him.' She leaned forward then to look Eve in the eye. 'If you loved him like you say you did, then you'll know that he was nothing if not completely honest about himself. Always.'

'What did he tell you?' Eve asked, her words muffled by the palms of her hands.

'He told me what you had him do six years ago. I can only wish he'd found me and told me at the time, then maybe we wouldn't all be in this mess.'

Eve pulled her hands slowly away from her face, but she didn't look at her. She couldn't. She feared Nicole Hammond now. Not that she might hurt her. Eve had been hurt so many times that she didn't fear that any more. She didn't even care that the woman might kill her. She seemed personally involved enough that she should want to and, honestly, *that* would be an ease now. What Eve feared were her motives. Was she going to use this information to hurt Pennie further? Was she just going to dangle Amelia in front of her and then let Eve die without ever knowing what happened to her? What *actually* happened, as opposed to what her mind, and her experiences, *told* her had happened?

'You had him kill Peter for you,' Nicole said, like this was something everyone knew.

Eve was shaking her head before Nicole had even finished her sentence. Her lip trembled but it seemed she'd finally run out of tears.

'More than a year after he'd managed to leave this place behind for good, wasn't it?'

Eve still didn't respond, but just kept shaking her head, eyes trained on the wall ahead. On the frozen, projected image of the dirty old wall in the dirty old Room.

'Peter died six years ago. So why now?'

'You think anyone gave a shit when Peter died? No one mourned him, Eve. But I didn't know about Jack's involvement and what that did to him. By the time I found out, Jack only had a few days left to live. Course, neither of us knew that either, did we?'

Eve kept her eyes straight ahead on the wall as Nicole's glare burned the side of her face.

'He managed to get a job for himself,' she continued after a quiet moment.

'A chance at a normal life and you knew that, didn't you? The Nuts 'N' Bolts Hardware Store, which came with room and board upstairs. He'd cleaned himself up and was turning his life around.' Nicole paused and tilted her head, trying again to meet Eve's eyes. But Eve refused to give her that. 'The owners of that place were good to him. They saw a lad who was just aged out of the system, who needed a hand up, and they gave it to him.' She reached out and took Eve's face in her firm hand and made her look at her finally. But Eve pulled her face away and buried it in her bent-up knees. 'But you found him,' Nicole continued. 'Of course you did. You sought him out, found him and cried on his shoulder about what Peter was doing to you since he left. How he was being starved for girls, now that Raven's Rock weren't being sent any more, and how it was all about you now.'

'Why shouldn't I get some help?' Eve all but screamed, her burning red eyes looking right at Nicole now. Who the hell did she think she was, this do-gooder who'd probably never known the kind of vulnerability that kids like Eve lived with constantly? 'Everyone else got to leave, but never me!' she cried with renewed ferocity.

'Why didn't you leave!' Nicole raised her voice to match Eve's now and threw her arms up in defeat. 'Why the fuck didn't you just walk out the door? That was *your* choice!' She jabbed a finger into Eve's chest.

Eve had no answer for that. She clearly remembered the night before her eighteenth birthday, when she'd packed all her belongings into a bag, ready to go the following day. Then Peter reminded her about what happened to homeless girls her age, and how their bodies became public toilets for the men of the city. Her birthday passed and then another day, and another. Then one year rolled into the next, Eve asking herself all the time when she was planning to leave. But it never happened. She never had the guts.

'Why didn't you ever tell? The cops, I mean, or social services? Not that bitch who dropped us all off here, then turned her back on the place, but I mean...'

Eve laughed a bitter laugh then. 'Do you want to know how many Raven's Rock kids went to social services? Hmm? Because at least one of them is buried under that wall at the back of this house. And as for the police?' She snorted a sarcastic huff of a laugh. 'They fucking loved the Hollands. They thought Ellen was some kind of saint, taking in the kinds of kids that they took hell from every day. They didn't listen to *us*. They weren't going to help *me*!'

'But Jack would,' Nicole said, her tone flat like her point was made.

'Fuck you,' Eve uncharacteristically growled.

'You were right when you said that he loved you.' Nicole rubbed her face wearily. 'But even *he* knew how twisted that love was. How fucking toxic. So, when you went to him and told him that Peter was hurting you, you knew what he'd do. God knows, he talked about it often enough, didn't he? Back in the day.'

'You would have talked about it, too, if you'd lived here,' Eve mumbled, lowering her head again, her breathing coming a little easier at last, and her hammering heart slowing, beat by beat. There was no point in shouting or trying to make her see. How could she? But Eve suddenly saw why Ellen Holland held reporters with such contempt. They thought they knew so much. When really, they knew nothing at all.

'I'm sure,' Nicole continued. 'But talking about it is one thing. Sitting in a stolen car and driving it to where someone works, then waiting for them to cross the road before shoving your boot to the floor and mowing them down... well, that's something else entirely, isn't it?'

'I didn't know he was going to do that,' Eve said unconvincingly. Almost sulkily.

'Sure you did. You knew that Sparrow blamed himself as much as Peter for those videos. He couldn't control his hard-on after all, could he?'

'Yeah, well, he paid the price, didn't he?'

'Who – Peter or Sparrow?'

'The only way Peter will pay is if he's still screaming and burning alive in hell.' Eve looked up, the venom back in her voice.

'Ah, yes. Well, Sparrow certainly paid, didn't he? Locked up in a place guaranteed to get him back on the gear. Then of course, there were the nightmares. He already had enough of those, but Sparrow was no killer. Not until you made him one.'

Eve said nothing. She just breathed heavily into her knees. Her eyes felt painfully raw, but a kind of numbness came over the rest of her. That was it. That was the worst part of her life's story. Yes, she'd gotten young Robin killed by creating such a... fuss about her. But knowing that she'd destroyed Sparrow? That was the beginning of the end for Eve. Nicole was right in everything she was saying.

'If you had just stayed away, gotten *yourself* away, then Sparrow could have made a real life for himself and so could you.' This was beginning to feel like a lecture now. A *consequences of your actions* type that came with a wagging finger. 'You just had to pop back into Sparrow's life, and once you did that...' she jabbed her finger in her chest again, '*you* turned him into a killer.' Nicole rocked slightly then, her gaze intensifying on Eve, who still refused to look at her. 'But that's not all you did, is it? In fact, watching these, I'm sure anyone would understand why you took that to Jack's door.' She touched her fingers to Eve's chin and lifted it, so that she was looking at her whether she wanted to or not. 'But you've done a lot more since then, Eve, haven't you, hmm?'

Eve sat rigidly still now, in the same position she'd been in for some time – knees pulled up to her chest, her chin still in Nicole's hand. Nicole said nothing more for a few long minutes before letting her go. Then she just sat there, studying Eve. Like all the answers she ever wanted might flow from her at any minute. But Eve had nothing left to give. She wanted to ask about Pennie, for her to be spared all of this, but she didn't give Nicole that satisfaction. She wanted to ask about Amelia, to beg for information, but she didn't for the same reason. Instead, she forced herself to be still and be quiet. To say nothing at all to this woman. Perhaps Nicole sensed her resolve, because when she did move again, it was to reach into the box beside her and pull out another old VCR tape. Eve had no idea what was on this one, but bile rose up her throat at the idea of reliving another awful day from her past. A past she shared with so many, yet felt completely alone in. But she swallowed it down and braced herself with the reminder that they were gone. They couldn't hurt her any more. They couldn't hurt any of them.

Nicole reached behind her and switched out the tapes and, when she pressed play, Eve knew from the angle of the recording being projected onto the wall in front of her that this wasn't one she'd seen before. Her stomach fell so suddenly that an involuntary sound escaped her lips and she had to press her hands to the floor on either side to steady herself.

Eve was not a religious woman. She knew that no God would allow homes like theirs to exist, and yet she found herself praying, begging the universe not to do this. But the universe never listened to Eve and when Ellen Holland moved across the screen, she knew that in the next couple of minutes, everything would change again.

33

'Where did you get this?' Eve asked in utter disbelief. She felt nauseated, and the dull *thud, thud, thud* of her headache made her want to scream for all of it to stop. But how many times had she done that before? Screamed for the end of something awful to come, when all it ever achieved was, well, nothing. Screaming never made anything stop, except maybe Robin's life. Screaming made that stop, but nothing else. She closed her eyes and squeezed her temples, reminding herself of the times she decided *not* to scream, and instead to act mute and unresponsive. Those times used to frustrate Peter so much and that frustration was the closest thing to a win that Eve could ever expect. So perhaps that's what she needed to do now. Just, not respond to what she suspected this might be. Or, to *her*.

'You didn't know about these other cameras, did you?' Nicole Hammond continued. 'Peter installed them in every room.' Nicole looked at her then to see a reaction that wasn't there. 'How do you think he always knew what went on in the house while he was out?'

Eve kept her eyes on the screen and the palms of her hands to the side of her head, applying just enough pressure to lessen the thud. Judging by what she was seeing, this camera was either in, or close to, the smoke detector on the ceiling down on the landing. Eve remembered Peter installing those smoke alarms in every room. There was one over Eve's bed, one over Ellen and Peter's bed. There was one over Pennie's bed and one over the bed in The Room. Had he been watching them the whole time? Even when he was out of the house and they thought they had some respite from him. Was he *always* there, watching?

'Ah. There she is, boot an' all.' Nicole's voice came from behind her again. She'd moved back and she sounded almost jovial. But it was all an act. Eve knew that now. None of her many emotions were real, except for the anger that she was just about managing to keep in check. But Eve could sense it. She suspected that Nicole Hammond, whoever she really was and whatever reasons she had for being here, despised the Hollands almost as much as any of the Raven's Rock kids had.

'But you can't do that! What about me and Pennie?' Eve recognised her own, whiny voice coming from the recording.

'They even had sound.' Nicole sounded almost impressed. But again, it was an act and no longer a very good one.

'Oh, don't be so fucking stupid, Eve.' Ellen Holland's voice boomed from beyond the grave. 'This house has brought me nothing but fucking ulcers and that auctioneer's ad in the paper said that they're *desperately* looking for houses like this one. I'm selling it, whether you like it or not. It's time I retired to the sun and started looking after *myself* for once! Now you're an adult and that freakish little runt is *your* problem, not mine.' She turned to face Eve then, with her signature snide look on her face. The one she got when she was about to spit nails instead of words. 'You're wondering how you'll manage without my ongoing charity, aren't you? Well, your mother was a whore. You know that. *Everyone* knows that. Her first instinct was to wrap her mangey legs around any man who went within six feet of her. Pick that up,' she ordered Eve, who only now came into view, carrying a load of dirty laundry from Ellen and Peter's bedroom. She bent to pick up the towel she'd dropped from her bundle.

'No, I...?' Eve watched herself and wondered if she was really that miserable-looking. Small for her age and slightly underweight at that time. Dirty, ragged hair and a clueless expression on her face.

Ellen sighed impatiently. 'Why are you pretending not to know this? Your mother was a whore and the apple didn't fall far, did it? Now if you're trying to tell me that you have no memory of fucking my husband and then shoving his bastard child out of you, then you really are as stupid as you look.' She held her hands up in surrender then. 'But that's not my problem any more, is it. Now all you have to do is start charging for your services and you'll be able to put some sort of a roof over your heads, I'm sure. And then when the time comes, your daughter *I'm sure* will be happy to follow in your footsteps. I have no doubt you'll both be fine. But either way, I'd suggest you start thinking about where you're going to go, because this house will sell fast, and I'll be on the Costa del Sol by the end of the month.'

'But Pennie's my sister.' The past-tense version of Eve stammered like an idiot, while present-tense Eve frowned in confusion.

She brought her hands to her face. 'Turn it off,' she said, her tone flat and muffled.

'Shh,' Nicole said with exaggerated dramatics. 'We're just getting to the good part.'

She didn't need to look at the twisted home movie to see Ellen's face contorting, that snide and cruel way that it did when she was taking pleasure in someone's pain. She could see it as clearly now with her eyes closed, as if she were back on that landing, on that day. She heard her voice in her mind, as well as filling the room around her.

'Pennie's my sister?' Ellen said, mocking Eve's tone. 'You dumb bitch. You don't fool me.' Ellen's face changed then and her hatred for Eve was as clear as day when she jabbed a finger and hissed, 'I know what my husband was like. But he's gone now and I'm done wasting what's left of my life in this godforsaken house. Why should I spend the rest of my days looking at the filthy fruits of his fucking loins?' She turned towards the stairs, shaking her head. 'No. I'm done. So you have until the house sells to pack your shit and get out.'

'Turn it off!' Eve shouted, as the same rage that filled her that day threatened to take her over again.

'I get it,' Nicole said from behind her. 'That bitch knew what he was doing and she blamed *you* for it. She was happy enough to keep you on as her personal housekeeper and help spend your benefits for you. I'll bet she made you hand it over to her each week, yeah? But only so long as it suited her, right? I get why you—'

'No!' She was all but snarling now as she watched her slightly younger self dropping the load of laundry, her eyes ablaze with fury. Eve straightened her back defiantly and lifted her head. She watched with wide-open eyes, as another version of herself charged the woman who raised her. She watched as she slammed her scrawny body into the much larger one, who was standing at the top of the stairs with a clumsy boot on her right foot. She watched as Ellen lost her balance, seeing it with a clarity that had eluded her in her memories. A small, almost imperceptible smile played at the corner of Eve's mouth. Ellen never saw it coming. She didn't even scream as her body tumbled down the stairs and came to rest at a most unnatural angle between the bottom step and the front door. It all happened so fast on the day that Eve's memory of it had always been hazy. She never expected to see it play out before her like this and, if she had, she could never have expected the way it made her feel. Calm and at peace.

They both sat there for a few silent moments, watching the naïve and arguably institutionalised woman on-screen. For countless minutes, she just stood there, at the top of the stairs looking down, her shoulders, her whole body, rising and falling dramatically with her heavy breathing. If she felt any sense of panic in that moment, it didn't show. Shock, perhaps. But not panic.

'And that,' Nicole Hammond said at last, 'was the day when the old Eve Holland became someone else entirely, too.'

Eve didn't respond as she remembered the enormous and conflicting feelings from that day, as she stood at the top of those stairs, looking down. Fear. Elation. Uncertainty and, yes, a hint of panic. And of course, indecision about what to do. Should she run away? Call Ashley Evans? Call emergency services? The rising and falling of her entire body now almost perfectly matched the other version of her, who would forever find herself standing at the top of those stairs.

'Do *you* want to tell the rest of this story, Eve? Or should we just keep going the way we are?'

'I made the right choice,' she said, more to herself than to Nicole.

Nicole didn't answer.

'You probably think I should have run away. It was the perfect opportunity. But where would I have gone?'

'Anywhere but here?' Nicole supplied, her tone questioning. She wanted to know why she hadn't.

Eve shook her head, but kept her eyes on the screen. That Eve was still standing in the same spot. 'Then I would have become exactly what she said I would. I'd have had no choice. I'd have been out on the street and I would have had to survive somehow. Plus...' She paused.

'Plus, what?'

'How could I have cared for my sister if I was whoring on the street?'

'Your sister?' Nicole asked, her tone softer suddenly.

'Yes. Pennie.'

There was a silent beat before Nicole said, 'Do you really not remember, Eve?'

Eve buried her face in her knees again, a shiver running through her suddenly.

Nicole went rummaging in the box again before returning to Eve's side. She placed a folded, yellowing newspaper clipping in Eve's lap. 'Look at that.'

Eve glanced and then looked away.

Nicole picked it up and shook it in front of Eve's face. 'Look at it!'

Eve snatched it from her and looked.

Hottest Summer on Record! the headline boldly announced. Below it was a short paragraph about the soaring temperatures and something about it being the perfect time to holiday at home. A photograph took up the entire width of the page: two smiling little boys in a holiday-caravan site. They were squinting in the sun and licking massive, dripping ice-cream cones.

'What?' Eve asked, disinterested. Raven's Rock children didn't get ice-cream cones. Eve didn't know those smug little boys.

Nicole pointed to a spot on the photo, behind the two boys. A heavyset woman walking from her car to the open door of their rented caravan. Bright green with a yellow stripe wrapped all the way around it. Standing in the doorway of that caravan was thirteen-year-old Eve.

Eve pulled the page closer to her, her face screwed up in confusion. That was definitely Ellen coming from the car. And the girl in the doorway looked a lot like Eve. She even remembered that awful, baggy denim dress that Ellen made her wear from her own wardrobe. But beneath the dress, that swollen belly...

Eve rolled up the paper and threw it as far as she could.

'You don't remember?' Nicole asked very softly now, as if understanding had just arrived in the room.

'I didn't *make* Sparrow do anything,' Eve said, dismissing what she'd just seen. She glanced over her shoulder to see Nicole Hammond staring at her, pity all over her face. 'Is that it? *That's* why you're here?' Eve swivelled slightly so she could look at her then. She was almost completely lost in the shadows, but Eve could see the shape of her clearly. She was sitting with her back to the wall again, her forearms resting on her bent knees. Was she crying? 'A heroin addict killed the man who abused him,' Eve went on. 'And I *accidentally* caused the death of the woman who let that man abuse *all* of us. *That's* your reason for stalking me and my sister? For creeping around inside my house for days on end and for—'

'No.' Nicole cut her off. 'That's not why I'm here.'

'Why then?' Eve demanded.

Nicole dug the heels of her hands into her eyes and Eve couldn't tell if it was because she was crying, or if it was out of tiredness, or frustration. 'I'm here because...' She exhaled and dropped her hands away from her face. 'I'm here to put an end to it all. I'm here to make it stop and to finally, *finally* tell you the truth.'

34

Eve sat and quietly watched her. To her left, Nicole Hammond, *Angel*, watched her back. To her right, the movie played on, and past-tense Eve Holland had just begun her descent of the stairs. Eve didn't need to watch that any more, but *she* was another matter. Eve took a moment to realise that her headache was gone. It vanished so suddenly that she wondered if she'd imagined having it in the first place. Her thoughts had gradually slowed down, too. At last, they moved at a pace she could keep up with. 'Who are you?' she asked at last. But this time, there was no fear or panic in her question. No desperation, either. Just curiosity.

'I am Angel,' Nicole replied.

'Who are you really?' Eve asked, in the same level tone.

'I am Nicole Hammond.'

'But who *are* you? Why would an unknown journalist go to such elaborate lengths, breaking,' she shook her head and shrugged, 'God knows how many laws, just to confront me with my past? And if you're an angel,' she huffed out a humourless laugh, 'then you're a pretty shitty one because you're twenty years too late coming to this house.'

She didn't respond, but she still watched Eve casually from the shadows.

'So, who *are* you?'

'You're wrong,' she said at last. 'I'm not here just to confront you with your past. In fact, we're not talking about your past at all, really. This,' she waved her hand around, 'is very much about the here and now.'

Eve reached over and pulled a videotape from the box between them. 'Really?' She held it up, tilting it so she could see the label. *This Little Piggy* was scratched on it in faded blue ink. Eve waved it in front of Nicole. 'Really? So we're just watching these for fun, are we? Is this how you get your kicks?' There was anger in her voice, but she didn't feel it much. Not really. These tapes didn't have that effect on her any more, but she wanted to turn the tables on *Angel* a little bit. Make *her* feel uncomfortable for a minute.

Nicole tilted her head to read the label, then she looked away.

Eve, sensing that she had in fact succeeded, pressed on. 'Oh, you'd like this one.' She held it towards her. 'Go on. Put it on. Let me introduce you to my sister, Amelia.'

'Mm. This little piggy,' Nicole said quietly and it seemed as though a blanket of depression had come down upon her.

Eve's slightly manic smile fell away, and she looked harder at Nicole, desperate to see through the darkness. To see her face clearly and to be able to study it in a way that she'd been too self-conscious to before. Who *was* she? It was the only question Eve wanted the answer to now. She lowered her eyes to the tape in her hand. She knew this one and it was particularly vile. Her sister, Amelia, being abused at Peter's direction. Eve frowned and glanced up at Nicole's darkened face again. She tried to remember the boy in this video, but she couldn't see his face either. 'Is it you?' she asked at last. Nicole had the frame of someone who could once have been a boy. Eve watched television. She knew how these things could be done. How routinely boys became girls and vice versa these days.

Nicole looked sharply at her.

'It is, isn't it?' Eve all but whispered. How could she not have known? Eve thought she remembered all of them, but even sitting directly across from Nicole Hammond, she didn't recognise her at all. 'You're the boy in this video,' she mumbled.

Nicole threw her head back and laughed then. An unsettlingly hearty laugh, a version of which she was sure she'd heard before.

'Why is that funny?' she asked sadly and Nicole stopped as suddenly as she'd started. 'You suffered, too,' Eve said softly, her anger melting away. 'We *all* suffered here, Angel.' She called her by her chosen name, and she could tell that this surprised her. But she wasn't thinking about that any more. She understood now. '*That's* why you're here, isn't it? It's the path you were put on and that isn't your fault.' She exhaled as steadily as she could. 'They set us all on a path and none of them led to anywhere good. It's not your fault. It's none of our fault,' Eve said, her tears returning as she gave Nicole a wet smile, her eyes conveying her sincerity and her sudden understanding.

Nicole was staring at her so quietly that Eve wondered if she was holding her breath. When she finally spoke, her words seemed like they were carefully measured. Controlled, even. 'You haven't watched this in a while, have you?'

'Why would I want to?' she asked, all her hostility gone now, too. Angel was one of her brothers. Or at least, she *had* been, and it hurt Eve that she didn't remember which one.

Nicole looked at the video in her hand, before flinging it back into the box. 'Because if you had, then you'd know that the boy in that video wasn't me, Eve. It was Henry Carver.'

35

Nicole was right. Of course it was Henry. He and Amelia were paired up more often than not for no reason other than they were both deemed to be overweight. There were people out there who loved that shit. Just like there were people out there who paid for Eve and Sparrow's love story. That's what Peter said once, pretty much word for word. Henry was a nice kid really. Quiet and self-conscious, which Eve always thought was unusual for a boy. Either he was the only boy she'd ever met who had issues with his body image, or he was the only one who didn't know how to mask them. But for those who'd never lived with Henry Carver, and instead only saw him on those recordings, they would think him a beast. A big bully who hated the girl beneath him, because that's the character that Peter created, while Amelia was just worthless livestock. Their time in The Room had as much of an effect on Henry as it had on Amelia. He hated himself, pure and simple. He always gave weeping apologies to a curled-up and unresponsive Amelia afterwards, when Peter had gone, but eventually, he gave that up, along with most other things. He gave up speaking at all for the most part. He just moved through life in an automated fashion, going where he was told to go, when he was told to go there and then doing exactly what he was told to do. Nothing more. Henry Carver was never a particularly happy person. But Raven's Rock utterly destroyed him.

'He's dead because of these videos, isn't he?' Angel asked.

Eve nodded. 'Probably.'

'There is no "probably", Eve. If anyone were to look through this box, what do you think they'd find?'

Eve shrugged, her eyes on the box and the teetering pile of old video cassettes inside it. 'I think they'd find a whole lot of suffering. More than anyone should ever have to endure.'

'Mm.' Angel nodded in agreement. 'What else would they find?'

Eve glanced at her, but only briefly. 'What else *is* there?'

'Oh, I don't know. A whole lot of dead people, perhaps?'

Eve frowned, remembering. 'Where's Pennie?'

'Why are they dead, Eve?'

'Why are you asking me that?'

'Henry Carver, Leslie-Anne Williams, or Leslie Granger, as others know her. What about Sparrow? And Brian Merriman, he's in here, too, isn't he?'

Eve struggled to her feet as pins and needles assailed the entire lower half of her body. Her legs refused to work properly, and she hobbled in the general direction of the hatch leading down to the landing. Where *was* Pennie? She hadn't heard a sound down there since Pennie had directed Eve to climb into the attic. So where did she go?

'Is there someone else down there?' Eve looked sharply at Angel, with another hint of panic. She'd distracted her from Pennie. Why had she let her do that?

'Pennie is safe, Eve.'

'You didn't answer my question,' she demanded, fingering the knife in her sleeve again.

'And you didn't answer mine.' Angel got to her feet as well. 'I can kind of understand Brian Merriman. He always seemed a little *too* enthusiastic during his time in The Room with Robin, didn't he. And,' she took a small step towards Eve, 'he came to see you, didn't he?'

Eve was ignoring her now, moving ever closer to the open hatch. She tried to block out the sound of Nicole's voice and instead listen for sounds coming from below.

'The day he died,' Angel continued, 'he came here to tell you that he was sorry.' She laughed then, but there was no humour in it. 'Cycled all the way from fucking Waterford, ten years too late, to apologise!' She stepped around to see Eve's face, but Eve refused to look at her.

Eve was leaning over the hatch, thinking about jumping down and wondering what Angel would do if she did that. Was there someone down there holding a knife to Pennie's throat or something? Would they hurt her if Eve ran away? Or if she hurt Angel?

'I get it,' Angel continued. 'People should just go away and turn their lives around in private, right? Fuck that making-amends shit. That only dredges it all back up for other people. Isn't that right, Eve?' She leaned towards Eve and lowered her voice to a conspiratorial level. 'It might even get you killed.'

Eve couldn't wait another minute. She had to take the risk and go find her sister. She lowered herself quickly into a sitting position, her legs dangling through the hatch. She took one look at Angel, almost daring her to do something about it, then she dropped down into the linen press. Eve landed in a crumpled heap, but quickly recovered herself and hurried to Pennie's room.

'Pennie?' she called, rushing through the bedroom door, which was ajar.

There was a loud thump as Angel came down through the hatch behind her. Seconds later, she appeared at Pennie's bedroom door, and as she did, another sound came from somewhere else in the house. A glass, or something falling over and smashing, downstairs. Eve froze. She looked from Angel to the space behind her, near the stairs. There *was* someone else. Of course there was. Nicole Hammond couldn't have done this alone and Eve could have screamed at herself. How could she not have realised that this one woman couldn't have controlled both Pennie and Eve at the same time?

Someone else was in the house.

36

'Who's here?' Eve demanded, shoving past Angel and taking the stairs down two at a time. 'Pennie?' she called, louder this time, as she hurried through the open-plan ground floor. There was a pile of books on the floor, which had been on the kitchen counter. Beside them, a smashed mug, left over from breakfast the day before. She looked around frantically. 'Pennie!' she cried. Where would she hide? Eve's blood pulsed loudly in her ears and her heart hammered against her chest. 'Where is she?' she roared. 'Where is my sister?'

'She's not your sister, Eve,' Angel said, as she arrived, very unhurriedly, at the bottom of the stairs. 'But she *is* safe.'

Eve looked accusingly at her. Clearly, Angel knew where Pennie was. Did she have someone else take her? 'Where is she?' she asked again, ignoring the jibe about Pennie not being her sister. She turned in frantic circles, looking for anywhere that could conceal a ten-year-old girl, and her eyes came to rest on the kitchen cupboards, the ones at floor level, and she ran to open them. 'Pennie!' she called, even though logic told her that Pennie had already been taken from the house. 'Come out, Pennie. It's okay!' she shouted anyway, pulling open every door. But of course, Pennie wasn't there. She wasn't anywhere. 'Where is she?' she all but screamed at Angel, her tears coming hot and pouring furiously down her cheeks.

'She's not here,' she said calmly.

'What do you want?' Eve demanded. 'What the fuck do you want?!'

'What did Brian Merriman say to you?'

Eve groaned loudly and turned away, bringing her hands to her head and scraping her hair back from her face.

'You want to know where Pennie is? What did he say?'

Eve turned angrily towards her, her eyes as sharp as knives. 'Why do you want to know? Why are you *so* fascinated with human suffering, *Angel*?' She stepped almost threateningly towards her. 'You need to hear me say the words, do you?' Her mouth turned down in disgust and her eyes travelled from Nicole's lying, deceiving head to her toes. 'You want to hear how Brian hated himself so much that he had to drink at least a bottle of vodka every single day of his life? How his self-loathing led to him beating his wife until she couldn't stand to be around him any more? How this *place*,' she gestured to their surroundings, 'is the reason why he has no relationship with any of his four children, two of whom he never even met? You need to hear how that man's life, and the lives of everyone who got close to him, were shattered by *this house*?'

'He'd turned his life around! He—'

'There is *no* turning your life around from this place!' Her raised and angry voice drowned Angel out. 'The misery of this house spreads like thick, black treacle, smothering us all.' She wriggled her arms away from her body. 'It ripples outwards, suffocating everyone it touches.'

'But you loved Sparrow?'

Eve turned and walked slowly away, towards the kitchen. 'Sparrow's love for me and his hatred for this house devoured him.' She turned slowly to look at Angel again. 'He was destroying himself with heroin, and when the drugs weren't eating him alive, the nightmares were.' How could anyone *not* understand this? 'Sparrow's pain was a living thing. A relentless, snarling, black dog that chased him through his waking hours and continued to torment him in his dreams.'

Eve was pacing the kitchen now, pulling on the sleeve of her jumper. The handle of the knife slipped down and was no longer concealed, but she wasn't thinking about it. She wasn't thinking about anything, except for that dog. He chased Eve, too, invading her dreams by howling and snarling through her bedroom door, and more often now, her waking hours. He'd been sleeping fitfully for years, only waking occasionally when provoked. Ellen had provoked it with her flippancy when she'd talked about Eve's time in that room. And Pennie. She'd spoken about her with such disdain. Her filthy husband fathered her, but Pennie was the one spoken about like *she* was dirty. The big, black mammoth of a dog growled at her now from the corner of the room. Ashley Evans had provoked the dog, too. The dog could hear the name bouncing around inside Eve's head and his low growl became a snarl.

'Eve?' Angel asked.

'She tried to say that Pennie was...' She frowned again and shook her head vehemently, the knife sliding further into her hand. She gripped it before it fell to the floor.

'What, Eve? That Pennie is what?'

Eve wasn't listening. She only heard the dog.

'She's your daughter, Eve.'

'Ellen wanted to kick her out onto the street. She would have been taken away from me and... she would have suffered every day of her life, like we all did, here.'

'That's why you did it,' Angel said softly. Too softly for the words to travel the full distance of the room, realisation dawning at last. 'That's why you had Sparrow kill Peter. Not because of what he was doing to you. But because of what you *knew* he'd eventually do to Pennie.'

Eve was shaking her head, wondering why the kitchen looked so different suddenly. Was it the introduction of this other person into it? Did Nicole Hammond change the air so completely that this old house was changing with it?

Nicole brought her hands to her head and looked towards the ceiling. 'You were putting them out of their misery,' she whispered. Not that it mattered, because Eve wouldn't have heard her anyway. Angel stepped tentatively towards her. 'You used Ellen's insulin, didn't you?'

'Where are my sisters?' Eve turned slowly to face her. Her expression said that the time for games was over. She *wanted* her sisters back. Amelia *and* Pennie.

'You were making her sick.' It seemed Angel was wondering aloud now, her brow furrowed and her eyes pleading with Eve to convince her otherwise.

'I was trying to show her the kind of love that neither of us ever had,' she said. 'Where are my sisters?'

'A mother's love,' Angel said. 'Because a sick child gets all the tender loving care that a mother can give, doesn't she?'

Eve continued to pace with one eye on Angel, and the other on the dog in the corner of the room, where she hoped he'd stay. The closer he came to her, the more despair filled her up. Eve brought her hand up and roughly tapped the handle of the knife against her forehead. 'Where are they?' she mumbled. 'Where's Pennie? Where's Amelia?'

Angel hunched over, bringing her hands to her eyes. 'You know Pennie would have died if you'd kept going? I had to stop her from eating your poisoned food, Eve. Why?' Angel shook her head, disbelieving. Then she opened her eyes wide and dabbed at her eyeball with her index finger.

Eve took a step back. 'What are you doing? And why aren't you answering me?'

Angel stepped quickly towards her then, coming within inches of Eve's face. She'd noticed the knife, but she didn't appear to be afraid of it. 'You want to know where Amelia is?'

Eve's features softened and her desperation returned. This was how Eve's mind and that big, black dog chose to torture her, always. By violently swinging her from fear to anger, to self-loathing, to desperation and then all the way back around again. She hated her desperation the most, yet it dripped from her words when she asked, 'Is she dead?'

Angel's eyes searched her face and Eve found herself looking self-consciously away from her scrutiny. 'You want to know where your big, fat pig of a sister is?' Angel hissed, the change in her surprising, even now.

But the words cut through Eve's heart. She'd had to listen to her beautiful, kind, generous and protective big sister being degraded in such a way throughout their whole childhoods. She would not listen to it from *her*. Eve swung her hand towards Angel's face, clutching the butt end of the knife. But Angel was quicker than Eve was. She grabbed Eve's wrist and held it with such a tight grip that Eve cried out.

'You want to know where your sister is?' she hissed again, more venomously this time, tightening her grip even more. 'Look at me. Look!'

Eve tried, but she was unable to pull free from her grasp. Angel brought her face within inches of Eve's, but the fear and uncertainty Eve felt made her unable to react. But at last, she saw it. The sudden difference in Angel. Her steel-blue eyes... were brown now.

Angel held one hand open, and a pair of blue contact lenses clung pathetically to her palm.

'*I'll* tell you where your sister is,' she said in a forceful whisper.

Bile rose up Eve's throat and she shook her head in confusion, as the landscape of her life changed again.

37

'Amelia?' The word stuck in her throat, barely making it out at all.

'Amelia died at that wall out there,' she said, her voice low and soft and suddenly *so* familiar that it shattered Eve completely.

Was it her voice that bred familiarity when Eve first met Nicole Hammond? It just didn't match the physical appearance. The last time she saw her sister, she was a broken girl who hated herself and the body she lived in. Right down to her pale skin, her curly, brown hair and the darkest of brown eyes. By contrast, Nicole Hammond appeared to be someone who took on the world and won. She was tanned, white-haired and built of pure, tattoo-covered muscle. How were they the same person? But those eyes... that voice! It was unmistakeably her. It was Amelia.

'She died when she was forced to dig a grave in the back garden, and help throw a dead girl into it...' her sister continued.

Eve stared into those eyes as they filled with tears, but she couldn't speak.

'Amelia died that day, along with Robin,' she said again, letting her tears overflow and run uninterrupted towards her chin. 'I buried the pair of them in that hole.' She released Eve's hand and took a small step back. 'Then I got the fuck out of here.'

Eve hadn't moved since Amelia started to speak. She hadn't so much as expelled a breath, for fear that she might stop. Only when she was sure that she'd finished, did she whisper in disbelief, 'Amelia?'

She shook her head. 'I'm Nicole now. This is who I was always meant to be, so don't ever call me by that name again.'

'But...' Eve's eyes were wide like saucers, 'how?'

'Eve, before anyone else...' She glanced towards the back door and then so did Eve. 'I need to explain something to you.' Nicole stepped tentatively closer to Eve again, holding out her hand like Eve was a wild animal who might pounce.

Eve blinked hard, desperately trying to catch up. This was real. She looked at her face again and into those eyes. Could it really be her? Could Amelia be in there somewhere? Had she buried her pain behind this elaborate mask?

'You're Pennie's mum. You know that now, right?' Nicole said it as gently as she could.

Eve stepped back, shaking her head, remembering again why they were here. Why *she* was here. 'Why did you come back?' she asked, unable to keep the sudden feeling of betrayal from her voice, thinking that the real question should be, *why did you leave me?* Perhaps the answer to that would come, too. But this was more pressing, so she continued. 'Why have you been doing this?'

Nicole took another small step towards her. She looked at her feet, just like Amelia used to do when she was thinking. 'Eve, you're the reason I stayed for so long after ageing out. But by the time I...' She brought her hand to her forehead. 'After Robin, I was no good to you. I was no good to anyone. Not for a long time. But Eve, I was the first person that Brian Merriman contacted,' she said quietly.

Eve frowned and shook her head.

'He contacted all of us. He wanted to take a case against Tusla and he wanted all of us to be a part of it.'

'Tusla?'

Nicole nodded. 'Who do you think put us all here, Eve?' She gestured to their surroundings. To the house that shaped all of their lives. 'You don't think Ashley Evans knew exactly what was going on here? Of course she did. Why else would she suddenly stop sending girls, but continue to send boys? And just, what,' she flung her arms up in a *what the fuck* gesture, 'let Peter and Ellen just get on with it? Let them keep locking kids up in a fucking room, starving them,' she laughed incredulously, 'selling videos of their abuse online!'

The room started to spin slowly around Eve.

'You know they're still out there, don't you, those videos?' She glared at Eve.

'Perverts of all shapes and sizes are still getting off on what happened to us in this fucking hellhole!' She paused to catch her breath, which was coming in short, sharp bursts. 'Why do you think Leslie came back from New Zealand, hmm? She wanted to be a part of it. She wanted to bring those fuckers down.'

'And you?' Eve asked quietly, still struggling to grasp any of this, even though she knew it was true. Or at least, some of it. Brian did come to her. He came and he apologised for his part in her life, even though none of it was his choice at all. He told her that it was time for all of it to end. His exact words were, 'I'm done with the pain of it. I'm done with the guilt and the shame that I've carried with me my whole life.' Eve remembered every single word of what was essentially a monologue on the doorstep of Raven's Rock, because she had so little to add to this unexpected conversation. Perhaps if she'd had a chance to prepare, she might have responded differently. She might have *responded*, full stop. Brian, too, had refused to step inside the house. 'They took away my ability to live a normal life,' he'd said. 'To be a productive member of society. Because of them, I needed a skin full of booze just to get through every hour of every day. I beat my wife because I was so angry all the time.' His voice replayed those words daily in Eve's mind, and she realised that he was speaking for all of them. For every child who came through this house. He was telling her that they were all in pain. Constant, ongoing, unbearable pain. Them, and their snarling, black dogs.

'Why did you kill him?' Nicole asked.

Eve reached out to steady herself against the kitchen counter, as she stumbled backwards. She still had a loose grip on the knife, but she'd just about forgotten it was there. For the first time, Eve heard Nicole's profound sadness. It chimed like a bell, and she knew she had to do something. She had to explain and take that pain away in the only way she could.

'Brian needed my help,' she explained. 'I had to do something.' She reached out to touch Nicole's arm, but she took a small step back. 'He was in so much pain.'

'What did you do?' Nicole asked, but it was Amelia she heard at last. She wondered in amazement how she hadn't heard her all along. It was *so* clearly her.

'He told me all about the misery he carried everywhere with him. How he passed it on to everyone else in his life,' she implored, eyes wide and hopeful. 'Brian was right that something had to be done. But the thought of my brothers and sisters spending years more of their lives dragging themselves through court, reliving the horrors of their lives over and over again, only to be told at the very end, that no one believed them...' She stepped away from the counter and reached a hand out to Nicole again, but still, she didn't take it. Eve looked questioningly at her. She didn't understand. 'Because you know that *is* what would happen. No one would have believed us. They never did before and the system is rigged against kids like us, too. You know that.' Eve pleaded with her to see it. 'If it weren't, then you would never have had to bury Robin Higgins in that garden. You must know I'm right?' she said, taking a small step forward, matching Nicole's backwards one. But Eve saw no understanding in her expression. All she saw was more pain reflected back at her. Pain. 'I couldn't let them go through that.' Eve lowered her hand and her voice, her own sadness pressing down upon her now. But her resolve was strong. She couldn't sit back and watch this house inflict any more misery upon the only family she'd ever known.

'You killed them all,' Nicole said, her tears free-flowing again.

'I took away their pain,' Eve beseeched.

Nicole shook her head slowly, looking at her like she was a complete stranger. Like she hadn't sheltered and protected Eve as a child. Like she hadn't wrapped Eve up in her strong arms and told her that everything would be all right, even when they knew that it never would be. Nicole brought her hands to her mouth and turned slowly away.

'I loved them,' Eve cried, walking step for step with Nicole as she started to pace, slowly. 'Brian coming here like that finally made me see it. How much they were all still suffering...' She reached out again and managed to take Nicole's arm this time. She startled and pulled her arm away. 'Don't you see?' Eve begged. 'I took away their pain.'

Nicole's hands fell away from her mouth.

Eve frowned and lowered her own hand, too.

Nicole closed her eyes and her tears ran silently off her chin. 'You know that Pennie wasn't a foster kid, Eve. She wasn't *placed* here.' She was hoarse with emotion, and she glanced again towards the back door. 'Pennie was born here and you... well, you were sent here specifically because you had a biological sister who was already living here. I know that you know this. You must remember!'

Eve looked over her shoulder, too, then looked questioningly back at Nicole.

'Eve, you had a baby when you were thirteen years old.' She sobbed loudly. 'That baby is Pennie. Your daughter. My niece.' She doubled over for a second as if in physical pain, her hands covering her face. When she straightened back up, she shook out her hands and looked Eve in the eye. 'I'm sorry we never talked about it properly and I'm sorry I left. I just... I didn't think I could ever be good enough for you. For both of you.'

Eve stared blankly at her, like she was speaking in a foreign language.

She cried. 'Eve... you're *my* blood. Why do you think I stayed so long after ageing out? And Pennie... Eve, we're your family.' She pointed towards the back door and, again, Eve glanced back, her stomach shifting uncomfortably.

'Where's Pennie?' Eve asked, as if Nicole hadn't just dropped a bombshell on her. All her life, she'd craved a flesh-and-blood family, but now her mind refused to bend around the notion that she'd had one all along.

Nicole's crying intensified.

'Where is she? Where's my sister?'

'You were making her sick,' Nicole said through the tuck in her heart.

Eve shook her head, no.

'You killed Sparrow.'

'I loved Sparrow.'

'You met him at the park, on those damn swings, and you injected him with insulin.'

'No.' Eve shook her head, adamant.

'You went to Henry Carver, knowing that he'd let you in.' Nicole coughed and cried. 'You did the same thing to him... and Leslie and Brian...'

Eve was still shaking her head. 'They invited me in.' Her mouth turned down then at the memory. 'They wanted to talk to me. They wanted to tell me their pain.' She pulled the knife out of her sleeve again. 'They wanted to tell me, because they wanted me to help them.' Eve imagined Nicole nodding her agreement on the inside, but on the outside, she was still, like a statue. Still, but pain and sadness emanated from her.

'Do you remember that Christmas when we all watched *Annie* on TV?' Eve asked with a small smile. 'Remember how we all looked at each other from time to time? The hope we all had, that someday, an Irish Daddy Warbucks would knock on our door and that might be one of us?'

Nicole looked to the ceiling and blew out a teary breath. She remembered.

'Remember the way Ellen laughed at us at the end? Remember what she said?'

Nicole nodded slowly. 'There are no happy endings for little shits like you.' She replayed Ellen's words, her voice completely flat. 'Or big shits like me.'

'Exactly.' Eve jabbed a finger in her direction to emphasise the point. 'It might be the only time I'll ever admit to agreeing with Ellen Holland, but she *was* right about that.'

Nicole shook her head and turned away.

'I asked her about it the following day,' Eve continued. 'And you know what she said? She brought out that little glass trophy again. The one with *Children's Hero* engraved on it. She won it the same year Ashley Evans won hers, remember? "We're award-winning foster parents, Eve," she said. "*We* are the best you can ever expect in this life."'

Nicole bit down hard on her bottom lip.

'Where's Pennie?' Eve asked again, her previous train of thought vanished once more.

'You made her sick,' Nicole cried towards the ceiling. 'You were trying to kill her.'

Eve shook her head. 'I'm helping her! She'll just go to sleep alongside someone who loves her, *knowing* how much she was loved. Is there anything in the world that could be better than that? Isn't that all any of us ever wanted?'

Nicole stood still, staring at Eve through her fingers, watching her moving closer. She was so sure in what she was saying.

'You have no idea how much I've wanted to see you again.' Eve smiled. 'For so long, I dreamed that you'd come back. I thought I'd lost you.'

Nicole's hands slid away from her face again and, this time, she allowed Eve to take her hand.

'I thought you did *actually* die, and I wasn't sure which one of you was buried out there.' She nodded towards the back of the house. 'But now I know.'

'Now you know,' Nicole agreed softly.

Eve nodded. 'I'm sorry, Amelia.' She squeezed her hand. 'I'm so sorry.'

'None of that was your fault.' The words caught in her jagged breaths.

'I loved you all so much,' Eve cried, moving in closer and wrapping one arm around Nicole's thick, strong waist. 'And you were all still suffering *so* much.'

The feel of the sharp blade punching its way through Nicole's skin and slicing through layers of muscle and fat beneath it was something that Eve would never get used to. 'I'm so sorry,' she cried into Nicole's chest, which heaved as the knife did its work. 'But it'll all be better now.'

Nicole's hand clutched Eve's tightly and wrestled with her. Even now, she was strong. Amelia was always *so* strong. But Eve stepped back, pulling the knife with her, and as she did, blood flowed frighteningly quickly from Nicole and pooled on the kitchen floor. Nicole stumbled against the kitchen counter, her eyes wide with horror, as Eve turned the blade towards herself.

'We're all free now, Amelia.' She smiled. 'We're all finally free.'

Nicole started to fall and the noise of the toaster hitting the floor, along with boxes of cereal, the radio, and several pots, was drowned out by Nicole's calls for help, as Eve drove the bloody blade into her own abdomen, in exactly the same spot as it had struck Nicole. There was a bright flash of white-hot pain as the knife fell to the floor. Eve's hands cupped her stomach like a badly thought-out receptacle at a drinking fountain. But with the pain came a great sense of achievement. She'd done it. She'd found her entire family, and she'd set them all free. No more pain. Not for any of them.

She hardly registered the sound of the back door bursting open and the noise that followed. Someone was pulling Nicole from the house, but as Eve hit the floor and darkness closed in around her, she saw Pennie in that same polka-dot nightie she'd been wearing when they sat on the bed in her room, listening to Amelia issuing soft instructions through Bluetooth headphones. She thought of how Amelia had cared enough to replace Eve's frightened words with Pennie's favourite songs, while Eve responded to her story. Did all of that only happen tonight? It seemed like a lifetime had passed since the sun last set in the sky over Raven's Rock.

As Eve's eyes began to close, Pennie's feet came closer still and in what she was sure, what she *hoped* were her dying moments, she wondered if she could still take Pennie with her. All she wanted to do was show the child the love she deserved, the love they *all* deserved, and then bring her the ultimate peace. But before she could put her final thoughts into any kind of action, Pennie's feet lifted off the floor and were replaced with the heavy, black boots and shouts of *Gardaí*.

And just like that, it was over.

38

NICOLE

Two Days Later

Nicole exhaled sharply as the door slammed behind the ill-tempered detective, whose name was as unmemorable as he was. He seemed like the type of man who liked his women compliant. But Nicole hadn't *complied* in more than a decade and that man was already gone from her mind. The cramped hospital room, however, was closing in on her and she wished to be free of it. To be free of *them* with all their *we're trying to help you* sentiments. Pain stabbed at her abdomen. She brought her hand to the wound, which was opened by her sister and had since been stitched and glued shut by someone claiming to be a doctor. Nicole didn't trust them. She didn't trust anyone.

The pain made her think about Eve and, not for the first time, Nicole half-wished she could have found the strength to finish the job. Death would have taken the weight of her failures off her shoulders. She'd failed at just about every aspect of her life and every plan she ever made, bar one. The plan to become bigger and stronger than everyone else. Her plan to never again be on the receiving end of misogyny, or someone else's power over her. In that, she'd succeeded. But in everything else, she'd failed spectacularly.

'Nicole?' A woman poked her head around the door, then smiled and stepped inside. 'I'm Detective Sergeant Melanie Boyde. But you can call me Mel,' she said, closing the door more gently than her colleague had. She was a very tall, thin woman with acne-scarred, black skin. She looked to be in her mid-thirties but still struggling with blemishes, while her clothes hung shapelessly from her bony frame. A black trouser suit, designed to do absolutely nothing for the female form.

Nicole took one look at Mel and deduced that her life must be shit. Women like her... like *them*, constantly had to prove themselves worthy of respect. She imagined it must be significantly worse in a male-dominated profession like An Garda Siochána. Still, if Mel had a chip on her shoulder, she covered it well.

'Do you mind if I sit down?' she asked, indicating the uncomfortable visitor's chair beside Nicole's bed, which had just been vacated by Detective Anger-Issues.

Nicole didn't respond. She was exercising her right to remain silent. Even though she hadn't been read those rights, because she hadn't been arrested. But Eve had.

Mel sat down anyway and looked around the room. 'So this is what it takes to get a private room in a public hospital, eh?' She looked to Nicole again, her friendly smile still there. 'A good old stabbing.'

Nicole would have smiled at the glib joke if Mel and her buddies weren't trying to hammer nails in her sister's coffin. Which was *her* fault, she knew that. Another failed plan in a series of many. She picked a point on the wall straight ahead and rested her eyes there.

'My colleague is a bit bullheaded, Nicole,' Mel said. 'I apologise for him.'

Nicole didn't respond in any way.

Mel watched her for a long minute, then she seemed to settle herself into the chair, crossing one very long, trousered leg over the other, hands loosely clasped in her lap.

'I get why Eve did what she did,' Mel said quietly. 'I saw the tapes. Bastards like them should never be allowed near children, should they?'

Nicole stayed quiet.

'I get, too, why you don't want to talk. I don't think I would either, in your shoes. So why don't I talk and maybe you can just stop me if I get it wrong? Or, if there's anything you'd like to add.'

Nicole kept her eyes on the wall and her hand on her stomach wound, which was throbbing now. She thought about the pills in her jeans pocket. They were better than the shitty ones the so-called doctors were giving her, but she had no idea where her jeans were. *They* might have them for all she knew, but she desperately wanted those pills now. She needed something to numb the pain. *All* the pain.

'I think Brian Merriman found you, just like he found Jack Logan, Henry Carver and Leslie Granger,' Mel got started. 'He tracked you down to tell you that he was planning on bringing a case against Tusla. I'm right in that, aren't I?' She shrugged and made a face. 'Can't say I blame him there. But he wanted all of you to join him, right? To strengthen the case.'

Nicole said nothing, but she didn't need to. They already knew this. They now had all the stupid fucking nanny-cam recordings of her conversation with Eve, through Pennie, as well as the smoke-detector recordings *and* the home-movie collection in the attic. Tears welled in Nicole's eyes as she was faced once more with her many inadequacies. The police were never supposed to be involved. She was *supposed* to confront Eve with her past, just like they did in every so-called *therapy* session she'd ever seen on TV. She was *supposed* to make her see that none of it was her fault. Not even the recent killings. Eve was *supposed* to see everything clearly for the first time, have some kind of a fucking breakthrough or something, and see that there was a life for her and Pennie beyond Raven's Rock. Then all three of them were *supposed* to get the fuck out of there and never look back. But no. Nicole had to lose her lunch after two days under that roof.

'Nicole, when did you first suspect that Eve might have killed someone?'

Nicole plucked at the blanket on the bed, just to give her free hand something to do, while she continued to stare resolutely ahead. She should have suspected it when Brian died. He told her that he was going to see Eve, and that was the last time Nicole heard from him. But then Jack died and, somehow, she just knew. Eve had finally broken after a lifetime of bending, but it was too late to link him for sure to Brian, who was already in the ground by then. She didn't want to believe it. Not any of it, which was why she had to get close. Too close, she now knew.

'Did you fear for your life, Nicole? And for Pennie's life?' Mel asked, moving from one question to another, unperturbed by the lack of response.

Nicole shook her head but remained silent. The second she saw the knife and whispered in Pennie's ear to get help, she regretted it. In that moment, she saw herself being sliced open by Eve and bleeding out in that hellish place.

'I'd imagine Eve's strength is no match for yours,' Mel said. 'Yet, you never tried to overpower her?'

Nicole shot her a look at last. 'You think I could have hurt my sister?'

Mel shrugged. 'Perhaps in self-defence?'

Nicole shook her head and looked to the wall again. She deserved to die for leaving Eve there all those years ago, so she wouldn't have tried to stop her. But that would have left Pennie all alone and *that's* why she had to get help. But now they were all alive and truly fucked, thanks to that one decision to *get help*.

'I get you don't want to talk about it,' Mel interrupted her thoughts. 'I just...' She frowned and shook her head. 'I guess, I understand why you didn't want us getting involved from the start. Eve is your sister. You didn't want to put her on the hook for murder. But why go to such elaborate lengths? Why hide out in your old house?' She shrugged and shook her head. 'What was your plan?'

Nicole's stoicism waned and she brought a shaking hand to her head. Hiding out in that house was a nightmare which was thrust upon her, and scaring Eve was the last thing she had set out to do. She'd suffered as much as any of them. More, given the fact that she'd imprisoned herself in that house even after they were dead.

'In fact, it seems like you put a lot of planning into it,' Mel said, as more of a statement than a question.

Nicole smiled a bitter smile. Her *plan* only extended to saving Eve from herself. She didn't know then that she was making Pennie sick. Only that she was shortening the list of people who lived to tell the woeful tale of Raven's Rock. Truth be told, Nicole didn't particularly care about any of them. She had nothing but vile memories of Henry Carver. Brian Merriman was a prick and Leslie-Anne was a born victim and a snivelling pain in the ass. Their deaths would never have been enough to bring Nicole back to this place. No. Her plan was never about protecting *them*. It was all about protecting Eve, and Eve adored Jack Logan. He might have been the only person she *ever* loved. So the only way Eve could ever bring herself to kill *him* would be if she were planning on following him to the grave. Nicole's *plan* was to stop that from happening. It was as simple and as stupid as that. Tears dripped off the end of her chin and she wiped them angrily away. Then she forced her gaze back to the wall ahead.

'You were trying to stop her, weren't you?' Mel said. 'You thought that by protecting Pennie, you could somehow come up with a way to make Eve stop.'

Pain shot through Nicole's abdomen, but she wouldn't allow herself to react, other than to bring her hand over it again. She deserved this pain. She deserved every ounce of it. And this so-called detective could think what she liked. None of it mattered now.

'We have a string of messages between you and Eve. *She* reached out to *you*. Why didn't you tell her then, who you were? Why pretend to be a journalist?'

'I never pretended to be a journalist,' Nicole snapped, and she could tell by Mel's face that she was surprised to have gotten a response. She still wasn't quite over the shock of seeing that DM coming from Eve. That was when she knew that Pennie was telling her what they'd talked about.

'No, of course,' Mel said, 'but you weren't honest about who you were either,' she rightly pointed out.

Nicole lowered her eyes to the bunched-up sheet in her lap. 'I just wanted to see what she'd be like,' she muttered, looking around again for her jeans.

'It had been a while, hadn't it?' Mel said softly.

Nicole nodded. She almost didn't turn up at Costa that first day and, when she did, it took all she had not to run when she saw Eve walking towards the café, her shoulders hunched and her eyes cast down, away from the world. She'd been watching Eve for a while by then, but that was the first time they'd spoken in almost ten years. Nicole wholeheartedly expected her to know who she was, even though she'd gone to such lengths to bury her old self.

'Being that close to her again after all these years,' she said softly, shaking her head, 'seeing how little she'd changed... I just wanted to *know* her again, you know? Not as someone who shared her pain. But like a stranger might get to know her. As the person she is today.'

'I get that,' Mel said, managing to sound like she actually did.

'I went to visit Raven's Rock for the first time since I left there, after Brian was found dead. I was hoping to see Eve,' she explained, despite herself. 'I couldn't believe it when I saw Pennie instead.' Tears dripped onto the sheet. 'She looked so much like Eve did at that age... it was like time had stood still at that house. Like,' she frowned and shook her head, 'like I'd never left the place. Like, *he* might walk out the door and see me at any moment.'

'But he didn't,' Mel prompted.

'She had blonde hair. That was the only difference. She was only a newborn baby the last time I saw her and,' she exhaled loudly, 'seeing her just pinned me to the spot. I couldn't move.'

'And that was the first time Pennie saw you?'

She nodded. That was the day Nicole had stupidly told the girl that she'd be her guardian angel. It seemed it was all she needed to hear and for a child who seemed so detached from life, she sure as hell clung to Nicole. But Nicole didn't tell Detective Mel about that.

Poor Pennie. She was who Nicole needed to worry about now. She was the reason why Nicole needed to keep her mouth shut and just get through this. Eve was caught. There was nothing more she could do for her now, only to look after her daughter as best she could. An utterly terrifying thought.

'So when Eve reached out, unexpectedly, to you, I get that you were curious about her. But we also have a record of *you* calling *her* a week later. That wasn't to come clean about who you were?'

Nicole shrugged, but she was right. That wasn't why she'd called Eve. She *had* to call her, because she was just sitting there in the woods, watching Pennie's room. Nicole needed to get her away from Pennie because she didn't trust Eve to manage her own stress at that point. She worried that Eve would try to end it for both of them, and she was right to think that. It seemed that actually was Eve's plan. To take them both away from their pain, together. But again, she didn't say that to Detective Mel. She wasn't about to hand her anything else to incriminate her sister. Instead, she said, 'I thought about telling her. But then I lost my nerve.' She glanced at the woman. 'I just wanted to see her again.'

Mel nodded, her gaze intense. 'I know I asked you this already, but... *was* it always your plan to hide out in her house like that? To confront her the way you did?'

'You know that word is ludicrous, right?' she snapped.

'Which word?' Mel asked, badly masking her delight at this conversational volley.

'*Plan*,' Nicole hissed. 'Do *you* make plans?'

Mel shrugged. 'Sometimes.'

'Do they ever work out?'

Mel looked thoughtfully at the floor before responding with a slight shake of the head. 'Not as often as I'd like, I suppose.'

'Exactly. So you can stop asking me about my plans, because most of them went to shit.' She looked down at her broad, muscular body. The only plan of hers that ever came to fruition, but not without a lot of narcotic help. Her other plans included never setting foot in Raven's Rock again, which was why most of her interactions with Pennie were through windows and out in the woods. Once she'd gone as far as the kitchen table with her, but on the condition that the back door stayed wide open. She needed to see for herself what Eve was feeding her and she had noticed the smell then, but not nearly as strongly. That house always smelled of something. Fear, probably, and Nicole's discomfort that night didn't let her think too much about it. But those two days spent in the attic were totally unplanned and were as torturous as every other day she'd spent under that roof. It happened because Nicole's curiosity got the better of her, when she saw an Amazon delivery guy leaving a package on Eve's doorstep. She came out of the woods to see what it was, and knowing that Eve was inside the house, she didn't expect Pennie to open the door. But when she did, Nicole was left with no choice but to go inside.

She inhaled sharply, hot tears stinging her eyes as she was transported back to that porch again. She could smell it even now. The stench of rot and decay that slammed against her face when Pennie opened the front door. Her hand flew to cover her nose and mouth, now in her sterile hospital bed, as it had that day, as she stepped inside the house.

'Oh... that's coming from The Room,' Pennie had said. Like, *yes, it's unpleasant, but it's nothing to worry about.*

She *had* to cross that threshold again and as soon as she did, fear and bad memories assailed her, as she tried to stop her eyes from soaking the place back in. She looked towards the stairs and then at Pennie, who'd nodded encouragingly.

Then without another word, Pennie walked to the stairs and started up, glancing back from time to time to see that Nicole was following her. Reluctantly, she did. And each step she took towards The Room sapped more and more of that new-found strength from her legs.

'Wh... who's in there, Pennie?' Nicole asked, her voice, barely a whisper, sounding smaller than it had in years.

Pennie didn't respond. She just stepped back and gestured for Nicole to open the door.

Had Nicole been alone in that house, there's no way she would have done it. She would have turned and run. But she had to help Eve's child. And she had to help Eve. She squeezed her eyes shut and turned the key in the lock. She took a series of shallow breaths before shoving the door open with her foot, releasing with far more fury, a smell, the likes of which she never knew existed. She felt it wash over her like a wave, as much as she smelled and tasted it. Her body violently convulsed, and she vomited on the floor.

39

NICOLE

Between heaving and gasping for breath, her bleary eyes found their way to the bed in the corner of The Room. Ellen might have looked like she was sleeping peacefully, if her corpse weren't rotting in a way that Nicole had so often dreamed of when she were younger. The sight in reality was enough to send her stumbling backwards away from the door. She couldn't remember if she'd said anything. Certainly, nothing coherent, but she remembered Pennie's voice, begging, 'Please don't leave. I'll clean it up, but please don't leave.'

As Nicole stumbled, crying and retching away from The Room, some form of muscle memory sent her scrambling towards her ancient hiding place, above the linen press. She vaguely remembered Pennie pulling the door shut on Ellen and running past Nicole, getting to the linen press before her. She grabbed an armful of towels, which she now realised were to clean up Nicole's vomit, while Nicole herself retreated like a coward to the attic.

'You grew up in that house. You must have known about the doorbell camera.' Mel's Cork accent intruded on her thoughts again. 'You must have known that you'd be seen.'

Nicole roughly wiped away her tears and picked up the little pot of jelly on her tray table. She sniffed it, just to mask the scent of Ellen, which she was certain would never leave her now. Each and every breath she took came with a hint of decomposition.

'You weren't worried about the camera?' Mel pushed a little further.

Nicole shook her head, but that was all she gave her. She was done talking. Of course she knew about the camera. But she also *thought* she knew Eve well enough to know that she wouldn't have activated the app. Her original plan that day was to wait for Eve to come out of her medically induced coma and confront her. But that hastily changed when Pennie opened the front door. *Then* she planned to quickly go inside, see what was happening in there, and leave again. Go wait in the relative comfort of the woods. In and out in the same short space of time. But that didn't happen either.

'How did it feel being back inside that house?' Mel asked, sounding like someone who knew pain.

Paralysing. That was how it felt, but again, Nicole stayed silent. She'd spent more than twenty-four hours in the spot she used to hide in as a child, unable to move. Pinned in by her demons. The nanny cams and the Bluetooth earbuds were the only way she could finally bring herself to communicate with Pennie, spurred on by the sound of her throwing up so violently that she worried she'd be too late. The use of technology was the only way she could try to protect her, while she herself reverted back to the scared little victim she'd always been inside that house. Her own fear was what kept her there for two days, while she'd been in no position to consider Eve's fear. Or anyone else's.

Pennie, she was sure, felt no such fear. Ever. She even made sandwiches and tried to give them to Nicole through the hatch to the attic. She worried how the worst of situations could seem so normal to that child.

Mel exhaled loudly. 'Wow, you really know how to keep your council, don't you?' She uncrossed her legs and leaned forward in the chair. 'Okay, well, look, Eve isn't pressing charges against you for being in the house. But she is likely to go away for a very long time, Nicole. She's pleaded guilty to everything. I just thought maybe it might help your sister's case if you were to give your side of things. That's all.'

Nicole shook her head and looked at the woman at last. 'I can't ever remember a time when my trying to help *actually* helped anyone. Quite the opposite, in fact.'

Mel rubbed her chin thoughtfully but said nothing.

'The best way for me to help my sister now is to find someone who actually knows how to do that.'

Again, Mel just looked at her for a while, thinking. 'Well, she will be entitled to free legal aid,' she said after a minute, pulling a card and a pen from her pocket. 'And I'd imagine a court-ordered psychiatrist will become involved, too. Perhaps you could talk to them when the time comes.' She scribbled something on the card, then got to her feet and took a step closer to Nicole's bed. 'I really am sorry that you all had to go through that.'

'What about Eve?' Nicole asked, a hint of a challenge in her voice. 'Are you sorry for her?'

Mel gave an almost imperceptible nod. 'Maybe most of all. Chances are, she wasn't born a killer, was she? She had a lot of help to become one.'

Nicole brought both hands to her face and let her tears fall. She felt the woman's gentle touch on the sheet covering her legs, before she heard her leaving the room. Only when the door closed behind her did she let her hands fall away and look at the card resting on her knee. She picked it up and read Detective Sergeant Melanie Boyde's contact information. She turned the card over and on the back, in neat, cursive writing, was a brief note:

Ask for Leonard Lowry to represent. Let the world know what happened.

40

PENNIE

Fourteen months later

Sitting in the packed courtroom that day, Pennie Holland looked around and wondered if this was what a circus looked like. She'd read that the circus had animals and all that, but if animals looked like people, then she was sure this was it. A wooden railing separated the circus ring from the jostling crowd and, today, Eve was the one in the ring. The crowd wanted to see her jump through a ring of fire, sure that she'd done it so many times, she wouldn't even feel it. But they didn't know Eve. Not like Pennie did. They didn't know how deeply Eve felt pain, even when that pain belonged to someone else.

Pennie first discovered that Eve was her mother, and not her sister, at the age of six. Ellen let it slip to her in a moment of frustration. One of many. She didn't tell Eve, though. See, Eve kept going on about them being sisters, especially after everyone died. She'd totally forgotten that she was a mum, and Pennie just knew that Eve would feel it too much if she told her. She'd been right. If only Ellen had kept her mouth shut. If only *everyone* could learn to just keep their mouths *shut*, then none of this would be happening.

She gently stroked her thumb against the smooth glass surface of the little bottle in her hand. She liked to have something to fidget with at all times. It calmed her somehow and helped her to settle her thoughts, as well as her hands. She stared at the woman who was sat in the little box beside the awful judge. She was tall and beautiful and looked like she'd never had a bad day in her life. Even her lipstick looked like it cost more than a week's grocery shopping at Raven's Rock. Pennie listened to that woman talking about Eve as if she knew her better than anyone, just because she'd been forced to sit with her for a few hours a week for one miserable year.

But Dr Louise Harris looked nothing like what Pennie imagined a doctor would look like. She was at least six feet tall, and yet she still wore four-inch stiletto heels and not just today. She wore them every day. Which was to say, she'd been reaching alarming heights for at least 425 days straight now. Eve told her that. But today, she looked exceptionally smart, in her tailored, blue trouser suit with her blonde hair pulled into the perfect low bun. Her make-up was subtle and flawless, and watching her now taking charge of the room, Pennie wished that Eve had just a fraction of the woman's self-confidence. That didn't mean that Pennie trusted her. Of course she didn't. Not when it was Eve's life hanging in the balance, but whether she liked it or not, the woman was about to speak *for* Eve. She was about to tell the world what was going on inside Eve's head and exactly *why* she had taken the lives of five people, while also trying to take Pennie's. Pennie didn't hold that against Eve. How could she, when all Eve ever tried to do was love her? For all either of them knew about love.

Now, whether they liked it or not, the time had come when the world would hear about life at Raven's Rock. Up until last year, it was the only life they'd ever known, and Pennie already imagined the circus frenzy that would ensue when those details emerged. Details she now knew were not normal. Eve told her that she looked forward to all the shame, pain and loathing emerging from the darkness, into the light at last. Maybe that was why she didn't look afraid any more. Eve had always looked afraid. Always. Pennie worried what it would do to her, knowing that they would all look at her and see her many humiliations in their mind's eye. Human nature would make them picture everything that happened. They would be fascinated by it, whether they wanted to be or not. Pennie didn't care. But she wondered if, despite her brave words, Eve would.

She listened intently as Dr Harris recited her credentials for the man in the drab, grey suit who was defending Eve on the state's say-so. Eve had tried to get rid of him. She said she didn't want anyone defending her. *He* didn't look like he wanted to be there any more than she wanted him, so Pennie didn't suppose he'd make much of a difference either way.

'Tell us, Doctor Harris,' he said at last, 'how long have you been treating Eve Holland, now?'

'For almost fourteen months,' Dr Harris responded. She was sitting in such a way that she looked completely at home in that box. Not straight-backed and stiff like others who'd sat there before her.

Pennie sensed that many of the men in the room were intimidated by Dr Harris. The grey suit beside Eve certainly was. He cleared his throat way too many times when he spoke to her. He wasn't like that with anyone else. Pennie was good at picking up on people's discomfort. In her experience, those subtle changes in people's demeanour could lead to just about anything. Though she suspected those things wouldn't be so extreme in the world of the grey suits.

'So would you say you've gotten to know her fairly well?' Grey Suit asked, after another clearing of the throat.

'I'd say so, yes,' Dr Harris responded politely.

'So, jumping straight to the point, Doctor: in your expert opinion, what do you think led us all to this courtroom today?'

Eve had asked him not to ask lots of stupid questions and, instead, just one that allowed the doc to tell the judge, and all the people, and all the reporters in that room, exactly what happened. Eve was very clear about the fact that she wanted people to understand, but she didn't want to get off. That bothered Pennie, but she said nothing. Pennie *never* said anything, because there was no point. People would always do what people were going to do, regardless of whatever she had to say. Eve said that all she wanted was for Brian, Henry, Leslie-Anne, Sparrow and Amelia to be believed. *She* wanted to be believed, and the rest didn't matter. Pennie stroked the smooth glass again.

'It's not so much what I *think,* councillor,' the doctor answered with such confidence. 'What I *know,* and what the jury *knows,* is that Eve Holland suffered years of habitual abuse at the hands of Ellen and Peter Holland. We know that her sexual abuse was filmed and sold online, where it will remain forever, no matter how hard the authorities try to have it removed. We know that the same thing happened to many of the children who were fostered by Ellen and Peter Holland.' She swivelled her chair ever so slightly and looked pointedly at the members of the jury, who hung on her every word.

'Go on,' said Mr Grey Suit lazily. As planned, Dr Harris was doing his job for him.

'I believe that the reappearance of Brian Merriman into her life was so triggering for Eve that, essentially, she suffered a...' she rolled her hand and looked again to the jury, like she was thinking of a way to explain it in a way they'd understand, 'a break from reality.'

'You're saying she didn't know what she was doing?' Mr Grey Suit asked.

Dr Harris bobbed her head and said, 'Mm, no. I'm saying that her reality became altered. Brian Merriman came to her because he was on his own road to recovery. A part of that for him was to talk about the past, and their shared time at Raven's Rock. For him, it was about reconciliation.' Dr Harris used her hands a lot while she spoke, bobbing them to one side when she was speaking about Brian Merriman, then to the other side when she spoke about Eve. As if this was needed to define the two. 'But throughout this conversation,' she continued, 'what Eve actually *heard* was how his life had been derailed by his time spent at that house. This, in turn, triggered a drastic train of thought, loaded with painful memories for Eve.' She swivelled away from the jury now and looked around at the crowd of journalists at the back of the room.

Pennie wondered if she was imagining herself as the star witness on a Netflix courtroom drama. She certainly performed like one.

Dr Harris lowered her hands and continued in the same confident tone. 'She started to imagine the pain that they all must be in. Not just herself and Brian Merriman. But *all* of the children who passed through that foster home. Eve knew for a fact that *she* was in pain. A twenty-three-year-old woman, living like a recluse. Eve has never had a consensual sexual relationship. She never had a *loving* relationship, not even with her daughter. She was denied all of that by Ellen and Peter Holland. Now she has a fear of other people and a fear of leaving the only home she's ever known.'

Pennie wondered if Eve could feel the dozens of eyes boring through the back of her head. She must have because she appeared to be shrinking into the hard, wooden chair beneath her. Pennie couldn't look at her any more, knowing that she was beginning to struggle, despite her resolve. She lowered her eyes to her fidgeting hands and the piece of glass gripped tightly in her palm.

'So, in your opinion, Doctor, what do you believe Eve Holland actually did from there?'

Dr Harris shrugged. 'Well again, it's not just my opinion, Mr Lowry. I've spent countless hours with Eve Holland now and I can tell you exactly what happened. Brian Merriman was training for a leg of the Tour de France. As part of his training, he'd cycled from Waterford to Cork that day in order to see Eve.'

She gestured towards Eve, like anyone needed reminding of who she was. 'He apologised to her for the part he played in her abuse.' She waved her hands around again. 'We've all seen the tapes that were entered into evidence,' she said, almost as a *by the way*. 'But like I said, all Eve heard was the devastation in his life and in her words,' she gestured again towards Eve and looked her way for the first time that day, 'she saw the pain and the misery that had been inflicted upon him by the Hollands, and in Eve's mind, she didn't think it was possible for him to ever move on from that. For his pain to ever end. So,' she blew out a long, dramatic breath, 'she made him a drink in which she deposited enough Rohypnol to cause him to lose consciousness.'

'But this didn't kill him?' Grey Suit interrupted her, which she didn't appear to appreciate.

'No. It did not,' she responded tersely. 'Eve explained that she gave Mr Merriman an injection of insulin while he was unconscious.'

'But Mr Merriman wasn't diabetic.' Grey Suit was at it again.

'He was not,' Dr Harris responded in the same confident tone as before. 'But Ellen Holland was and there was a quantity of insulin at the house, to which Eve had access. From living with Ellen's insulin dependency for so long, she would have gained enough knowledge to know that too much insulin in the body can lead to death.'

'And the Rohypnol? Where did Miss Holland get that?'

'Again, it was already in the house. Ellen Holland had a supply of just about every drug you can think of.' She gestured towards Eve again, but just with her hand this time. 'Eve explained that many drugs were confiscated from foster kids over the years, and while Ellen claimed not to believe in doctors, she had access to all the prescription medication you could think of. We believe that Ellen Holland was illegally obtaining many of these drugs for her own personal use.' She looked to the jury again. 'An inventory of those drugs has been entered into evidence.'

'Indeed.' Grey Suit looked down at his notes, cleared his throat and then carried on. 'So, she rendered Mr Merriman unconscious and then injected him with a fatal dose of insulin. What then did she do with the body?'

Pennie didn't like these questions. They were basically just reminding everyone that Eve killed people. But apparently, when he was explaining this tactic to Eve, he asked her if she'd ever seen a movie called *8 Mile*. Pennie had no idea what that was, but he explained that someone named Eminem, like the sweets, basically took all his enemy's ammunition and used it against himself, leaving his enemy with nothing else to say. That didn't make much sense to Pennie, but again, she said nothing.

Dr Harris glanced at Eve, looking somewhat worried for her. 'She put him in her car, along with his bicycle, and drove him towards Waterford. On a sweeping bend in the road, she managed to get his body over the crash barrier and damage his bike enough to make it look like he'd simply left the road while cycling at speed downhill. Accidents like that have happened in that location more than once.'

'So then why was Brian Merriman's death ruled as an accident?'

Dr Harris shook her head. 'Insulin is not routinely looked for in post-mortem toxicology reports for one thing. But also,' she shrugged and gave another sad shake of her head, 'his death appeared to be the kind of accident I just described. An accident believed to have been caused by a medical emergency.'

'The fact that she disposed of his body afterwards, do you think she planned to kill him?'

Dr Harris had been shaking her head in denial since he started asking the question. 'Absolutely not. Eve had no idea that Brian Merriman was coming to see her that day. He hadn't called ahead, and she hadn't heard from Brian in more than a decade. Not since he left their house. His sudden reappearance in her life caught her completely off guard, so you see, she couldn't possibly have planned it.' She rolled her hands around again, letting everyone know that she was about to launch into yet another detailed explanation. 'Eve used Rohypnol and insulin to give Brian Merriman a painless death. In her mind,' her hands paused mid-air, 'it was to ease his suffering. She then took him away from Raven's Rock. From the place where his pain originated. Eve Holland killed Brian Merriman. She's freely admitted this. But she didn't do it out of malice.' She turned towards the cameras at the back of the room again. 'She did it out of love.'

A ripple of conversation made its way through the room and the judge banged his gavel heavily to silence it.

Pennie rolled her eyes and looked into her lap again. Those were the words that would be sprawled across every newsfeed in the world tonight. *She killed them out of love.*

Pennie didn't have a mobile phone. Nicole wouldn't allow it, and she hadn't been letting her use any devices in the run-up to this trial. But Nicole was glued to her screen day and night. Her emotional outbursts left Pennie with plenty of time to glance and see what people were saying. She was surprised by the number of posts calling for Eve to be shown mercy. People seemed to care suddenly, which was almost laughable. Where were those people all their lives?

'And what about the others?' Grey Suit asked. 'What about Jack Logan, Henry Carver, Leslie Granger and Ellen Holland? Does she also admit to killing them?'

Dr Harris looked at Eve then, and Eve returned an almost imperceptible nod. The only reason Pennie saw it was because she knew it was coming. Eve had told her.

'She does. All except for Ellen Holland.'

41

PENNIE

'But Doctor Harris, we've all seen the footage of Eve Holland pushing Ellen Holland down the stairs. Yet you're saying that she denies killing her.'

Pennie rolled her eyes again and let out a quiet sigh. Grey Suit asked the question in such a way that he sounded like an imbecile. Feigned confusion, when he knew exactly what Dr Harris was about to say.

'That's true,' Dr Harris confirmed. 'And that footage also has audio, so you would have heard the conversation that had just taken place between Ellen and Eve Holland.' She swivelled to look at the jury again. 'One could even argue that this was what first triggered Eve's psychosis.' She said this like they were all just having a chat around a fancy dinner table. 'You see, Eve had blocked out her pregnancy entirely, which really is understandable. She was thirteen years old and pregnant with her foster father's child. Around the same time, she strongly suspected that one of her foster siblings had been killed by the Hollands and buried in the back garden, where indeed the remains of Robin Higgins were later discovered.' She paused to let this sink in. 'Eve's mind was protecting her by locking certain details away. So, at the time of Ellen's fall down the stairs, Eve fully believed that Pennie Holland was her sister. Not her daughter.' Again, her hands were firmly moving from one imaginary box to another. She left out the bit about Ellen moving to the Costa del Sol without them, which was probably just as well.

An excited hum of conversation filled the room at that sordid little titbit, and again, the judge had to bang his gavel to shut them up. He probably loved doing that, too. Mr All-Powerful up there with his stupid-looking wig. But the doc carried on as if she hadn't heard a thing.

'Her response was purely a reaction to this overwhelming revelation, which was delivered so flippantly,' she said, finishing with a minor flourish. Or maybe she just raised her voice to be heard over the din.

'So, she pushed Ellen Holland down the stairs,' Grey Suit asked.

'Indeed,' Dr Harris confirmed.

'But she did not kill her?'

The doc shook her head. 'Ellen Holland died from hypoglycaemia.' She looked to the jury again, perhaps trying to see from their faces whether or not they understood what that was.

'Low insulin,' Grey Suit clarified, just in case. 'Ellen Holland was diabetic.' He gestured to the jury, like they might have forgotten the whole insulin thing. 'So she did not die from that fall?'

'She did not. If you continue to watch that footage, you'll see that Eve went downstairs after the fall, and moments later, she can be seen helping Ellen Holland up the stairs and into a nearby bedroom. This is where she was later found to have died from complications associated with her insulin dependency.'

Pennie guffawed and the man beside her shot a quizzical look in her direction. She covered her mouth with her hand and manufactured a cough. Eve locked Ellen in The Room and then forgot about her. Just like Ellen had done to so many kids, so many times. *That's* what she'd died of. That's what she'd deserved to die of. But unlike Ellen, Eve had genuinely forgotten. That's why she'd never got her precious insulin, and now Pennie could see the benefit of having someone else explain all this. Someone with fancier words than all three of the Holland girls put together.

'In your professional opinion, Doctor Harris, was Eve Holland criminally responsible for committing these terrible crimes, to which she's pleaded guilty?'

Again, she turned to the all-important jury, who really just looked like a bunch of people at the movies. Glued to the action, mentally eating buckets of popcorn while Eve's life hung on whatever opinions they formed. 'Eve Holland endured a lifetime of trauma at the hands of Ellen and Peter Holland,' she said, her hands resting peacefully in her lap at last. 'So, it's not really surprising that she's been diagnosed with post-traumatic stress disorder and delusional disorder.'

'I'm sorry, Doctor,' Grey Suit interrupted her, 'can you explain that, please?'

The doctor did a long, slow blink which Pennie reckoned was one of those tricks people used to hold back their annoyance.

'Delusional disorder is characterised by persistent delusions, as the name suggests.' She gave a small, patient smile in the direction of the jury. 'These delusions often focus on a specific theme and, in Eve's case, that theme was suffering. She believed that each of her victims were still suffering as a result of their shared experience at the home of Ellen and Peter Holland. She believed that she was freeing them from that pain. Setting them free.' She turned towards the crowd then, but rather than looking at the likes of Pennie and Nicole in the pews, she looked directly over their heads and straight at the row of cameras at the back of the room. Once the flashes died down, she continued. 'It's important to note that people with delusional disorder may not experience other psychotic symptoms and can function relatively normally otherwise.' She looked to the jury again, clearly enjoying being able to take in her entire, captive audience. 'Not that anyone would have noticed anyway, because thanks to her PTSD, Eve did not interact with other people, and thanks to the reputation of her house, people did not actively seek to interact with her.' She paused then for dramatic effect. 'The world had essentially turned its back on Eve Holland.'

'Don't mind me,' Pennie muttered, and Nicole squeezed her hand.

'So to answer your question, do I think Eve Holland was criminally responsible for her crimes? No, I do not.'

A frenzy broke out in the courtroom as cameras clicked and flashed, all the whispers grew louder, and people jostled all around them. Someone elbowed Pennie in the back of the head in their excitement, but she didn't turn around. She didn't take her eyes off Eve, who was sitting as still as she could, apart from the dramatic rise and fall of her shoulders that told Pennie she was close to hyperventilating. But she'd control it. She could when she had to.

'It is my opinion,' the doc continued loudly, and the noise settled again. Pennie couldn't imagine what it must be like to have that kind of power in your voice. The doc cleared her throat and lowered her voice again. 'It is my opinion that Eve's actions, as terrible as they were, were a direct result of her psychotic symptoms, which impaired her ability to understand the nature and the consequences of what she was doing.'

Grey Suit thumped his fist on his desk and smiled like an idiot. 'Thank you, Doctor Harris. I have no further questions.'

42

PENNIE

I don't remember being born, but I do know that I came out with the best of *all* the superpowers. I was invisible. Do you know what that meant? It meant that I could go anywhere I wanted. I could see just about anything, and I could hear *everything*. And best of all, no one ever knew. Mammy Ellen would be shouting in the kitchen, real angry the way she used to get sometimes. She'd be scream-ing, *Eve, get this house cleaned up and have dinner on the table in the next twenty minutes...* and then she'd really let rip to say, *or so fucking help me!* Then she let out another roar like, *you fat fucking whore, get in The Room* and all that sort of thing. And there I'd be, standing at the top of the stairs, in plain view, not hiding or anything really... but *no one* saw me. No one shouted at me to do anything or go anywhere. Sometimes, they even forgot about me when dinner time came around. No one would come get me from my room and there wouldn't be any food left for me when they all finished. I could tell that Eve felt bad for me on those days, when I might walk into the kitchen as she was clearing up and then she'd be the first to remember I was there. Eve would always say, *Pennie! Where were you?* And I would have been there the whole time. Invisible. Also, I don't really talk much, so as well as not seeing me, no one ever really heard me either.

I cried sometimes when I heard all the awful noises coming from inside that room. I'd hear one of the girls crying out and there'd be all this banging around.

I cried the most when I saw what they were like after. They walked in like normal people, but when they came out, I could see that they'd been bitten by the Soul Sucker. I read a comic book about him once. He was lovely. Always smiling and I think he worked in an office or something. But then at night, he turned into the Soul Sucker and if he bit you on the neck, he sucked your soul out through the little hole and then you were left just walking around like a zombie. I think the Soul Sucker lived in our house and that was his room.

Anyway, that all changed the day Mammy Ellen fell down the stairs. When she went into that room, I lost all my powers. Worse than that, I became the *opposite* to invisible. It was like suddenly, when it was just me and Eve, Eve wasn't able to see anything else at all. Only me. That felt weird. Imagine going from having no one at all seeing you, to having someone seeing nothing else *but* you. *In*visible to *over*-visible. I didn't like that. But luckily, that was around the same time that Angel came. You should have seen her. She was the most beautiful thing I'd ever seen. Her skin was made up of all these bright and colourful pictures. She even had a huge picture of Eve's face running from her knee, right up to the top of her leg. I never knew angels had pictures of the people they minded on them, but she said that it was to make sure they never forgot. Angel said that she was going to get a picture of my face on her other leg. She said that God saved a space on her body, just for that. Can you imagine?

Now pretty much everyone can see me. Most of them know that I still don't like to talk much, and yet they spend *all* their time trying to get me to *talk*! It makes me mad sometimes, but I try my best to keep that to myself. Take Dr Harris, for example. I'm in her office right now and she's sitting in a super comfy-looking chair right across from me. It's yellow and it has kind of wings on the sides, so that if she falls asleep, she can just lean her head against it. I'm on a blue couch and that's nice, too. But I've told her over and over again that I don't like to talk. She just won't listen.

'Did you know that Eve's food was making you sick, Pennie?'

That was the third question she asked me today after, 'How are you, Pennie?' and, 'Would you like some juice?' Usually I said no when she offered me food or drinks, and I think that's why she asked me about Eve's food. Like maybe she thought that *that's* why I always say no. I mean, I didn't actually know that Eve was putting stuff in my food. I just knew that I felt sick every time I ate it. Then Angel told me to stop eating it, and she started bringing those little mini boxes of cornflakes, so I just ate them instead. I don't really like corn-flakes, but I didn't tell Angel that. She was doing her best.

'How does it make you feel?' Dr Harris asked, after I nodded yes.

I shrugged. What did she want me to say? I didn't blame Eve for that. She was doing it because she loved me. She wanted to love me to sleep. That's what she told me afterwards, when they let me see her. She told me that she was going to go to sleep with me, and then we'd be together forever. But that didn't really work, because I don't like things like hugs and kisses and hair-rubbing and back-rubbing and all those kinds of things. Actually, I don't like anyone else's skin touching me at all. It makes my stomach go all hard and angry and I don't like it. So Eve didn't get to do the love thing that time, which I was sorry for. But there was no point in telling Dr Harris any of that. After all, Eve had told her everything already and I saw the way she looked at Eve in that court-room. She looked at her like she hated her with everything she had. Angel... I mean, Nicole... I find it hard to get used to that, but Nicole said that Dr Harris only took us on so that she could get the front page. I think what that means is that, she wanted to be famous. And Eve was famous, so maybe she thought some of it could rub off on her. I don't know about all that. But I do know that I don't want to be famous. Not at all. I want my superpower back, and that's why I had to just stop all of this.

Dr Harris's office is really nice. The walls are painted really dark blue, but they have snow-white wood on the bottom halves. There are big, leafy plants all over the place and a painting on the wall with so many bright, splashy colours on it that it must have been painted by someone who was five years old. She had a big, old, brown desk that I don't think she ever sat by, this comfy, blue couch and her big, yellow chair. She is leaning to the side now with her head resting against one of the big wings. Her eyes are closed, and she looks really happy and comfy.

I've been carrying this little glass bottle around with me for ages. Since before the police took everything away, and it looks like it's filled with water. But I know it isn't. This is the stuff Mammy Ellen used to take every single day. Eve told me that she gave it to the people she loved so that they could go to sleep and be happy. But you need to give more than Mammy Ellen used to take. Much more.

Mammy Eve was very clever. She used the little white pills first, so that they could just go to sleep. She must have told Dr Harris how to use those, because Dr Harris explained it to everyone in court. So I knew that if I just popped one of those in a drink, she could go right to sleep. The kind of sleep where nothing at all would wake her. That's why I said yes today when she asked me if I wanted some juice. You should have seen her face. You'd swear I told her she won first prize in the front-page competition or something. She was thrilled.

She *always* has a drink. Every time I'm here, she has a cup of coffee while we talk. Or at least, while *she* talks. It was resting on the little table beside her yellow chair, where she always puts it. When she went to the little fridge by the window to get my juice, I just moved very quickly and very quietly, and it was in there in no time.

I don't want to be here, in her office. If they didn't make me, then I wouldn't have to do anything. But the court said that, basically, I couldn't be right in the head coming from that house. Or at least, that's how Angel... I mean, Nicole explained all the big words they used. They said I had to see her twice a week for however many months, just to make sure that I *was* right in the head. Nicole wasn't very happy about that. She said that Dr Harris was going to use me to get back on the front page again, after she already locked Mammy Eve up in some mental hospital for four years. Honestly, I don't think Mammy Eve will mind that too much. Except for not being able to leave it to go for very long drives and walks every day. That bit might bother her, all right.

Anyway, Dr Harris is asleep now. Nicole lets me use the Internet again, now that they've mostly forgotten about Eve, so I know how to fill up the needle with the medicine from the little glass bottle. Dr Harris was sleeping so soundly that she didn't move a muscle when I stuck the needle in her leg. She didn't look like she felt any sting from it either, and I was happy about that. Dr Harris would like this, actually. She said as much to the court one day. She said that the rohyp... the roh... I can't remember what the name of it is, but it's these white pills anyway. She said that by giving these first and then the injection, that those people wouldn't have felt anything at all.

The room gets cold all of a sudden, just as I am about to leave. It is nearly one o'clock, and Nicole will be downstairs, waiting. I take the blanket off the back of my blue couch and place it over Dr Harris. Then I put the needle and the empty glass bottle back in my backpack and let myself out. I make sure the lock clicks into place on her door when I leave, because I don't want her getting robbed or anything.

Anyway, that is the last time I'll see Dr Harris.

'Hey, how'd it go?' Nicole goes to place an arm around my shoulder when I walk out onto the street, but then she stops herself, remembering that I don't like that.

She is wearing shorts and has what looks like cling film wrapped around her leg. My picture is being put on there, on the leg opposite Eve, and it looks like a little more of my face might have appeared today.

'Good,' I say.

Nicole throws a look at the upstairs window, where Dr Harris's office is, just above one of those expensive pharmacies. 'She better not be trying to make out there's anything wrong with you,' she says, like she is threatening the woman. Only Dr Harris can't hear her.

I shake my head.

Nicole looks at me then with the kind of smile that says, *You're weird, but in a good way*, and I'm all right with those kinds of looks.

'You're not worried that she's just hunting the fame of the notorious Eve Holland's little girl?'

I shake my head again.

'You did tell her that you don't want to be her poster girl, didn't you?'

I look at her then, because I don't really know what she means by poster girl.

'I mean, does she know that you, Pennie Holland, do not want the infamy?'

I look at her again.

'That's the opposite to fame. Infamy. It's when you're—'

'She knows,' I say.

Nicole doesn't look so sure, but she nods anyway and doesn't say any more about it. She knows I don't like loads of talking and questions and all that kind of thing. So anyway, now that that's done, I think I'll get my superpower back. No front page means no Pennie Holland and, pretty soon, Eve will start to disappear, too. I cross my fingers every day that Angel will vanish, with us. She takes loads of pills, so I think she will. Then finally, we can all be free, just like Eve wanted. We can all be happy.

* * *

MORE FROM MICHELLE DUNNE

Burning Secrets, another gripping and twist-filled read from Michelle Dunne, is available to order now here:

https://mybook.to/BurningSecretsBackAd

ACKNOWLEDGEMENTS

Keeping it short this time, I must begin by thanking the incredible team at Boldwood Books for their expert guidance and their passion for my work. In particular, my fabulous editor, Vic who is an absolute dream to work with – I look forward to all that is to come!

Thanks to all at WGM Atlantic and especially my wonderful agent Nicky Lovick. You've been in my corner, championing my work from the very beginning, and it means the world.

To the most supportive group of women, the Irish Murderesses – you know who you are. (The first rule of WhatsApp group – you don't talk about WhatsApp group!)

Finally, thank you to the readers, booksellers and those who sing from the rooftops about the books they enjoy. Without you, none of it would mean a thing.

Thank you all from the bottom of my heart.

ABOUT THE AUTHOR

Michelle Dunne is the bestselling author of hard-hitting thrillers, whose early work was inspired by her time as a soldier and UN peacekeeper in the late nineties. When she's not busy writing, Michelle is the founder and organiser of The Spike Island Literary Festival, and also works on Dublin's International crime festival, Murder One.

Download your exclusive bonus content from Michelle Dunne here:

Follow Michelle on social media here:

facebook.com/MichelleDunneAuthor
instagram.com/michelledunneauthor
x.com/NotDunneYet
bookbub.com/profile/michelle-dunne
tiktok.com/@writereadrepeat

ALSO BY MICHELLE DUNNE

The Imaginary Friend

Burning Secrets

THE *Murder* LIST

**THE MURDER LIST IS A NEWSLETTER
DEDICATED TO SPINE-CHILLING
FICTION AND GRIPPING
PAGE-TURNERS!**

**SIGN UP TO MAKE SURE YOU'RE ON
OUR HIT LIST FOR EXCLUSIVE DEALS,
AUTHOR CONTENT, AND
COMPETITIONS.**

**SIGN UP TO OUR
NEWSLETTER**

BIT.LY/THEMURDERLISTNEWS

Boldwood